In Love
with the
Past

Viola Dawn

For my mother, Rosalie. A kind, loyal, clever, patient, quiet and exceptionally witty woman.

Table of Contents

Author's Note: The Banat

Today, the Banat is a region of Europe around where the borders of Hungary, Romania, and Serbia meet. Beginning in the eighteenth century, the Hapsburgs, rulers of the Austro-Hungarian Empire, invited German-speaking farmers and craftsmen to settle in lands that had been won from the Ottoman Turkish Empire. A 'Schwob,' or in some cases a 'Banater,' is a common way of referring to the descendants of those settlers. The author has used the German names for the European villages in chapters set in the Old World, as would have been used by the characters in this story. The European chapters are set in what is now western Romania.

Chapter 1

2017. The Homestead. North Dakota.

Amber's long, legs were spread in a V on the wooden floor of her open living room. The scraping of the spoon against the pumpkin was the only sound in the one-story home. The orange fruit between her knees was nearly hollowed out when wavy blonde locks fell in front of her eyes. She paused to tuck them behind her ears and tightened her ponytail.

It was a Monday night, the sun had set less than an hour ago. The room behind her was dark. It felt as though the room she sat in was still wrapped in summer, while winter's stark chill emanated from the kitchen. Amber peered towards the back and cellar doors, wondering if either was open.

They weren't.

"Wish I'd chosen a different color for the kitchen now." Amber huffed and tried to ignore the tightness in her chest.

Amber slowly turned away to stare at the front door. She sighed, wishing that her friend Theresa would show up.

It was the night before Halloween, the one evening when Theresa could get away from her husband and kids to have a mini-housewarming with her friend. Amber had finished at her computer early to carve a jack o' lantern.

Clearing her throat, Amber carved the triangles. Yet her back, which still faced the dark kitchen, remained tense and cold. The fragrance of fresh pumpkin and orange-scented floor soap filled her nostrils.

This was the first house Amber owned. An original homestead that had been derelict for a decade. The real estate agent had told her that if it had remained empty much longer, it would have been torn down.

Amber had had her time having housemates, living in bland apartments in suburban areas. This house had history, and she wanted to make it her own. It had been worth all the work it took to fix it up. Even in its dilapidated state, it had a warmth that drew her.

There was even a creek and trees some distance behind. There were a couple of trees to the side of the house. Those features and the road that led to the place were the only landmarks cutting up the sea of land.

Why does it seem like the darn door is open in the kitchen?

Amber stood and collected the carving knife, spoon, towel, newspaper and bucket. She walked into the kitchen. She switched on the light, peering around for any leaks or cracks that decided to occur moments before she was due a guest. She disposed of the stringy pumpkin flesh, saving the seeds and some of the firmer pale orange pieces for a soup.

Born and raised in southwestern North Dakota, Amber enjoyed a romanticized version of her homesteading heritage. It wasn't this specific homestead where her folks had settled. It wasn't a common choice to live in such an unpopulated area. Most of her friends from school went away for college and never came back.

The wind picked up and Amber peered through the window over the sink as she turned on the tap. The air outside howled as though expressing a reminder of its ancient reign over the prairie.

Amber turned the tap on, steam rising as she watched the faded grass twitch against the gusts. The sun disappeared and the sky shifted to a dim shade of gray. The afternoon's fading light warned her of night's impending arrival.

Amber washed and rinsed her carving knife, holding it before her, checking that all orange residue was gone. Someone stood reflected in the metal.

Amber cursed, dropping the knife into the sink. Steaming hot water splashed her face.

"Oh!" she cried and turned around, her hands bracing the sink behind her for dear life. No one was there. Yet she could tell that the woman, the shape of whoever that was, had been standing behind her.

A woman wearing a house dress, the sort that grandmothers wore in decades gone by.

"Hello?" Amber asked the surrounding air, she moved to turn the tap off, her chest heaving.

What...who was that?

The doors are locked. I never noticed anything spooky when I viewed the place, all those months of working on it.

It was as though *she* was being noticed for the first time.

Amber stood with her hands still grasping the front of the sink but now staring out the window. Then she shook her head and cleaned with a shaky hand.

Curiosity ate at her, like a veil had been lifted and then suddenly put back in place. Straight-backed and padding towards her door, she lit the tea light and placed it inside the now glowing orange fruit. It grinned back at her. Though unease made the hairs on her arms stand up, she cleared her throat and moved to find it a place.

At the larger window to her right, red drapes floated and danced above the floor.

Shit...

Her breaths were shaky.

Knock, knock, knock.

"Oh, jeez!" she said, trembling as she placed the pumpkin down and put a hand over her pounding heart. A muffled yet familiar voice came through the heating vent.

"Hey, honey, you in there? Happy Halloween!"

Amber opened the door to find her friend Theresa dressed as a witch, complete with a hat, and black-and-white striped tights. She was lit only by Amber's flickering porch light.

"Hey! Gosh it's so dark already...seems more like the witching hour than six pm. Theresa smiled.

"Yeah...hi Theresa," Amber said, her hand on her chest the corners of her mouth forced up in what was supposed to be a smile.

Theresa stood with her arms crossed, regarding Amber with a tilted head. Then she reached into her bag and pulled out a container of salt. Theresa poured it over the threshold of the door, snapped the metal pourer down, and winked.

"There, see? Salt to keep out evil spirits. I see you put out a pumpkin. Good girl. Can't be too careful. You doing okay? You look white as a sheet, like you've seen a ghost." Theresa patted her friend on the arm as she passed.

Amber laughed, battling to hide her nerves. Torn between embarrassment and fear.

"Oh, I'm okay. I think getting this place livable and keeping up with work has finally started to take its toll." Amber smiled, trying not to look forced.

"Well, we can do this another time, honey..."

"No, no. Come on in. Please. I've been looking forward to a visit."

"I'll bet," Theresa said as she walked in with her overnight bag and a smaller gift bag.

"Oh!" Theresa exclaimed as Amber shut the door. "This room is so warm. You did such a great job with the floors..." She peered down the hallway to the left, then came back out to inspect the pale-colored kitchen.

"Are you going to use the root cellar?"

"I...I don't know. Maybe, once I get a garden going here next season. I'm getting kind of freaked by the place right now. Must be because it's Halloween."

Theresa lifted an eyebrow and nodded. "Hmmm. You didn't seem right just now. What happened?"

Amber smiled almost regretting mentioning her fear.

"I was...washing the knife and I swear I saw something behind me. But it...it must have been just that I'm tired. I hadn't turned the light on in the kitchen. So it was creepy in there I guess."

"Well, it *could* be your imagination, Amber. This is an old house though." Theresa furrowed her brows and looked around the house. She pressed her lips together then changed the subject. "How is work going?"

"Fine. I've got a few covers to design and a backlog of manuscripts to edit and format. So, money is coming in."

"You might have been better placed working in a city. I'm glad you're here, but why not somewhere like New York or Chicago? Plenty of need for editors and graphic designers there. And you wouldn't be so...secluded."

Amber put up her hands. "Okay, I get it. I've chosen to live in the middle of nowhere. It's just that I've tried towns and cities. I went to college in one. I have enough clients now that as long as I have internet, I'm good. It's less expensive here. Mom and Dad are close. It...it'll be fine. "

Theresa nodded, surveying the room before replying. "So...editing, graphic art, and homesteading it is then?"

"Looks that way." Amber pursed her lips, trying to remove the image of the lady in the knife from her mind.

It was just my tired mind...that's all.

"And here we are...mid-thirties. The only thing you need now is a man. Maybe some burly cowboy or farmer will turn up and sweep you off your feet."

"I'm just fine without all that. I've got too much work to do."

Theresa laughed as she pulled out a bottle of wine. "That is so typical of you. Don't you ever get lonely?"

"Nope. Kinda nice being able to work and not deal with the hustle and bustle. I missed the quiet when I was living out of state."

"Well, let's at least give you a little housewarming," Theresa said, pulling the cork out of the bottle. Amber began slicing some summer sausage and cheese.

Amber sat chatting away with her old friend as night fell on the cold prairie. They brought the pumpkin in with them when it was time to choose a movie to watch.

Later, with her head resting on the arm of her chair, Amber stared at the screen as the credits rolled. Her eyes flitted to the glowing pumpkin.

"That thing is grinning at me, Theresa. It's got it in for me," Amber said, half joking.

"Oh, stop it. You carved it. I hope you got the futon all made up for me. I'm looking forward to a night of sleep, toddler free." Theresa yawned from the couch.

"Sure." Amber blew out the tea light in the jack o'lantern, leading Theresa past her bedroom, the bathroom, and down to the office and guest room at the end of the hallway. Amber glanced at the blank canvas poised on an easel in front of the window.

"You could paint the moon and the stars," Theresa said drowsily as she placed her bag down.

"I don't get that much time to paint these days. Too much—"

"I know I know...too much work to do," Theresa interrupted.

Amber smirked. "Goodnight, Theresa."

"Goodnight, Amber."

As Amber walked the short distance to her bedroom and collapsed on the bed, she heard a voice.

Amber...

She pulled the covers up to her chin and turned towards her window. The curtains were open, fluttering slightly over the vent. In the starry night she could just about make out one of the trees in the distance.

Amber...

She winced then opened her eyes wide, staring out the window. "Theresa?" she whispered. There was no answer.

The creaks in the walls, the fluttering of the drapes over the heating vent suddenly struck her as unexplainable. She'd always found the little noises an old house makes comforting, like it had a personality.

She dozed of slowly, slipping into sleep layer by layer. The memory of the whisper never quite left her even as she drifted.

Amber fell asleep, thinking *"Who are you?"*

Pumpkins, Halloween, and the final realization that this was going to be her home—that's all it was, surely. On some level she was trying to sabotage herself, her brain convincing itself that this was a haunted house. Her family had expected her to move to Chicago or New York, to some kitsch apartment with easy access to publishing house headquarters.

Living here wasn't a rash decision. The house was in good condition, for the most part. The bedroom was the one room in the house she didn't have to rip the floors up in. She'd only had to treat, sand, and polish, just replacing the odd board.

Amber drifted in and out of slumber. At one point, her hand fell out of the covers. She was barely aware of the backs of her fingers resting on the cold wood.

The floor creaked as though someone walked around the hall. Or behind her on the other side of the bed. Amber felt like a child, squeezing her eyes shut to avoid seeing a shadow or shape.

It's probably Theresa using the bathroom.

But Amber didn't speak. In a way she didn't want to know. Curiosity mingled with her goosebumps.

This was the first week she had in forever where there wasn't some painting to do, a plumber to wait for, a furniture delivery, etc. And Amber, who thrived on solitude, was grateful for the company of Theresa tonight. Even though tomorrow and most every night, she'd have to deal with whispers and creaks on her own.

Chapter 2

2017. All Hallows' Eve. North Dakota.

Amber stirred in bed. As consciousness arrived, she realized how icy her arm felt. Turning on her left side, she pulled it beneath the quilt and rubbed to get her blood flowing. Pulling her knees up into a fetal position, she opened her eyes. Then something bumped beneath the bed, like a heavy piece of wood dropping.

Trying to keep her quilt over her shoulders, Amber scooted closer to the left side of the bed and peered underneath.

Oh, for goodness sake…

She let the quilt slide away as she looked underneath the bed.

There was nothing there apart from the shadow of her head, framed by sunshine.

She sighed and pulled herself up, smoothing down the waves of her hair. As she did so, a shadow passed outside her window and Amber gasped, looking up. The back of a man was just passing her window, turning to walk around the front. Amber blinked and he appeared to have already gone around the corner.

Amber placed her hand over her mouth and lay back down, eyes wide. The sun hid behind a cloud and the sky cast a gray light over the prairie. She didn't have neighbors, and there were no deliveries or service calls scheduled for today.

Amber pressed her lips together and crept out of bed. When she reached the hall, she whispered, "Theresa?"

There was no answer.

"Theresa, are you there?" she said, slightly louder. Worry knotted her stomach.

She moved farther down the hall until coming to the office door. Her feet creaked on the floor and Amber winced as she dived in front of the doorway, not sure what she would find.

The futon was made up, with no sign of Theresa's overnight bag. Then, she sniffed the air and noticed the aroma of coffee brewing.

Amber walked to the other end of the hall, through to the warmer tones of her living room, then turned into the open partition that led into the pale blue kitchen.

Theresa was not there, but coffee had been made. Amber's chest pounded and the back of her head prickled. The kitchen floor creaked as she padded to the coffee maker, looking over her shoulder. Apart from the coffee having been made, all signs pointed to the interior of the house being empty.

I could check the cellar, she thought, but a choking sensation arrived and her breathing sped up in an attempt to counter the tightening of her throat.

That was when she noticed the note by the coffee maker.

Morning Dear,

Thanks for the wine and laughs last night. I let you sleep in because if you are starting to feel spooked it's probably because you are overtired. You work too much! ;)

You've done a great job on the house! I've gotta go because one of the boys has to stay off school. Dave is waiting for me so he can go to work.

Give me a call if you need anything.

Happy Halloween!

Theresa

Amber put the letter down. Maybe the 'man' was actually Theresa. She had only just woken up, so it was possible she hadn't been seeing straight. Amber shook her head, poured some coffee, and sat in front of her computer.

Amber stared at the screen as her programs loaded. In the few seconds before her desktop images came up and the room behind her was visible, her gaze flicked around screen.

There's no one there. There's no one there.

Her heart rate slowed as the screen lit up and her e-mail server came on screen. There was no reflection that way.

She started working, editing a client's manuscript. Amber's eyebrows knit, focusing on the screen.

Knock, knock, knock. "Oh!" She jumped in her seat, hand clapped over her mouth.

Heart pounding against her chest, thudding in her ears, she willed herself to calm down before another knock sounded.

It's just someone at the door for goodness sake, Amber...you're a grown up. Amber's legs shook as she walked towards the door. She cleared her throat and pulled open the door, a tall man she'd never seen before stood on her porch.

His mouth was open and his breath misted in the air. He smiled and took off his hat. His lips turned from an almost plum color to a peach. Amber swallowed, her heart rate slowing.

"Hi, I'm Martin. I'm new to the area. I saw this place had been done up and wondered if you needed any building work done? Oh, uh...here's my card."

"I see...I'm...I'm Amber Kilzer. I've done most of the work on the house myself. I did get an electrician and a plumber in. Had a roofing guy over last summer..."

Amber gazed absently at the flyer then looked back up at Martin. He had brown eyes that crinkled when he smiled. He looked around her age.

"I see, I just...well I have to admit I was curious about this place as I saw it when it was falling apart. I work all over the state and I find the abandoned structures interesting."

Amber nodded. "Well, this place isn't abandoned." Amber didn't want to come off as rude, but door to door salesmen in this day in age smelled a bit fishy.

This guy, Martin, however, smelled like soap, a faint tint of spicy deodorant and warm skin.

So he's a nice looking guy who showers every day. Doesn't mean you should invite a stranger in for coffee.

Still, Amber found herself pleasantly distracted by how huggable he looked.

You weren't expecting him. Quit being weird.

Yet no alarm bells went off. Martin shifted on his feet and looked at the ground for a moment. "Yeah...well sorry to trouble you. If you decide you need any work doing, I'd appreciate being considered for a quote, free of charge of course. Have a good day Mrs..."

"It's Miss. Or Ms. I don't bother too much but I'm not married." She gave a closed mouth smile and blushed, wincing. *Was it weird that I made a point of letting him know I'm single?*

"Miss Kilzer, pleasure to meet you. Happy Halloween." He grinned again and nodded.

"Happy Halloween" she responded. She'd wanted to reach out and shake his hand, but that seemed inappropriate. The oddity of fearing getting too much enjoyment out of a mere handshake wasn't lost on her.

Amber stood on the porch with her arms across her chest, watching him get back into his truck. Part of her justified watching him to ensure he left and wasn't going to stick around the property. Part of it was that he was pleasing to look at. Not like a male model cum lumberjack or a gym sculpted Adonis. He was big but...friendly. Amber realized she was staring and stepped back, closing the door. Clutching Martin's card in her hand, she held it up and looked.

"...Structures. Garages, Barns, Temporary Car Shelters and Floor and Roof Repairs.'

The wind picked up outside, whistling as it whooshed over the house.

Amber shivered and walked back to her desk. "Well ghost...if you're here I suppose you saw that.." She giggled and shook her head. The smile fell from her face slowly as a chill went up her spine.

"It's Halloween, Amber...that's all it is."

Then, something else dawned on her. Something so mundane.

It was something her mother had picked up on when she first looked at the place the winter before.

'You're onna need a garage or something. Your truck will get buried in the winter.'

"Crap. And she told me at the beginning of the summer. I could have said something." She huffed. *If you weren't so busy checking him out, you might have been in the right frame of mind to think of it.*

Then again, she thought he must be quite desperate for work if he's going door to door.

Especially all the way out here...

 beginG   ဆ

Hours later, Amber was still sat in front of her computer, her desk light on but the rest of the house had gone dark.

She sat back, pinching the bridge of her nose. "Guess I'd better light the pumpkin!" she exclaimed, her feet thumping over the polished floors to get a tea light.

She'd flipped on the living room light and leaned into the dark kitchen to grab a book of matches. Amber retrieved the pumpkin from beside the door and set it on the kitchen counter. The living room light partially illuminated the kitchen yet the corners and side where the cellar door was were still dim. Amber ignited the match with her right hand and while placing the tea light into the pumpkin she caught a face with wide eyes to her left.

"Shit!" Amber both burned herself and almost knocked the jack o'lantern over. She gasped and clung to it, her feet frozen. Where could she run?

"Who's there?" There was no answer. No face, no eyes.

It was that woman again.

Knock, knock, knock.

Amber couldn't move for a few seconds. Then with shaking hands and harsh breaths she lit the tea light. Old superstitions about the illuminated fruit keeping spirits away raced through her mind.

There was no good reason for anybody to trick-or-treat all the way out here.

She licked her lips and swallowed. Someone knocked again, and she heard muttering that sounded like children. A particularly young one whined.

Amber sighed in relief as the voices sounded familiar. She went to get her chocolate stash and padded to the door. Opening it up, she saw her friend Theresa with a group of boys, the youngest of whom sniffled and fussed in his ninja costume. Her knees shook as she plastered a smile on her face.

"Trick-or-treat!" they exclaimed and a nervous laugh escaped her mouth.

Amber dropped small chocolate bars into the children's open pillow cases.

"We weren't sure if you were going to open up," Theresa said.

"I wasn't expecting anyone to come all the way out here. How's...how's the little ninja doing?"

Theresa tilted her head and narrowed her eyes at Amber, noticing her friend's jumpy demeanor before answering,

"Crabby, but okay. This is our first stop. He wouldn't even *think* about missing trick-or-treating. Are you okay Amber?"

Amber said "Sure. Oh yeah. Just nearly burned myself lighting the pumpkin is all..."

Then the boys started exclaiming, "Wow...cool! How'd you do that?"

They were all shrinking back behind each other, then one would peer out and say 'wow' again.

"You've got a ghost lady...like a hologram." One of them pointed a grim reaper-cloaked limb in the direction of her kitchen.

Amber's eyebrows went up and she looked behind her. She just caught a woman's sleeve slinking out of view in the kitchen. Her heart stopped and the prickling sensation at the back of her scalp started up. She worried she might pass out in front of her friend and the kids.

She turned back to the boys and Theresa with an open mouth. Theresa was furrowing her brows and looking in the same direction as her sons and her friend.

"She's scawee," her youngest said, starting to cry. Theresa picked him up and shook her head. "Boys, that's enough now. I don't see a darn thing."

"She's gone now, but, Mom...she was there!" the eldest pleaded and his friends and second youngest brother agreed. The little ninja started to cry.

"You stop that now!" Theresa told the kids, feeling her youngest's forehead.

"I'm sorry, Theresa...I...I don't know," Amber said, yet her heart pounded. *Kids have crazy imaginations, and I might have to make a doctor's appointment.*

"Don't worry. I thought they'd like to come out to a secluded homestead for some candy, but they're just being naughty."

"Oh, it's okay. Don't be too hard on them. It's a spooky place, and they have such imaginations." Amber's laugh was forced.

And please stay because I'm freaked out too. They aren't seeing things! Yet Amber wouldn't utter the words. She put a smile on her face and said good-bye to all the kids, complimenting their costumes.

Theresa said, "I'm afraid the only scary old lady who lives here is Amber." Theresa winked at her friend, and looked at her boys and their friends with pursed lips.

"Thanks a lot." Amber smirked, but her heart beat ever faster.

The boys said good-bye, yet continued to look in the direction of the kitchen with open mouths and wide eyes.

She smiled and nodded, shutting the door.

Amber stood with her forehead on the door, listening to the boys argue and the youngest cry as Theresa ushered them all to the car. She stared at the floor for a few moments after she could no longer hear its wheels rolling in the distance.

Then, she straightened herself and turned around. All was quiet. Avoiding the selection of horror movies on television, Amber went straight back to her office. Sitting down on the made-up futon, Amber took her pad out to work through some sketches. When the internet failed to suggest an image for a cover, she could easily design one herself.

The wind howled and the window creaked from the pressure. Amber watched for any movement outside. The blank canvas mounted on the easel in front of the creaking window drew her attention. It was as though the prairie and the very sky outside were angry when the entire house creaked again. Amber sat cross-legged on the futon, staring at the glass, wondering if it might crack.

"I don't know who you are or what you want...but I'd like it if you'd stop spooking me."

Nothing happened. Amber continued working until she fell into an uneasy sleep, a circle of papers and her laptop surrounding her. Before she fully drifted off, she reminded herself to ring Martin's Structures tomorrow.

Chapter 3

2017. North Dakota. All Saints Day.

Amber woke up on her futon, surrounded by notebooks and sketching papers crinkling in her ear. She reached up to rub her temples. The fleece blanket fell off as she sat up with a groan.

"Ugh," she said aloud. It had been a rough night's sleep. She kept imagining herself opening the cellar door and peering down into the darkness of the one room in her home she avoided.

In the dream her heart had hammered in her chest while looking down into the dark abyss of the cellar. Tears stung her eyes and she fought for control of her breath.

Did I actually go and look? Was it a dream?

Yet what wasn't a dream was the fact that Theresa's sons and their friends saw the lady. The same lady she saw. That was a total of three appearances now.

She walked down the hall and paused at the bathroom.

Placing her fingers on the wall, she peeked into the kitchen. Light filtered through the window over the sink, giving the nearly sheer curtains a cold glow.

There was a sudden clicking and humming noise. Amber placed a hand on her heart before realizing it was the heating kicking in. She went into the bathroom to brush her teeth, shower, and dress.

Finally ready, Amber took a deep breath and walked into the kitchen. Her chin was up as she set about making coffee. She looked this way and that, and still there was no one.

Amber sat in her kitchen, sipping her coffee and reading the news online. She looked around, half expecting an apparition. She stuck her arms out feeling for cold spots. Scenarios from ghost documentaries she'd watched and made fun of before suddenly felt relevant.

"Okay..." Amber said then pursed her lips together.

I did not buy this place and put all that effort into fixing it up just so I could get scared off.

From time to time her eyes would travel in the direction of the cellar door. Blowing a breath out of her nose, she stood up and walked to it. Amber opened the creaky, white wooden door and flipped on the light.

The back of her neck prickled and her heart pounded so hard that her ears buzzed from the pressure.

She couldn't see anything down there. She swallowed and closed the door with a trembling arm. Something fell over on the window ledge near the sink. Amber's head snapped toward the direction of the noise as she leaned against the cellar door...

It was one of the portraits in front of the window over the sink. Amber quickly grabbed her coffee cup and placed it on the counter. She lifted the portrait of her Grandma Caroline. There was another picture behind it of her great grandmother and grandfather on their wedding day. It was taken in Europe, and was likely the oldest picture of her father's family.

There were portraits of her Norwegian great grandparents, via her mother's side. Yet it was the fallen portrait of Grandma Caroline she handled with the most curiosity.

Amber couldn't *see* anything yet breathed in sharply and whirled around. There was no one.

"Who are you?" Amber panted. There was no answer. Everything was silent; there was no movement. Not even a flickering of light over the rectangular table and chairs.

She grabbed her keys and flew out the door, hands trembling as she locked the door and went to her car.

Despite being a baptized Catholic, it had been some time since Amber had been to church. Now seemed as good a time as any. There would be a mass for the feast of All Souls today.

ℂℬ ℬℂ

There was a harsh chill in the air, but no snow yet, as Amber pressed the gas pedal and drove as fast as she could. Her eyes darted up to the rearview mirror.

If this is anything like the movies, I should see a creepy lady in the backseat, or staring at me from the road.

This wasn't what she imagined a haunting to be like. This was more of a sudden visitor, like somebody needed to tell her something.

No one's head is spinning around but this is still creepy.

She pulled up to St. Vincent's Church and entered just as the mass was starting. It was only midmorning, but Amber was drained and shaky.

She came and sat in the pews in the middle. As it was a work day, there weren't many at mass. She sat down as the priest walked up to the pulpit.

Amber expected to go through the motions, but there was comfort in the old and familiar. The ritualized nature of it all was soothing. The priest spoke of the day for honoring the saints, and the example they set for all Catholics. As he was discussing Saint Vincent, the sky outside darkened so the morning service felt more like an evening one.

A sudden lightheadedness caused her to grip the pew in front of her. Her back warmed and a sheen of sweat gathered around her hairline. Amber removed her coat. Then she turned to her right, looking at the other side of the aisle. There was a man with a shock of black hair looking at her. It was Martin.

He smiled in the casual sort of way one might when any person accidentally makes eye contact with another. Only he looked down and flashed another glance her way, like he thought he could sneak another glance without her noticing. His eyes were brown, a good shade lighter than his ebony hair. Now he was looking down at the kneelers in front of the pew, then back up at the priest. He blinked a couple of times. He was obviously very aware of her presence. Whether or not that was a good thing she wasn't sure.

Amber realized she was staring. It took him looking at her again and widened his dark honeyed eyes for her to notice her gaze was less than appropriate. She turned away with hot cheeks.

Amber shook her head and squeezed the pew in front of her, making enough of a noise that a couple of people looked her way.

The service went on, and she said a few prayers for the soul of whoever was haunting her. As soon the service finished, she waited around to speak to the priest before she lost her nerve. Martin walked across the aisle and she turned towards the sound of his voice.

"Miss Kilzer?"

She turned to him. "Martin...please call me Amber. How are you? I actually needed to speak to you."

His brows rose and he tilted his head. "Sure...would you like to..."

"I actually need a car shelter." She interrupted him and winced to herself. *Jeez you're rude.*

"Oh. Sure. I'll have to head back to the office to double check my schedule as my phone might not be up to date. Well...I gotta get back. Gimme a call, I'll come have a closer look for a quote. You won't be obliged of course."

"Thanks...I will." She did her best smile as Martin nodded and headed out of the church.

Now she was the only one left.

"Can I help you, Miss?" The priest seemed to have appeared out of nowhere.

"I...umm. Yes, Father..."

"You moved onto the Schreiber homestead, right?"

"I...yeah the real estate agent mentioned that's the nick name."

"Yep. I believe those are the folks who built the place. Settling in alright? I heard you had a lot of work to do on it."

"You bet..." Amber was losing her nerve. Even if this was a priest who surely at least had an opinion of the paranormal, she didn't want to be forever be labeled as the lady who thought her house was haunted.

"I'm Father Zenf, by the way. You know...come to think of it, the Schreibers are buried at the Catholic end of Sunnyslope."

"I see. Thank you, Father." Amber's eyes widened. She itched to see the graves.

Father Zenf, seeming to sense that Amber was ready to go, said "Is there anything else I can help you with?"

"No...no Father. But, um I think I'll stop by the cemetery and pay my respects. It only feels right."

"I understand. Have a blessed day." He nodded to her.

Amber also nodded, smiled and headed to her car. She stopped at the store to pick up some flowers and drove back to Sunnyslope.

The cemetery was located on the northern border of the town of Mott, and it was connected to St. Vincent's Cemetery. Amber drove over the gravel road and through the gate. She could see a truck parked up to the side. She stood in front of her car for a moment, clutching a bouquet of roses.

Her booted feet swept over the dying grass and Amber tilted her head up at the rumbling, rolling gray clouds. It was like the earth was rising to meet the sky as she moved farther and farther back to the earlier dates on the stones.

Then she saw the names:

Hans Schreiber: June 1888—11th August 1945

Klara Schreiber: February 1890—12th August 1945

They had died within a day of one another. Now she wished she'd asked the priest more questions. Yet how would he know? Surely he was a baby or at least very young when the Schreibers were alive. She'd heard some older people in the area mention 'The Schreiber Homestead.' After the Schreibers died, there were some bachelor brothers who lived in the place for decades. They were the last inhabitants and if they had any strange experiences during their lifetime, the estate agent hadn't told Amber.

The wind picked up, whistling over the plains and past her ears. Her eyes watered against the biting cold. The clouds still rolled, making the sky seem lower.

Staring down at the graves, she noticed that there was a fresh wreath laid down. It couldn't have been there barely a day. She laid her roses next to the wreath and ran her hand over the gravestones.

A car started behind her and drove away. Amber turned around and saw that now she was alone on the prairie cemetery. Amber walked to her car and made her way back home.

Well, I went to see you, Hans and Klara. I hope you can find peace.

Chapter 4

1902. Learning to Paint. Deutschbentschek or 'Bensek.'

Seeds flew from the hand of an excited thirteen-year-old girl, scattering over the ground and now at the mercy of hungry chickens and geese. Margaritha Koenig bustled about the yard, smoothing her skirts and apron.

"Have your breakfast, quick! I have an important arrangement today." Little Margaritha imagined the excited clucks and warbles of the waddling, feathered animals as a sign of their interest in her plans.

"Anton's Walter Onkel sent some paints from Temeswar for Anton's birthday and he is such a nice boy, he is going to share them with his friends! We all get to paint a picture today. There wasn't enough for the whole class, so it's just myself, Klara, Hans, and Anton. We *each* get to paint a picture. Frau Handl will watch us. Isn't that wonderful? Eat. Eat!"

Then her little booted feet scooted over the dusty yard and went into the kitchen where her mother was working.

"Mami?"

"Yes, Margaritha?" Her mother looked at her tenderly.

"I am finished feeding the geese and chickens. Please may I go to Herr and Frau Handl's?"

Frau Koenig's face fell just a little, and she pursed her lips. "Very well, dear, but please only just the once. You are getting too old to be going to friend's houses alone."

"But, Mami, Klara is going and Hans is going...we will all be together..."

At this, Frau Koenig put up her hand and closed her eyes. "No, it won't be appropriate after this, only on this special occasion. I want you to understand this. And here, give this to Frau Handl." Her mother turned and took a round, freshly baked loaf from the shelf.

Margaritha's mother nodded and pursed her lips again before saying, "They are a very generous family, the Handls. I worry they are being too generous in letting you children use those paints. Such expensive items! Please give this loaf to Frau Handl. It's the only way I can pay them. I know they would be too proud to accept money. Don't you repeat that." Frau Koenig raised her forefinger at her daughter as she said those last words.

Margaritha nodded and took the loaf. "Okay, Mami, I will. Please may I go now?"

"Yes, you may, but don't linger too long. There are still chores to do."

"Okay, okay." She ran off out of the kitchen, her little booted feet moved in a blur below her skirts. Her face split in a smile as she adjusted her headscarf on her way to the Handls's house.

Leaving her yard, she almost didn't notice her father talking to Peter Lulay, a man of almost thirty who had recently wed one of the village's young women. Her little brother Michael was kicking the ground next to her father, who ignored the small boy as he continued his adult conversation.

"Bye, Tati! I'm going to the Handls's house. Mami said it's okay." She looked sideways at the two men with a huge grin as she ran past.

"Did she now? Well, you be sure not to stay long! I will come get you soon!" her father shouted as she ran. It felt particularly good to be free of her father and pesky little brother.

"Margaritha!" a different yet familiar voice shouted from behind.

"Klara!" Margaritha exclaimed. "What did you tell your mother?"

"Bah, she told me I am a stupid girl to go and waste my time on stupid things, but she let me go. She actually let me go!" The girls clasped hands, grinned with glee, and set off.

Running through town with her friend felt like the greatest of adventures. They were free from chores and got to spend time with their favorite people.

"Mami says soon I can't visit the Handls."

"No, you won't be able to." Klara slowed as they passed the Catholic church, both catching their breath. The Handls's house was only a few places down from the church.

"I...don't look at Anton like that." Blood rushed to Margaritha's cheeks. She adored Anton.

"It doesn't matter. It won't be considered proper by all the wagging tongues. My sister Anna says that Anton wants to marry you, and my mother thinks the Handls are after your dowry."

"Your sister is..." Margaritha bit her tongue, not wanting to be unkind. Yet with the mention of Anton and marriage, her stomach fluttered with joy.

Margaritha's heart flipped inside her chest. Anton was one of the more handsome boys. Not the most handsome, yet he was kind and never took part in any of the other boys' crueler games. He was tall and slim, with a shock of black hair and warm brown eyes. His family, though known for being intellectual and artistic, were poor.

Her feelings for Anton were ones she wouldn't dare utter to another soul, not even Klara. Anton's smile made her think of freshly baked cakes, with how warm and content he made her feel inside when he approved of anything she said or did.

"What's that?" Klara commented.

"What's what?" Margaritha replied rather abruptly, worrying that Klara would see inside her head.

Don't be ridiculous, Margaritha. She doesn't realize you are thinking of Anton's lovely, sweet smile that makes you happier than anything.

"You are bringing some bread. Oh...I wish I would have thought to bring something. I know they don't have much..." Klara said.

"Shhh. We are here now. Don't worry," Margaritha soothed her friend. Klara's family also had very little money or food to spare.

The Handls' house was one of the smaller ones in the village. What little they earned from their fields and Herr Handl's other work now went for physician's fees. Herr Handl had done his best to help with roof repairs and renovations in the village, particularly since tiles had begun replacing thatch, but Frau Handl's ailing health often kept him home.

The girls knocked on the Handls's door.

"Gruss gott, Frau Handl," they said in unison.

"Ah, guten morgen, girls," Frau Handl replied. She was a stark contrast to many of the older women in Bensek, most of whom were plump with rosy cheeks. Frau Handl was tall, with wispy brown hair loosely pinned up. There were purple shadows beneath her hazel eyes, yet her smile was so kind, despite her weak constitution. When Frau Handl grinned, her lips shifted from a deep plum to a pale peach color.

Frau Handl lifted an eyebrow at Margaritha, having caught the young lady looking up at her. The older lady winked, then turned and said, "Anton! The rest of our art class is here."

"Klara and I brought you some of my mother's bread, Frau Handl," Margaritha said, handing her the loaf as they were ushered into the small house.

"Oh, thank you. You must thank your mother for this. She makes wonderful bread. Our Anton has always said so."

As they stepped inside, they saw Hans and Anton. The boys both stood at the Handl family table, discussing something with Herr Handl, who had unwrapped the package from Temeswar. The paints and canvas sheets appeared as such wonderful, luxurious items to Margaritha.

"Are you sure, Anton? You don't have to do this. These are expensive," Hans said.

Hans was a contrast to Anton, smaller and with the palest of blonde hair. Being almost fourteen years of age, there was a dusting of yellow fuzz above his upper lip. His gentle blue eyes settled on Klara as she walked in, and both girls immediately began to adjust their headscarves.

Herr Handl cleared his throat. "Well, Anton? Your friend is asking you a question. This is your special present. You can choose to share or not share."

"Yes, Anton, it is okay if you want to save them. None of us will mind," Klara said.

"No...I want to share the canvas and paints. We have enough brushes. I think...the memory of this will mean so much more than me just holding onto these things forever."

"Very well." Frau Handl still bore her peach smile, yet her voice held an edge of fatigue. Margaritha watched how gingerly she walked, as the older lady made her way to place the loaf in the kitchen.

"Frau Koenig sent us a loaf, to say thank you for having the children over to paint," Frau Handl said to her husband.

Herr Handl nodded and ran a hand through his black hair. He was quiet for just a moment too long, and it was Anton who broke the silence. "I love your mother's bread. She is a wonderful cook."

Margaritha grinned at Anton as though he had complimented her personally.

She was just about to reply when Herr Handl said, "Yes, well, that wasn't necessary, but it was kind of her. Please tell her we said thank you, little Margaritha. Anton...I think you have been over to the Koenigs' house too often, eating them out of house and home. But come now...let's see if any of you have any artistic talent, shall we?"

The children all sat down, gushing over the colors and the feel of the canvas.

The youngsters were quiet for the next hour. In the second hour, the odd bit of chatter interrupted creaking chairs, sighs, and coughs. Some of the chatter revolved around their school teacher.

"Anton, you are the only one who is getting anywhere with the Hungarian lessons," Hans said.

"Anton has always been clever, haven't you, Anton?" Klara teased him.

"Yes, well...cleverness comes in many different forms, Klara." Hans did his best to sound sour, yet the corner of his mouth went up and his periwinkle eyes twinkled at her.

Klara, meanwhile, turned to ensure everyone's head was in a different direction before she winked at Hans, whose normally wan complexion turned a shade of rosy pink.

Hans blew a breath out as he focused on his painting. It was of a large house, with some tall trees surrounding it and a couple of barns. There was an air of practicality and comfort about it.

"What's that then?" Frau Handl quizzed Hans.

"It is where I will live one day," the slight, blond teenager replied.

"I like it very much. It looks very spacious and free," Klara said with a dreadfully wicked grin. Hans turned a shade of pink again and Klara felt very satisfied as she noticed his hand trembling just a little.

"My Klara, what a beautiful garden you have." Frau Handl came and placed her slim hand on Klara's shoulder, already muscular from hard labor.

Klara grinned. "I have all sorts of herbs and vegetables. I don't know if I will manage fruit trees or not, but I would love one day to have my own big garden...like this. One thing Mami is happy to leave me to do is the garden."

"Anton has some trees...though they aren't fruit trees. Oh my goodness, what is that, Anton?"

Margaritha stopped her own brush strokes to gaze at Anton's beautiful portrait of a Temeswar street. Given he hadn't had any formal training, apart from what his mother taught him, his ability to capture every little cobble, the leaves of every tree, the stone and brick work of the buildings in the distance was impressive.

"You are really talented, Anton," Margaritha exclaimed, looking at his city scene leaving her mouth hanging open.

Anton turned to Margaritha. "You know, in Temeswar? They have electric street lights."

"I see...so beautiful," Margaritha exclaimed, looking into Anton's eyes.

"So are...so...so is your painting." Anton swallowed and cleared his throat, a reddish hue spreading over his cheeks. He looked back to his own work, furrowing his black eyebrows.

"Margaritha...you have drawn a field...and the sky!" Frau Handl exclaimed, clapping her hands together then spreading them apart as she said, "It's so open and free."

Margaritha leaned back and grinned. "Yes. I love it. Just imagine all that room. No chores. No one telling you what to do! Just a place to run. Then you could lie down and just look up at the sky. Nobody would ask what you were doing, and no one would find you strange."

"Yes, what a wonderful place that would be. Perhaps Hans could help you build a shelter, though. All that open sky. You could get rained on or get too much sun perhaps?" Frau Handl coaxed like a practiced school teacher.

"In *my* painting...it never rains and the sun is always gentle," she giggled.

"Wonderful," Frau Handl praised.

"It's nice, Margaritha, but it is terribly impractical," Hans said in his no-nonsense voice. Then he teased, "I'm sure Anton has more than enough buildings to lend you. Just for a place to rest your head."

Anton kicked Hans playfully. "You've always made terrible jokes."

Now it was Frau Handl's turn to clear her throat. "Right, well, I am impressed with you all. And I think that you should keep these pictures forever, to remind you all of this day. Happy Birthday, my dear Anton." Frau Handl reached out and touched her son's shoulder.

"Thank you, Mami." Anton placed his own hand on top of his mother's.

"How is your mother, Hans?" Klara asked. Everyone stopped, and Margaritha could tell Klara regretted her question as soon as Hans didn't answer for a few moments and the silence grew uncomfortable.

"She...she is getting better. Unfortunately, it looks like I will not have any brothers or sisters any...any time soon."

"Hans, I am so sorry. God bless them all." Klara blushed and looked back at her portrait. Hans was the only surviving child of his parents, despite several attempts at having a large family. The loss of young children wasn't an uncommon phenomenon, yet with every burial, it was as though a part of Herr and Frau Schreiber died too. And Hans, their serious yet caring son, who was ever determined to be practical and not emotional, did his best to bear the weight of his parents' endless grief.

"If there is anything we can do, Hans, you have only to run over and ask, yes?" Herr Handl broke the silence.

"Yes, of course," his wife agreed.

"Thank you. Thank you very much. And I think I speak for Margaritha and Klara when I say thank you so much for having us over and letting us use these paints. It is a great luxury, something the titled children in Vienna do."

At that, everyone agreed, nodding and voicing their sincere thanks.

Knock, knock, knock at the door. Frau Handl moved to answer it. Her feet shuffled and she put her hand out to steady herself. Margaritha was about to get up and help her when Herr Handl moved towards her, placed his arm through hers, and they both went to the door.

"I'm here to collect Margaritha." It was her father.

Margaritha cringed, moving from her painting and towards the door. She thought for a moment how she could avoid her father embarrassing her by looking down upon the Handls' poorer abode. Hopefully, he would give her another few moments and let her walk home with Klara.

Then again, her parents never much approved of Klara either. As she walked past Anton, he reached out and wrapped his fingers around her wrist, as though to keep her with him. Margaritha's heart soared and their eyes locked on one another.

Anton did not remove his hand, and he did not take his eyes from hers. He smiled.

I should have painted a table...laden with cakes. Her sugary fantasies were interrupted by the voice of Frau Handl, and Anton removed his hand from her wrist.

"Yes, she is here. We have quite the group of artists on our hands."

And the door opened, letting the reality of daylight and her father into the small abode.

"Hmmm. Well, I wouldn't know much about that. We don't get much time to paint. Too much work to do in the fields and with the animals. At any rate...where is my girl? Let's see what you've all done then." Her father's heavy footsteps sounded closer as he inspected all of the paintings.

Her friends all greeted Herr Koenig politely. He nodded at all of them and said, "Ah, yes, I see. Well, you have been having some fun in here. I like your barn, Hans. Good. And, Klara...that's a garden. Anton, that...actually does look like Temeswar. I've been before, you know, to take our goods to market." He twitched his mustache as he looked at his daughter's painting. "You've made a field. With nothing in it."

Margaritha kept her head down. "It's a place to play."

Her father laughed and placed his beefy hand on her back. "Typical of my girl. A place to play, eh? Nobody to bother you. Well...unfortunately, your mother, brother, and I have much to bother you with. Thank you again, Herr and Frau Handl, for entertaining the children. Of course, they are getting a little old for this sort of thing. You understand. Herr Handl, I have to say the roofs you've done are far better than that new fellow who has started. You take more time. Let's pray you get better soon, Frau Handl."

Frau Handl smiled politely, though it appeared she barely had the energy to speak. She stumbled a little at her husband's side and Anton went to stand with his mother. Anton looked at Margaritha beseechingly.

"Can we walk Klara home as well?" Margaritha said.

Her father ran his finger over the light coating of dust on the table. Herr Koenig rubbed his thumb against dusty fingers and sniffed before he spoke.

"What? Oh yes...yes, of course. Come, Klara, let us take you to your mother. Thank you again." He nodded and walked the girls out, leaving the Handls and Hans to see to Frau Handl and clear up after the visitors.

Klara, Margaritha, and Herr Koenig walked in silence past the church and other homes down the main street in Bensek. Margaritha was doing her best to memorize the feel of Anton's fingers around her wrist. The temperature of his skin.

His hands were just a bit sweaty. I didn't mind at all.

Her father's voice brought her out of her reverie.

"You know, Peter Lulay commented on what a beauty you are. I've heard a few comments about how my daughter is getting so pretty."

Margaritha shook her head and looked at Klara, who stared ahead.

"And you, Klara. What a nice job you do looking after your mother. Why, if only our Margaritha were as diligent in her gardening and taking care of the chickens."

"Thank you, Herr Koenig," Klara said as they approached her house.

"Well, this is your place, Klara. I should imagine your mother and sister need you."

Margaritha reached to her friend, whose face had fallen at the sight of her own home. She wanted to beg her father to allow Klara to come stay with them for the rest of the day, but he had already been tolerant enough in allowing the unusual luxury of going to Anton's to paint.

Klara appeared to be doing her best to smile as she turned to her friend and bid them good-bye.

Margaritha and her father stood in front of the small home as Klara entered. They could hear the shrill voice of Klara's mother and the shouting of her younger sister, Anna. When a noise of some kitchen implement smashing sounded, Margaritha's father said, "Well, let's go, Margaritha."

"Her mother beats her, Tati," Margaritha muttered.

At this, her father sighed. "There is no visible proof, and Klara seems a strong girl. All of the village is keeping an eye on the family. She will weather the storm of her life. She is a skilled young lady. Perhaps the two of you could work on more useful things? That would mean we don't meddle in their life and you gain a useful reputation for growing things and cooking, instead of daydreaming and being so pretty."

At this, her father reached down to playfully pinch one of her cheeks.

This only aggravated Margaritha. "I would love to paint a picture of cakes, a table laden with cakes, like what the nobles eat when they aren't even hungry. They are just so pretty to look at."

Her father roared with laughter and Margaritha only crossed her arms. She'd fully intended to be abrupt, but instead it'd come out as a joke.

When her father finished chuckling, he said, "Well, I will let your mother deal with you." The mirth was still in his voice.

"Tati?"

"Yes, my dear?"

"Would I still be able to visit Anton, if he asked me again, to paint at his house? Frau Handl is so..."

"No, Margaritha. You are too old now for such things. We allowed this, but you can no longer run about with the boys, especially Anton Handl and Hans Schreiber."

Margaritha blushed as though she'd just committed some great sin. "Yes, Tati." And they walked the rest of the way in silence.

Later in the day, whenever Margaritha spoke to her father, he responded with grunts and furrowed brows. It was as though she had done something terribly wrong, yet she couldn't think exactly why he was correct in being angry with her.

Chapter 5

1905: Kirchweih Festival. Bensek.

Margaritha never thought she would get sick of baking. Except when Kirchweih time loomed. The baking and cooking never seemed to end, right up until the day itself. It was an annual festival celebrating the consecration of their church. Other villages would hold their Kirchweih celebrations on different weekends, thus allowing friends and family to attend.

Margaritha heard Frau Handl say once that the nobles grew frustrated at how little work would happen in the fields when the villagers were busy cooking, baking, drinking, dancing, and generally merrymaking.

But this year was different. Now that the vast amount of food preparations were finished, it came time to get ready. Her heart raced when she imagined wearing her very best layered skirts and shawl with frills on it.

I will dance with Anton for sure. School had since finished for them both and his mother's continually declining health meant he was either at home assisting his mother or helping his father with the odd job of roof repairs around the village.

Margaritha was tending to the hanging baskets with her mother outside, giving the porch a final sweep before the sun went down. Her mother and most of the other hausfraus around Bensek were obsessed with making everything spotless.

Soon the town center would be like a mini-market place, and the entire village would be ready for the party.

Her father was repairing some of the floorboards on the porch as Frau Koenig swept and washed around him.

"My goodness, woman, you've done this patch already. Wait until I finish the board," Herr Koenig grumbled.

"You should have done this before! Just let me clean it," Frau Koenig hissed. Herr Koenig complained, but under his breath this time.

Margaritha, holding the other broom, pressed her lips together and turned away from her parents, hoping they wouldn't notice her shaking from suppressed laughter. Their bickering had been amusing her for most of the day.

She wiped her eyes, sniffed, then crept along the side of the house so that she could see if anyone was out and about on the main street.

Her heart began to pound and a warm sensation spilled down her arms, like her blood found new license beneath her skin. A tall young man walked beside an even taller, yet stooped, older one. She could just make out their silhouettes in the setting sun.

It was Anton and Herr Handl, carrying their tile repair equipment over their shoulders.

Margaritha dropped her broom, and it smacked on the long L section of the porch. She placed a hand over her mouth and gazed behind her to see whether her parents had noticed.

Thankfully, her parents were still bickering.

Is he looking at me? Is he coming over?

Just then, a little boy shouted 'boo!' Margaritha jumped again, and noticed that Anton stopped walking, his head tilted before he continued in her direction.

"Mami, Tati! Margaritha is staring when she should be working!" Margaritha's younger brother Michael giggled with delight at this discovery of his sister. He ran around the other side of the house, intending to pass the back courtyard where her parents were.

"Oh, you little!" she shouted. Blinded by anger towards her sibling, she ran behind him, brandishing the wooden handle of the broom. "Wait till I catch you!"

Her parents wearily followed the commotion. Margaritha growled as she closed in on her giggling brother, now on the other side of the house, but the sun was suddenly in her eyes and a much taller body was in her way. When her bottom met the end of the side porch, she winced and said, "Oomph! Ow!" She shielded her eyes and looked up.

"Margaritha, I'm so sorry."

It was Anton. She gaped up at him. Time stood still and all her rage faded.

Anton reached his hand out and she took it. Her parents arrived just in time to see the pair of them, staring at one another, Margaritha's hand in Anton's. Neither could control the guilty look upon their faces as they both turned to Herr and Frau Koenig.

"Anton?" Herr Handl called for his son from a small distance.

Oh no...Mami and Tati are already in a foul mood.

"Well?" Her father spoke sternly, though not unkindly. He folded his arms. "What can we do for you today, young Anton?"

Frau Koenig stood with her hands upon her hips, pursing her lips. Her eyes were wide in an expectant way she had after being interrupted in her work.

Meanwhile, Herr Handl had arrived on the scene, his face registering the situation. Anton finally dropped Margaritha's hand. It landed, lonely and cold, on her apron. She couldn't stop herself from looking at him with a pout.

Stop it, Margaritha. What could he do? Take your other hand?

Anton finally began to speak. "Good evening, Herr and Frau Koenig. I'm afraid you caught me helping Margaritha up. She was chasing Michael and..."

"No! He was going to kiss her! I saw him, Mami!" Michael beamed with wicked delight.

At this point, both Margaritha and her mother shouted at Michael. Herr Koenig rolled his eyes and threw up his hands, one of which still held a hammer.

Herr Handl spoke, "Peace, please. I can assure you we raised our Anton to be nothing but respectful. Now son, I believe there was something you wanted to say to the Koenig family?"

Anton winced for a moment and looked at his father beseechingly.

"Our Anton is a good boy. Go on, son."

Herr Koenig now had his hands refolded over his large chest, one eyebrow raised. He hadn't put down the hammer.

"Margaritha?" Anton's timid voice sounded.

"Yes, Anton?" Margaritha found solace in his brown eyes. The sinking sun bathed the surrounding leaves and porch in an orange glow. Anton gave her his full attention, speaking with a smile.

"Margaritha Koenig? I would like very much if you would decorate my hat for the Kirchweih. And I would appreciate it even more if we could walk together in the parade. And with your parents' permission of course, under their supervision, if we could dance together during the festivities."

"Yes. Yes, of course you can," she blurted out before her parents could say a word.

"Now..." her father said sternly.

Frau Koenig interrupted him, "Yes, with our supervision of course. Please forgive our little Michael for his outbursts." At this point, the sound of feet scurrying away sounded from the youngest Koenig's hiding place. Frau Koenig continued with her chastisement. "He gets into mischief when he is supposed to be helping his father and I!"

"Oh...leave him be. He is a boy," Herr Koenig said.

"You would let *him* be a devil, but our Margaritha can't even dance with one of her dearest friends?"

Then all was silent save for the insects and poultry. The noises of animals heading back out to graze somewhat filled the awkward moment.

No one could see the expression on Herr Koenig's face as he turned to his wife. Frau Koenig turned a shade whiter and took a step back. Margaritha's mother then smoothed her hands over her apron, blowing out some air before turning to Herr Handl and asking, "So? How is your wife?"

Herr Handl's face fell. "She is most unwell. I'm afraid she won't be able to enjoy the Kirchweih...this year..." He cleared his throat and said, "But, with all the repairs required in the village, it has been a good time for work. Hasn't it, Anton?"

Anton nodded and said, "Yes. Yes, it has."

Herr Koenig grunted and said, "We are sorry about your wife's health. It is good to hear that you are working around the village again. I've said before, Handl's work is second to none. Yes...of course I give permission for Anton and Margaritha to be together at the Kirchweih. Our Margaritha will do a wonderful job decorating your hat."

Margaritha, grinning ecstatically, turned back to Anton, who was giving her the brightest smile. Her knees went weak, but she stood firm, and was sure to be as helpful as possible up until the day of the parade arrived.

○3 ℬ

Inside the church, Margaritha stole glances at Anton. Her mind wandered to the village weddings she had been to. When she turned and found his golden-brown eyes on her, Margaritha wondered if he imagined the same things she did. A hard pinch from her mother forced her to keep her eyes on the priest as he spoke of the anniversary of their church's consecration.

Later, the brass band filled Bensek with a jovial marching tune and it was time for everyone to line up. All the young ladies on one side and all the young men on the other escorted one another through the village. Margaritha from time to time looked back at Klara behind her, and Klara would wink. Her apron was well stitched by her own hand. Klara's mother and sister glared at her.

They can't even bring themselves to give her a smile during Kirchweih.

Margaritha now turned back, worried that Klara would be sad after seeing the spite and bitterness evident on her family's faces. It was a relief to find her dearest friend grinning at Hans, who grinned back.

Margaritha sighed and looked at Anton, who was looking at her. His mouth slightly open. When he blinked, his lids opened slowly.

Perhaps he and Hans got into some raki and the fruit brandy is making him look so happy.

"Are you alright?" Margaritha asked him.

"What? Oh...oh, yes. Sorry." He shook his head, and Margaritha noticed how red his cheeks became.

Margaritha bit her lip.

He was staring at me. He was actually staring at me.

I wonder if he continued to stare at me in church after Mami pinched me? Her grin widened.

Anton's hand was sweaty as he held onto hers. She squeezed him.

Now Anton chuckled. It was the first time she heard that, his chuckle. Like a deep, rumbling man's laugh. Anton was a man now. Her childhood friend now had a mature chuckle. It delighted her.

Anton was responsible, diligent in helping his father. These thoughts made her warm inside, in a way she didn't entirely understand.

Over the brass band, she cleared her throat and asked, "Anton?"

"Yes, Margaritha?" Anton replied.

"Do you still paint?"

He smiled and seemed to relax. "Yes, I do. Though, my Walter Onkel doesn't have much money to send me paints all the time. And you know? I miss having someone near me to paint with." Anton raised his voice a bit.

"Hans doesn't like painting, do you?"

Margaritha grinned and giggled.

Hans said, "No. I don't have time for it. I am trying to see what I can make of Mami and Tati's crops and the animals. The future isn't so promising." Hans's voice faded as he looked in the distance.

Klara sighed and rolled her eyes. "Hans is too practical. Aren't you, Hans?" She continued, "He wants to be a farmer in America."

Margaritha lifted her eyebrows and smiled. She relished every moment of Anton's hand touching hers. She waved at her parents.

Later, it was time for the main events in the town square. There were stalls for food, drinks, and goods. And competitions.

The favorite activity for most was the dancing.

Every time she could manage, Margaritha found herself being whirled around in Anton's arms.

She and Klara stopped together for something to drink. "It is like heaven." Margaritha sighed, talking to her friend.

Klara laughed, then her face became serious.

"What is it, Klara? What is wrong? Is it your mother? Has your sister said something? Oh, you mustn't listen to them..."

"No, Margaritha, it isn't that. It's just...Oh, you haven't noticed, have you?"

"Noticed what?"

"Peter Lulay. He has been staring at you. I don't like the look on his face."

"Herr Lulay? But he is married."

"His wife is unwell. I can see she won't be around long. It's been one short pregnancy after another. And I'm afraid...Frau Handl will be leaving us soon. Poor Anton."

"Oh, Klara..." Margaritha reached out and embraced her friend. People everywhere around Bensek laughed and danced. The air was heavy with the scent of fruit brandy, fresh breads, and roasted meat. Older men smoked pipes and visited with one another. Women handled fabric and other goods at the stalls.

Yet in all this reverie, Klara was sad.

"You've always known when people are going to go," Margaritha said.

"Yes, just like I knew when my father was going to leave this earth. I just didn't know Mami would lose her mind when he did."

"I knew it!" A shrill voice pierced the crowd near them. Some people stopped to look at fourteen-year-old Anna, glaring at her older sister.

"You killed him. I knew you did it. You are a witch. Mami knows it too." The younger girl pointed at the older one.

Klara and Margaritha stood, horrified that they hadn't noticed Anna shadowing them.

"Anna, stop talking nonsense. Go find your mother," Margaritha snapped.

"And you, you think you are better than everyone else. So proud and haughty, Margaritha Koenig, with your wide hazel eyes. Do you know? The men are fools to fall for your tricks. Poor Anton will always be poor Anton; he'll never get to your dowry!"

"That's enough, Anna!" Hans stepped in and put his arm through Klara's. Margaritha's mouth still hung open, her eyes still wide with shock.

Anna shrank back a little, her head looking from side to side at the witnesses to her outburst. Then, one corner of her mouth curved up.

"Oh, Hans Schreiber, you have fallen under my sister's spell. You should be ashamed of yourself, Klara! On this day when we celebrate the consecration of our holy church, *you* are making death predictions. What have you done? Poisoned Frau Lulay *and* her baby? Slip something into Frau Handl's tea?"

"Don't be ridiculous, Anna! You are making a fool of yourself!" Margaritha's ears rang and she clenched her fists at her sides.

"Anna, today is your day to mind your mother and make sure she isn't ranting to anyone who will listen, but perhaps someone should be minding you!" Hans growled.

Anna closed her mouth and looked down. She then turned as if to go, but before she did so, she approached Margaritha and sneered. "You wait. Your precious Anton will have to go to the army soon. So will Hans. Then who will protect you both from what everyone knows about you? That my sister is a blasphemous witch and you are a seductress."

Anton was just about to speak when Margaritha leaned down to Anna, speaking through her teeth. "I don't need anyone to protect me. Certainly not from the likes of you or your wagging, false tongue. Foul little creature."

Anna's eyes widened at the venom in Margaritha's words and the piercing glare in the older girl's amber eyes. She turned away and fled through the crowd.

Herr Koenig had made his way towards the two couples just as Anna had left.

"What's all this? I heard your sister Anna is making a fuss," Herr Koenig said to Klara.

"She has been a mean little thing ever since Tati died. I couldn't...I couldn't help that I knew. It was awful knowing..." Klara ran off in tears, and Hans went after her.

Anton was wide-eyed as he looked at Margaritha, then he turned to Herr Koenig. "Well, your Margaritha sure frightened her off."

Herr Koenig pursed his lips before he replied, "Hmmm. Well, I think your mother is off having a word with Klara's mother, not that she will get much sense out of the woman. This village cannot tolerate such nonsense! Sooner Hans and Klara get married and she is out of that house the better." Then he said to Margaritha, "Your mother will want to speak to you soon. You can't linger here."

People had slowly turned away, and soon enough, the crowd was caught up in music and frivolities again. Though, Anna's outburst would provide plenty of gossip for some time to come.

Anton cleared his throat.

"I would like to continue dancing with Margaritha, with your permission, Herr Koenig?"

Herr Koenig's eyebrows went up and he rubbed his bushy mustache. Some people glanced over briefly, yet the brass band continued to play.

He spoke, "There will be a few of you boys turning eighteen soon, is that right?"

"Yes, sir," Anton replied.

"You will be doing your time of service. No knowing what a young man will encounter during that time. The brass band will play for you and Hans and a few of the other boys, then these girls don't have their companions."

"I will be back, sir."

"Yes. I just want you both to keep your head. We've...worked hard to ensure Margaritha has a good future. You young people you don't really know what you want."

"Tati!" Margaritha admonished.

Anton said, with his chin up, "I can assure you I care for Margaritha a great deal. My family might be poor, but we've always gotten by."

At this, Herr Koenig furrowed his brows and looked down. He nodded and turned to walk away, yet before he did, he said, "Very well, enjoy the festival. But don't forget yourself, Margaritha."

Margaritha balled her fists at her sides. Anton reached out and took her elbow as her father walked away. She fumed, "It is an outrage! I'm tired of this. He must know how deeply we..."

Care for one another. How I love you. How I always have.

She didn't say the last words out loud, but Anton's golden-brown gaze must have read her thoughts.

"Come, dance with me, Margaritha. We won't be young like this forever." His voice had the effect of chamomile tea. She held onto his arm as he escorted her to the main dancing area.

They got closer and closer to the music. Margaritha couldn't help but feel by Anton's side that they were as an old couple. She was comfortable with him, like they were already a family. His company was so easy and made her happy.

Anton's hands were no longer sweaty as he held her back firmly, swinging her around in time to the band.

Yet reality was never far away. "You will have to go do your service though, won't you, Anton?" It was impossible to keep the sorrow out of her voice, despite the euphoria coursing through her blood.

"Yes. I will have to do my duty," Anton said.

"Duty, bah! They will take you away from me just to ensure the rich men far from our village have enough men trained to be slaughtered in the defense of their territory."

"Margaritha..." Anton admonished gently. "The Hapsburgs have been good to us. As Swabians, we owe them our allegiance."

The euphoria fading, Margaritha wrapped her arms around Anton's shoulders and rested her head on his chest. Most of the folks around were too distracted by drinks and revelry to notice the young couple cuddling.

"For what, Anton? We sweat and bleed and die. All so they can draw new dots and lines on paper."

"But think, my love...there is no war going on now. Nothing serious is happening. I will be doing training maneuvers. A bit of marching. Nothing else. Don't worry." He rubbed the back of her head. Margaritha closed her eyes in bliss at being so close to him.

"No...there is no war. Not now..." She let herself be calmed. Anton's words *my love* echoed in her head.

Chapter 6

1908. Soldiers and Enemies. Bensek.

Margaritha was on her knees in the kitchen, collecting scraps of onion peel and cabbage, when there was a knock at the door. She stood abruptly. Frozen. Over the past couple of years, she hadn't usually enjoyed who came to visit.

Knock, knock, knock. There it was again. She hoped it wasn't Peter Lulay, coming to drop off more fruit.

'For you or your mother. As I don't have a wife anymore to tend the garden, and my garden is full of these things.'

Or leave a message for her father, as it seemed Peter Lulay was one of the regulars in the Wirtshaus, or was at least always present when her father went in.

Her mother would close her mouth and appear distracted whenever Margaritha asked the question, "Does he think he can marry me?"

Many of the village women found him handsome. Margaritha found him intimidating and annoying.

Klara's prediction that Frau Lulay would pass had come true. The poor young woman had barely been in her grave when Peter took a more obvious interest in Margaritha.

Another problem was that it could be someone coming to complain about Michael. Her younger brother had been starting fights at the Saturday dances, which Papa seemed to find quite amusing...until parents came to complain about their son's bloody nose or black eye.

Perhaps I can avoid answering the door. Pretend I'm not home. Perhaps I can hide beneath the table.

Knock, knock, knock. There it was again, followed by a voice. "Hello? Anybody home?"

Margaritha knew that voice, though it had been over four years since she had heard it.

She ran to the door and opened it so quickly that she nearly knocked Anton off the porch. She threw her arms around his neck and he caught her, wrapping his arms around her. He reached up and stroked the curls that escaped her headscarf.

They could feel each other's heartbeat and were breathless with joy in one another's arms. Then, they realized the danger if anyone saw them in such an embrace.

Papa would never forgive me.

They pulled away from each other, smiling at the ground.

"You are back!" she squealed with delight, looking at him. In such a short time, he appeared to have aged. There were shadows beneath his eyes. She reached up to touch his face.

"Anton..." she said, struggling to contain her joy at seeing him back in their village safe and sound.

He caught her hand and held it in both of his.

"Hans is back too. I told you everything would be fine. It was some training, some marching, that was all." He fidgeted a little with her hand on the porch, then she remembered and her eyes filled up. The funeral had been only a few months ago.

Both Frau and Herr Handl were now gone.

"Oh, Anton. I am so sorry. I really, really am so sorry."

"It's okay. My father will be happy that he is with her. They are both free now." Anton told her that he and Hans were granted early release; both were the only sons and heirs of family properties, and both had ailing parents.

Anton's release, sadly, had not been granted in time to say a final farewell to his mother or father.

"They were both such wonderful people. I have so many wonderful memories. Your mother in particular, she was a lovely woman."

Anton was looking at the ground, nodding. Margaritha braced herself against the ache in her chest. His hands still held one of hers and she reached out her other hand to stroke the tops of his. "I can't tell you how much I've missed you. Oh, Anton..."

She couldn't resist. She threw her arms around him again and kissed his cheek.

"Margaritha…please. We will both be in trouble." Yet he didn't resist.

Margaritha stepped back, pursing her lips, but when she looked up at him again, she noticed how he was grinning.

"Mami is inside. Why don't you come in? I'm sure she would love to see you."

"Margaritha, it won't be appropriate. Truly. I need to speak to both of your parents. Margaritha…I want to…."

"…yes?" She stood on her toes with wide eyes.

"I would like to get your father's permission to court you."

"I would like that too." She smiled.

"So…we must do right. There is also the problem of me having nothing."

"It's not a problem with me, Anton. I don't need any fancy life. I'm happy to be a maid or take in washing." Margaritha's mind began to whirl. An adventurous future, one that shunned tradition, gleamed before her and Margaritha spoke quickly, before the beautiful image faded. "We could run away together, to somewhere like Budapest or Vienna. We could paint! The both of us. I don't care about all the expectations…"

"Margaritha, I care for you. So much. We must have approval. I know you don't require lavish things, but you will want to eat."

With that, Anton reached out and stroked her cheek. She leaned into his touch and held his wrist as he stroked her face. She stilled for him, for his unspoken request to study her every feature.

"Did I ever tell you that your smile and your eyes make me think of freshly baked cakes? I'm sure I could live off of that alone."

Anton laughed and Margaritha beamed, both caught in love's spell.

Until a cough sounded from a distance and a sharp voice said, "See here, young Anton…you and young Schreiber are back from your service, are you? I should think you have far better things to do than harassing Margaritha."

Peter Lulay walked towards the couple. He balanced a huge bundle on one shoulder and carried a small satchel slung around the other.

"What is that you have there?" Anton asked.

"I've collected some things from the fields. Plus, my cousin in America sent me a few samples of his crops. I wanted to show Herr Koenig."

"He isn't home right now, Herr Lulay," Anton said, insolence lacing his voice.

Margaritha felt the blood drain from her face. Peter placed the bundle down with a grunt and wiped his brow. He folded his arms across his chest as he looked at Anton.

"Herr Lulay, Anton is one of my oldest friends and he is not harassing me at all. We should be happy that one of our village sons is back safe and sound."

Margaritha looked to Anton, who was watching Peter closely. Peter returned the younger man's dark stare with a glare of his own.

Anton said, "I have no intention of harassing Margaritha."

Peter shook his head and said, "At any rate, you'd better speak to her father about their plans for her. They might not include a poor boy from Bensek, destined to be a poor man in Temeswar." Herr Lulay spoke as a concerned elder, not as a jealous suiter.

Two-faced swine who should still be mourning his dead wife and unborn child. Margaritha loathed the sight of him. Anton's voice broke into her thoughts.

"I'm not frightened of hard work, Herr Lulay, to get to where I need to go."

Peter chuckled as though amused by two foolish young people.

"I hope that you will manage when you get to Temeswar, young Anton, but it isn't fair to drag Margaritha down with you. She deserves more out of her life."

Anton took a steady breath and moved as though to say something to the older man, but Margaritha placed a hand in the crook of his arm.

They watched Peter slowly walk away and down the road, heading in the direction of the church.

"How long has his wife been dead?" Anton asked darkly.

Margaritha sighed. "She truly hasn't been in the ground long, God Bless her." She crossed herself.

"Margaritha, I will need some time to get things in order, but I will speak to your parents..."

"Anton? Are you planning on going to Temeswar?"

"Yes. I will have to go there to work. I will stay with my Walter Onkel and Susannah Tant. They will give me accommodation. If I can get settled in employment...I'm hoping your parents will give me a chance. That is, if you would wait."

Margaritha's gently arched brows drew together and she chewed her lip. She reached out and grasped Anton's arms, just above his wrists. "The problem, Anton, is that Herr Lulay is trying to get my parents' approval to marry me. I don't know how long before father insists. He likes Herr Lulay. I can't imagine why."

"He would give you a life of stability. Right now, I can't offer that. But oh, Margaritha...If you would have me, I would love you forever..."

And I you, Anton...

Chapter 7

2017. Early November. North Dakota.

Thump, thump, thump.

Amber was in bed, drifting in and out of sleep in the wee hours, when she was sure she heard a voice. A murmur.

Then the noise came again. Thump, thump, thump. Amber sat up, holding her hand over her chest. She stayed completely still in the darkness of her room. The thumping ceased. Amber's gaze flicked around, waiting for the silence to be broken.

Her eyes ached with exhaustion as she got up to pull on her robe, padding over the cold wood floor. There were no signs of entry at either the front door or the kitchen.

She pulled her robe tighter. Her vision adjusted to the darkness. Amber stopped walking and sighed.

Now, she stood in the middle of her living room. The pillows and throw on the couch, the coasters on the coffee table, all lay in the same position they were in when she left.

It's been two days since I've seen anything...

There hadn't been any sightings of the Schreiber couple, if that was who she was seeing, yet there were odd voices and noises in her dreams. Or rather, somewhere between being asleep and being awake.

It could just be from being so darn sleepy.

Thump, thump, thump. Amber turned in the direction of the hall. She walked behind the couch and down the hallway to her office.

Was it from there?

She thought if it had been coming from her bedroom, she would understand the source of it.

She walked into the futon room/home office. The heating kicked in again with a click and a hum.

"Oh! Geez!" She startled at the sound that, a month ago, wouldn't have bothered her.

Amber laughed and placed her hand on her forehead, then dropping her hand from her head, she stared at the blank easel.

Maybe painting will relax me. It always used to.

There was something satisfying about the oil-soaked brush gliding over the canvas. It sent tingles up the back of her head.

She sat in front of the window, swallowing and blowing out a sigh.

There is nobody there...nobody outside.

There was enough moonlight to illuminate the canvas itself, and to see the beginning of her long gravel driveway.

Amber leaned towards the set of drawers where she kept brushes, paints, and pens.

Oh...crud. After rummaging through, she realized how low she was on paints.

Amber left her office and headed out to the living room. Tentatively peering out of her front window, her car stood, lonely and uncovered in front of the house.

Oh no...car shelter. The breeze picked up again, whipping the blades of grass on the edge of her driveway. It was a reminder of the impending freeze, and the mountains of snow that would bury her vehicle if she didn't sort out something for the winter.

Apart from the road cutting through it, the land outside was like a sea of faded green waving in the darkness.

Amber resigned herself to have a trip into town tomorrow.

She went to sleep, thinking about Martin. She imagined his midnight-colored hair, and the kindness in his eyes. How difficult it was not to stare at him. Just the memory of him made her warm, like a protective blanket she could crawl under to escape the ghosts in her house.

○ ॐ

Amber pulled up outside the variety store attached to the grocery store. The sun created just a little warmth on her head, in defiance of the icy air. There were garlands of leaves and friendly scarecrow figures on the doors of shops.

The door chimed as Amber entered and headed straight back to the art supply section. She gathered a few containers of oil paint, alongside some new brushes.

Thump, thump, thump.

Amber stopped in her tracks, looking around.

I'm losing my mind.

Then she saw that it was the rolls of fabric being unraveled for a customer. A dark-haired woman turned around and said, "Hey, you!" It took Amber a moment to register that it was Theresa.

"Hey," she said, walking slowly and clutching her paints. Her knees felt weak. The door chimed again with the arrival of another customer, Amber didn't look at the door.

"How're ya doing?" Theresa beamed at her.

"Oh, fine...fine. I realized I was low on paint, so I came into town."

"Ah. I thought you do everything on a computer these days." Theresa tilted her head.

"Well, I do mostly, yes. I still like to do things old fashioned, though. Painting and sketching helps me to de-stress."

"*You* are stressed? You? What's the matter? Don't you have enough work? Are you still seeing ghosts?"

Amber cringed at her friend's bluntness. "I..." A motion out of the corner of her right eye caught her attention. Standing at one of the checkout counters was Martin. He was wearing his blue coat, and was staring right at her.

The lady serving him had her back to Amber. "Sir?" she said. He blinked and said, "Oh, sorry...sorry...uh..." And he proceeded to get his money out to pay.

Amber turned back to Theresa, who was looking at her with a raised eyebrow.

Theresa whispered, "He is way too cute to be in a fabric store. It isn't right. I'm glad he's here, though." She poked Amber, who glared in response.

Martin had obviously finished with the cashier and walked towards Amber and Theresa. Her eyes widened as he approached.

"Amber, good to see you. How's things?"

"Oh, fine...fine. Yourself?"

"Great." He wet his lips with his tongue, his mouth open slightly as though he wanted to say something. There was an awkward silence as both of appeared at a loss for words.

Theresa broke the silence, "You must be new around here? I'm Theresa, Amber's friend"

Martin looked at Theresa with a smile and extended his hand.

"Hi, I'm Martin. I uh...I am new. I found out someone was living at that old homestead and I'm a builder you see. I'm from Chicago, I've always had an interest in abandoned structures."

Theresa nodded and replied. "Oh, she's done a great job on it already, not sure what she'd need..." Theresa's brows knit together, finger on her chin as her words tapered off.

"Car shelter. I didn't even think of a garage. Quite an oversight." Amber interrupted her "hmm" noises.

Theresa's mouth dropped open and she said "oh...that is an oversight, Amber."

"I know." Amber mouthed before turning back to Martin and continuing, "So...I take it you've had a chance to look at your diary?"

"I have. I can come over tomorrow." Martin replied.

"Wow, that's quick." Amber's heart rate sped up and she smiled.

"Ten tomorrow morning okay?"

"Absolutely." Amber replied.

"There's really no obligation to use me and I won't charge you for the quote." Martin held up his hands.

"Well, we'll have a talk when you come over tomorrow."

"Great." Martin was still smiling. There was another awkward silence between them as they looked at one another.

They were interrupted by Theresa clearing her throat and saying, "Looks like it's a date."

Amber's cheeks heated in a way she hadn't experienced since high school and Martin coughed. Amber caught a pinkish hue spreading across his face.

"Well, I'll see you tomorrow Martin for a quote." Amber accentuated the last word, looking at Theresa with narrowed eyes.

Theresa grinned back. "Nice to meet you, Martin."

"You too, Theresa. Well, I'll be heading off. See you."

With that, Martin nodded and headed out of the shop.

"Well now..." Theresa turned her gaze on Amber.

"He did stop at the house. And I saw him at church."

"You went to church?" Theresa's eyebrow went up.

"I wanted to go and say a prayer for the..."

"The ghost?"

"I think there are two." Amber trembled with the admission. She'd been feeling so elated moments ago, with Martin's face in front of her.

"Amber, you know...the boys were adamant that there was someone there. I know they have imaginations but..."

Amber pressed her lips together and shook her head.

Theresa reached a hand out and placed it on Amber's shoulder, saying

"Oh my goodness. Just move. Come on. You can't live out there on your own all scared."

"I don't know how to tell you this, Theresa, but they don't exactly *terrify* me. I feel like...there is something I need to find out."

"Well...I know you've put a lot into that house." Theresa said with a sigh. "If you need anything, you let me know. Call me anytime."

"Will do." Amber forced a smile, and bid Theresa good-bye.

She paid for her things and then left to run a few more errands in town. The sun was shining and despite the impending stark winter, the sky gave a reminder of summer with its vibrant blue.

The thought of Martin coming to her door filled her heart with excitement.

He's coming for to give me a quote for a car shelter. That's it.

She put her items in her truck and headed home.

A smile was on her face as she walked up her porch steps. The sound of Martin's voice was a tonic against any chills that threatened when she entered the house. Her haunted house.

Chapter 8

1909. The Wirtshaus. Bensek.

Anton pulled his worn overcoat closer together as he walked from his parents' old house towards the Wirtshaus. Since returning to Bensek, he had managed a couple of paying roof repair jobs, but nothing sustained. He'd noticed more and more children running through the streets. The family sizes had grown during the time he'd been away. There simply wouldn't be enough work or land for everyone here. No wonder many had begun to leave.

The Wirtshaus, or village pub, was a place that the inhabitants of Bensek had been rather proud of, perhaps even boastful of, in comparison to other villages.

Tonight, Hans and Anton hoped to have a reason to celebrate. Anton was finally going to speak to Herr Koenig. From his previous visit to Margaritha, and Peter Lulay's irritating appearance, Anton gathered that the older man was seeking Margaritha, the village beauty, for his wife.

I must speak with Herr Koenig and make it clear how we feel for one another. AND that I will do whatever is necessary to care for her.

The weather was getting colder, and he hadn't been able to have much lately in the way of food. Tonight, he would visit the Wirtshaus to purchase a hot meal and have a drink or two with his friend. And he would speak to Herr Koenig, prove to him that he was a hard-working man, who would look after his only daughter.

Just as he knew Hans would always care for Klara.

When Anton pushed the doors open to the Wirtshaus, he was greeted with the smell of cooked pork, smoky paprika, and onions. His mouth watered despite the scents of pipe smoke and sweat. The fragrance of food made it all worth it.

As he progressed into the room, fruit brandy and beer permeated the musty air as well. It was mostly a room full of men. A couple of gypsy women were there, smoking and discussing the possibility of horse sales.

He looked down at his worn boots traversing the floor.

Herr Koenig will be here. He usually comes in on a Friday night.

As he passed table after smoky table, he heard a couple of phrases. "This...Dakota, in America. They are almost giving land away...My cousin, he insists it is worth going. I haven't seen him for years, but he has stayed in contact."

Anton had heard this sort of talk before. His chest ached. Many people were leaving Bensek for the cities of America and for the 'homesteading' opportunities that were in the farming areas. Much like when the Hapsburgs put the call out to German and French-speaking peasants to come work the land just reclaimed from the Turks, now American politicians were calling for 'yeoman farmers' on lands only once inhabited by migrating Native people.

Of whom he'd heard all sorts of terrifying stories. What was fantasy and what was truth was hard to discern.

I should imagine the American natives are people, just as the Turks were and still are just people. Most good. Some bad. Like us.

Anton never voiced these feelings out loud. Not even with Hans, who was a decent fellow but very practical. He saw things day to day, season to season. What would grow; what would not. Hans had always found his friend's interest in philosophy and art amusing. Politics was a messy topic that only interfered with work and planning.

The conversation continued, "The difference is that that land will be ours. Well and truly. All we have to do is make something of it."

Anton looked to the source of this talk, and was instantly met with the coal dark stare of Peter Lulay, who lifted his drink to his lips and stared at Anton. Peter flitted his eyes back to Herr Koenig.

Anton gritted his teeth.

Just this one night, can't he stay at home? From the impression Margaritha gave me, he is forever down the ear of Herr Koenig.

It sickened him to see Margaritha's father nodding and listening so intently to every word Peter said.

The door opened and Hans walked in. A grin was on his curiously rosy face as he spread his arms open and looked at his friend. He nodded and

Anton instantly realized the source of his friend's joy. Hans, upon their return to Bensek, had talked about asking Klara to marry him.

She's said yes.

Anton swallowed and smiled. There was a small part of him that was a little jealous. Sadly, Hans's parents were now gone too, but they had left him with something of a small inheritance. And likely, Klara's disturbed mother was only too happy to be rid of her eldest daughter.

Anton turned to the barkeep, ordered some food and two drinks. The bushy mustache of the barkeep twitched a little and he began to give orders to his staff. He then wagged a finger at Anton.

"Good you didn't order your drink in Hungarian. I would have thrown you out. Apparently, you even started speaking that blasted language. I am a Schwob forever, and this is my place!" The man pounded his bar with a meaty fist.

Anton winced. Yes, he had been one of the few students successful with the Hungarian tongue, during the government incentive to unite the people under one Magyar language. Many considered it to have been a slow process of bullying any Serbs, Slovaks, Romanians and Germans into conforming to one culture. His Walter Onkel spoke of Schwobs he knew in Temeswar changing their names so that they would sound more Hungarian.

He looked the bartender in the eye and said, "Sir, there is nothing wrong with being or speaking Hungarian. It is the land we live in. However, I am happy with the language and culture I was brought up with, and happy to speak it here."

The barkeep grunted and gave him his drink.

Just then, a hand clapped him on the shoulder and he was met with the pale, twinkling eyes of Hans.

"She said yes! She said yes to everything!"

Anton chuckled and clapped his hand on his friend's back.

"Klara will marry me. She will come be with me. We will move, Anton. Anton...you must emigrate!"

Anton looked at his drink and then back up at Hans, who grinned when he saw that Anton had purchased him one as well.

Anton said, "You have a fine house and fields here."

"I don't want to dishonor my parents, but every last one of my siblings died in their house. It is a sad place." Hans nodded, looking ahead before continuing. "I know that I can sell it; someone else will make something of it. Then with the money, I can get supplies to build a place in Dakota. I will take advantage of this...homestead act. Many are doing it. It is a good option. I understand it will be hard, but...I will do it. Klara can make anything grow anywhere. We will be so happy!" Hans grasped Anton by the shoulders and shook him a little before letting go.

"But...you could be happy here. You have a house. And I could visit you from Temeswar," Anton said.

"Bah! You know how things are here, Anton." Hans took a swig of his drink. The laughter of other men sounded in the background. "But you know what people say about Klara...because of her mother being strange, that spiteful thing of a sister. I want her to be free of gossip. I want the best for Klara. As I know..."

Anton felt Hans grip his arm and shake him a little.

"As I know that you want to do the best by Margaritha..."

At this point, Anton looked to Peter Lulay, who now glared at the pair of them from a few tables away. Peter must have heard Hans mention the name of Margaritha. Herr Koenig remained oblivious, busy waving his hands and talking about the size of wheat fields.

Anton looked back to Hans, interrupting him, "Yes, I do. You know I do." They both turned, putting their backs to the rest of the pub. Anton lowered his voice to a whisper, "I was hoping to have a word with Herr Koenig tonight, but it would appear that Herr Lulay has his sights on Margaritha and has been doing his best to secure a marriage with her while I have been away."

Just then, the doors opened and Michael Koenig walked in. The light and dark heads of Anton and Hans turned in his direction then back again.

Hans rolled his eyes. "He is only just old enough to be in here, the fool. And he often causes trouble."

Michael walked up to the table of his father and Herr Lulay. Anton's stomach turned as Peter's face lit up at the sight of the young man. More drinks were brought and Michael sat down next to his father.

Michael turned around and waved to the two men watching them. "Hello, Hans. Hello, Anton. You are back! Soon it will be my turn!" He referred to his time in the service, which he appeared to have avoided for an extra year. Anton had an idea that Michael intended to go to America as well, to avoid conscription. There were a few who emigrated purely for that reason.

They ordered another drink. Herr Koenig stood up from his party and, to Anton's delight, walked towards Anton and Hans. It was Hans whom he clapped on the back. "So, you boys are indeed back. How wonderful. Not many come back so soon. My condolences for your parents. What are your plans?"

Hans spoke, "I wish to go to America, to homestead in this, North Dakota. There are other Schwobs in the area. There will be lots of hard work and a period of adjustment, but we will be fine."

"We?" Herr Koenig, his teeth—each slightly spaced apart—showing themselves below his mustache.

"Well, Klara and I are to be married. She has agreed."

"That's good. That's good," Herr Koenig said gently. He lowered his voice more. "I always thought it best she marry someone goodhearted enough to take her away from that woman and that unkind sister. She is below your station, you know. She won't bring you anything. But with your parents not being here anymore, it is only you. You can do as you wish. I wish you luck, Hans. You too, Anton. What will you do?"

Anton took a big sip of his drink. "Herr Koenig, I will go and stay with my aunt and uncle in Temeswar. He has long been working for a wealthy family in the city. They pay them well and I will join him, learning his trade. I..."

Hans coughed and set his drink down. Herr Koenig stood still, nodding in anticipation of what Anton would say next.

"Herr Koenig, please forgive me. I am aware that Herr Lulay seeks Margaritha as a wife. It seems plain to me..."

Herr Koenig crossed his arms over his chest and furrowed his brows. A few men roared with laughter in the background.

"You know that Margaritha and I care for one another. I would be respectful and provide for her. I am sure Margaritha would wait while I get situated in Temeswar. We might live a simple life, but it will be what we both want. If you speak to her about this, you would see."

There. That's the best I can do.

Herr Koenig let out a long sigh from his nose and stroked his chin. "Anton...I am aware of how you and Margaritha feel for one another. Yet you must understand that this not only goes against tradition, but it goes against my own feelings. Her mother's feelings."

Anton's heart began to race and he interrupted Herr Koenig, "Frau Koenig is fond of me..."

"Anton." Her Koenig's voice was firmer now. "You may feel this way now. You are both young. We are not...rich people, but Margaritha has a decent dowry and Peter, like Hans here, has a considerable amount to his name. He has cousins in America. He has the wisdom of age."

Anton blew out a breath and said, "She does not love him. She doesn't even like him."

Herr Koenig put up his hand and pulled his chin in. "It is not for Margaritha to decide on her husband based on childhood fancies. As the years go by, she will grow to care for him. It will be better for her in America. You likely don't even have the money for passage. You are putting on poor relatives so you can live in Temeswar. One day, you will be able to provide for yourself and maybe even afford a wife. But it won't be my Margaritha. I won't give her that life."

Anton's face grew hot with anger and he felt prickles of impending danger at the back of his scalp. Hans placed his hand on Anton's shoulder and moved closer to Anton. "I am sorry for my friend, Herr Koenig. You must understand he has always loved Margaritha."

"You will be fine in time…it will be better. For both of you." Herr Koenig clapped Anton on the shoulder and walked away.

Anton's eyes flitted to the table, and again he saw Peter Lulay looking at him as Margaritha's father returned to their table.

Anton turned to Hans, hoping his friend would have some advice or plan. Some sensible way of convincing the man that insisting his daughter marry Peter Lulay was a mistake. Instead, Hans stayed silent and gestured for them to sit at a different table as the food was served.

"My friend, you appear to have no appetite," Hans finally said, noting Anton's sullen face as he poked at his sausages.

"The old man doesn't see reason. He thinks once property and finances are in order, then happiness won't be an issue. He doesn't care how Margaritha feels. All this tradition! Even if my father were alive, Herr Koenig would still look down his nose at my family."

"Come to America. Follow on after us. There is more there."

"You know that I cannot. Herr Koenig is right, I don't even have enough for passage. I want to stay here. This is my home. It's *her* home. Yes, we have to leave Bensek because it is too small, the population is growing and there is not enough work. I don't speak English…"

Anton stumbled over his words and slammed his fist on the table, causing the cutlery to shake.

Hans reached out and patted his friend on the back. "Michael and Peter are looking at us. Perhaps we should go, you can re-think how to go about this."

"No. Let's have another drink. I don't care that they are staring. Let's celebrate your marriage to Klara."

Hans sat back and began to eat. Anton took a few mouthfuls and their conversation turned to Anton's plans in Temeswar and his aunt and uncle there.

With every swallow of wine, anger lurked in Anton's heart, but he allowed nostalgia to also set in, and the talk was of their childhood exploits.

The time ticked by, and the pub's volume grew as the alcohol flowed. The smoke, brandy, and sweat began to outweigh the cooking smells.

Anton's skin felt numb from the drinks. He stared at the rich red sauce and remains of onions on his plate. When he reached to the side to pick up some bread and soak the rest up, he noticed a shadow.

Michael Koenig stood at the side of their table with a smile on his face.

"How are you, young Koenig?" Hans said with a raised eyebrow.

"Ah. I'm not so young anymore. So, my father tells me you will emigrate with your soon to be wife, Klara? You will go to the same place my sister will be?"

Hans looked up, squinted his pale eyes a little as he replied, "Yes... it appears that way. Will you go through with your service or will you emigrate?"

"How dare you suggest that I would avoid my duty!" Michael slammed his hands on the table and glared at Hans, who only widened his eyes.

"Look, I mean no offense. I speak honestly. In hindsight, if I could have chosen to stay with my parents before they passed, I would have. That's all." Hans took a drink.

Michael shuffled his feet and took a deep breath in through his nose. "I would be careful, you know, marrying that Klara." He leaned in and whispered, "People say she is a witch. She could have even put a spell on you to get you to marry her."

"That's enough, Michael. Why don't you go back and sit down with your father and future brother-in-law?" Anton spoke sharply, bitterly. Michael turned to him and grinned.

"Yes, good that you see reason. You will always be nothing but a pauper, and we are better than you. Stay the hell away from my sister."

Hans shook his head and sighed. "Please, young Koenig, go back to your table. We want no more of your taunts. Perhaps there is someone else for you to pick a fight with." Hans's voice was weary.

But Michael leaned closer to Hans and lowered his voice. "You know, I bet she can't even give you children. What use will she be? A witch with a dry womb, who you wish to bed due to some spell."

Hans's chair scraped the floor as he stood, grabbed two handfuls of Michael's shirt, and said in a low whisper, "You shouldn't say such things, Koenig."

Michael punched Hans right in the stomach. Hans doubled over, eyes bulging and bile and spit coming out of his mouth as he groaned.

Anton pulled Michael away from Hans. Michael smiled, seemingly gleeful over the casual violence.

Anton pulled Michael up and threw him across an empty table.

"You are a stupid boy, Michael Koenig. You never mind your tongue when you should. It will be end of you!"

At this, Herr Koenig stood up and approached the younger men. "What's all this? Michael? Hans? Anton?"

Hans was still pale from Michael's fist. Then Michael, who had since pulled himself up, said, "Anton is dishonorable towards my sister. Perhaps you will find those sort of women in Temeswar, Anton, but not in Bensek. Leave *my* family alone!"

Anton could no longer bear the injustice of it. His punch was swift and sharp, smashing into Michael's face.

He saw red, lunging again. But he was held back as Michael stumbled, the younger boy holding a cloth to his bleeding nose.

It was Peter and Herr Koenig holding Anton back. Hans shouted for calm. Anton was murderous, and could have strangled Michael Koenig to death.

The Wirtshaus owner ran towards them, shouting, "Enough! Enough! Get out! You! Schreiber and Handl! And Herr Koenig, get your boy out! I've had enough. It's you, Handl! You are the one who threw Michael across the table! Stupid boy!"

Herr Koenig ushered Hans, Anton, and Michael out with the help of Peter Lulay.

Once they were outside the Wirtshaus, Margaritha's father scolded the three of them. "I've told you, Michael, about that. Our family is above such behavior. And as for you, Anton, you are lucky I don't get the authorities involved."

Peter Lulay blinked serenely and stepped towards Herr Koenig. "If I may, sir, I don't think any one in particular is to blame. I used to have such silly confrontations when I was younger too. Perhaps forgiveness is in order on this occasion."

Herr Koenig nodded and said, "Well, I'm ready for bed now anyway. But you, Handl, you for sure stay away from my daughter. For shame, you behaving like that!"

Anton stood next to Hans with his mouth open, his brows furrowed. He had since calmed and realized the gravity of his mistake.

As the three other men walked away, Peter Lulay turned back to Anton, a smirk just detectable on his mouth. Anton's stomach twisted at the look of triumph in the older man's eyes.

Chapter 9

2017. The Shelter. North Dakota.

Amber had been at her desk for over two hours. She rolled the chair back and walked into the kitchen, squeezing her eyes shut and stretching her arms while moving towards the sink. Her gaze met the portraits on the windowsill before her.

Her grandparents and her great grandparents stared back at her. Amber filled the coffee pot with water as she stared at the old portrait of her Grandma Caroline, then over to the wedding portrait of her great grandmother, her father's grandmother. Amber swallowed, expecting to see a shadow in the glass.

Her eyes darted to the portraits of her mother's Norwegian grandparents, then back to her paternal grandparent's wedding photo, taken in Europe over a century ago.

Icy water ran over her arm as the coffee pot overflowed.

Knock, knock, knock.

Her arm jerked and she looked down to the broken coffee pot.

"Oh!" It had smashed onto the bottom of the sink and she was still holding the handle.

Knock, knock, knock. Amber slipped her hand out of the handle and found some of the glass stuck her palm. She grabbed a dish cloth and went to the door.

She fumbled with the lock and opened the door, pushing some hair out of her eyes with her unwrapped hand.

Standing there, on her front porch, was Martin.

Then, he took a step back and smiled. When he did, his lips stretched and lightened into a pale peach color. Amber was still staring when he began to speak.

"Hi Amber, good to see you…" he looked down at her wrapped hand then back up at her and said "Are you okay?"

"I'm fine. I just…" She looked down at her palm, removed the dish cloth, and saw the minor yet bleeding cut.

Amber cleared her throat and spoke. "Oh, this…I just smashed the coffee pot. So, unless you are into tea or the instant stuff, I'm afraid I can't offer you a cup."

He smiled again. Amber swallowed. He said, "That's okay. I really just need to have a look around to get a feel for where you would want your shelter."

Amber nodded and said, "Ah…" She looked down at her porch. Just to the right were some grains of crystal sea salt. She focused on them, sure that they had been swept up since Theresa came over.

"So, it was nice to meet your friend, Theresa," Martin blurted out.

"Yeah." Amber giggled, shaking her head. "She's a character alright. So…what were you getting from the variety store?"

He chuckled. "Um, I like to paint."

"Really?"

"Well…yeah. When I get time. Landscapes and stuff. I go fishing and watch football too."

"That's nice." She smirked a little.

He grinned and said, "I have to admit I was disappointed when I came out here before. I had an eye on this place myself a while back, then I saw somebody got it. I wanted to meet the person who owned it."

Amber laughed and squeezed the dish towel around her hand. "Well, if your quote is reasonable, then you'll be able to spend more time here." Amber blushed and looked down. Everything she said to him seemed have an over-friendly ring to it. She wasn't a flirt and certainly not with workmen so what was wrong with her?

Martin cleared his throat and shifted his feet on the porch, making the boards creek. Amber took a slow breath in and said, "Hold on a moment, let me grab a coat and I will show you around. You wanna wait inside?"

"Sure."

He took off his woolen hat and his large boots scraped over the mat as he entered. Amber closed the door and went to grab the fleece from her bedroom.

She heard Martin sigh through his nose and she returned to the front door to find him looking all around her home.

"You've done a good job here."

"Thanks. I forgot about the garage, though. Felt kind of silly when the weather started turning and I realized…"

"It happens. I've seen it before when people take on doing up an old house on their own. I'm glad you got in touch." Martin cleared his throat again. Then they were silent as they exited the house to head out into the yard.

Amber's cheeks heated as their feet crunched over the cold, dry grass.

"I'll give you a tour around, okay?"

Martin was silent for two seconds then said, "Sure." His gaze flicked all around, like he was amazed by the surroundings.

"Are you from out of state?"

"Yeah. I'm from Chicago. I've lived just outside Dickinson for a couple of years. I'm only just starting to do business in this part of the state." They walked around the side of the one-story house.

"You can see out there where the creek is. And the trees."

Amber shielded her eyes from the sun and squinted, scanning the landscape.

"What's that?" Martin asked.

"What?"

Martin pointed to what appeared to be some gray wood at the very far end of her yard.

I'm sure I never saw that before.

The wind picked up and blew hard enough to make Amber's fleece stick to her front and blow out at the back. They walked towards the strange wood pile.

"Man…I thought Chicago was cold," Martin said.

"Yeah. I was raised here, but I'm still never ready for winter when it comes."

The wood looked like a collapsed section of house or of barn, the paint on it long since destroyed. It lay mainly in the wilder bit of prairie behind her house.

Martin reached down and examined the wood. "Ah!" he shouted.

Amber yelped too and jumped back. There was a mouse sheltering beneath the wood. It ran off into the overgrown prairie, scurrying as fast as its tiny legs could carry it.

Amber and Martin laughed.

"You're afraid of a mouse?" she said.

"You were too!" he chided with a grin.

When their chuckles subsided, they stood silent before the vast expanse of land behind Amber's house.

Amber found herself unable to look away from him. The sun had gone behind a cloud and without the glare, it was easy to study one another's features. Martin smiled and tilted his head. Amber's cheeks warmed despite the cold. She cleared her throat and gestured that they should move.

They walked around the other side of the house, and Amber shivered as they passed her bedroom window. She recalled the vision of the man walking past when she had just woken up the other morning.

It had to have been Hans. But could it have been Martin?

Her breath caught in her throat, wondering if Martin had been lurking around her property. She hardly knew this man. And here she was, on her own with him at her isolated dwelling.

Amber stared at the back of Martin's coat, wondering if there were any similarities between Martin and the man she saw.

Her body tilted back slightly as she observed the movements of his arms, the way he held himself.

He is much bigger than...Hans.

"Oh God..." she said aloud, then clamped a hand over her mouth.

"What is it?" Martin said, snapping his head in her direction.

"Oh...well, I was just thinking...I don't remember seeing it," Amber said, truly confused. Should she be relieved it couldn't have been Martin? Should she be happy her property is haunted?

"Yeah, looks typical of some of the old places I've seen around here. The odd bit of wood hanging around that used to be a barn. There's lots of interesting ghost towns in the state, aren't there?"

Amber was quiet for a moment too long.

"I..."

It was Hans. It wasn't Theresa. Unless I've got a stalker. And that is probably what is left of Hans's barn.

She continued, "I guess there are. Most people who I grew up with left and haven't come back. It's always been a rural state. When I was younger, people used to talk about how depressing it is here after you've visited somewhere else. I lived away for a while. But I like the quiet. *You're* kind of unusual for having decided to live here after growing up in Chicago."

Martin nodded. "I guess. I suppose I wanted quiet too. Plus, it's less expensive to live and set up a business here."

"Oh yeah," Amber agreed.

They turned the corner of her house back to where her vehicle was parked.

Amber watched Martin as he examined the lay of the land around her truck, on either side of the long gravel drive that led to the road. "We can get something up pretty quick. We'll erect it a bit farther back from the house. It will only take a few hours to get the thing up. When the ground thaws, if you still want a permanent structure from us, we can re-assess then too."

Amber nodded as she looked from her truck to Martin, who gave her a closed-lipped smile. She stared at his mouth, searching for the pleasant peach color, seeing only a flash of it. Amber pressed her mouth together, gazed up, and was met with a stare from Martin, the look in his eyes almost heated. Then he smiled and they both laughed. Both of them were nervous. They couldn't quite say out loud what was transpiring between them.

They discussed price and Amber was pleasantly surprised.

"Oh, that's so much better than what I thought it would be." She sighed.

"Yeah...well, that was part of my reason for moving out here. I hated having to charge what I did back in Illinois."

The wind picked up and blew Martin's hair over his head.

"How about next week? Monday? Then you're under cover before the snow happens," he said.

Amber nodded, reaching out so they could shake on it. Martin removed his glove and grasped her smaller hand.

The sensation of his palm and fingers sliding over hers gave her butterflies.

He has the perfect handshake.

Amber hoped that he didn't have the same expression on his face when he shook other client's hands.

"I'll look forward to Monday then," she said.

"Me too," Martin replied, clearing his throat and turning to get into his truck.

Before Amber entered her house, she turned around. Martin's eyes met hers from his rearview mirror before he drove away.

Chapter 10

1909. Klara and Hans. Bensek.

Hans woke up and placed a hand on his heart. He breathed in, noting the fragrance of Klara's warm flesh. His breath out was a contented sigh. His pale mustached mouth lifted in a smile as he turned to see his new wife next to him. Klara also sighed, letting him know that she was also awake.

"This is truly the happiest day of my life," Hans whispered and leaned in to kiss her cheek. Klara's eyes did not open, but her mouth curved in a smile.

"Are you sad we didn't have a big party?" he asked, turning his body to face her.

Klara's tanned face, neck, and forearms were a stark contrast to the rest of her body's white flesh. Her thick hair spilled in wild waves over the pillow. He'd never seen it completely down before.

"No, of course not," Klara replied groggily, finally opening her eyes to look at him. "My mother and sister hate me. And you know what the rest of the village thinks of me." Her words held bitterness, then her voice picked up with affection when she said, "Save for Margaritha and Anton."

"We shouldn't care at all what the rest of the village thinks. What a fool of a brother Margaritha has," Hans said, clenching his fist.

Klara reached down and placed her hand around his wrist, holding him gently.

"He is nothing. Though a bit of a beating off of Anton might have done him good." Klara's eyes narrowed and she chewed on a nail. "He is often a fool, but from what you told me...it's like he was encouraged."

Hans shrugged. "Yes, but there is little we can do about it now, Klara. I'm afraid Anton will have to set aside his love for Margaritha. I pity him. But Peter Lulay will certainly..."

His new wife interrupted him. "How I *hate* Peter Lulay. Do you know? I think my sister had eyes for him once, but of course she hasn't the looks nor the sweet nature of Margaritha."

"Anna is a nasty piece of work. How you got the reputation as being a witch rather than her, I don't know." Hans instantly regretted his words.

Klara huffed and placed a hand over her forehead.

"I spilled the salt. It was an accident! And she...*she*..." Klara's eyes began to well up.

"She spread the rumors...I know, Klara, I know...I'm sorry." He leaned over to her and tried to comfort her by kissing her mouth and stroking her arms. But while they had this time together, he didn't wish to discuss his new wife's horrid sibling or the cold opportunist who was Peter Lulay.

"Hans?" she said in the moments his lips were not upon hers.

"Yes, Klara?" he said, somewhat breathlessly.

"Would you be sad if we found that I couldn't have children?"

"Klara...I...I know we didn't discuss this. Children are wonderful, but I...I don't relish the day I have to worry about such things."

Hans was the only survivor of his siblings, and the first child of his parents. The other ten children his mother bore had died either minutes or far too few years after entering the world.

Hans's poor mother and father suffered greatly with each and every loss. As they registered the death of every babe at the church, the life drained from their eyes a little more.

Klara reached out to him, yet her silence told him she awaited further explanation.

Hans pressed his lips together before saying, "It was awful, Klara. Watching the slow decline of their happiness. They managed around others, but at home...they were not with me. They were with all my dead brothers and sisters."

"Forgive me, Hans." Klara leaned over, pressing her body against his as she kissed his cheek.

"We are out of favor in this village," Hans said, sighing and changing the subject.

"Will we be invited to the wedding, do you think? If it really goes through?"

"I don't know, Klara." Hans wished to set aside all their problems and enjoy these precious moments together.

It was her who brought him to life, his ferocious Klara. If she was a witch, he didn't care. He'd always loved her, always defended her. Yet it wasn't him who had beaten Michael Koenig for the insult, though he'd tried. It was Anton, defending him and his Klara. Hans couldn't help but think that it wasn't anger towards Michael that spurred him on, rather his fury over the arrangement of Margaritha and Peter's marriage. His friend had hoped to persuade Herr Koenig to allow him to court Margaritha, but Peter Lulay had been campaigning, promising Herr Koenig that his dear daughter would have a prosperous and successful life in America.

Ever since the incident in the pub, Anton had grown far too quiet.

"Hans?" Klara reached over his body and placed her hand on the side of his abdomen.

The heat of her touch spread through him. He smiled. Klara was the kindest, warmest woman in the village.

He loathed Klara's mother. The bitter old woman was more than happy to 'get rid' of her eldest daughter. She'd grown mad with grief at the loss of her husband, and resented her children for surviving when her love died.

Klara's mother always said, "She's brought me nothing but trouble. Spilled a whole jar of salt. It's been the ruin of us. She killed her father. Not long after she spilled that salt...*he died.*"

Her younger sister was simply desperate for approval, any approval, any chance of the slightest reward. That was motivation enough for her to accuse her sister of sorcery.

The day he'd come to ask Klara's mother for her daughter's hand in marriage...Hans grit his teeth, remembering the smirk on Anna's face

"You need to be careful, Hans. I saw her do it. She did it on purpose! Tati died the next day. She would spill flour, sugar...on purpose. She talks to the devil! I've seen her!"

Hans shook his head and leaned into Klara. He inhaled the fragrance of her skin mixed with the flower petals he'd found crushed against her flesh, when he'd first removed her clothing hours after the priest married them.

Warmth rushed through his chest as he touched the smooth, slightly sunburned flesh of her forearms.

Her skin was hot to his touch, not from any fever, just from where he'd lain against her for so long. Locked together in matrimony, they'd devoured one another once alone. They were new to lovemaking and Hans suspected he had been clumsy, but it didn't matter because they were together.

"Mmmmmm…" Klara moaned, accepting his distraction. Hans's mouth curled up at the already familiar sound.

'She will never give you children. Do you know that? She is cursed. She sees things. Things no one should see.'

Anna's words taunted him, and his small smile faded. Not that he did want children, but that Klara had lived with being taunted every day upset him.

"What are you thinking about?" Klara suddenly said, and her green eyes opened.

"Would you like me to show you?" Hans grinned. Klara sat up, leaning into his hand, and said, "I know what my mother and sister told you. You didn't have to marry me."

Then her voice dropped low and she whispered, "I could have met you secretly. We could have had many a sinful encounter together with hardly anyone noticing. And if they did, I wouldn't have cared." She leaned in and gently bit his neck.

Hans gasped with pleasure at the gentle force of her teeth. He rolled her over and said, "Oh but, Klara, I want to take you away from here. I want to give you a big house in America. Your garden will be huge! And we can still have many encounters together. It's just that the church says it's not sinful now." He winked at her and chuckled.

Klara smiled dreamily at him, then it was her smile's turn to fade. Her green eyes ceased the lustful sparkle that had just been delighting him. Then she spoke, like she'd slipped away in a daze.

"You will miss it here. You will miss the village." There was such sadness in her voice that Hans paused. Removing the weight of his body from hers, he went back to his side, staring at her with wide eyes.

Hans couldn't imagine her saying something further from the truth. There was nothing for them in the Banat. At least with the money his parents had left him, they could go somewhere with opportunity.

"Hans?"

"How can you possibly think that, Klara? We are officially unwelcome here. It will be much better if we leave."

"You know that Anton isn't going."

Hans winced. "I know. But Margaritha might be, once Peter Lulay has his way."

Klara's face went still as stone, staring up at the low ceiling. It came to life with anger, her eyes filling with tears. "I would rather bid farewell to my dear friend forever, knowing that she is happily in Anton's arms. Because that is where she wishes to be."

"I understand your feelings, Klara, but there is nothing we can do."

Suddenly, Klara sat up. "What sort of man insists upon bullying a younger woman into marrying him, knowing her heart belongs to another?"

"The sort of man who lives in this village." He understood his wife's feelings, but was always wary of her when she was like this. Hans shifted back when her wild green gaze met his.

"Could you have, Hans? If you hadn't found me? Would you insist on marrying a woman you'd watched grow up knowing her heart ached for someone else? Am I the only one who finds this perverse?"

"Well, no. No, of course not. For me, I'd rather be alone than force someone who had feelings for another. But there is the simple economics of the situation, Klara."

"I hate him, Hans. I hate Peter Lulay. I won't forgive him. Never."

Hans furrowed his brows and lowered his voice. "Klara, you should be careful. You might not be a sorceress, but your anger towards Peter Lulay could endanger Margaritha. If you think of nothing but cursing him, it won't do any good. It's much better to focus on love, on better times."

Klara sighed and lay back on the pillow. Hans moved closer to her, his hips pressed against hers. While he was feeling so happy and content, he wished to make the most of it. That meant not discussing matters they couldn't control.

"Do you remember, when Anton and I used to chase you and Margaritha?"

Hans felt her face shift into a smile as she lay against him. "Yes, of course I remember. I'd never been happier when you caught me."

He stroked her thick waves, then gently twisted them into a rope that fell down her bare back.

"It took me some time. I swear you could predict my movements."

He could feel her body relaxing against his, the blood coursing beneath her skin heating with womanly instincts. He smiled, turned her over, and nuzzled her neck. She wrapped her arms around him, her knees bending and her feet sliding up the side of his body as he moved in between her legs.

Hans was already lost in the pleasure of young love, enjoying the exclusive privilege that he and his bride were a love match. That she would want him always, and he her.

As his lips began to worship her, he barely registered her words

"There are some things, Hans...some things that I do know for sure..." Then her breathing quickened as he continued and she said, "I love you. I love you, Hans," in the dazed, soft way she had.

"I love you, Klara," he whispered feverishly against her neck.

Chapter 11

Amber was at her desk, in the middle of designing the cover of a fantasy novel. She'd just sketched a river winding through a dense forest. The details of a wooden, almost raft-like boat were clear in her mind before the image was created. Now it was time to fill the boat with its inhabitants.

Drawing back slightly, Amber could see the shape of her eyes reflected in the computer screen.

A man, who needs a wife. Though...he wonders if he can find a suitable one. Someone he could love. Who could love him back. Not some poor lady who has no choice.

That was the request for the character type from the author. Amber closed her eyes and tried to picture the man.

The boat would bob from time to time, and the man would look down at the brownish water flowing beneath the bow of the boat.

Knock, knock, knock.

Amber shook her head and stood up, taking note of the time.

It's ten o'clock...

Amber answered the door to see Martin on her porch. His peach-tinted smile was wide, and he gestured to another man unloading materials out of a much larger truck than Martin's smaller one, which was parked next to it.

"Hello, Martin."

"Mornin'. That's the monster work truck." He gestured behind him, still grinning. "My colleague John is here to help get the shelter up as quickly as possible."

Amber watched as John lifted materials to the spot where they would be building.

"I hope not too quickly; I don't want the thing collapsing on my truck."

Martin laughed. His earthy chuckle sent ripples down her abdomen. Amber placed a hand on the cold doorframe.

"Don't worry," he said.

"Yeah...we'll do a good job!" John called, getting a huge toolbox out of the truck. "But the forecast is saying we are in for some serious snow tonight."

Amber looked at the sweeping, wan sky. It was bitingly cold. Cold enough to snow.

"Well, we better hurry up. Looks like we're gonna get it up just in time."

"We're a long way out too, boss."

Amber shifted on her feet and said, "You guys want to wait for another day? I don't want you to get trapped out here."

"No, it's okay. We'll manage," Martin said.

Amber nodded and said, "Well, alright then. I'll leave you to it. If you want any instant coffee, let me know."

"We're good. We've got a thermos and sandwiches." Martin winked as he went to assist John.

For a few hours, she was lost again in her work, alternating between finishing the cover of the fantasy novel and editing the content.

She organized projects that were next in line, and received e-mails requesting her services. Thanks to her low cost of living in comparison to editors and designers working in places like New York or Los Angeles, Amber was able to charge very reasonable prices for her time. That was one of the reasons her clients always came back to her.

That and the fact that you do nothing but work. Theresa's voice echoed in her head.

The sound of Martin and John digging and hammering eventually faded into the background.

Amber leaned back in her chair, stretching her slender arms above her head, and closed her eyes.

The floor creaked behind her. Amber dropped her arms and swiveled on her chair.

"Hello?"

She could hear Martin and John shouting to one another outside.

Amber got up and walked down the hall. Wearing thick socks, her feet barely creaked over the polished wood floor. The farther down the hallway she got, the chillier the air became. Amber wondered if she'd left the front door open.

The door was still shut, but a movement in the living room turned her head.

There, looking out the living room window, was the lady. Her wild gray hair was loosely pinned up, and Amber could just make out the apron tied around her waist, over her house dress. She stood between the couch and the window.

Klara...

"Missus...Missus...Schreiber?"

The lady turned and looked with eyes that were a vibrant green, despite age. Chills ran up and down Amber's spine, and a cold sweat broke out on her body.

This was the clearest apparition so far. Not a reflection, or a passing shadow.

The next thing Amber knew, she was on the floor, with Martin kneeling over her.

"Hey, are you okay? Amber? Do you have some medication or something? Do I need to call the doctor?"

"I...I'm okay." Horrified, she sat up.

"Don't get up yet, you'll pass out again. I just found you like this."

Amber lay back on his hand. "I've never fainted before."

They were both silent for a few moments, then Amber pursed her lips and said, "How did you know I..."

Then Amber remembered seeing Frau Schreiber stood at the window. *Klara.*

Martin looked around the room like he was distracted. "Well, I thought I saw you looking out of the window, like you needed something."

"I wasn't at the window."

Martin shook his head. "It's...pretty strange around here, isn't it?"

Amber nodded, conscious that his hand was still cradling her head. She pursed her lips together and said, "Well, it's an old house. It has a few memories, I suppose."

Martin cleared his throat. "Do you know much about the house? I mean, who built it?"

Amber grimaced, unsure of how much to say.

"Some...German immigrants, I believe. They were homesteaders in the earlier part of the twentieth century. I, um...This is going to sound strange."

Amber felt odd, divulging this to a man she hardly knew, but something compelled her to tell him.

"You know after I saw you in church? I went to the graveyard, to leave some flowers on their graves. Klara and Hans Schreiber. They built the place."

Martin's mouth was open, as though he was going to say something, then he closed it. He sniffed a couple of times, furrowing his brows.

"Something wrong? Do I stink?" Amber asked...then she recognized something in the air as well.

"Do you have a lot of rosemary in here?"

"No. I haven't bought any rosemary."

He looked right down at her.

"That's very odd. The air smells like you have a rosemary-scented candle or something."

"I use orange oil soap," she said in a monotone, her mind starting to swim from his hand touching the back of her head.

Martin absentmindedly licked his lips, appearing to mull something over, and said, "Are you any relation of the Schreibers?"

"No, not at all. Well, not that I know of," she responded.

"Oh."

"Why?"

"Just curious...maybe if you were a relation, it would make sense for them to try and contact you."

Amber was about to answer when heavy footsteps came from near the door.

"Hey, boss? Is she okay? We need to call an ambulance? We're gonna have to speed things up, whatever we do. There are some flurries already. Forecast is bad for tonight."

"I'm okay. I'll rest on the couch till I feel better. I didn't eat anything. That's probably all it was."

Martin didn't look convinced. He reached into his pocket and pulled out a granola bar, handing it to Amber.

She took it with a smile. "You eat granola bars? You look like a meat and potatoes kind of guy."

"Well...meat and potatoes are hard to carry in my pocket. Plus, I like granola. Don't tell anyone." He grinned and helped her up. Amber placed her left arm around his left shoulder as his right arm wrapped around her waist. She settled on the couch. "Really, I don't have any medical conditions or anything. It was dumb of me not to eat lunch."

Martin looked over at John, who still was torn between concern about Amber and the incoming snowstorm.

"Well, okay. We'll finish getting your shelter up. I'll be back inside within the hour."

As soon as Martin was gone, Amber grabbed her laptop to continue working from the couch. She munched the granola bar and fixed typos in the fantasy manuscript.

ଓ   ๛

Martin continued to work beside John after he'd reassured himself that Amber was okay. He was sure he had seen her in the window looking at him. His eyes were blurred by the cold, though. It was John who said that he saw a lady staring out the window, thus causing Martin to look.

"Hey, John?"

"Yeah?"

"I think I'd better get her to call a friend or something, in case she has another fainting spell. It's dangerous, not like anyone could find her for a while if she would have been all alone."

"She's not alone," John responded.

"What?"

"She's not alone. Her mom or someone is with her. She was looking out the window. That's why I said there was a lady there. Looked older, though. Maybe Amber looks after her."

Martin stood completely still, uncertain what to think. He hadn't wanted to tell her before why he wanted to meet the owner of the old Schreiber homestead, when he knocked on her door a few weeks ago, he was distracted by Amber, generally. He was trying to get a grip of his instant attraction to her.

It wasn't entirely due to thinking of buying the place himself. It wasn't exactly the best location for him. He imagined that it was fine for Amber since she worked from home.

"I'm gonna have a look around. It's kind of weird. There isn't an old lady in the house."

John stopped for a moment, looked at Martin, nodded, and said, "Okay. There's someone else there though."

Martin walked around the left side of the house, clockwise, the opposite direction he and Amber had walked the other day. He came to the remains of the old barn, his boots crunching over the frosty ground. Snow flurries were spinning in the air, landing on the gray, rotting wood.

Martin couldn't remove his gaze from the remains of the old structure.

This would have been their barn. Sad there's not much left of it. There's not much left of their place in the Old Country either.

Martin looked up the vast expanse of wild prairie behind. His voice caught in his throat, swallowed by icy wind and shock.

An old man, wearing clothes more fitting to over half a century earlier, was staring at him. The man had pale blue eyes just visible beneath his hat.

"I guess you are Hans. My name is Martin…" Martin hadn't spoken the German dialect his parents used at home much at all recently, but he did his best.

The ghost's light blond mustache twitched, like he was smiling beneath it. "Klara's inside…" He pointed into the house and disappeared.

Martin's throat was dry and the cold air bit at him.

Martin turned, in a world of his own now, to walk around to see John finishing up. John broke into his thoughts.

"I gotta go, boss. The wife will go nuts if I don't get home soon. Hey, are you okay? You look like you've just seen a ghost," John said.

Martin sighed and opened his mouth. There was still a layer of ice beneath his flesh. He licked his lips and got the words out, "I'm fine. Just cold. Uh, hey, John, you might have to tell your wife that working in bad weather is kind of part of what we do. This business won't survive out here if we can't handle working in snow. This ain't Hawaii."

John held up his hands. "I know, I know…I'll talk to her."

"You knew that when we decided to set up out here." Yet the words were hollow. He could still see the blue eyes. Piercing him. Like he knew him. But Martin couldn't say that. He knew of Hans, but he didn't know him personally. The man had died long before Martin was born.

John said, "Yeah, Martin. I know the weather in Chicago isn't a picnic, but out here, you can get caved in. Hey, are you sure you're okay?"

"I'm fine. Sorry, John. I...got a lot on my mind." The wind began to whip snow flurries all over. Several white mini-whirlwinds danced around the prairies.

"Geez, it's gonna be a bad one. Alright, take care, Martin. We got the lady's truck undercover so that should be good. Don't wait too long to go."

After John left, Martin finished checking the structure. Every now and again, chills would race up his back and he would look behind him. Then he went inside to get Amber's keys in order to put her vehicle beneath the shelter.

Amber was sitting upright with her legs folded and her laptop resting on her thighs. She'd just turned to him, pushing her reading glasses back into her hair, and said 'sure' when he'd requested the keys.

Wow. He was impressed by how focused she was. After another half an hour outside, the wind's bite became sharper.

Martin, out of breath after scrambling to finish the job, knocked and entered the house again.

Amber wasn't on the couch.

"Hello?" The house creaked and the wind whistled outside.

Apart from that, there were no replies.

"Amber?" Martin called more loudly.

Then there were light footsteps coming down the hall. Amber emerged, her skin stark white in comparison to the hunter green fleece she wore.

The house creaked from the force of the gales outside.

"Hey, are you okay?" Martin moved towards her.

Amber had a hand over her heart. Her wide-eyed gaze rested on him and she said, "I'm so sorry. Would you mind looking at something for me? You might think it's strange, but..."

Then there was a huge bang! It came from her bedroom.

"That. I mean that," she said through the hand she'd placed over her mouth.

 C3   ❧

Amber had still been working after letting Martin have her keys, then the banging started. Her fingers ceased their keyboard clicking and her head popped up. She'd looked out the window and Martin was busy double-checking the car shelter and getting into her car.

Bang!

She got up in a huff, heading down the hallway. There was no sign of any movement in her office. She checked the bathroom, looking everywhere for anything that might have fallen.

Hurrying to her bedroom, she saw the bedspread still in place. It didn't even ripple over the hardwood floor.

The house creaked again and air whistled through the cracks. She put her hand over her heart, then heard Martin call her name.

This is so awkward. He must think I'm crazy.

Then, the bang sounded again when he was there.

Martin came in, checked everywhere he possibly could.

"Bet you think I'm nuts," Amber said shakily.

"No, no, not at all. I heard the noise too. I just…It's all kind of strange. John seemed anxious to go. While we were workin' out there, he said this place gives him the heebie jeebies. I agree with him."

"Yes, I think it's established that I have company," she replied.

"I think you do too."

Amber noticed Martin blowing into his hands to warm them.

"Would you like some tea? Or instant coffee?"

"Actually, black tea would be good."

It was around 4:00 pm now, fading light filtering through the lace curtains. The day had been weakly illuminated throughout, and the blue and white tones of the kitchen now took on a shadowy gray.

Yet Amber could feel Martin's eyes on her as she made tea for both of them. They sat at the table, watching the steam rise from their cups.

"Martin?"

"Yeah?"

"You are being so nice. Anyone else would call me a wacko and say I'm inventing all this. You should go; the weather is getting worse."

Then, frantic footsteps went to the door. They heard it open and shut. All the while, their eyes remained locked on one another, wide and shocked. By the time they turned to face the door, there was no evidence of any footsteps or the door being opened.

They slowly got up and walked through the wide opening between the kitchen and living room. It was Martin who placed his hand on the handle so they could both look outside.

It was a complete whiteout snowstorm. They could barely make out the shape of Martin's truck, though it wasn't far from where they stood.

"Well, it looks like the car shelter is really going to get some use tonight," Amber commented.

"Yeah, it sure does. Amber?"

Amber looked to Martin.

"Would you mind if I stayed put a while?"

"That's okay. I don't think driving is a good plan right now."

"No. No...But I will stay out of your way. I..."

He'll have to stay for dinner. And sleep over. None of these things alarmed Amber, she had a sense of trust towards him. She just hoped that after spending time with her, he wouldn't think she was odd.

"Martin, it's really okay. I should have insisted you cancel the job when John mentioned the bad weather."

Martin put his hands up and said, "No, no, I've never canceled a job due to weather. Never."

"You've never had to sleep over at a client's house before, have you?"

Martin's dark eyes went wide, his eyebrows lifted. "Uh, absolutely not. This is a first."

"Well, there you go. Do you like Chicken Paprikasch?"

She looked at Martin, whose mouth hung open before he shook his head in surprise and answered, "I...I like that a lot. You know how to make it?"

"Yes. My grandma taught me before she died. I really haven't eaten much all day, so we can have dinner early. How's that?"

"That...sounds great," Martin replied.

Meanwhile, Martin was thinking,

Does she know?

Chapter 12

Anton sat in the crumbling kitchen where his mother used to cook meals when he was a small child. Before she'd become sickly. The few plates that lined the shelf were no longer worth saving. If his parents were alive, they would be forced to throw them away.

The limited candle and lamplight made the run-down place appear even more dingy.

Anton stood and handled the cracked, once cherished plates. They'd been loved enough to be displayed. They were evidence of better, prouder times. Anton's long fingers held the back of the plate whilst his thumb stroked the delicate vines and flowers painted on the edges.

There isn't even a point of taking them for memorabilia. I can only take what I can carry.

Despite Frau Koenig's kindness, his mother had always felt embarrassed after being in Margaritha's family household. Frau Handl knew they were poorly regarded in the village. Margaritha's family wasn't exactly wealthy, but Herr Koenig had done well as a farmer. Koenig pride denied him his Margaritha.

Thinking of Peter Lulay's twinkling gaze, after the fight with Michael Koenig, a haze fell over him. He could still hear the landlord shouting at them as Herr Koenig appealed for calm.

You are never to come in here. Ever! The girl would be a fool to marry you anyway, Handl. Get out! Get out! You too, Schreiber! Pair of fools!

Anton smashed the plate in fury, then pushed his hands through his hair roughly as he stared at the ground, willing himself to calm.

In the end, he'd bloodied Michael a little and bruised his face. But Michael had done worse than that to boys younger than him! Young Koenig was a natural bully, encouraged to be arrogant by his father. Yet the boy knew deep down, he'd not yet earned any status.

Anton hated bullies. He and Hans had to save Klara a few times from cruel children after school finished.

They would be the ruin of us all, if no one ever taught them a lesson.

Yet more than a few times, Anton found himself intimidated by the more aggressive people in the village. Too often it was too easy to say nothing. Do nothing. How beautiful, kind Margaritha could be related to such a stupid boy as Michael Koenig baffled him.

Anton pulled at the top of his hair, staring at the smashed plate littering the already dusty floor. Anger burned in his chest and tears stung his eyes. He mourned his sweet, intellectual, yet underprivileged parents.

They would have been better in a city, working in some bookshop. They'd tried their hand at taking over the family farm whilst dreaming of owning a small bookshop in Bensek. Roof and structure repair was a natural skill passed down through the Handl family. His mother had an eye for art and beautiful things, which she had passed to her son, but poor health had overtaken all dreams and aspirations.

Now, to Anton, the shattered remains on the floor revealed to him lost hopes. He wanted to imagine his parents at peace in paradise, not suffering due to struggles during their earthly life.

How he longed for his Margaritha, his sweetheart. The yearning was painful.

Margaritha will marry Peter Lulay. They will go to America. Hans and Klara will also go. Just the thought of the impending Lulay/Koenig wedding was more than he could stomach.

When the stinging feeling began behind his eyes, he did the only thing he could do. Anton picked up one of his two last pieces of blank canvas and the remaining paint. His parents' last act of love for him had been that they kept his beloved art things safely for him, ensuring no damage came to them while he was away in the service.

He'd have rather been able to embrace his mother and father upon returning than have the canvas and paint.

They could have sold the art supplies, bought more medicine. Perhaps they would still be here...

Anton placed the canvas on the easel. When his brush dipped into the paint, a wonderful sensation spread from his fingers all the way down his arm. It was like igniting a healing fire.

Not far from him, the ornate, gold-colored crucifix glittered on a chest covered with a tattered lace cloth. The wooden chest was also damaged. Furniture purchases and repairs had to go to physician's fees and food long ago.

Anton began with long strokes of green, varying the shade of it, creating the heaths and rolling hills, the river. The patches of trees in the distance.

It was from the perspective of leaving town. With the effect of little Swabian houses and the Catholic church passing by. He wanted to remember his home village in better times. Life had never been easy for him, certainly not for his parents and the family that came before them.

But it had been his world, for better or worse. And now, he had to leave it. Those he felt closest to were also leaving. All the links to his family's longtime home were fading.

Anton sniffed and worked on the church. It reminded him of the ceremony he'd attended only the night before. He'd been so happy for Hans and Klara. Margaritha had kept her distance, under strict orders from her family, and likely Peter. Exactly how strict those orders were, he could see once he came out.

Herr Koenig had been waiting for her outside the church. He'd been curt with Hans and Klara. Ice cold with Anton. It didn't stop his heart from melting when, upon leaving, Margaritha had cast one last look at him. His favorite pair of amber eyes.

He sighed and chose an intense gray for the sky. Like the color before a storm. When things could be renewed and refreshed. Or utterly destroyed. Like an end and a beginning all at the same time.

He would depart for Temeswar within a couple of days, once all his parents' affairs were in order.

Anton paused, resting his forearms on his long legs as Hans's voice echoed in his head.

'Why don't you come with us? We could homestead together...'

'You are a good farmer, Hans. The call of the land isn't the same for me. I will go to my relatives in Temeswar. It's all been arranged. After what's happened, I will have to go even sooner now.'

The hours ticked by whilst Anton created as clear a view as possible of his village.

Anton stared at the familiar fields and houses in Bensek upon the canvas. As though he wasn't sitting in the source of his inspiration. As though he was already so far away.

He thought back to his time in the military. He and Hans were often treated snobbishly by higher ranking nobles when asked where they came from. Swabians were true peasants, apparently. Albeit with a reputation for hard work.

They'd met a Prussian officer who made it very clear he found their 'Germanness' to be of an inferior quality. He commented about the Schwob's primitive dialect and hunched over, babushka-clad women. That they were more like Slavs than Germans, as if that was such a dreadful thing.

The haughty insult was met by Anton and Hans with raised eyebrows and shock at such shortsighted ignorance. They did their best to ignore his comments about Jews, which were far worse.

Blowing a long breath out of his nose, he reminded himself that these were exceptions. Most folks they'd encountered were normal. The Serbs, whom so many Schwobs and Germans resented and who never cared for anyone loyal to the Hapsburgs, were just normal people wanting to get on with life.

Now, he sat in the ruins of his family home, in a village that had no place for him. Bitterness churned in his stomach. The world was a mad place, and rulers, nobles, so detached from the majority of people, yet holding the reigns of the madness.

His Margaritha was being forced to lead a loveless life for the sake of family reputation.

Of course, this is how it's always been, but does that make it right?

Anton drew his long slender fingers over a blank section of canvas and thought of the land Hans and Klara would go to. He'd heard it was empty and vast, only used by nomadic tribes.

Not one building, no structures. In the tavern, the men there started saying that there weren't even any hills or trees. There was barely a river or a lake in sight. A few Bensekers had gone to North Dakota, and that was their complaint. The loneliness.

They'd compared it with their ancestors who came from the German-speaking principalities to make the vacant marshlands of Hungary, previously overrun with Ottoman Turks, into decent farm land.

Yet there was success enough for people to continue going.

Anton wished he could convince Hans and Klara to come with him to the city, but his friend was determined to have his own farm and his own home.

A knock sounded and Anton looked up. He rose from his seat, wiped his hands on a cloth, and grinned. The village would be asleep now, so this could only be Hans.

Yet again hoping I will reconsider and move to this...Dakota place.

As he opened the door, holding a candle, he said quietly, "I would think you would have far better things to do than to come and see me, Herr Schreiber..."

The half-grin on Anton's face dropped when he found his very favorite pair of amber eyes.

Her hair was covered in a large babushka, and an even larger, padded out black dress. It was the sort that the very old women wear to church.

"Margaritha? You are dressed so..."

"So that no one will recognize me. Now let me in," she whispered frantically.

He opened his door and backed up as she entered, shutting it as though a monster lurked outside.

Her light footsteps echoed in his house. He stood speechless as she removed her headscarf, releasing her beautiful curls. He could smell her sweat as she undid the top fastenings of her black dress; he heard her anxious breaths. She looked to him.

He shook his head.

"Oh...oh, please, please, Margaritha. You will get us both into trouble just by being here." His voice was weak and forced.

She ignored it and said, "Why did you do it? Why did you fight with Michael? You know he is a fool. It was not like you." The smooth flesh of her chin and lips trembled, her large hazel eyes began to water.

She continued, raising her arms in exasperation.

"Of course I understand *why.* There's been many a time I've so longed to punch him."

Anton struggled for words, relishing her being in his home...*alone.* It made all his sadness evaporate. At the same time, he feared her father and brother would be pounding on his door any moment. If that happened, there would be no running away.

"M...Margaritha. He was insulting our friend right after Hans announced his intention to marry her. Why did you not speak to me before in the church?"

"I did not want to ruin the wedding celebration of our friends. My father would have been so angry had I spoken to you," Margaritha replied.

"Margaritha, this will get us nowhere. You should leave."

"I know that you love me!" She drew close to shouting before pausing and continuing, "And I know that I love you as well! I have since we were children. You didn't want to believe that there would be hope. But now, because you…"

Margaritha's tawny gaze went wide as he closed the difference between them and gripped the top of her arms. He shook her gently, in frustration as well as passion.

He hated how right she was.

Then his lips crashed against hers.

His heart soared and broke at the same time in the throes of this surrender. His fingers slid down her back and pressed her to him. Margaritha made a sobbing sound against his mouth, and he had to hold her steady to ensure she remained on her feet.

Yet she acquiesced to every caress and melted into his embrace.

When he curved one arm all the way around her shoulders and slipped his other hand into her hair, doing his best to memorize every tendril, the very idea of breaking the contact of their lips was too tragic.

As though they had finally made it home together. To remove their lips from one another would be to become lost again.

It was Margaritha who had to remove her mouth from his, yet she stayed in his arms. She reached to his cheeks, touching his face tenderly, kissing his jaw with feather light pressure.

"Anton…" she whispered. "There truly is no hope now. You know what will happen."

"I couldn't bear it. The thought of *him* with *you*…Your brother bore the brunt of my heartbreak." Anton's words were broken as they spilled out.

"His face will heal. My heart will not," she said quietly.

Anton winced.

"I have to go…even sooner to Temeswar. I'm afraid I've caused more trouble for you as well as for Hans and Klara…simply by being here. You will all go to America. I will insist that Hans checks on you."

"Yes…" she said and Anton shuddered as her fingers moved to stroke his arms through his shirt. This was the closest they had ever been.

Being so near one another felt natural and like heaven. It wasn't the fear of sinning that stopped them from going further. It was more the danger of being caught, and the consequences it would bring. Anton would be beaten or worse. Margaritha could be ruined and shunned.

"Margaritha, I can hardly bear your touch...the joy you give me," he whispered.

"Oh, Anton...how will I face a life without you? I know what I must do to be a wife and mother, but I can't imagine...I can't..." Tears begin to flow down her cheeks.

Anton swallowed down the gut wrenching feeling that came when he thought of Peter wedding Margaritha, the horrible reality of it.

He took his hands and placed them on her cheeks, rubbing the tears away. "Ssshhh, please, Margaritha. Our lives will have to go on. But I will never forget you. How I would love to take you to Temeswar with me."

"We wouldn't even get as far as the train station, Anton. And I understand now there is no way we could both eat if we were there. We couldn't ask such a thing of your relatives."

She stopped for a moment, looking down before looking immediately up again.

"Did you mean what you said?"

"Yes?"

"That you grew so angry by the thought of me with Peter?"

"Yes," he croaked.

"I dread to think of you with another. Anton, my heart will always be yours." And she placed his hand on her chest, where he could feel it beating, as though it were a part of him.

"I do love you, Margaritha."

"I so love you too, Anton."

Her head turned in an attempt to wince away more tears. When she opened her eyes again, they were wide in amazement. Anton realized that she had seen his canvas.

"It's like a view of someone...leaving the village. Looking back at the sight so they will always remember. It is so beautiful."

She walked slowly towards it then traced her fingers over the blank bit of canvas.

Margaritha turned her gaze back to him. The golden hue of her eyes never ceased to amaze him. They glistened, still wet with tears.

"I will always remember it, Anton. What a beautiful painting."

He longed to give her this work. "Perhaps if I finish it tonight, I will somehow pass it over to you."

"I couldn't bear for such a beautiful thing to be destroyed. And..." She looked down.

"I know. If your father doesn't destroy it, then your husband surely will. They'll..."

"They'll know it was you who gave it to me."

"But they can't rip me from your heart. Can they?"

"Never. Never, Anton. Your memory will comfort me, live with me always."

He couldn't speak for the moment. In truth, he was trying too hard to stay on his feet. He was hungry, exhausted, and heartbroken. The last weeks had been hard.

"Ah. I almost forgot." She reached into her skirts to pull out a small, wrapped piece of bread. She handed it to him. "You must go to Temeswar, find work, and eat more." She reached out to touch his too slim frame.

"Margaritha, I can't give you anything in return for this. What if someone notices?"

"They won't. And yes, you can."

He shook his head.

"I want another kiss. And a promise, that you will try to be happy in your life. I will do my best, despite my betrothal to one whom I haven't chosen and don't love. Despite having to leave my home, despite having to carry my longing for you with me until the end of my days. It will be my greatest sin, Anton. I will be good in every other way, but I will not stop longing for you."

Her determined expression stirred him.

"Nor I you, Margaritha. I will remember your face...forever."

His footsteps sounded as he approached where she stood near the canvas. Again, his hands went through her hair, over her face, worshipping every moment of this precious contact. Until finally his arms crossed over her back diagonally. One hand gripped her shoulder while the other grasped her hip.

His lips found their home again, against hers. Margaritha had desired him to kiss her as though they were already husband and wife. As though he'd carried her to bed many times and this would be one more sweet encounter. As though it was a great pleasure they'd ever seek comfort in amidst the toil and trials of life.

In just this one kiss, it was as though he understood the very thing she wanted.

But it had to end. And it had to be tucked away in the memories of their youth.

Unwrapped and mentally devoured when life allowed for a little indulgent fantasy.

When his lips finally left hers, he whispered, "You are sweeter and more wonderful than any bread or cakes."

Margaritha smiled at him. She padded to the door and tied the black babushka underneath her chin. Fastening her hair and ensuring that it was well hidden, ensuring the scarf shadowed her face. When she looked down, he could not see the tan plumpness of her cheeks.

He saw her as an old woman, how she would be in the future. And he still loved her.

His heart panged when he thought of her future without him. In a place where he'd heard tales of great loneliness.

Margaritha Koenig left the Handl household.

Anton's head pounded as he lay down on his small, shabby bed. Candle light flickered over his half-finished painting, teasing him.

Her face, her eyes, her flesh were alive in his mind. Her smell was still in the room. Her retreating footsteps in the dusty road just outside his house. He could envision her every move.

"I'll love you forever, Margaritha," Anton whispered like a prayer, looking at the crucifix that glittered in the lamplight.

ℭ ℬ

Meanwhile, Margaritha was slipping back into her parents' dark house. Everyone else was snoring, too exhausted to notice her sneaking out in the night.

Margaritha crossed herself as though preparing some penance, as though to say a prayer of contrition.

Instead, she whispered into the darkness, "I will love you forever, Anton."

And she thanked God for the stolen moment with her true love.

Chapter 13

2017. The Storm. North Dakota.

Martin watched Amber ignite a match. His gaze quickly found the floor when she caught him staring at her face over the flame.

"I just wanted to light a few candles, in case the power goes out. It hasn't happened yet, but we don't want to be caught in the dark. I've got a generator too." There was a hint of embarrassment in her voice, and Martin guessed that she wasn't used to having guests over. Particularly male ones.

Is it my imagination, or is she checking me out too? Martin knew he was guilty, but every now and again, he caught her glancing his way.

With the fading light and the roaring storm outside, it was as though they were on the edge of the earth together.

Martin shifted on the wooden bench that ran along her rectangular dining table. When she reached upwards to get some glasses, her fleece lifted, revealing her slim waist. He looked away and said, "Amber. Can I ask you something?"

Amber's movements were lithe as she stooped and rose to gather meal ingredients from her cupboards and fridge. She turned and leaned against the counter,

"Sure, go ahead," she replied.

"Why on earth did you fix up and live in an old homestead in the middle of nowhere?"

Amber laughed. "I tried cities. I tried medium-sized towns. I still like to visit them, but not to live in. Out here, it's like I can claw back more time. I don't have to travel often. I don't need much. And...."

Amber looked at the floor and blushed.

"And what?" Martin prodded gently.

"I always wanted to live in a simpler time. Don't get me wrong—indoor plumbing, electricity, and the internet it's all great. But when I saw this place, it filled a void. I had planned on moving back to my home state, but not on living *so* far out of the way. Not until I passed this place."

Martin nodded, staying quiet for a few seconds. Then he said, "Are you frightened?"

Amber replied, "A little. But I don't want to leave. I want to figure out what they want."

Martin stood and approached Amber at the counter. Her breath hitched.

He said, "I can help you with the meal. I don't expect to be waited on. I know a thing or two about Paprikasch."

The corner of Amber's mouth went up. "Oh, do you now?"

"Yeah, I..." His mouth froze. He saw the old framed photos on the windowsill behind the sink. He couldn't look away from the unsmiling bride with striking eyes.

"Who is she?"

He referred to the picture of Amber's great grandmother. "My great grandmother with my great grandfather. I think this was taken on their wedding day back in Hungary."

"So, you're Hungarian?" Martin asked.

"German-Hungarian via my dad. Norwegian via my mother. A Lutheran Scandinavian marrying a German-Hungarian Catholic caused quite a stir back then amongst old folks. Seems so silly now. My dad's mom loved the whole thing. She told me that love is a gift from God, however a person prays. And...she said that despite the gossip, she had an obligation to ensure nothing else stood in its way."

"I see." Martin found it difficult to take his eyes away from the piercing stare of the woman in the Old World style wedding dress. It was normal for folks in old photos to be straight-faced. With her, though, he could discern her sense of duty and sadness. That day wasn't a happy day. Martin swallowed and finally looked away.

"Apparently, she was a very nice lady, my great grandmother," Amber said.

"And she was beautiful," Martin replied.

"Yes..." Amber's voice was soft as she began to chop an onion. She sniffled and wiped her eyes with her sleeve.

"Here, I'll do that. Do you have flour, eggs, and milk?" Martin moved close to Amber and as he reached to take the knife and chopping board, his fingers grazed the tops of her knuckles. She looked up at him. He was a few inches taller than her. Now, he leaned so close, the warmth of his breath was tangible on her skin.

"Sure," she replied, but didn't move.

"I'll make spaetzle," he spoke softly, but also didn't move. He looked into her eyes. She tilted her head.

"My grandma, she used to say it...almost...just like that. The same way..." Amber's voice was slow; she obviously hadn't thought about spaetzle in many years.

Martin's eyes were resting on Amber's lips. They looked firm but still pretty.

"Where were your grandparents from?" she asked.

Martin stepped back and began chopping the onion, focused on his task.

His grandparents had been a difficult subject back home in Chicago.

"I'm sorry. Have I offended you?" Amber asked. He looked up at her. The day had passed and the kitchen light shone on the kinks of her almost white-blonde hair. He could just make out the straight teeth behind her strong, pink lips.

Martin didn't particularly want to talk about his family's troubled history.

She's so damn pretty...

"I...No. I never knew my grandparents. Most of them died before they left Europe. My dad's mother made it, but she passed away before I came along. They were from Eastern Europe." His voice was quiet.

"I'm sorry. I believe life was a lot harder back then..." Amber fumbled with the chicken legs. She got out some sour cream and a container of paprika. "...but you pronounced spaetzle in such a German way."

Martin nodded as he continued to chop the onion. "They spoke a dialect of German. Actually...today, the villages where my grandparents came from are in Romania and Serbia. But, at one point, it was all part of the..."

"Austro-Hungarian Empire." Amber finished his sentence, placed her hand on the counter, and looked ahead before turning to him. "You're a

German-Hungarian too?"

Martin looked down. There was something he wasn't quite ready to reveal to her. "Well...yes, I'm a Banat German. My folks were from there."

"What is the Banat?"

"The Banat was one of the main regions filled with German-speaking settlers originally invited by the Hapsburgs in the eighteenth century."

Martin drew an invisible picture with his fingers on the counter and said, "Imagine that this is a border. Here is Hungary. Here is Romania. Here is Serbia." He swallowed.

A howling, whistling noise surrounded the house. Martin tensed and could see that Amber did too. The sound eased and Amber laughed nervously.

"Really, it's just the wind," she said.

Then a huge bang sounded again and Amber yelped. Martin looked down to find her in his arms.

He could feel her heart beating against him.

BANG! He gripped Amber's tight shoulders, pressing her against him.

"What the..."

"Oh god, what *is* that? I don't understand it," Amber said.

"Amber?"

"Yeah?"

"I think we should check your cellar."

The blood drained from her face and he feared she might faint again. "I would rather check anywhere else than there."

"It's the only part of the house we haven't checked since that noise started. Had you heard it before today?"

Amber backed away from Martin, gripping the counter and wincing. "On and off, but it has never been like this. Like it has today..."

Martin opened his mouth, wanting to tell her about his experience beside the old barn remains when he saw Hans.

Then the bang sounded again, this time more muffled. With the incessant wind howling and whistling outside at the same time, it was difficult to tell *where* the noise was coming from.

Amber's eyes were squeezed shut, like she was hoping once they opened, the racket would cease.

Martin watched, not wanting to push her too hard but knowing they had to look. She opened her eyes and looked at him.

"Alright. We'll go down there."

ↈ   ৪০

Amber's heart was slamming against her chest as adrenaline raced through her body. Between her intense attraction to Martin, whom she barely knew, the vision of Klara Schreiber staring out of her living room window, and the rosemary smell and the banging...and...

Martin. It was the oddest thing, finding out that they shared some similar ancestral background. Yet talking about it seemed to bother him, like when she'd asked about his grandparents. He closed up.

I hope we're not related, she thought as they inched towards the cellar door on the other side of the kitchen. She stayed behind him, placing her hands on his shoulders as he opened the door and flipped on the light.

Slowly, they descended the wooden steps into the earth-scented cellar. Martin shone the flashlight in every dingy corner.

"You might not believe me, but I did get this place cleaned out when I started work on the property. When I first looked down here, there were still old cans of food. They were from the bachelor brothers who occupied the house through the second half of last century."

"Those guys never saw anything?" he asked tensely, still shining the flashlight in every corner.

"Not that I was told," she replied.

"You...you've already started putting vegetables down here? It smells like root vegetables, earth, onions, cabbage and stuff..." Martin said.

"I haven't put any food down here."

There was a moaning sound in the corner. It sounded like a wounded animal, or the muffled groan of a person. An icy prickling sensation flared up beneath her skin.

"Who's there?" Martin said. Silence, and the flashlight beam revealed nothing in the corner. Only the stone floor and remains of some old shelves.

"Is this it? Nothing else to this place?" Martin's voice was agitated. The flashlight beamed all around the dark room. Now the only sound was the creaking house above, and their breathing.

"Martin, there's no one. There's nothing here." Amber approached him, placed her hands on his shoulders, and looked into his frantic face.

He shook his head and cursed, then said, "Let's go upstairs. This is freaking me out."

Amber couldn't argue. Distress tugged at her insides. They both returned upstairs and shut the door.

They leaned against the cellar door. The beginnings of their meal were still on the counter, waiting to be assembled and cooked.

Amber blinked back tears that stung her eyes. "I feel terrible. Something so sad happened down there. I just felt..."

She fretted against the waves of emotions. Amber inhaled deeply, puffing out her chest. She had always prided herself on her steadiness. That she never got overly emotional. She continued, "I did. I felt..."

"Cold. Helpless? Worried? Me too. Amber...I...I am not so sure you should stay here," Martin interrupted her.

Amber interrupted him by placing her hand on his. "I'm not leaving. Everybody leaves. That's the problem here. Seclusion, snow, failed farms... now ghosts. I'm not going anywhere. She isn't scaring me for the fun of it. She wants me to find something out."

"What about him?" Martin asked.

She knew he was referring to Hans. "He doesn't scare me for fun either. He never comes in. I've only ever seen him pass my bedroom window outside. Like he's still doing chores on the farm."

"Amber?"

"Yes, Martin?" She found comfort in saying his name.

"I saw him outside. By the barn remains. He looked real. Then he just... disappeared. And I think John saw Klara, but he thought she was your mother."

Amber looked at him, then tilted her head back. "Good to know it isn't only me losing it then. Martin?"

"Yeah?"

"Why on earth would a city guy choose North Dakota? Surely you could have still cut costs and gotten enough business in a place like Iowa, Nebraska, or I don't know...Wisconsin or something? You don't have any family here..."

"Okay, I'll talk. But let's cook. I don't want you fainting on me again."

Amber smiled, though her uneasiness lingered. They continued their work together at the counter.

Chapter 14

1909. The Portrait. Bensek.

How long Anton lay in bed, he did not know. Sunlight had begun filtering through the dingy cracked window of his parents' home. The ornate yet faux gold crucifix on the wooden chest glittered, reflecting the rays.

He could still hear Margaritha's retreating footsteps, down the dusty road and back to her house. He had never experienced such joy as when their lips met or when her hands were upon him.

Yet his feelings for Margaritha went beyond how beautiful she was. Most men in the village noticed that to the point where her father was pushing his daughter into a marriage with a man he knew she did not love. But Peter Lulay had some money, and would take her to a new country where there was more land available.

Anton stared at his painting of the village. For some reason, looking at its fields, the tops of the houses, school and church left him hollow. He looked forward to painting more in Temeswar, with its cobbled streets, grander buildings, and electric lights.

He closed his eyes, imagining Margaritha's hand in the crook of his arm as they strolled the streets. If he had money, he would take her to the theater. They could sit beside one another, and he could see her face react to the performance. Watch her laugh and smile.

His Margaritha. She was a woman who appreciated the deepest of emotions. She was kindhearted and passionate. One of the more successful farmer's daughters, she could have befriended girls from 'better' families. Yet she chose Klara, the poor girl from the troubled family.

Because Klara too valued the freedom to be one's self.

And Margaritha loved him. The poor boy from an unsuccessful family.

She loves me. And I, her.

His heart ached and pained so much that Anton could no longer lie in bed. His eyes were sore with fatigue and stung with tears. He sat up, his long torso leaning over as he drew his knees up and buried his head in his hands.

A slow groan of despair left his lips.

How will we live without one another?

The agony was too great. Anton spotted the other canvas in the corner of the room. He stumbled out of bed, lightheaded with hunger and need. He had used most of his greens and blues. Now only blacks, grays, and a couple of lighter shades remained.

But he had to imagine her. He wanted her to know that he would always think of her. Knowing his own heart, and seeing his days before him, staying with his aunt and uncle, having to learn and work alongside his relatives just to scrape by.

Coming to grips with his poverty-stricken situation, he was growing to accept that his future as an artist was growing bleaker. As was his future with Margaritha.

What he'd heard of this North Dakota, when people in the Wirtshaus spoke of letters from relatives, was of how vast the land was, how cold the winters, and how few the people, how frightened some were of the natives. He wanted her to know she was forever seared in his heart.

I will think of you every day, Margaritha.

He slowly put his partly finished 'view of Bensek' painting down in the corner and placed his very last blank canvas on the easel.

As the morning passed, he created a portrait of the woman he loved. He imagined her in America, her piercing stare and the thick waves of her hair when he saw it pinned back without her scarf. The shape of her nose, her jaw, and the arch of her brows. He'd always found Margaritha's beauty of such intensity, it was almost alien. Her mouth was strong, perfectly shaped.

And wonderful to kiss. He released a long sigh then continued to paint.

She is strong enough to withstand this. But we will always think of one another. Some days, when life and loneliness are too much...the struggle will be great. But I will always remember my love, as she will remember me.

He was creating the space around her when a knock came to his door.

He turned slowly, still in a daze as he went to the door. He opened it to Hans, who stood looking at him with raised blonde brows.

Anton's shoulders relaxed upon greeting his lifelong friend. "Good morning, Hans."

"Anton," Hans returned his greeting. Anton moved back inside and gestured that his friend could follow.

Hans's boots made muffled clicks on the dirty floor. Anton could see Hans looking all around the room. He turned to the disheveled bed. Anton moved towards it and sat down, fearing he might pass out.

"You are a fool, you know. You look as though you might faint from hunger, yet you have bread here while you paint like a madman."

Anton looked at his friend and put his hand on his chin as he pondered the comment.

Bread? Ah, yes. Margaritha left it for me. He smiled, though no happiness lit his eyes.

He looked to the loaf sitting on the table in the dank room, the only light coming from the dirty window and the reflected religious ornament atop a ruined lace tablecloth.

Hans sighed and handed his friend the bread. "Eat." He leaned against the bed. "What were you doing last night?"

"I...Well..." Nervously, he took a bite of bread, his mouth too full to speak.

Hans continue to look around the room. He breathed in sharply when he saw the portrait of Margaritha.

"I am rather glad it was you who came to the door," Anton said.

"Hmmm. I can see why. Though, it would appear there is one visitor you would rather have."

"She came to me last night." Anton spoke as though he had been visited by an angel.

Hans cursed. "You can't be serious, Anton. I came here to warn you. Word around the village is that Peter and Herr Koenig have expressly forbidden you from being anywhere near the wedding."

Now it was Anton's turn to curse. "As though I could even bear to witness her marrying that selfish old bastard." His blood boiled.

He wanted to take her away.

"So?" Hans's voice cut into Anton's thoughts.

"So, what?" Anton found himself growing frustrated with his friend.

"She was here?" Hans said. Now, Anton knew what his friend wished to know.

Anton sighed, recalling Margaritha's lips against his, the way her hands caressed him through his shirt. The feel of her curls, the scent he caught of her skin. He vividly recalled her unbuttoning only the top buttons on her heavy black dress. The way her throat glistened with perspiration in the lamplight.

Yet that had been all. They hadn't made love. Yet their feelings and desire for one another had been bared as much as possible without removing any clothing. Still, he wanted those stolen moments of passion with Margaritha to remain somewhat secret. Even from Hans. Even if they had not gotten into bed together, keeping the kisses, the sighs, the scent of one another and their exchanged words of love secret made them more intimate. As they shared something no one else could understand.

He stared at her portrait and said, "She wanted to say good-bye. We embraced. That is all. She left me with some bread; she knows I always liked her and her mother's cooking. I will have to leave today. There is little choice. I would never dishonor Margaritha."

Hans looked at him. "I am sorry, my friend. Herr Koenig only believes he is doing right for his daughter's future. He is ignorant to the misery you both feel and believes it will go away in time, like a passing childhood whim. Perhaps he is aware that for his daughter and his potential grandchildren, there are limits here to how far they can go."

Anton waved one of his arms and said, "If he still believes his daughter to be a child, then why on earth is he demanding she marry now?"

Hans sighed. "It's always been the way for the girl to be married off. And good parents will always see their children as children. Take Klara's mother, for instance. She is not a good parent. She sees her daughter as either a burden or a servant, depends on the damn woman's mood. Even if I was a drunken violent bastard, she would give Klara to me and say good riddance. They won't admit how she's helped keep the family afloat all these years."

Anton softened his shoulders. Sighing, he said, "I am happy for you and her, my friend."

"I know. As we are sad for you. My God...how Klara hates Peter Lulay. I can't tell you. I believe she would kill him if given the chance."

"Does she now? Well, she is a force to be reckoned with, that lovely wife of yours. Kiss her on both cheeks for me. I will miss her."

"Bah. You are a scoundrel. I will shake her hand for you. Then I will kiss my wife, thank you very much."

Anton laughed. "When will you go?"

"Soon. Klara wants to be with Margaritha on the day of the…you know."

Anton's face paled and he swallowed, as though feeling sick.

Hans changed the subject. "You must leave us the address of your aunt and uncle."

"I will give it to you before you go."

"You will take these paintings with you?" Hans gestured to the two canvases.

"Actually, one of them I wanted to give to you. I…am not so sure about the other."

"Right…we will travel early in the morning. We'll go through Germany, and sail from Bremen. Imagine…we will see the land of our ancestors. In passing, of course."

"I will miss you both greatly," Anton said gravely.

"I know. And I know you will miss her more."

Hans gestured to the nearly finished portrait of Margaritha.

"Ah, well…as you can see, she is much prettier than you."

Now Hans laughed. He slapped his friend on the back and said, "We'll say farewell once more before you go. Maybe you will meet us in Temeswar?"

"Maybe…" But Anton was lost, thinking of Margaritha. "You will do well in America, you and Klara. You will be fine."

They embraced one another, slapping each other's backs and swallowing against the wave of emotion rising in their chests. They had been friends since boyhood. They had served together in the army, and managed to get out and start new lives. There had been many men who found themselves unable to get away from years and years of service.

"Be careful, Anton. Peter Lulay is likely to watch you like a hawk until he has Margaritha secured by his side."

"And halfway across the world," Anton added, sitting on a rickety chair and resting his hands helplessly in his lap. He stared at his portrait of Margaritha as though he would become lost in it, then turned back to his friend.

"Yes…" Hans said, shifting on his feet and looking at the ground.

Anton took a deep breath and said, "You watch him too. I don't like the bastard. I've always been biased, of course, after he set his sights on the woman I love." Anton's mouth curved into a bitter smile.

They shook hands and Hans left. Anton listened to the sound of his friend's retreating footsteps before returning to his portrait of Margaritha, placing some more features on the dress, revealing the very top of her throat. He looked down to where her heart would be. A ringing began in his ears. It was like someone had cast a spell over him.

By creating Margaritha's portrait, Anton sealed her soul as a part of his. As much as her heart always had been, and would continue to be so.

Chapter 15

2017. Cooking an Old Dish. North Dakota.

"Do you have a grater?" Martin asked.

"A grater? Yeah, but why? There's no cheese in Paprikasch." Amber set about frying the paprika and onions and putting the chicken in the pot.

Martin drew his eyebrows together and said, "I know that...It's for the spaetzle."

Now Amber felt confused. "Well...a grater? My dad just rolled up the ingredients then dropped them in the water. He used to call them 'lazy noodles.'"

Martin laughed. "I thought you said your grandma made this."

"She did...but I don't remember how she did spaetzle. She died when I was pretty young. Dad did his best when I requested Paprikasch, though cooking wasn't his thing. The whole spaetzle thing I figured out later and connected it with...the *lazy noodles.*"

He nudged her with his elbow and said, with a smile in his voice, "You're a rough frontier woman."

Amber swatted at his arm. "Oh, really? Well, I can make Paprikasch so there. Grandma was born here in North Dakota, but her mom was from the Old Country. Not sure how much my dad ever paid attention in the kitchen."

Martin chuckled and Amber inhaled slowly, relishing the sound of his laugh. She watched him put a pan of boiling water on the stove. Then he made a much smoother dough than her father ever did.

"Wow...you really can cook. It's sort of like homemade pasta," Amber exclaimed, watching him put the dough through the grater with a spoon.

Martin's smile faded slightly. "Yeah..." he said, as though lost in thought. It was like he was pretending to concentrate more than he needed to on the food.

Amber checked on the chicken, adding a bit of water. When she looked at him again, she noticed Martin still looking at her great grandmother's portrait.

"Who taught you to cook then?" she asked.

"My Mom mostly...but Dad would chip in sometimes."

"Where was your mother from?"

"Serbia. But when she was there, it was called Yugoslavia. Where's your strainer?"

She found it and handed it to him.

"Are your folks still around?" She swallowed.

"No. They both died a few years ago."

"I'm sorry."

"Thank you." His voice was soft, and his eyes focused on his task.

"So...why North Dakota? Some folks moved up here because of all the fracking business..."

He laughed again, and Amber relaxed, happy as he let go of some of his tension. "No...oil money didn't motivate me. I suppose I craved solitude too. But folks still live up here and there's enough agricultural communities, lots of buildings that need fixing up. I made the move a couple of years ago and I liked it. I started out closer to Bismarck and then came down here. John is a huge help. The winters are something else, but...I don't know. I grew up in Chicago so it's not like I expected a tropical paradise. After Mom and Dad passed away, everything I looked at reminded me of them."

Amber nodded. "I see. Never been married?" Amber kept her gaze averted as he drained the pasta. She stared intently at the pot.

"No. You?"

"No. I...never had time. Most men I met expected a real housewife. My dad was great and all, but he still likes being waited on. I saw how my friend Theresa's life went...I realize not all men are the same but I never wanted to wind up in the role of waiting on someone."

"Ha! Well, for the record, I don't like being waited on. It makes me nervous. Mom would do it for Dad because it was traditional, but he always got twitchy if he had to sit still. He had to help his mom out a lot after they came to America because he was the one with better language skills..." He paused, pursing his lips and tidying things on the counter.

Amber nodded, noting that he appeared to be relaxing a little. She decided not to push his family story out of him. Perhaps in time, he would tell her.

"I would die if I couldn't work. The thought of having no projects gives me the chills." Her voice came out more serious than expected.

"More than working in a haunted old house in the middle of nowhere in one of the least visited states in the nation?"

"Yes. *One* of them. Not the least." She giggled and turned to him. He placed the spaetzle on a plate and leaned against the counter, staring at her.

Amber blushed. He cleared his throat and said, "So, Chef? How long until the Paprikasch is ready?"

"Maybe another half an hour...Would, um...would you like some wine?"

Martin smirked a little. Every time his lips stretched and turned that pale shade of peach, her stomach did a somersault and her knees weakened.

She grasped the table and said, "I'm sorry...Maybe it's not appropriate. And if you don't drink, it's okay."

"No, no. I love wine. I drink beer though too. I'm very manly," he said, being deliberately silly. He chuckled again.

"Great then...great." She found herself beaming. Martin was playful and easy to be around.

From time to time, the house would creak from the wind as the storm raged outside.

As Amber opened a bottle of red wine and set out two glasses, she watched Martin peering through the curtains at the window over the sink while washing the utensils from his spaetzle making.

Amber tilted her head, unable to stop herself from admiring him. He'd since removed his heavy fleece and had rolled up his sleeves. Amber wasn't exactly short, yet in this room, Martin's height was imposing. The top of his head reached past the middle level of her three-shelf cabinets. When he flicked some dish water off his hands, she watched the muscles in his forearms flex.

By the time he turned around, she approached him with a glass and a smile.

Martin stilled and said, "I'm not going anywhere tonight, so...why not."

He took the glass from her slowly, letting his fingers graze hers. Amber's face heated at the look in his eyes. He looked away and started tapping his foot, looking at the ground.

"You probably had to peel back a layer of two of linoleum from this place, huh?" he asked.

"Oh goodness, yes. It took me a while. The wood in the living room needed replacing. Some of the hall too. The bedrooms were in decent shape, though. It's weird how any of the flooring survived the neglect. I just sanded and treated everything in the bedrooms. The bathroom and plumbing needed gutting. This place was built with a lot of love."

A strong, cool fragrance overwhelmed the smoky Paprikasch. Rosemary. Martin's breath hitched. Amber scanned the kitchen with wide eyes.

"Are you...sure you don't have a bottle of oil or something that spilled?"

"I don't have any rosemary. I have the odd cinnamon scented candle, but nothing that smells like this..."

Martin released a breathy laugh. "You know...there are times when you talk that you almost sound Irish to my ears. Your inflections and stuff."

Amber giggled. "I've heard some folks from other places say that. I don't get it."

Martin grinned at her. Amber neglected to disguise how closely she monitored his mouth.

Yet she didn't look away when his eyes met hers. And she didn't flinch at the heat present in both their gazes.

"Well, cheers," Martin said as they clinked their glasses.

The smell of chicken, onions, and paprika filled the house. The rosemary fragrance had faded. It had happened in such a burst before.

Amber sipped her wine, looking to the side.

It was like Klara wanted to remind us that she was still here.

"What are you thinking about?"

"Um..."

"Yeah. The smell eased up. It was like a reminder that we aren't alone."

Amber blew a breath out of her mouth, relieved he was just as aware of everything.

"Yeah," she said.

"I prefer the rosemary reminder to the banging. I'm not a fan of that one."

"Me neither."

They spent the next few minutes, clearing and setting the table. Amber arranged candles and set a couple of flashlights out.

From the living room, there was a cracking sound, like the wind was straining the glass. They both went to look, turning to one another silently. Amber finished the Paprikasch by adding sour cream to the sauce.

"It's not low fat, is it?" Martin asked as he spooned spaetzle onto two plates, to which Amber eventually added the finished Paprikasch.

"No." Amber smirked and replied.

"Oh, thank God," Martin replied in mock relief. "You're such a skinny thing, I hoped it wasn't because you go for all that low-fat stuff. With you fainting earlier and all…"

"Ha!" Amber nearly snorted with laughter. "Well, you don't look like a guy who indulges in heavy cream *too* often."

"No…I'm sensible." He gave her a boyish smile as they sat down, like he was proud of himself and not afraid to admit it. He lowered his voice, adding a serious note when he said, "I sure don't skip meals, though."

"I can see that," Amber replied, not realizing till it was too late that he might take it the wrong way.

Martin gasped in mock offense. She giggled. He was theatrical yet subdued in his humor.

"I really didn't mean you are overweight. You appear healthy, not skinny. That's all."

This was the awkward bit where she should reassure him, yet not let on how very attractive she found him.

"Well, I do like to eat. But I move around a lot too. I don't like sitting still for long."

He's…adorable. Amber shook her head at the revelation, finding it odd a man of his size, outdoor occupation and all, could strike her as *adorable.*

At the table, their talk turned to the ups and downs of living in North Dakota. They sipped their wine and exchanged stories of their grown-up lives, college and the earlier part of their thirties.

Amber found herself growing more and more relaxed. Soon, the plates were empty save for a few smears of pinkish paprika-laced sour cream sauce and chicken bones.

"Mmmm. Well, I'm impressed. Thank you for the meal," Martin said.

"You are welcome, and you helped. I loved your spaetzle," Amber replied and Martin smirked, his cheeks flushed.

"Thanks," he said.

"Martin?" Amber asked.

"Yeah?"

"When did your parents leave the Banat?"

He tensed up a little. "Um, after the Second World War. They were... sort of trapped for a while. They came over as refugees."

"Oh..." Amber was confused.

"It's okay. Most Americans I know don't talk much about *after* the war in Europe. What happened during it was awful enough."

"I am sorry. I'm afraid I only read up to a certain point on the history of where my dad's family had come from." She bit her lip.

Martin sighed. His eyes seemed to rest on one side of her hair. His arm twitched and she was certain he would touch her. Instead, he pulled back and folded his hands together on his legs.

"Amber? Do you remember learning about how after the war, when the Germans lost, Europe was divided into zones...like the American zone, the British zone, etc.?"

"Yes?"

"Well, the Banat fell under the Russian zone. This was where communism defeated fascism."

Amber nodded, furrowing her brows.

"Well, Hitler was defeated and that was obviously a good thing. Our families were ethnic Germans, but had no ties to Germany. The Nazis called them Volksdeutsche, which more or less means they were German people by blood but born outside the Reich. The term has a connotation of racial superiority over other groups living in Eastern Europe. Apparently, there were even German 'tourists' from the Reich documenting German culture in the Balkans in the early nineteen thirties. When Hitler invaded Eastern Europe, Nazis occupied many villages in Romania and Yugoslavia, places like Poland, classed as Prussia or Silesia then, and Czechoslovakia, which had a big ethnic German population too. The situation varied depending on the country's status as an axis or allied nation. Some of the 'ethnic Germans' welcomed the Nazis. They were eager to prove themselves 'real Germans' by being 'real Nazis.' Some people didn't like it, but they stayed quiet about Jewish folks going missing, their property being taken, and so on. Folks who didn't like it and said something got their business ruined, were put in jail or worse. But still...some did subscribe to it all.

"Long story short, Amber, after Hitler's defeat and the German army's retreat, because of the Nazis' war crimes and also due to their status as 'Volksdeutsche,' they found themselves enemies of the state in the country of their citizenship. In the Russian zone. In places occupied with soldiers filled with memories of fallen comrades, tormented on the Eastern front, in places occupied by communist partisans who had no sympathy for anything remotely German. After what Hitler had done to the Jews—the torture, starvation, families ripped apart—there was a lot of hatred. It didn't matter whether you participated in the crimes or not. If you were of German extraction, whether young or old, soldier or civilian, pro-fascist or anti-fascist, there were plenty of people in Eastern Europe eager for revenge. Schwobs eager to embrace their superior status and Nazi war crimes basically damned those communities. It was a bit like assuming every white face from the American South was in favor of the Klu Klux Klan."

"Oh..." Amber didn't know what to say. Her skin had gone cold, and the chicken bones on her plate made her nauseous.

"Yeah. I'll tell you all about it, okay? It's just that I grew up with the mental consequences in my parents of all that stuff. It's not all horrible. The fact that I exist says something. And there were some kind people, Romanians, Hungarians, and such who helped ethnic Germans escape. I even read about Russian officers who stepped in when ill treatment went too far. Some non-Germans helped at great personal risk to themselves. It was a lot worse for Mom in Yugoslavia. Serbs and Germans were old enemies. Romania had changed sides toward the end of the war..."

Amber turned to Martin, who ran his hands over his head. The beginnings of dark stubble darkened his jaw and shadows were beneath his eyes. Like talking about this aged him. He smiled bitterly. "Please don't *ever* think I have any sympathy for Nazis...or that my folks did. I can't tell you how much they hated them up until the day they died. The horrible irony is that a lot of the Volksdeutsche who had done bad things, who participated in persecuting their Jewish, Gypsy or Slavic countrymen whom they had lived with for generations...I mean...the real bad ones? Most of them took off as soon as they got wind of Hitler's impending defeat. The people who stayed, who didn't flee...they honestly thought it would be okay because they didn't do anything. They spoke a dialect of German, but they never *liked* the Nazis being in their village. My maternal grandmother was insistent that they hadn't done anything wrong. They were Yugoslavian citizens. Tito didn't care. Apparently, my great grandpa in Romania *hated* the Nazis...."

Just then, the lights flickered and went off. A creak was heard down the hall. The bench creaked as Amber scooted closer to Martin. He placed his hands on her arms and squeezed. She could smell his skin, masculine deodorant, and antibacterial soap. There were still candles lit and Amber knew she had a generator at the ready if her power died.

For now, there were no noises except for the storm raging outside. Amber faced Martin, her gaze flickering to the window over the sink. Over the outline of her ancestors' portraits, she could see the rapid movement of flurries in the night.

Her eyes went back to Martin. Their faces drew closer. Their lips touched and she felt Martin's hot breath against her mouth. His fingers pressed deep into the flesh of her upper arms, and her body went languid in his grip.

In the next moment, the power came on. They found themselves in the light again, staring into one another's illuminated, heated gazes. They drew away, each looking down, but Martin still held Amber's arms. He removed them, inhaling and exhaling deeply.

Amber worried if he noticed the powerful effect he had on her.

Oh, Amber, this is moving too fast. But he seems to like me too...Change the subject...Don't talk about his family's past.

Then words began to fall from her mouth.

"I do have a generator, so we'd be okay. That wasn't supposed to happen...the lights going out. I spent good money on re-wiring the place," Amber said. Her lips still burned where he had barely touched hers with his.

Martin nodded. "I'll do the dishes." He stood quickly, and Amber followed him. Amber was sure she could feel his gaze on her while they tidied up. Then when she looked at him, he appeared lost in thought, his eyes sad.

"Martin, I'm sorry I brought up your folks' history..."

He turned to her and held his hands up. "Amber, it's okay. It's not like I was there or anything. And I...did enjoy your Paprikasch, by the way. It made me think of better times." He smiled, but it didn't quite reach his eyes. Amber nodded, worried that she had encouraged him to speak about something he didn't want to think about.

☙ ❧

Martin's head swam with memories from Chicago.

Martin swore internally as the memories of arguments, of his mother closing herself off from both himself and his father, played through his mind.

They often involved her refusal to visit Europe. He tried not to let these thoughts override his enjoyment of Amber's company.

When he was doing the dishes and Amber was wiping the table, he pressed his lips together, savoring the feel of her lips on his.

It was only a second...barely that.

After the light flickering, there weren't any more 'incidents.' There was still no sign of Hans in the house.

He wanted to continue with their kiss. Yet he also wanted to look John in the eye at the office tomorrow when his colleague inevitably realized he stayed the night on the Schreiber homestead.

As Amber led him down the hall to her office/guest room, he cursed himself for watching the way her slender hips moved beneath the fabric of her jeans. She'd removed her fleece while they were cooking, and her cotton t-shirt allowed for a much better view.

He helped her turn the futon from a couch into a bed. She set him up with an extra quilt and a flashlight.

He looked over to her canvas and easel by the window. "So...you paint too?"

She smiled. And the light from the hall lit up the pulled back waves of her hair. Martin's fingers twitched.

She replied, "Well, sometimes I get stuck for cover ideas when I'm only using my gadgets. Plus...it's stress relieving, to focus on the purely creative side of what I do. Let go of all the technical things." She turned from the easel to him.

Say goodnight, Martin. That's the appropriate thing to do.

Then he caught her chewing the inside of her lip.

Is she checking me out again?

Her gaze flicked up to him.

"I suppose we should say goodnight now." She smiled, somewhat sheepishly, he thought.

Martin opened his mouth to reply. Her lids lowered just slightly.

He took one step towards her, unable to stop. It was her who closed the distance between them, wrapping her arms around his shoulders. Martin's arms circled her waist, pulling her to his body, and their lips found each other.

The sound that then overwhelmed the snowstorm outside was that of kisses and gasps. She was so slight in his arms, and when he pressed even closer to her, she moaned and bent in acquiescence. Amber clutched at his shoulders, pulled him closer by the lapels of his shirt. He could taste the wine and paprika still on her tongue. He groaned and dug his fingers into her waist.

"Martin..." she gasped as he proceeded to kiss her throat, her skin hot and tender against his mouth.

"Oh god, Amber...." It was liberating to have her in his arms. That was how he felt—as though he was finally free.

But I'm not. I've got all kinds of stuff in my head...

They stopped for breath, resting their foreheads against one another.

"I'm sorry...I'm so sorry. Maybe we shouldn't do this." Amber's hands were on the sides of his head.

Martin reached up to stroke her hair. "I don't want to push this either...I mean, I want to but...I want to get to know you."

"I want that too, Martin..." They took a couple steps away from one another.

"Thank you for, uh...giving me shelter for the night." His voice came out more intimate than he intended, but it was how he felt.

"You're welcome." She reached up to touch her lips and smiled behind her fingers.

He reached up to grip the top of his own hair and blew out a breath. "Well..."

"Goodnight, Martin."

"Goodnight, Amber."

Chapter 16

1909. The Prayer. Bensek.

Margaritha had only just drifted off before the sun came up. She imagined Anton next to her, his long body weighing down the mattress at her side. She was sinking from his weight, rolling over to touch his slim frame...but he wasn't there. And her bed was too small. She woke, stricken with grief over the absence of her lover.

Alone and horrified that soon she would have to lie next to Peter.

She never liked the way Peter smelled. Or the way he looked at her. There was a knock on the doorframe and her mother stood, with folded arms.

"Good morning, daughter," Frau Koenig said.

Margaritha winced and squinted at her mother. She'd been so exhausted, and then so deeply asleep, that now the reality of her impending marriage and her mother's scrutiny were overwhelming.

"Morning, Mami."

"Well? I need you to help today. Soon, we will begin preparations."

Margaritha rolled over and stared up at the ceiling. "For what?"

"My dear, you know for what. For your wedding. Your father and I have negotiated with Peter. His parents have long since passed away and he is a successful farmer; he just needs a good wife."

There was a bitterness in her voice, and Margaritha guessed it wasn't directed towards her, yet anger began to burn.

Margaritha's eyes stung and her chest clenched. "Did you love father, when your parents told you he was who you would marry?"

Her mother remained silent for a few seconds before answering. "Your father is a good man. And he makes decisions based on what he feels will be best in the long run, not based on how you feel this morning."

"That's not what I asked." Margaritha spoke through her teeth, her fury so strong, and this disobedience towards her parents so foreign.

Wincing again, expecting her mother to shout, she braced herself. Yet what followed was, "Margaritha, I learned to love your father. As he learned to love me. We were of the same status in the village. And we accepted one another. That is the only way to be happy—accepting what you have. That is what we do here. In America, in time, you might be able to advance as a family. There will be more chance there. But know this: acceptance is the only way. Longing for what you cannot have will only make you miserable."

Margaritha clenched her fists, digging her nails into her palms as the ceiling above her began to swirl.

Suddenly, there was a frantic knock at the door. Margaritha shot up past her mother, who scolded her. "Margaritha!"

He'll come for me. We will run away together. I don't want any of this.

She was lightheaded as she opened the door. Klara appeared, looking pale and as though she had not long been up.

"Good morning, Frau Koenig. Hello, Margaritha. I wondered if we might spend time together. I will help you with your work this morning. With Hans and I leaving soon, there isn't much to do, much of our preparations are in order. I offered to help Mama this morning, but neither she nor Anna are speaking to me today."

Margaritha looked to her mother, whose lips had been pursed but were now beginning to loosen. Even her gaze softened. "Very well." The older woman released a long sigh. "Klara, dear...perhaps your mother really will miss you."

Klara kept her chin up and her face straight as she nodded at Frau Koenig. "I will be sad to leave our home here in Bensek, but I am happy with Hans."

Frau Koenig said, "Yes, well, he is such a good young man for taking you..." Then she stopped and looked down at the ground, as though unhappy with her own words. Frau Koenig looked back up and continued, "Well, we will miss you and Hans for sure. Yes, if you would help Margaritha, that would be good."

Margaritha quickly changed into her work dress and went out to the garden with Klara. Their boots and skirts swished over the soil.

The geese and ducks clucked in the background, but the two women were otherwise alone in the back garden.

"Almost everything is pulled up. The weather will turn too cold soon anyway..." Klara smiled at her and pulled her friend's hand towards the large rosemary bush that was just to the right of the rain barrel.

"Oh, dear Margaritha. Even in heartbreak, you are too dutiful. In times like these, there is only one thing to do. We will pray together." Klara held her friend's hand and the two knelt near the rosemary bush.

"Pray?" Margaritha watched her friend pull out a rosary and a prayer card as they knelt behind the large bush.

"Yes. Come...we'll make it look like we are protecting the roots of the bush from the colder weather. But really, I pray for strength for you and Anton." Klara also pulled out a small white candle and lit it, holding it just far enough away from the rosemary needles.

She joined hands with Klara as they prayed together, hoping for some kind of intervention for her and Anton.

Margaritha's full attention was in her prayers. The wind picked up and rosemary-scented air flowed around them, lifting tendrils of her hair. Margaritha's ears began to ring as though Klara wasn't only praying to the Holy Mother and the Saints for intervention, as though Klara was casting some sort of spell.

Margaritha smiled with the pure joy of it. God above would sort the injustice of thwarting true love.

Surely, surely, we will be together. I can't really marry Peter Lulay and move halfway across the world.

They were about finished with their prayer when a sharp intake of breath behind them made both women turn around.

They could see the slight, skinny form of Anna, Klara's sister. Her sunken cheeks brought out large eyes glinting with malice.

Margaritha's stomach sank as she watched the corner of Anna's mouth curve up. Klara stood, her chin high, looking defiantly at her sister.

Margaritha also stood, despising every tooth in Anna's head. Where one sister had remained a good soul despite the sorrows she suffered at the hands of a half-mad mother, the other had turned to bitterness and spite. Finding joy only in the destruction of others.

"What are you doing here?" Klara asked her sister.

"Mami said you could come and help with a job or two, even though you are leaving us in the lurch. It's the least you could do. Frau Koenig said you were both out here. I didn't think you would be performing witchcraft."

"I pray with my friend for the success of her marriage. Perhaps you are only jealous that Peter Lulay didn't choose you. You are too lazy to do any work. That's the only reason *you* will miss me," Klara hissed.

At this, Anna's smile fell and she glared at Margaritha. "Peter Lulay will regret choosing a wayward woman such as you, Margaritha. You are a fool, cavorting with my heathen sister. He will be interested to know how much of a tight rein he needs to keep on his pretty wife!" With that, Anna turned and marched away.

"Anna!" Margaritha shouted, panic coursing through her blood.

"Leave her. He won't take any heed of her anyway. My sister has always believed she is entitled to the same treatment as a Hapsburg princess. She'd be happy eating cakes and wearing delicate frocks while other people do her dirty work. Bah!" Klara picked up a handful of dusty earth and tossed it in the direction Anna had marched off in.

Margaritha could see that her friend was shaking as she rubbed her now soiled hands together. Margaritha reached out to take her friend's hands and looked deeply into Klara's large green eyes.

"I will miss you so."

"And I you," Klara replied, her eyes shining with tears.

○3　৪০

In the wee hours of the following morning, the rooster crowed in the distance. Margaritha lay on her side. Her eyes were swollen with tears and her mouth was dry. Her father had shouted at her, saying that Peter Lulay couldn't afford to have Anna gossiping about the two women.

"How are you cross with me? My friend and I prayed together. Klara is a very devout woman, a good married woman now..." Margaritha had insisted.

"You are to behave! If you want those friends of yours to come to your wedding, you will see nothing of them before the day. Do you understand? Hans and Klara cause trouble, whether or not they mean to." Herr Koenig threw up his hands.

"Of course they don't!"

"You are better staying away from her in America as well. Perhaps move somewhere else. The things that came out of that Anna's mouth..."

"No!" Margaritha had wailed.

And the argument had carried on. How their prayer wasn't appropriate. It wasn't in church, or even in the home. It could have been perceived as sorcery, even if it wasn't so.

A knock sounded on the front door. Acting on pure instinct, Margaritha scrambled for a wrap, lit a candle, and left her bedroom. There she saw her mother and father talking quietly to a figure on the porch.

She heard Anton's voice. His gentle tones were like honey traveling down her insides.

Perhaps they will see sense now.

The light she brought with her caused her parents to turn. Her hair was in a loose braid hanging over her right shoulder. She stepped forward and caught sight of Anton.

His dark eyes settled on her, unblinking as though frozen in a gaze of love. She could see he carried a large bag over his shoulder. She also recognized the leather bag, which would be filled with his canvases and art supplies. She wondered if he would give her one of his portraits.

Her father cleared his throat. "Margaritha, Anton is leaving for Temeswar this morning. He would like to bid you farewell."

Margaritha looked to her mother's face. Frau Koenig's brown gaze was watery and she quickly looked down at the floor, nodding in agreement.

Margaritha quietly stepped forward. "Good morning, Anton."

"Good morning." His voice was raspy. "I've heard there has been trouble because of Anna."

"Yes…really so ridiculous," she replied. Her parents were still on either side of her.

"I've spoken to your parents. I told them I know what a good woman Klara is. I know Hans would never have chosen anyone wayward to be his wife. They are both good people."

"Yes, absolutely. It was all nonsense. Anna is jealous of her sister's good fortune to be with Hans."

Her father's voice almost boomed behind her.

Margaritha realized that with Anton outside on the porch, and her there with only a shawl covering her night dress, neighbors would notice as the village woke up.

She bit her tongue against her father's petty worry over the opinions of neighbors.

"I hope they will get to see you marry, still. Hans and Klara." His voice broke slightly at the end.

Margaritha's knees weakened. His lips said one thing yet his eyes spoke of something so different.

I love you, Margaritha.

"You will be missed here. And I hope you will write to Hans in America. Then perhaps, he will tell me how you fare in Temeswar." She couldn't speak of the wedding.

"Yes. I will write. Hans knows the address of my aunt and uncle. I am sorry, Herr Koenig, for the trouble in the Wirtshaus. I forgot myself. I hope you will be happy, Margaritha, in your life."

"I honestly hope the same for you, Anton. I would want to think of you as being happy. Always."

Margaritha placed the candle down and held out her hand, keeping her gaze locked on Anton's.

Anton reached his hand out, grasped hers. His thumb grazed the inside of her wrist. The tiny caress meant the world to her.

Anton spoke in a voice low enough for only the Koenigs to hear. "I want to kiss you, Margaritha, because I love you and I always will. But I don't want to disrespect your parents or cause you trouble once I go. If we were free, I would kiss you and I would marry you. No matter what, even if this truly is the last time I set eyes on you, I will always love you. I wish you and your family well."

Her father moved quickly behind her, placing a hand on his daughter's shoulder, as though staying her from flinging herself into Anton's arms. But Herr Koenig said nothing.

Then Anton smiled and said, loud enough for the village to hear, "I wish you well, dear Koenig family. Thank you for all you have done for myself and my parents when they were alive."

He sniffled a little bit as he squeezed Margaritha's hand, hard enough for it almost to hurt, before letting go.

Anton shouldered his bags and reached to shake Herr Koenig's hand. Margaritha's father said nothing, but returned the handshake.

Frau Koenig came forward and shook his hand too. "We will miss you. Take care of yourself, dear boy."

Margaritha watched Anton leave, staring at his tall frame as he disappeared in the sunrise that seemed barely there.

Margaritha blew out her candle, accepting the gray light that surrounded her. All warmth and sweetness seemed to leave the village with Anton's departure.

She rushed past her parents and flung herself on the bed, weeping.

Her parents did not knock on the door or try to speak to her. Her mother only brought her food and water in silence.

Margaritha understood, in her misery, that this was their way of being kind.

Chapter 17

2017. The Aftermath of the Storm. North Dakota.

Martin woke up in Amber's office, staring out at the distant iced-over creek and trees across the field behind Amber's house. He leaned against the window and looked to the far left, where the remains of the barn lay under a high snowdrift.

Nearly knocking over Amber's easel as he moved away, he walked out of the office/ guest room and bumped into Amber.

"Oh!" She smiled. "Morning," she said and blushed, looking down.

"Morning. Did you sleep okay? Any problems?"

Her eyes were almost black in the shadow of the hallway. Her mouth fell open slightly. He wondered if either of the ghosts had showed themselves to her.

He'd heard nothing. His dreams had been intense, but didn't involve ghosts. They featured the pale pink lips he found himself staring at right now. He adored their arched softness. How strong and responsive they'd been against his.

"No...No, I slept...fine," she said. He caught her eyes staring in the direction of his mouth.

Liar.

Martin grinned.

Amber shook her head and looked back up at him before speaking, "I... The plows have been out here already. Those guys amaze me. They are so nice, they clear right up to the house. We can clear a path for your truck in under an hour."

Later, after they had shoveled around his truck to the clear a short path to the plowed road, both pink-cheeked, they faced one another. Panting slightly, the heat of their breath made distinct steam as they stood still.

"You're, uh…pretty in shape for a woman your age."

"Ha!" She slapped his arm playfully with her gloved hand.

"Well…to be fair, you did agree with me when I commented that I never miss a meal."

"I didn't mean it like that." She rolled her eyes.

"Only joking." He winked.

"Yeah…" She giggled, slightly out of breath. It was obvious she enjoyed physical activity, and the thought made him delirious with happiness.

"Well, listen, I've gotta go get to the office now that the weather has turned so nice. But, um…I'd like to see you again, Amber."

"I would like that too. Very much." She beamed.

"I will call you tonight if that's okay? Just to check in?"

"Sure."

As his truck negotiated the freshly plowed snow, he watched her go inside the house from his rearview mirror. It was the oddest thing, but he didn't fear for her safety, living alone in a haunted house.

He feared for her sanity a bit, but not her safety.

Because Martin knew that Hans and Klara had been dear friends with his great grandfather, Anton Handl. From what his father had told him, his great grandfather had been a good man. Someone who wished no one harm, save for some guy who insulted his friends in the tavern once.

The old story went…

He loved a girl, in Bensek, but her family had higher status and they were determined to keep them apart. I've no idea what happened to her. But if you could go and see my Ota's friends, maybe even their children, tell them what happened. It would mean a lot…to me.

As Martin drove down the highway, surrounded by thickly blanketed prairie, he shook his head.

"Why did I come out here really, Dad?" The fields had no answer. There was silence, save for the hum of his engine. The grief squeezing him was in stark contrast to the euphoria he'd felt less than an hour before with Amber.

"I got sick of remembering all the sad stuff you guys used to tell me from Mom's childhood. Thought I'd get a business going and put your ghost to bed. Instead, I've met new ghosts."

The sun was rising higher, making some of the snow glitter. "...And I've met a nice lady too."

When Martin walked into the office, he was met by John's raised eyebrows.

"So, boss, how did you get home?"

Martin stood straight and looked directly at his colleague. "I had to sleep in Miss Amber's guest room. She made me dinner. That's all. Okay?"

John nodded. "Okay, boss. I believe you. From what I've heard, she's pretty straight-laced. Didn't want a cad like you taking advantage of a nice lady." John's voice was deadpan, then he proceeded to type on the keyboard.

"Hmmm," Martin said. "She *is* a nice lady. And a client."

John stopped typing. "Hey, boss?"

"Yes, John?" Martin spoke tersely as he went to his desk.

"I, uh...You remember when I said I saw the old lady in the window there?"

"Yes."

"I reckon she might have been...Well, it wasn't only her. I...It sounds crazy, but I felt like someone was watching me."

Martin nodded.

"Don't make fun of me now." John sulked.

"I won't, John."

"That place gave me the heebie jeebies. Not real bad, just...eerie. How... how was..."

Martin turned on his chair, his head full of visions of Amber sitting at her desk, glasses askew, the focus in her eyes as her fingers clacked on the keys. He'd much rather be staring at her than John right now.

"How was sleeping there overnight? Were you scared?" John finally asked.

"I know what you mean about the place. I'm not sure she's alone there. But no...not gory R-rated horror scared. More..."

"PG-13 scared."

"Right."

"You didn't go more than PG-13 with Miss Amber, huh?"

"That's enough, John." Martin's voice was abrupt. He didn't want to discuss Amber as anything more than a client, though he couldn't deny there *was,* without a doubt, something between him and his client out on the Schreiber homestead.

Martin still changed the subject and asked John, "Did you send the guys over to the site north of Dickinson?"

"Yeah. But we'd better go check it out too. One of our fellas is only a kid."

"He's twenty-four. That's how old I was when I started after school."

"You're old."

"Shut up, John."

John laughed, and to Martin's relief, finally took the hint to keep the conversation focused on work.

After lunch in the office, and a long afternoon that rolled into early evening checking on a much larger temporary shelter project, Martin finally made his way home.

After showering and changing, Martin shivered despite his thick sweatpants. He went to find a thicker fleece to put over his t-shirt. He stood in his closet, pulling plaid work shirts aside, then reached up to the wooden shelf on top of the clothes rack.

Martin was rummaging through old boxes when something hard bumped his forehead as he reached towards the back. "Ow!"

Cursing under his breath, he pulled the dusty old suitcase down. It was from the late nineteen-forties, and had been one of the few things Martin brought from his parents' house in Chicago. There were other old photos, clothes, and pieces of memorabilia in the attic.

Things he couldn't get rid of yet couldn't look at either.

He still owned the house they'd left to him, though he rented it out to some friends who had trouble affording a place in the city but needed to be there for work and their kid's schooling. Martin couldn't imagine living there again, not after coming to appreciate the total lack of traffic and quiet existence out here. Visiting the city would serve him just fine.

He sat on his bed and clicked open the suitcase. Inside were some ancient toys, old German books, and a book of sketches. Some of the sketches weren't the work of his father, but of his great grandfather.

Martin's mind wandered to before his mom got sick and passed away. Before his dad died.

'It's safe to travel there now. A couple of people from the club are going, so we wouldn't be alone. You can speak some Serbian; I speak Romanian. We would be able to get by.'

His mother's short, gray perm stuck in his mind. She'd refused to look at his father for a moment. Martin recalled the tears in her eyes when she turned back. How she'd spoken like uttering the words was a task far greater than he noticed at the time.

'I won't go. It was different in Romania. In Yugoslavia, it was a horror film. Do you know what they did to some of the men in my town? I won't go...'

'Please, Katy...please. I want to see where my grandfather lived as a young man. He always talked about his boyhood village. It would do you good. You could make peace, to see the place as it is now...'

'You can find your grandparents' grave at least. I don't even know where they dumped my grandparents' bodies. In some pit with all the other starved children and old people. That sort of thing was supposed to stop after the war! But if I start to ask, I have to prove that we weren't Nazis. If I tell anyone in this country, they think I'm one of those Holocaust denier people. If the Nazis hadn't done the Holocaust, we wouldn't have been punished for their crimes! I got starved and hit with a rifle butt just for crying for my murdered father in German. It was the language we spoke at home!'

Martin remembered his father holding the beaten-up suitcase he'd brought with him as a child, a pleading, almost pitiful look in his eyes. His mother remained shaking and tearful.

His parents had met in Chicago at a local Danube Swabian club. Though when they'd fled their hometowns, they technically were in different countries, they were from the same culture of agricultural German Catholic settlers in Eastern Europe.

People who'd lived there since the seventeen hundreds, when they'd migrated from other German-speaking regions of Europe, before Germany as a nation state existed.

Martin leaned back on his bed, placed his hand over his eyes, and squeezed them shut against the next onslaught of memory. He'd resented his father for pushing his mother to travel when she didn't want to.

Martin had yanked the suitcase out of his father's arms and shouted, *'Enough, Dad! She doesn't want to go. I'm done with you upsetting Mom. Her memories are darker than yours.'*

'Mine were not all so nice either! And the people who have gone back say it was a positive experience. It helped them to put the past into perspective. We could...'

Martin hated to admit it, but he resented his father for getting tearful. For showing weakness while his mother was falling apart.

His father had said through his tears, *'We could all go. It will be good for us...as a family.'*

'No, Bastian. No.' His mother's refusal had been final.

'Sorry, Dad. I won't let you push Mom on this anymore.'

Sebastian Handl's bottom lip went up. Just as it had begun to quiver, he'd turned from Martin.

Like he knew I was ashamed of him.

Martin's eyes started to burn and he shut the suitcase, as though he could shut out the memory.

He rubbed his stomach and grimaced; the burger he'd grabbed on his way home from work did not have the pleasing after effects of Amber's Chicken Paprikasch.

Martin removed his hand and glanced at the closet, happy there were no other memory triggers waiting to torment him. He pulled his phone out of his fleece.

He pressed Amber's number.

"Hello," she said. He leaned back on his pillow as a smile spread across his face.

"Hey," he said, sighing, relieved to hear her voice.

"How are you?" Her voice picked up at the sound of his. They had such an instant reaction to one another.

"Doing okay. It's been a long day. How've you been?"

"Guess so, it's ten-thirty now. I've been okay."

"Oh. Man, I'm sorry. I didn't realize it was so late."

She laughed. Her sleepy, breathy laugh that made his heart beat faster.

"Well, I'm happy to hear your voice," she said.

"I'm unbelievably happy to hear yours." He found himself using a tone he used with girls back in college.

He'd been told he should have been proud of his reputation as a lady's man in college. At times, he was. Sometimes, it made him feel hollow and pressured to live up to a certain image.

With Amber, it was different. He was different. He wanted more from her than a fling.

And she didn't feel like a temporary escape. She wasn't a rebellion against his Catholic upbringing or a 'conquest' his fair-weather friends would tease him about.

"So...thanks for my car shelter. I'd forgotten to get a few things from town, and I was able to get out without digging out my frozen truck. I'm all stocked up now. Ready for the next storm."

"I hope I get stuck with you again." He winced at the longing in his voice.

She laughed, not in a mocking way, more a sound of amusement.

And a hint of delight, he liked to think.

"Well, me too. I need a good spaetzle-maker in a snowstorm."

He chuckled, biting his tongue against the innuendos that came to mind.

Martin, you aren't some twenty-something horn dog. You are a mature, sophisticated man.

He coughed.

"I would like to take you out for dinner, actually. This weekend, if you're free?" Martin asked.

"Absolutely..." Amber replied. She'd paused as though caught in mid-sentence.

He heard her breath hitch.

"Are you okay?" He sat up.

"I...I'm okay. I smell rosemary again. Really, I..." She let out a laugh, as though shocked. It was like somewhere between laughter and weeping.

"I believe you. Are you okay with it?" he said.

"Yes...Yes. Like we said, I don't think it means...harm." He could hear her swallow and shift her position, wherever she was. He stood and started to pace around his bedroom.

"I...Are you sure?"

"I am totally sure. I can't wait for this weekend."

"Me too. Give me a message or whatever if you need anything."

"I will. Goodnight, Martin."

"Goodnight, Amber."

And Martin sat back down on his bed, looking at his phone and wishing he had a picture of her in his photos, to admire before he fell asleep.

I've never been this weird over anyone before...

He drifted off with her voice in his head and a vision of her lips, spread in a smile behind a wine glass, on his mind.

Chapter 18

1909. The Koenig-Lulay Wedding. Bensek.

Michael Koenig lingered outside the front door of his parents' house, watching the village begin preparations for the wedding. It was doubling as a good-bye party for Margaritha and Peter. Soon, Michael would have to go into service.

The experience of being punched by older, bigger Anton Handl did not make him as eager to serve. He'd previously enjoyed 'teaching a lesson' to smaller, younger people.

Michael hoped to secure passage to America himself one day, though he wished to go to a city. Somewhere he could enjoy himself. His father expected him to take over the farm. Michael yearned for adventure and beautiful women.

He leaned against the whitewashed walls of his parents' house and closed his eyes.

Hopefully, tonight will rid the house of the awful atmosphere. We are supposed to be looking forward to a party. Instead, my sister mopes, Mami cries, and Tati broods. Tati said nothing when Margaritha struck me...

Yes, this place wasn't for him anymore either. He thought of Anton in Temeswar, and a foreign emotion came over him. Pity for Anton. How poor he was and how he was pushed aside for older, richer Peter Lulay. Michael shook his head.

Bah. He will soon forget my sister. There will be women enough in Temeswar, and they will be more fun. Not like the virtuous village girls. He would only have ruined her.

Michael looked to his right. He breathed out, expecting to see his breath in the early morning chill yet it wasn't quite there. He was frustrated. In the rising sun, he saw the broad figure of Peter Lulay coming from the direction of the church.

His head was down, as though looking at the ground. Michael squinted and could tell Peter's brows were furrowed, his steps quick and harsh, almost like a march.

Michael admired Peter Lulay. He'd served in the military, having helped repress Czech nationalists challenging Austria-Hungary's authority in the region. Why his sister preferred lanky Anton Handl, he couldn't imagine. Michael seethed, recalling how Anton had thrown him across the table in the Wirtshaus.

Good riddance to the skinny pauper.

The older man came closer, his arms held slightly away from his body and his fists clenched. His work boots came to a halt before him. Michael looked up.

"Good morning, Herr Lulay. Ready to marry my sister today?"

Herr Lulay nodded, and his bushy brown mustache twitched. "I am. I thought I would say a few prayers on my last morning as a single widower. I hope your sister is ready to marry *me*, and put all childish things behind her."

"Of course, Herr Lulay." Michael paused, thinking of the depressing atmosphere in the Koenig house over the last few days. He continued, "She will come to her senses when she realizes how much more of a man you are than Anton. But...Herr Lulay, if I may comment..." Michael began to fidget, and reached a hand behind his head.

"What is it, young Koenig?"

"I do wonder why you have allowed the Schreibers to come. Klara isn't normal. And Hans was loyal to Anton..."

Peter crossed his arms and stroked his chin. Sighing, he said, "Well, the Schreibers are also going to North Dakota. It's likely we could be neighbors, and I don't want any ill feelings between us. But you know, I also do not trust Klara. I don't think she is a good Christian. Her sister and mother might be crazy, but they did see what they saw and..."

Peter paused and shook his head.

"Yes, Herr Lulay?"

"I...well. I am a tolerant man. But if it were up to me, I would run them out of the village anyway, as it's been proven they cause trouble. Misery follows Hans, and Klara is wayward in her faith. But they are leaving, as are we. Yet we will be neighbors. It isn't a simple issue, you see, Michael. I cannot be seen to be an aggressor."

Michael puffed his chest out and said, "Well, I can perhaps send a clear message that I don't want them anywhere near my sister in America. I would be happy to do so."

Herr Lulay held his hands up and. "No. No, please. You have already taken a beating partly because of those two. I won't have it. Just enjoy the party, young Michael. You never know, the next wedding might be yours!" Michael watched the lines around Herr Lulay's eyes crinkle.

Yes. Yes, he is a good man. My sister is lucky. And she should behave so.

"The world awaits me, Herr Lulay. I will be a proud soldier and kiss many beauties before I find myself taking vows with just one of them in a church."

Peter Lulay chuckled, patted Michael on the back, and walked away, whistling a jovial tune.

He is overjoyed to be marrying my sister. At nineteen, she is blessed to have such a man to care for her.

He thought no more of Margaritha's wan face, his mother's tears or his father's brooding. Hc looked forward to a good wedding party.

ငၽ   ဆ

Klara Schreiber had never seen her friend in a finer dress. Even Frau Koenig, who always dressed for working in the fields or the kitchen, now wore a new skirt and a pretty blouse and jacket. Klara's heart broke when she noticed the rosemary pinned to their garments, just below the shoulder.

Rosemary is supposed to symbolize love.

She'd also never noticed Margaritha looking so pale. Nor had she ever noticed Frau Koenig's eyes to be bloodshot. Herr Koenig smiled and nodded politely when he greeted her, though she was certain there was brandy on his breath.

Michael glared at her as usual, and Klara stayed on Hans's arm.

During the ceremony, she was sure Margaritha faltered on her feet for a moment.

Now, at the celebrations after the ceremony, Margaritha handed out cups of wine, ringed with sprigs of rosemary. Klara passed her gaze over the guests gathered before Margaritha as the bride recited her words of devotion. How her duties now lay with her husband, and she could no longer make merry with old friends.

Her white bridal veil was exchanged for the headscarf of a married woman.

Guests chuckled as she recited an old poem of how she was now with her beloved, and how they would treasure one another always. Frau Koenig leaned her head to the side, her eyes glassy. When a guest would speak to her, she smiled and nodded. No mirth reached her eyes.

Herr Koenig's cheeks and nose were red as he chatted with other men taking part in the raki drinking, while the usual formalities and theatrics were observed by his daughter and new son-in-law.

Herr Lulay proclaimed his devotion to her with glittering, dark eyes.

Food had been served, and for a time, many of the women, including Frau Koenig, left the party hall for an hour or so to feed the animals. The men stayed and kept the party going.

A couple of the villagers teased Hans, saying, "What of your dear wife? Doesn't she have something to do?"

Hans smiled, squeezed Klara's arm, and said, "We have sold most of my parents' animals, and the chickens we kept in for today. As you know, we go to America soon."

The inquisitors nodded and took another drink of their beer or brandy. Klara looked to where Peter and Margaritha were.

Peter was laughing and talking to Michael and Herr Koenig and a few of the other village men.

Margaritha sat in the middle of a white cloth-covered table, her tawny eyes staring at a candle. Klara looked at Hans. "I will go and speak to Margaritha. She appears miserable."

Hans nodded, already having had a couple of glasses of raki. An elderly neighbor of his parents wanted to speak to 'young Schreiber' about his plans to emigrate.

"Okay, but don't take long, Klara. And for the sake of your friend, mind what you say." Despite the warning, Hans's voice stayed kind and he gave her arm a reassuring squeeze.

Klara smiled and approached her friend. "Are you well, Margaritha?" Klara asked. Margaritha looked up as though she didn't see who was before her. Then, recognition lit her eyes and she smiled. The first real smile Klara had noticed all day.

Margaritha answered, "I am so tired. There has been so much to do over the past few days and weeks. And now Peter and I must prepare to go away. Mami is very sad. She will miss me."

"Won't your parents emigrate too? Many families have all chosen to emigrate, even if they don't all depart in the same year."

Margaritha shook her head, the candle light playing on her skin. Though she should have glowed from happiness, it gave her a maudlin appearance.

Klara noticed her friend squeeze her eyes shut and saw the tears that filled them when they opened.

"I don't know how much more of this I can take..." Margaritha whispered in a trembling voice.

"Come, we will go for some air." Klara took her friend's limp arm.

Klara grabbed two glasses of raki for them. Pulling Margaritha outside, Klara saw her friend take the rosemary wreathing the handle of the cup and toss it on the floor.

They found themselves on the back side of the hall, leaning against the outside wall and looking up at a sky full of stars.

It seemed a brighter and wider sky than any they had seen before in Bensek.

"Have a drink," Klara said.

Margaritha lifted the cup to her lips with trembling hands. She closed her eyes and sighed.

"I've been crying so much. I didn't think I would be able to cry more. I can't cry at my own wedding. I've been trying so hard...He won't be pleased, I know it. I don't really understand what sort of man he is, but already I don't like him."

They both took another sip and exhaled, their breath visible in the chilled night air.

"When will you go?" Klara asked.

"Before Christmas. Peter has family we will stay with. What about you?"

"We've decided to go in the spring. Hans wants to ensure that his parents' home and all their effects are in loving hands. He won't talk about it. I know he feels a sense of guilt about leaving them behind, even though they are in the ground."

"Oh. Poor, dear Hans. He was always a good boy. I'm ashamed of Michael for attacking him. I told him so."

"I can't imagine he took that well."

"He told me to shut up and get on with my destiny of making little Lulays."

Klara grit her teeth. "What did you say?"

"Nothing. I slapped him. Quite hard, and he was already bruised. I thought for a moment he would hit me back, but Tati stepped in. I suppose that was Tati's gift to me before I marry a man I don't love. Letting me get away with slapping my horrible brother."

"Oh dear. Well, neither of us were blessed with kindly siblings."

"No..." Margaritha unbuttoned the top buttons of her blouse. Klara knew this was something her friend did when she felt stressed, strained. No matter how cold it was, Margaritha always sought a bit of air on her neck.

Margaritha sagged against the wall, as though having finally been allowed to breathe. "I wish I could have gone with him. I hate this village now. I am leaving. He is gone. I just want to get to America and get on with it, whatever it is. Anything will be better than this. We will see each other there, won't we? You will homestead too?"

Klara didn't say anything for a few moments. "I hope so...I certainly hope so. Come, finish your drink. We should re-join the party."

Margaritha nodded and Klara led the way back into the party hall. Upon entering, she was met with the face of a smiling Hans approaching her. Then, Michael Koenig was at Hans's ear and Hans's smile fell.

Hans's face contorted and he turned to Michael. Klara moved close enough to hear.

"Why are you so bothered if my wife wishes to speak to your sister? They are old friends. What harm can it do?" Hans asked innocently.

Klara could see Hans's blue eyes glittering, displaying the effects of one drink too many. To her right, she could see Herr Koenig leaning against a wall, almost falling asleep.

Michael pushed Hans. "You would let your witch lead my sister astray on her wedding night?"

Hans pushed Michael back. "Get away, brat. The sooner you become a soldier the better. A bit of discipline will sort you out!"

Margaritha was right beside Klara, clutching her arm. The room was filled with pipe smoke and brandy. The ceiling of the hall felt too low, too confining. Klara patted Margaritha's back, noting how her friend clutched at the bottom of her throat in panic at the sight of the quarrel.

"What would you know! Weak fool taken in by the worst woman in the village. You might as well have taken her skinny, half-mad sister!"

Time slowed as Hans grabbed Michael by the lapels and hoisted him up. He shook the younger man and punched him in the left eye. Hans's eyes were blazing as he shouted, "What pain you cause your family! You little swine!"

Michael was stunned on the floor, then got up, groaning.

Peter Lulay came forward. "That's enough. Enough!"

Peter Lulay's gaze settled on Klara. Her heart pounded and there was a ringing in her ears.

Margaritha's new husband looked from his bride to her friend and glared.

"Okay, Schreibers. I think you should go. I have been generous enough."

Klara looked to Margaritha, who squeezed her arm still. Klara had to pull herself away to get to Hans, who appeared confused and contrite.

"They were talking outside. Michael is coming to me and insulting my wife. What do you expect, Herr Lulay?"

Peter ignored Hans. He shook his head and held up his hand in a haughty dismissal.

As Klara and Hans exited, she looked back to Margaritha. She watched the light in her friend's golden eyes dull with every word Peter Lulay said in his bride's ear.

Chapter 19

2017. Bumps in the Night. North Dakota.

Amber lingered somewhere between sleeping and waking for most of the night. The curtains on her bedroom window were closed. Friendly ghosts or not, the thought of a person who passed away in the nineteen-forties looking through the window didn't make for easy sleeping.

As Amber turned away from the window, one thump after another sounded and she turned to see what books had fallen onto the floor.

Yet when she scanned the shelf, all their leather and paperback spines faced her, undisturbed. Her head ached with tiredness from staring at a screen for most of the day before. Amber preferred living alone, yet these days, she found herself wishing for the company of Theresa.

Even more so, she missed Martin...though she hadn't slept easy the night he had been there.

The memory of Martin's heated yet tender kiss had kept her awake. That and a fear of seeing someone looking at her.

Now, with her eyes adjusted to the dark, she scanned the bookshelf again. Nothing had fallen. Bracing her hands on the mattress, she leaned down and looked under the bed. There was nothing save for some plastic containers of wrapping paper.

She flung herself back onto the pillow, looking out into the hallway, lit by a lone nightlight plugged into the outlet near the bathroom.

Amber expected to see Klara walking past. Her chest rose and fell softly with every breath. She pushed her fingers through her hair. The house creaked. Amber reminded herself that every door and window was locked. Apart from her computer and graphic design tools, she had little worth stealing.

Her thoughts turned to Martin. Amber closed her eyes and shifted her focus away from the effect his hands and mouth had on her. She thought of how easy he was to sit beside. How he made shoveling huge piles of snow fun. His laugh was comforting.

Then there was the way his brows would knit together and he looked away at the mention of his parents. Her heart hurt for him. He was a son of immigrants who came from a little-known situation in Europe after WWII. When Amber did research on the internet, she found sites dedicated to Danube Swabian history, and books written by survivors of Tito's internment camps in Yugoslavia, and others like Nick Tullius, whose families were displaced in Romania.

There were some pictures of life before the war. Images of farming families' days before they would be disenfranchised. Poems, paintings, and books by ethnic Germans who had been born and raised in Eastern Europe like Nikolaus Lenau, and Herta Muller. Muller's prose was dark and confrontational. Just as with American culture, there were demons and less flattering portrayals of everyday life in fiction and poetry.

She also found sites by neo-Nazis who denied the Holocaust and insisted the genocide of ethnic Germans was the 'real Holocaust.' Amber's stomach turned at the outrageous conspiracy theories on sites dedicated to such things.

There were academic articles about Hitler's use of the 'Volksdeutsche' as instruments in perpetuating Anti-Semitism and atrocities against Jews, Slavs, Gypsies, etc. in Eastern Europe.

Amber's paternal grandfather had died in the war, flying planes over Germany. He had been German-Hungarian by background, though born in North Dakota. Her Grandmother Caroline, who came from the same community, had remarried, though they hadn't had more children.

War is never a romantic thing. Amber had never viewed it as such.

Amber had edited stories detailing Nazi atrocities and crimes; how organized the disenfranchisement, torture, and killing was. She'd read about the revolting reasoning behind it, the embracing of racism in a fury of nationalist zeal.

That people had to live with the knowledge of such things occurring around them didn't seem like something that could have happened in recent history.

Or something that occurred in her lifetime, but Amber knew awful things were happening in the Middle East and Africa. Even if the details were blanketed in practiced tones of journalists, there were the common screen images of empty, crumbling buildings, dust and smoke.

It all disappeared with a swipe of the hand.

Amber groaned, willing her mind to quiet.

Dammit, dammit, dammit.

Life in cities where news reels, papers, magazines and political conversations were ever on display was something she actively sought to avoid.

It was this sort of thing which made her seek out more work from fantasy authors. Fiction writers. History and non-fiction were too upsetting. She thought she'd be safe here, back at home.

Living on this old homestead in North Dakota, amongst evidence of the past...but being haunted by it wasn't something she expected.

Amber threw back her covers and padded down the hall in her socks. She glanced out of the living room window, the moon allowing for a view of snow-blanketed prairie that led to the rural route which was her address. And Martin's car shelter.

She ran a hand through her hair and collapsed on the couch. Her phone chimed and Amber startled. It was a text message.

I really, really can't stop thinking about you. Hope you're doin' alright. See you this weekend. – Martin.

It was three am.

Should I reply?

Thump, thump, thump.

There was that sound again. Only there were several in a row. *Thump, thump, thump, thump.*

Goosebumps rose on her arms, icy prickles traveling up her scalp. The heat left the room and Amber shivered. Sorrow filled her and panic seized her chest. Still sitting on the couch, she looked down to her phone, which had ceased glowing with Martin's message. Her feet were frozen to the floor.

The wind whistled over the earth and turned into a low groan. The sound altered, until it was more like a shout, a call.

Amber shrank back onto the couch, worried she was in front of her window.

It sounds like...help...he...

It was a woman's voice lost in the wailing wind. The name became clearer.

Hans...Hans, the voice called. The air around her was still freezing. Amber took a deep breath in and shoved herself up from the cushions.

She marched towards the front door, grabbing her boots, coat, and the flashlight. The motion light went on as soon as she exited the porch and walked around the house. The snowdrifts surrounding the right side of the house came up over her boots, creeping into the top as they crunched through. Her light shone all over the pure white ground.

There were no footprints, except for her own.

She came to the back where the remnants of the original barn now lay buried beneath the snow.

She shone her flashlight in the direction and was met with a pair of light blue eyes, just visible beneath the rim of a hat.

Amber screamed and jumped back, her backside landing in snow. She aimed her light in the same direction, frantically shifting the beam in the air. There was no one. No sign. No footprints. No sound of human retreat.

Now, she pulled her knees up and bumped the side of her fist upon her forehead.

Go back inside, Amber. The atmosphere calmed around her, and the wind ceased whistling in her ears.

She was the only person around for miles. Her hands grew numb as she'd neglected to put on gloves.

Amber cursed and pulled herself up. The panic had passed.

Amber re-entered the house, removing her boots and coat. She changed into fresh sweatpants and a t-shirt, cursing the absurd time that it was and how sleepy she would be once the sun came up.

And she *never* slept late. Then a chime sounded from the couch. She grabbed her phone and held it like a talisman, returning to bed.

Two hours, two hours more sleep and I will be fine.

She lay back in bed, biting her lip and hoping for a message from Martin.

It was only an e-mail notification.

Damn.

Feeling sleepy yet edgy, her thumb tapped out a reply to Martin to his messages earlier. She decided not to mention the incident outside.

Bit of trouble sleeping. I can't wait for this weekend either, Spaetzle chef.
–A

Just as she was putting her phone down, it chimed. This time not with an e-mail notification, but with a reply from Martin.

Happy to cook, or chat with you any time ;) my treat this time. Pick you up at 6 on Saturday? – M

She replied. *Yes. Dinner out sounds great. Night...or good morning ;) - A*

Amber fell asleep, one side of her mouth curved up, finding some peace that Martin was thinking of her. And that he welcomed her thinking of him during the loneliest hours of the night.

Chapter 20

1910. Passage to America. Temeswar Train Station.

Klara waited near the station while Hans finalized their arrangements and the sale of their property. He was also selling the family wagon and horses to someone in town. She had never visited Temeswar before.

Hooves clacking over the cobbles and the rumbling of street cars nearby made her gaze jerk in different directions, she felt she wasn't situated in the right place and would inconvenience the drivers.

People spoke 'Temeswar German,' which Hans told her was considered a cut above the smaller village dialects. Klara wished the train would come sooner. She kept her mouth shut, fearful that if someone heard her 'common' dialect, they would look down their nose at her.

There were Hungarians and Romanians speaking nearby. Their rolling tongues mingled in a symphony of languages, clacking footsteps, and clip-clopping horse hooves. It was a beautiful thing, as Klara realized she understood more Hungarian than she'd ever given herself credit for. She would have no choice but to learn English eventually.

Though her future home still lay thousands of miles away, she felt trapped on an unfriendly border.

What if America is worse? We'll understand no one. People will dislike us for being poor immigrants.

The journey across the ocean wasn't one Klara relished, but Hans was right. They had to leave.

She looked at the bags Hans had left her with. She swallowed and her throat constricted dryly with the effort. A warm drink of tea would've worked wonders, yet she daren't leave the luggage. They had a long journey ahead of them and they'd been assured there would be food available on the voyage, part of the price of their tickets.

My God, there are so many people here...

There were people in much finer, more modern clothes than her, speaking different languages. Sweat began to build on her forehead.

Oh, perhaps this is a mistake...leaving like this. Bensek isn't perfect, but at least we know it. Temeswar is sophisticated, but doesn't seem friendly at all. If I can't handle this, how will I handle a different country thousands of miles away?

A gentle tapping on her shoulder caused Klara to startle. Turning, she saw a slim-fingered hand. She placed a hand over her mouth, wondering who wished to speak with her. Relief washed over her when she met Anton's smiling brown eyes.

"Oh, Anton! How good it is to see you!" Klara reached out to clasp his hands.

Anton chuckled, and Klara noticed he carried something. Boots clacked on the ground around them.

"It is good to see you too, Klara. All ready for America? How is your English?"

"I don't know any English! Hans insists that we will learn in time, and that there will be enough Germans where we are going. I am happy we won't be living here...I mean. We would rather be near you, but this city life isn't for me. So hectic! You...look well."

He smiled, and Klara noticed some crinkles beside his eyes. Like he'd matured in a short space of time.

"Thank you. My aunt has been doing her best to fatten me. It's an impossible task, she says."

"Come to North Dakota once we are settled. I will feed you until you burst." Klara squeezed his hands. She smiled and willed back the tears that stung her eyes.

Anton chuckled. "Have you seen the street cars?" He gestured towards the streets.

Klara wrinkled her nose and shook her head. "It's so loud!"

She couldn't begin to say how different she found Temeswar from Bensek. She knew he wanted to ask her about Margaritha. They released one another's hands, and Klara kept hers at her side.

"Oh, Anton...we will miss you. You mustn't forget to write."

"Of course not, dear Klara." His eyes softened and looked down for a moment. The sadness of good-bye bore down on them like a heavy weight on their shoulders. He patted her, saying nothing else for several moments.

Hans returned then, saying, "Handl, get your hands off my Klara, you city dwelling scoundrel." Hans's voice was droll, despite the warning.

Klara smiled at her husband, seeing the grin on his face as he approached his boyhood friend. He set his cases down and embraced Anton. The sounds of their slapping one another on the back added to the cacophony of noise.

"You are getting fat in Temeswar. Aren't you working?" Hans said.

"Yes, yes. My Walter Onkel is teaching me the way of things here. It keeps me out of trouble. Meanwhile, my aunt stuffs me. But they don't have much. I hope to be out of their way soon."

Anton set down his canvas bag. Klara noticed him looking at it, his brows furrowed and lips pressed together.

"We went to the wedding, Anton," Hans said and he patted his friend on the upper arm. "I punched Michael Koenig."

Anton shook his head. "It was inevitable. I have a feeling Peter Lulay knows how to wind up young Michael. Not that it's difficult. And he..." Anton paused and looked at Klara with his mouth slightly parted.

"He was one of many who never liked me," Klara finished.

"With no good reason, Klara. Snobbery and superstition," Anton said, his expression fierce.

"Yes, that's right, dear." Hans looped his arm through Klara's and she leaned against him, letting her lids close briefly. Like she could savor the moment of the three of them being together.

"So...now what once was four becomes two. I wish you all the best." Anton still smiled, but Klara could tell it was somewhat forced.

Compelled to reassure him that he wasn't alone in his feelings, Klara said, "Anton, she hardly made it through the wedding day. We spoke of how desperately she would miss you..." The words fell from her and she clamped a hand over her mouth.

Anton winced and looked away, as though there could be some salvation in the distance.

"Sshh, Klara." Hans gave her a nudge before continuing. "What's done is done. Margaritha and Anton need to get on with their lives."

"They are already there, aren't they? In America?" Anton asked, sniffing a bit.

"Yes," Hans replied.

The crowd entering the station appeared to be growing. There were more random shouts and chatter. Families with children, likely heading on a similar journey to Hans and Klara, started to arrive.

"I thought I might see her, one more time, when they passed through Temeswar."

"They went through the port of Fiume," Klara said.

"Ah yes, many people are taking that route now," Anton said, before he looked ahead and nodded, as though mulling something over.

Hans spoke, "Peter wrote to Herr Koenig. I had gone to speak to him after the wedding, to apologize. I wanted to make things right with the family after all our trouble with Michael. Herr Koenig seemed quite passive. He was so drunk at the wedding he hardly recalls anything. It seems they aren't best pleased with Michael at the moment. He filled me in on the letter."

"I think Frau Koenig regrets sending Margaritha with Peter. She misses her dreadfully. They won't emigrate because the Koenig farm does well. Herr Koenig insists Michael will mature and make something of it." Klara bit her lip.

"Michael is far too foolish. As for Herr Lulay, he will have wanted to ensure there wasn't a chance of running into me," Anton said.

"Well, yes. He said something about Margaritha still clinging to 'old friends.' That she needs to move on in their new life in America. 'A husband requires a dutiful wife', so Herr Lulay said. He likely hoped Herr and Frau Koenig would encourage her to be so in their reply," Hans said.

Trains rumbled over tracks and the steam engine called for its new passengers, including Klara and Hans. Klara didn't look to the trains, rather her eyes remained on Anton. His face fell, his eyes on the trains behind them. He said, "You will have to leave soon. You don't want to miss your departure. I...I have something for you..."

Anton's tall frame bent to retrieve his canvas bag. "It's a portrait of... our friend. I want you to have it. If it's ever possible...I want you to show her. Keep it for me. I will never forget her face. Please tell her that I will always think of her."

Klara expected Anton to weep, but he did not. Instead, his gaze held sincerity, such an oath that her chest ached and her breath was stolen for a moment. Klara nodded and took the bag.

Hans reached his hand out to grasp Anton's. They embraced once

Klara pressed her lips together and squeezed her eyes against the tears. When she looked at Hans and Anton, she noticed Hans looking to the ground and blinking several times.

Even Hans is trying not to weep.

"No portrait of me then?" Hans said with a sniff.

Anton chuckled.

"You're not nearly so pretty," Anton said to Hans, who pushed his lower lip out.

Klara giggled, taking advantage of the moment to bid farewell on a lighter note.

She said, "Come now, stop this. Anton has more important things to do than apologize to you, Hans. We have to get going. I will start sobbing and your last vision of me will be with my red, runny nose." She kissed Anton on both cheeks.

"I will always recall how lovely you are, Klara, with your green eyes. You and Margaritha were more like sisters with your matching wild hair," Anton said with a wink.

"Right, now. That's enough. We're going. No more words of flattery from you." Hans sniffed at the end of his pretend scolding.

The train's persistent whistle and the conductor's call caused all of them to look away from each other. They finally parted.

Klara and Hans just made it on time with all their belongings, now including Anton's portrait.

Once they sat down, the couple clasped hands. They were unable to speak for a few minutes, both lost in the grief of a final farewell. With Hans's parents and siblings dead and buried, Klara's family flitting between hostility and indifference, and the village having snubbed them, Anton had been more like family than a friend.

The train departed to make its way towards Arad, where they would change trains a few times going from Hungary and through Germany. They would sail from the port of Bremerhaven.

When they neared the port, they underwent a medical examination. Before Hans went to be examined, Klara noted how quiet he was.

"I hope I pass...I don't know what I'll do if we can't get to America. We've sold everything." He laughed nervously, blowing a breath out of his nose and tapping his foot.

"Hans, don't worry. They let you in the army quickly enough."

"Yes, but I wasn't upset by the idea of being refused. I would have only insisted they let me into the army so I could serve with Anton. My weak chest as a child could have saved me from that, then I wouldn't have had to listen to his lovesick talk of Margaritha during those years away from the village." He sighed.

Klara rubbed her husband's slender arms.

They both passed the exam and were given clearance to continue their journey. The time had come to leave Europe.

Hans said, "Finally we have been to visit the land of our ancestors, and now we really bid farewell. We'll never come back."

Klara shared Hans's feelings. "Lands change a great deal through the years. A century from now, we probably wouldn't recognize the country of our birth. Our forefathers likely wouldn't recognize this *Germany* today," she said.

"They wouldn't. We are far north from where they lived, Klara." He winked at her.

They had traveled through this *Germany* they had never visited or been to, yet were associated with by their Romanian and Hungarian neighbors. "I've always imagined we are more like Hungarians; after all, we've never even lived in Germany. In Temeswar, I could understand some of the Hungarian," Klara said.

Hans studied the German money they'd received in exchange for their Hungarian coin.

"Well, that isn't the language necessary for where we are going, dear," Hans said.

Most people on the vessel were also Germans, though they spoke with varying accents and dialects.

With the seas being so foggy, the ship had to emit several loud noises to alert any other oncoming boats.

Klara breathed a sigh of relief when the weather cleared. After one day, they saw England.

Seagulls flew and called in the air days after passing Britain. Fishing vessels could be seen in the distance, like floating villages. Soon, there were no birds or boats. They were out on the great Atlantic Ocean.

There was food and drink provided on the vessel. Klara was happy to eat summer sausage and drink tea, until her stomach began to turn. The boat's rocking was novel at first, then her head swam and the food revolted against her.

She found herself staring into the gray foamy waves below, retching and cursing the ship. Thankfully, the seasickness did not remain a constant companion.

Klara wondered how the passage had been for Margaritha a few months before. Throughout the journey, Klara kept a close eye on Anton's bag.

After almost two weeks, birds became prevalent again.

Hans patted Klara frantically.

"There…there it is, Klara!"

Despite the easing of seasickness and the camaraderie aboard the ship, she was ecstatic to be near dry land again.

They were not greeted by the lady statue they'd heard of in New York. Rather, they arrived in the port of Baltimore. Their first English greeting was from a ruddy, stern-faced immigration officer.

"Welcome to America," the tall, uniformed man said to them after examining their documents and belongings.

Klara smiled and nodded. She was impressed when Hans said 'thank you' in English.

"I didn't know you knew that."

Hans smiled. "Anton taught me a little. He was always good with language. Remember how clever he was with Hungarian? It's a shame he is so poor. With more money and education, he could have gone far." The smile faded slightly.

"Yes," Klara agreed. She knew in Europe you had to have the right connections; that generally, being of a certain status meant you would remain…of a certain status.

From there, things got more difficult. German speakers were more spread out. Hans's English was basic while Klara's was non-existent.

"Oh, it's so difficult. I can't imagine speaking it well. How will we manage, Hans?"

"It will be fine, Klara," Hans reassured her as they began their train journey across the country.

After over two weeks on the ocean, more travel seemed impossible. She cursed her frailty when Hans reminded her that they were blessed to have steam vessels and trains.

"We are lucky, Klara." Hans held her. "In the days of sail, ocean travel was far worse. Imagine months on a sailboat, rather than weeks on a steam one. Then there were no trains. Only wagons and teams of horses or oxen. The trip was longer."

Klara nodded, determined to make the most of their lot. The journey across the Midwest continued. Every time she looked at Hans, he was rubbing his chin, squinting at any fields, commenting on there being too many trees or the land being too hilly.

When they finally arrived at the station in Dickinson, North Dakota, fellow passengers trickled off the train, all of them being collected by family or associates.

Hans and Klara were alone on the platform, watching the figures of other people grow smaller and smaller.

The wind picked up and howled over the prairie.

"The land is like a sea. It would be easy to get lost here," Klara said and shivered.

For once, Hans did not have a reply. It was March, yet winter still held the air in a bitter grip.

"A lot of the passengers who got off sounded like they only spoke English, Hans." Panic clutched at Klara. This was like being deposited at the end of the Earth.

"He will come, remember? I contacted a cousin of my parents' old neighbor. They agreed to accommodate us. Don't worry, Klara." Hans's voice was calm, yet Klara was sure she heard a tremor of uncertainty.

Klara clutched Anton's bag, wishing to get it inside shelter and away from the biting cold.

Then a sound of wheels and hooves approached. A compact man disembarked from the seat of his wagon and removed his hat, revealing short curly hair. He addressed them in a Swabian dialect, not entirely unlike their own.

"Hans and Frau Schreiber? My name is Josef Petter. I'm a cousin of your neighbor, who contacted me on your behalf. I'm not from Bensek, but I am a Hungarian. I will take you to our place. We haven't much, but we have space enough to help you get along until the ground thaws and you can get your own place going."

Klara's eyes watered as the wind picked up and whistled over the land around them. She'd never seen so much land with nothing on it. The absence of trees, rivers, or buildings made the cold more invasive. Her memory of Temeswar struck her as suddenly friendlier than how she'd perceived it at the time.

She turned to Josef.

"Oh, thank you, Herr Petter. You are so kind. How good you are to accommodate us. We are only strangers," Klara said.

"It is nothing." The compact, curly-haired man held his hand up dismissively and said, "It wasn't long ago that my brothers and I were new to this country. We were thankful that someone gave us shelter when we needed it."

Josef helped Klara and Hans hoist their things onto the wagon. Klara looked at the man who would be their temporary host. There was a friendly twinkle in his brown eyes, and Klara imagined that if someone could still have such a happy face, then perhaps this place wasn't as lonely as it first seemed.

Soon, the horses were moving over the cold country road. Klara huddled next to Hans, who asked Josef all sorts of questions about the soil and the seasons in comparison to the Banat.

As Josef replied and the wheels and hooves took them farther from the train station, Klara kept her hands on the leather bag given to them by Anton. As though, by holding on to the image of Anton's lost love, she held onto a beautiful piece of home.

Josef was a quiet man, yet when he did speak, he made them laugh with his comments about the weather. "Sure, there's no mountains or forest here. But on this land, you are closer to the sky. God can hear you better, ja? He doesn't say much. Then again, neither do I." He chuckled.

Having been cheered by Josef's pleasant demeanor, now thinking of Anton made her heart fall when she realized how far they were from their friend. Klara vowed to one day show Margaritha his picture of her.

She would keep her promise.

Chapter 21

2017. The Date. North Dakota.

Amber had spent far more time than was normal checking her phone for messages from Martin.

Do you realize we are too old to be flirting like this? –A

I like flirting though. See you tomorrow. Can't wait. –M

She'd gotten into bed holding her phone, hoping it would buzz with another message from him.

Her favorite this week had been,

I know that you live with ghosts. But you are haunting my dreams. -M

That is corny and wrong in so many ways. -A

You like it though right? -M

Yes. –A

You kinda are. *Ghost emoji *loveheart.* - M

Amber closed her eyes and grinned.

Slumber crept over her as she settled beneath the quilt. Her grip relaxed on her phone and she became less and less aware of her surroundings.

Amber found herself on the porch, staring out at the prairie. She inhaled deeply of the breeze flowing over her from the land, like a wave from the sea. Her fingers slid over the smooth wood of the porch railing, as though it was a ship.

She turned her head to the right, leaning just slightly over the rail. Hans was there, adjusting his hat and walking out of her line of vision.

"Hans?"

He didn't answer. Amber left the porch, unsteady and inhibited. The air was thick, like heavy skirts clinging to her legs.

"Hans?" Her voice wasn't clear in her ears. Panic struck her when Hans didn't answer and she couldn't reach him.

"I need to talk to you!" she shouted, though the words were muffled, her emotions dominated by worry.

Amber turned around and re-entered the house. Her chest was heavy when she noticed the cellar door was open. Tears stung her eyes as her feet echoed over the hardwood floors.

"Hello?"

She was answered by a groan and a whimper. She swallowed dryly and blew out a shaky breath. The air was muffled and heavy, like the human sound she'd heard.

It was as though she wasn't alone.

Then, a loud banging noise came from the floor. Amber looked down at her booted feet, unable to move. She couldn't shift her gaze as the noise grew louder.

The floorboards are going to burst!

Panic coursed through her.

And she woke up, sweat gluing her shirt to her skin. Amber swung her legs out of bed and stood up. The dream had made her feel stuck, claustrophobic. It had been like being trapped in a glass box—she could see and hear who she needed to speak to, but couldn't quite get to them.

She changed her shirt and sank back into her mattress. The panic eased and the fragrance of rosemary was just detectable on the air. Amber grabbed the back of her neck and looked around. Her phone had fallen to the floor.

Setting it beside her pillow, Amber closed her eyes and turned over.

The rosemary smell didn't scare her anymore.

She associated it with Martin.

ఇ   ☙

An irritating buzzing was infiltrating her head. Amber groaned and opened her eyes, realizing it was her phone. She tapped the screen. "Hello?" Her voice croaked.

"Morning, honey," a perky voice greeted her.

"Morning, Mom."

"Well, can I reserve your place at the table for Thanksgiving?"

Amber blew out a breath and turned towards her bedroom window. Gray light filtered through the curtains.

"Yeah, I'll be there. Sorry, Mom, I've been kind of busy."

"You could come over tonight for dinner?"

"I can't do that, Mom. I've got..." She wanted to say 'work.'

"Do you have work?" her mother's breezy voice asked.

Almost too innocently.

The woman who gave her life had such a sweet, lilting voice, it was impossible to lie.

"I have a date." Amber slapped her hand over her forehead.

"Oh...Oh, well now. Is that so?" A combination of surprise and interest laced her mother's tones.

"Yes." Amber pressed her lips together.

"Does Theresa know about him? How did you meet him?"

"Actually, he installed the temporary car shelter."

"Oh...Oh, well now, did he?"

"Yes, Mother. He's from Chicago."

The responses were now more in the form of noises, like 'oh' or 'hmm' or 'huh.'

She'll need time to process this. And time to ring Theresa and find out what she knows.

"Where is he taking you?"

"To a steakhouse in Dickinson."

"That's nice, honey. Who knows, maybe I'll get to meet him. Maybe I'll be a grandparent after all."

"Mother..." Amber groaned. When she admitted to having a date, which wasn't often, the reaction came with a query about if she would be needed for babysitting.

Her mom's voice interrupted her thoughts.

"Okay, okay. Anyways. I called you for something else. I was cleaning out the closet the other day and I found the darnedest thing. They are old letters, all in German and addressed to your great grandma. The one from Hungary?"

Amber had been wincing and pinching the bridge of her nose. Now her eyes widened and her hand dropped to her side.

"Amber?"

"Oh...um. Well, who are they from? Why don't you ask Dad?"

Her mother sighed. "He says he doesn't know. They were just old letters in a box we took from his mother's house when she died. There weren't any addressed envelopes."

"Who are the letters from, Mom? It should at least say a name?"

There was a rustle of papers across the line and the sound of her mom's whisper, the one she used when she skimmed any form of literature.

"Klara. They are from a lady called Klara."

Prickles traveled up her arms and Amber sat up.

"I'll...I'll come pick them up tomorrow."

"But you can't speak German. Anyway, I was just telling you I might have them interpreted by someone."

"My date speaks German."

"Is he foreign? I thought you said he was from Chicago?"

"His parents spoke it. I'll come over tomorrow and pick up the letters."

"You can fill me in on your date too."

"Okay, Mom. See you soon."

"Bye, honey. Love you."

"Love you too."

Amber's phone buzzed.

*4:15 *grin**

Amber noticed his reminder.

She couldn't wait, and only just restrained herself from texting him again.

ෆ   ත

Amber fussed with her hair in the mirror. She had wanted to leave it down, but the waves were too unruly so she pinned it back at the nape of her neck. Swiping on some gray eye shadow and adjusting her more formal hunter green sweater dress, Amber jumped at the knock on her door.

Martin's peach-tinted grin was accompanied by a scarf tucked into a woolen black coat. It really complimented his hair.

"Oh, look at you." She beamed. "You need a top hat to finish it off. I hope I'm not underdressed."

Amber paused as his gaze traveled over her from head to toe.

"You look beautiful."

"Thanks."

Amber pulled on her brown leather boots over her black nylons and grabbed her coat.

"See? We match." She walked towards him, holding up her black woolen formal coat.

"Gorgeous. I wasn't sure anybody dressed up this far north."

Martin leaned in and rested his hand on the side of her waist. He gently kissed her cheek then pulled away. The gesture made Amber aware of how the sweater dress hugged her waist and hips.

Heat spread through her cheeks despite the open door. Amber slid her coat on and then locked the door and grinned at him.

"When the occasion calls for it. Can't accuse me of putting on airs, though." Amber winked.

The heat in Martin's eyes made her blush.

"I like formal stuff sometimes. Shall we?" Martin held out his arm. He opened the door of his truck for her.

Amber noticed how tidy the footwells were. Smells of oil and leather wafted from the seats, and something else. "Do I detect some pine scent in here?"

"I cleaned it up for you, okay? I don't do that for just anybody. But then, I don't have many beautiful women in my truck."

"Not...*many*?" she teased.

"Okay, not any. Except you."

The engine fired up and the wheels rolled onto the gravel road, then eventually onto the highway. The sun had peeked out in the afternoon and now sunk lower and lower. It washed over the snowy prairie with an orange glow.

As the light faded, Amber turned to Martin, whose gaze was fixed on the horizon. "Sure are pretty sunsets here," he commented.

Every now and again, he would glance at her with a grin that warmed her from head right down to her toes.

The journey was silent apart from the hum of the engine. On other dates, this would have been awkward. With Martin, she was relaxed, relishing their proximity in his truck.

The forty-minute drive went by too fast. They pulled into town and Martin pointed at the restaurant as he found a parking space.

"Best steak I've ever had. You'll love this place," he said, sliding out of the car.

He opened the door for her. Amber slid her own gloved fingers into the hand he held out. He squeezed it, before tucking her arm in his.

"Wow, you are a gentleman."

He chuckled. Another heat wave cascaded down her stomach. Their breath steamed in the icy air and their boots crunched over the snow.

After they sat down, Amber perused the menu. When she looked up, Martin was staring at her over his.

"I caught you," she said with a wink.

"I caught you too," he replied.

She opened her mouth to respond when the waiter turned up.

"Evening, what can I get you two?"

Martin kept his eyes on Amber for a second longer before smiling at the waiter and saying, "Ladies first."

They ordered an appetizer to share and a glass of wine each.

"Shame you have to drive," Amber commented.

"Aw, I'm good. I like wine, but I'm more interested in the food." He took a bite of the fried cheese curds and had a small sip of his wine.

Amber giggled. "You're really taking tiny sips, huh?"

He pouted. "I'm saving it." He took a big gulp of water. "I'm a big man," he said in a sulky, childish tone.

She laughed again at his pretend sulking. "Sorry, just an observation. I'm cool with big men being dainty wine drinkers. There should be more of you."

After ordering their main meal, they continued munching the fried cheese curds and taking very self-conscious, tiny sips of wine.

It was Martin who broke up their silent, playful game.

"So? How has it really been this week on the old homestead?"

"It's been okay. I've had a couple of strange dreams and...." She froze, not sure whether to talk about going outside, looking for Hans.

"Yes?" he asked.

"I can hear her calling him." The memory of Klara's voice, nearly swallowed by the wind outside, and her attempt to speak to Hans brought a sinking sensation inside. She looked down at her food.

Amber continued, "I could feel her grief. That's probably worse than the banging or the apparitions. The way she feels."

Amber laid her forearm on the table, and Martin placed his hand on her. He stroked her, rubbing the softer skin of her arm through the fabric. Amber trembled. Her eyes met his and the cold grief melted like the liquefied candle wax between them.

Martin opened his mouth. "I'm sorry. I wanna help you figure this out. Work takes up a lot of time, but I...I feel like I'm part of it."

Amber tilted her head. "Well...actually, you can help. You can read German, right?"

Martin's eyebrows lifted and he nodded. "Yeah, I can. Mom and Dad spoke it at home. I took advanced classes in high school and community college. That was one thing they agreed on. They wanted me to speak the language. Dad insisted."

Martin's eyes were cast down to his plate, though it wasn't as though he was studying it.

"Did they argue a lot?" Amber asked.

Martin shook his head. "Not exactly a lot. They loved each other, but there were sore topics between them. Mom had come from Yugoslavia, you know, the place that's Serbia today? Dad came from Romania. Remember I told you the situation wasn't good for ethnic Germans living in either place?"

"Yes."

"Well, it was far worse in Serbia. Mom had some pretty awful memories. Dad really wanted to do this family trip back to Europe, visit the village he was a boy in. Mom was *terrified* of going. She felt that people there would still hate them and call them Nazis. She *wouldn't* go. I stopped Dad from pushing her on it."

"I'm sorry. That can't have been easy."

"No, things were really tense with my dad for a while. I think he made peace with it all by the end. I think." Martin opened his mouth as though he was going to say something. He looked back up at Amber.

Then, their food arrived.

Martin said, "How are you with your folks?"

"Okay. My mom is a kind of crazy, but she means well. I have the total inability to lie to her, so she called today and I had to reveal I had a date."

"Oh, you were gonna keep me as your little secret, eh?"

He put his napkin in his lap. More people were in the restaurant. A steady murmur surrounded them.

She'd never liked crowds, but in this case, the social atmosphere was pleasant.

Amber curved one corner of her mouth up before replying to Martin, "You don't understand. If I tell my mother any man has the slightest interest in me, she is...well...she's nosy."

Martin nodded and inhaled the aroma of his strip steak, then said, "Does she want grandkids or something?"

Amber nearly choked on her steak. She stopped to take a drink of water, noting how Martin grinned at her while happily chewing his New York Strip.

"Um, well...I guess she does. I've always been work-focused, which she's been proud of, but it's bugged her sometimes."

Martin nodded. "Lots of my buddies rushed into getting married and having kids just to do the traditional thing. It wasn't ideal for all of them and they realized this too late. For some, they are happy. Kids are great... hard work, but...you can't blame the kids for when balancing work and family and other stress is too much."

Amber smiled.

He actually would make a nice father. Then she rebuked herself and tried to steer the conversation elsewhere.

"Are you still in touch with friends in Chicago?" Amber took a bite of her steak.

"Yeah, I'm debating whether to join some for Thanksgiving for the weekend. Believe it or not, some of the kids call me Uncle Martin. I'm not their real uncle. I was an only child. I came along later on in my folks' marriage." Martin reached for his water and looked around at the slowly filling restaurant.

Soft piano music mixed with the murmur of voices and the clinking of silverware.

Amber nodded, taking a sip of wine. The combination of rich red and gorgonzola and filet mignon made her mouth water. She sighed, continuing to chew.

Just then, a waiter passed with a dish of steaming rosemary potatoes. Amber turned to Martin.

"Martin? I have a favor to ask you. It's in relation to the fact that you can read German."

"Okay?"

"My mom found some old letters. They are addressed to my great grandmother."

"Where are the letters from?"

"Well, the address isn't on there. It's only the letters. They are from someone called Klara. I really have a feeling that it...it is Klara who wrote them. I haven't seen them yet. I understand if you don't want to get involved. You might think this is all kind of weird."

Martin exhaled through his nose and scratched his chin.

"Amber, I don't think that at all. I've seen and felt stuff at your place. Heck, even John said he felt...watched. I...There is something I need to tell you."

"What is it?"

"I visited North Dakota when I was looking into relocating my business. But part of my motivation was different. I'd been to the homestead before, when it was abandoned. I was tempted to buy the place myself, but, I don't know, something stopped me. It made me feel so sad. You see..." Martin stopped and looked at his lap, like it was difficult to go on, but he did.

"When my dad was dying, he told me about some childhood friends of his grandfather's. I wasn't even sure if Dad was mixing up his memories, but he had their address. He loved my great grandpa, you see, and had fond memories of him. He'd cry when he talked about him. I..."

"Go on..." Amber said, her eyes fixed on him.

"Amber, I'm saying that I knew about Hans and Klara because...I know that they knew my great grandfather. When I came to your house, I thought you were related to them or something."

Amber was silent for a few moments. "No, I am pretty sure we aren't related, but...I don't know...How come you didn't mention this before?"

"Well, I thought it would sound strange. Hey, can I hang out in your house because I think my great granddad who I never met was real buddies with the folks who built it? By the way, my parents were ethnic German refugees in the forties and fifties..."

"Is that why you..." Amber said, fearing that her feelings for him were one-sided.

He doesn't seem to be feigning interest in me...but, maybe...

"No! Amber, when I first saw you in...I was...It wasn't normal the way I felt. Then when I saw you at the homestead...I almost forgot why I came there."

Amber nodded.

"I like you too, Martin. I don't mind, you know, if you just want to read the letters and do some research. That's fine..."

"Amber, I am being sincere. But yes, I did want to find out if they had any descendants. My information about them is all via my dad and his childhood memories of his ota, er, grandpa, who used to reminisce about his dear friends, Hans and Klara. I did leave a wreath on their graves."

"That was you? On the day we saw one another in church? I went afterward..."

"Yeah...I went before Church. I don't always go...I'm not an awesome Catholic. But I wanted to say a prayer for them."

"I'd spent All Hallows' Eve being freaked out. That's when I realized Klara was there."

They were silent for a few moments. The restaurant patrons carried on and waiters passed them with iced cocktails and steaming plates of food.

They each had a small amount of wine left in their glass.

Amber raised hers.

"Well...to Hans and Klara."

"To Hans and Klara," he replied. She could tell he was still concerned about revealing his information to her.

The look in his eyes over the rim of his glass reassured her of of his attraction.

Amber whole heartedly returned his feelings. It was risky, but right then, she decided to take a chance and continue to open herself up to Martin.

She rather looked forward to the long drive home.

Chapter 22

1910. Margaritha and Peter. North Dakota.

Peter had fallen out with his cousin over how impressive North Dakota was. Peter said his cousin had misled him, whereas the cousin insisted he'd been as honest as he could have been about hardships in the New World.

To avoid any further unpleasantness, they now stayed with one of the first Banater families who came to homestead in North Dakota—the Brauns.

Margaritha stepped out onto the wooden porch of the Braun family home. In the past weeks, the ground had begun to thaw. Peter had gone with some other Banater men to construct a 'soddy' on the land they had chosen. Now, Margaritha stared at two Braun boys, aged nine and twelve, who were wrestling and chasing each other around the farm.

She placed a hand on her belly that was just beginning to change shape.

Her thoughts turned back to the painting she'd done years ago, in the Handl household. When she was the same age as the eldest Braun boy.

How jealous I would have been. To see this then, to have so much room to run and play.

But now, her heart sank at the thought of no neighbors, nothing nearby except some animals and her husband. And she hadn't expected such biting wind. When they'd traveled from Peter's cousin's to the Brauns', she thought it possible to die from the bitterness in the air.

A breeze picked up, milder and filled with the boy's laughter. Margaritha sighed, looking down at the wooden railing and the boards of such a different style than the porch at her parent's house. Many houses in Bensek had tiled porches. She couldn't imagine those being here.

She wondered how Hans and Klara's journey had gone. So far, she'd heard nothing. Her parents had written back that Hans Schreiber had been to visit them some time after the wedding. *'To apologize for the unpleasantness.'*

"Are you alright, dear?" Mrs. Braun came out.

"Yes, fine, Frau Braun. I needed some air. I felt in the way. Your elder girls do such a good job managing the little one and the kitchen, you will be happy to be rid of me."

"Don't worry about that, it's been fine having you here. We are happy of company other than our own. I'm sure you noticed that it isn't every day we get to see other folks. Pretty different from the Old Country."

Frau Braun spoke, gesturing towards Margaritha's barely swelling abdomen. "The first few months are always the hardest, but you get accustomed to carrying the baby. Then before you know it...it's one after the other." The older woman chuckled. "With God's grace, they will keep you company." The lady smiled. Margaritha liked how the skin near her eyes crinkled, like an affirmation of her kindness.

From inside the kitchen, she heard the girls talking. They bickered in a mixture of English and German. The baby began to fuss. Margaritha and Frau Braun turned at the sound. Through the open curtains, they could see the eldest Braun girl hoisting the small child on her hip.

They turned back in the direction of the barn, smokehouse, and fields. In the farthest distance, there was nothing to reassure them that they weren't alone in the world.

"Do you miss having neighbors?" Margaritha asked.

Frau Braun exhaled through her nose and gripped the railing of the porch. She pressed her lips together and said, "There are still times when I do think of my old village. I am sad I won't see it again. Still, it's been almost twenty years now, and we've been busy."

Margaritha nodded and thought again of Klara and how certain her friend had been in saying she would be unable to have children.

They must be here.

"Frau Braun? There is a couple who moved to the area, Hans and Klara Schreiber? They are from the same village as Peter and I. I know they moved to North Dakota, but I'm not sure where exactly..."

Frau Braun was silent for a few moments. "Well, if they were homesteading, most of the Banaters are in the southwestern part of the state. I've heard of many settling in Hettinger County."

"Thank you, Frau Braun. They were good friends. I miss them." Her chest clenched.

"Well, the best thing to do is get Peter to ask around when he goes to conduct his business, at the post office for example. And my husband might be able to shed some light."

"Oh. Yes, if I could ask Herr Braun. And...yes, I will ask Peter." The thought of only being able to go through Peter caused a stir of panic. Frau Braun's kind face made her think of Klara even more. Tears fell down her cheeks. Margaritha sniffled and wiped the wetness from her face, looking the opposite way of her host.

The boys, who had gone into the barn to feed the animals, came out again, pushing and shoving at one another. Margaritha watched them, looking forward to a day when she would have older children. The older boy stared at her for a moment. Margaritha smiled, but gasped when the younger one shoved his distracted older brother into a muddy patch in front of the barn.

The older boy appeared to have learned English insults as he slung them at his fleeing, giggling younger brother.

Frau Braun shook her head and shouted, "I will wash your mouth out with soap! You think I don't know what you said!" The boys rushed past the side of the house.

Margaritha placed a hand over her mouth, trying to hide her amusement as Frau Braun turned back.

"Yes, they are funny, I suppose." The lady shrugged.

The two eventually approached the front of the house, looking at their mother sheepishly as they removed their muddy boots. From his pocket, the elder pulled out a small wildflower. With his eyes cast down at first, he lowered his head and took a few steps towards Margaritha. The younger boy snickered.

"He wants to give you the flower, Frau Lulay. He thinks you are pretty." The older boy gave his younger sibling a stern look before turning back to Margaritha, his cheeks flushed.

Margaritha smiled at the boy and took the flower. "That is so sweet of you, such a handsome boy. Why, soon the girls will want to decorate your hat for the Kirchweih."

"Oh, the Kirchweih! We haven't been to one of those yet. But there will be one in Lefor this year!" said the younger boy, whom Margaritha could only guess was likely thinking of baked treats and a chance to play with other children besides his siblings.

"Oh, Mama, can we go!?" The girls heard the word 'Kirchweih' and clambered out onto the porch.

"We will see. And in fact, Margaritha, you might be able to meet up with your friends there," Frau Braun said.

A smile spread across Margaritha's face, until one of the children shouted, "Papa!" She turned and on the horizon, there appeared two men driving a wagon and horses. It was Peter and Herr Braun.

"Well, we'd best make sure dinner is finished," Frau Braun said to Margaritha and reminded the boys not to enter the house until they had washed at the outside pump.

"Yes, of course." Margaritha followed the older woman and the Braun girls into the kitchen.

Margaritha and Peter sat at the Braun family table, as they had done every evening for the past couple of months. The children loved teasing Margaritha and teaching her English words for all the different foods. She would miss being around the family.

She didn't look forward to being alone with Peter again. She placed a hand on her stomach, staring at the remaining sausages and potatoes on her plate. The few bites of kohlrabi she'd eaten were giving her indigestion.

Peter's mood had darkened not long after their wedding night, and it had grown worse on the journey to North Dakota. He'd demanded they travel via the port of Fiume. She'd heard it was easier, but believed he wanted to avoid Temeswar completely for different reasons.

Anton...

She tried to think of his picture. The painting of European tiled roofs, and the cobbled streets with electric lights.

Margaritha looked up from her plate and saw Peter staring at her, chewing his meal as though he was chewing on his daily assessment of her.

"So?" Frau Braun began the conversation. "The children and your dear wife are aware of a Kirchweih that will take place in Lefor this year. It isn't exactly the same as in the Banat, but it is a nice way to have contact with neighbors..."

"...and there is food," the second to eldest son said.

"...and dancing..." The eldest girl beamed.

Herr Braun put up his hand and said, "It might be an idea to take Margaritha if it's possible. Always a good place to talk to other farmers too. Good for business." He stabbed at one of his sausages.

Peter's mustache shifted as he smiled. "Yes, I remember. Kirchweihs were good fun in Bensek. Wouldn't you agree, Margaritha?" His friendly words didn't ring true. She wondered if it was only her who noticed Peter's falseness.

Margaritha's thoughts traveled to when she had danced with Anton at their first proper Kirchweih, the one where they first took part in the parade. Before he went off to do his service.

He had held me so close...

"What? Oh, yes. Yes, the children should go. I would like to attend too, Peter, if we are able. Perhaps we might even see our old f—"

Peter cut her off, addressing Herr Braun. "You should marry your eldest girl off soon. Get her a good match. She is lovely. Believe me, I know...such beauty doesn't last long. While she is so pretty, you will have many options."

The elder Braun girl smiled. Peter was still a handsome man, despite his age difference from Margaritha. It stung when he often assessed what he saw as her 'failing beauty.'

Herr Braun said, "Well now, Peter, we won't just give her to anyone. I want to be sure my daughter will be with someone kind as well as successful."

Frau Braun watched the exchange with wide eyes. "Yes, of course. We aren't in a rush to marry her off. You are certainly a lucky man to have Margaritha. Such beautiful hazel eyes she has, and so sweet. I will miss both of you."

Finally, Peter smiled at her. Margaritha's back prickled at the sound of her husband's voice. "Indeed, she was the village beauty for a long time. But I swear..." Peter paused and waved his finger in the air. "As soon as we married, she began to fade. Only enough for a husband to notice." He leaned towards her and winked. "I think she does it to spite me. Her best friend in the village was a witch, you know. She'll never forgive me for parting them."

The children grew excitable at the mention of a witch.

"Could she do spells?" The girls started to giggle.

Peter leaned back, twitching his mustache. There was a playful glint in his eye, as though his words were mere lighthearted teasing.

Margaritha said nothing, didn't smile, and kept her eyes on him.

When we get back to our soddy or whatever it is, I am going to give you what for.

Herr Braun cleared his throat and said, "Well, enough of talk about witches. You will scare me, Peter! Let's leave the women in peace for a few moments and go outside with our pipes. You should take an early rest. You will have an early start to get there and ensure the dwelling is comfortable."

"Thank you for your hospitality, Frau Braun. I hope Margaritha will maintain her cooking standard as well as yours."

Again, his kindly expression betrayed his stinging words. Their hosts smiled and explained how the newly arrived couple had been no trouble and indeed had kept them company throughout the lonelier, colder part of winter.

Margaritha could only mumble her thanks with a forced smile. She wished to stay with the family.

Why doesn't he go live in that soddy, and I will stay here.

Yet her changing abdomen and the band around her finger reminded her, Frau Margaritha Lulay, that she was not free to think of such things.

ଓ ଛ

After they had set off the next day, Margaritha wiped her brow and tried to stop herself from being sick. The weather was mild, but the sun overhead made her blouse and skirts too warm and heavy. The horses trotted with a methodical clip-clop sound.

"I will be happy when this condition is at an end," she muttered. Peter looked at her as though he forgot she was there.

"You look dreadful," he commented.

"I'm so glad that is your main concern," Margaritha hissed before unleashing her frustrations from the night before. "You should not gossip about Klara, you know. They won't live far from here. It is most unkind for one of her countrymen to be calling her a witch."

"Bah, Margaritha. We will become Americans now. The Brauns wouldn't know who I referred to. Your dear Klara *would* have cast a spell to keep you from me. And where would you be? Starving in Temeswar, a fallen woman, likely in the same condition you are now, only with no hopes and some pauper boy to starve with. Provided he even stuck around with you that long. Ha! What do you know, anyway?"

One of the horses neighed. The sound jarred her nerves along with Peter's reference to Anton. She couldn't bear to give him the satisfaction of knowing how he hurt her.

She spoke as matter-of-factly as possible.

"I could have looked after myself, you know. I could have taken in laundry. Worked as a maid. And I could have…I could draw. I was good at it. Perhaps I could have sold a painting or two…"

Her voice trailed off. She recalled Anton holding onto her wrist for the first time. The yearning in his eyes.

Peter stopped the wagon and looked at her. "You are a foolish girl, to think you could survive with a pencil. You would have lived and died a maid to some rich family. Your abilities are common. And cheap. Your beauty was considerable, yet lately, I notice how you fade as soon as I set eyes on you, as though you wilt for me." His voice lowered and he said, "Don't think that I don't notice that when I touch you, you do not relish the event."

Margaritha spat back at him, "What do you care? You got what you wanted. Why does it matter?! Whether or not you think I'm a beauty doesn't concern me. I don't trouble myself over your appearance."

His coal eyes burned into hers as though he intended to strike. Peter tore off his hat and threw it on the footwell of the wagon. His hairline was receding and just beyond his temple was a pulsing vein, shimmering with sweat in the sun. His nostrils flared above the wiry hair of his mustache.

Peter still said nothing. Margaritha did not break eye contact with him at first, until she looked around them and noticed the pale green sea of prairie. If he were to abandon her here, she would perish.

He wouldn't. Surely not while I am with child.

For the first time, fear overcame her. She'd never felt this. Now he was all she had. Peter. Not Anton. Not Klara or Hans. Not even her dear parents or her wayward brother.

Only Peter, whom she could barely stand.

He flung his upper body down towards her. Margaritha jumped back and yelped. The horses startled.

He was only getting his hat. His eyes flashed contempt for her and he shook his head.

Peter worked the reigns and soothed the animals.

"You are an ungrateful brat, Margaritha Koenig. Need I remind you that you were a farmer's daughter in Bensek, not a Hapsburg princess? Perhaps a life as a fallen woman in Europe was what you deserve. Now come, see the shelter I've built for us. I nearly broke my back doing so. And you know there is more work to do. Will you help me or will you constantly complain like this?"

"I suppose there is no use in complaining. I am your wife, after all. I shall be steady in my duty. But I would like to see my friends at the Kirchweih."

"By the time the Kirchweih comes, you will be indisposed, I think. You have far better things to do than pleasure-seeking with old friends. Come now and prove your loyalty for once. Smile. Let me see your pretty, shining eyes every now and again. Though, they never did shimmer in my direction, did they?"

No, because I never wanted you. This was my parents' doing. They couldn't have possibly known how it would be for me.

But Margaritha said nothing. She simply folded her arms over her abdomen. The sun mercifully went behind the clouds as they traveled the treeless land. The gray skies comforted her, yet her life lay before her like the prairie they traveled on.

Immense and without any joyful definition.

They reached the soddy. It was cool inside and not unpleasant looking on the outside. Peter had set up a table and chairs. There was a makeshift bed with clean linens the Brauns had donated.

It reminded her of what she'd read of the shelters Vikings would have had. Peter was like a Viking—cunning and dangerous—which, with his handsome face, should have been thrilling, she supposed.

The notion that she was his captive wife did not fill her with romantic fancy. Yet it was a distraction. A different way to look at her situation. On this great blank canvas.

One that she would fill and define in her own way whenever possible.

No matter what Peter thought or did.

Chapter 23

2017. The Letters. North Dakota.

Amber pulled up into her parents' driveway in Mott, the morning after her and Martin's date. With the sun shining so brightly on the snow and a lack of trees around, Amber wore dark glasses to avoid the glare. Pulling the key out of the ignition, she placed her forehead on the already cooling steering wheel.

It was difficult not to think of Martin sipping his coffee, swallowing and smiling at her, wiping his peach-tinted lips with the napkin. One of his hands held the handle, the thumb of his other hand stroking the cup.

She could feel the pressure of his hand on her forearm. Amber sighed, her breath turning to vapor in the car as the temperature dropped.

He'd been conscious of not having mentioned that he knew of Klara and Hans, and that they'd known his great grandfather. Amber understood that it was unusual for a person to fix up an abandoned homestead that was an average of thirty minutes from anywhere. After gathering that Martin had an interest in property and a passion for structures, she accepted the notion that perhaps he was a little unusual, like her.

It was an odd thing, that his great grandfather had been dear friends with Hans and Klara. There hadn't been an ideal opportunity to reveal such information, until she'd mentioned the letters.

As their conversation moved along, from what little information Martin had about Hans and Klara via his father, to their personal beliefs and lifestyle preferences, it was revealed that they had a connection transcending their Banat German ancestry.

His family could be from Mars. I'd still like him.

It was well after midnight when he dropped her off. She could still feel his lips pressed against hers outside her front door. His face had still been warm from the heating of his truck.

And as she'd suspected, the long ride home had not been long enough.

Even at her age, she was grateful to herself for not inviting him in and to Martin for being such a gentlemen and not expecting anything.

Amber's mother opened the door of the family home. Her bobbed blonde hair had just been blow-dried into an extra fluffy style.

"Morning, honey. Oh, you look tired. I've got coffee brewin'." She gestured for her daughter to enter.

Amber glanced at her mother's brown sweatshirt. It had a picture of a cartoon turkey hoisting a mug of beer.

Amber looked at the picture then back up at her mother.

"It's not Thanksgiving yet, Mom."

Her mother giggled. "I just wanted to wear it. I've got earrings to match, but they're kinda heavy so I'm gonna wait till Turkey day to premier them."

"Sounds good. Dad around?"

"Hi, Amber," her dad called from the kitchen. He was dressed for the day too, but still sitting at the kitchen table, reading the paper.

"Hi, Dad. Mom says there are some letters addressed to your grandma?" She gave him a hug and sat down by him.

He looked up. "Oh, yeah. I don't know that she ever mentioned them, though. Mom kept them, but...she'd never said anything to me."

"Well, she did to me!" Amber's mother piped in from near the stove. She was microwaving strips of turkey bacon and scrambling eggs. The smell mixed with brewing coffee.

Amber looked out of the kitchen window her Dad sat in front of. Lengths of twig poked out of the blanket of snow covering the yard where she'd played as a child.

Her dad spoke, "What did she say to *you* then?"

"Well, your mom said your grandpa was a real jealous type. He never really liked her having friends. Shame Grandma Caroline's brothers passed away too. They might have known something. The fact that these letters are in German is odd..." Her mother's voice trailed off as she retrieved some dill, salt, and pepper from the cupboard.

"Oh yeah, I remember that. Mom said that her dad wanted them to stop speaking German after a while. Lots of German-speaking folks around here were like that when the wars came around. WWI passed by without too much incident, but WWII pretty much sealed the deal for my family to forget the whole German thing. They were from Hungary anyway." He waved one hand then took a sip of his coffee.

"But they never spoke Hungarian," Amber said.

"Not that I know. They liked to cook with paprika, though," her father said.

Amber was inclined to correct her father about the changing borders and political climates in that part of Europe over the years, but she held back. Her mother placed mugs and plates of bacon and eggs on the table.

Amber got up and went to the silverware drawer. She quickly brought knives, forks, and napkins back to the table.

"You sure do move quickly. Then again, you always have," her father commented.

Amber gave her father a closed mouth smile and picked up her silverware.

"So? How was your date?"

Amber dropped the knife onto her plate with a jarring clink.

Her mother's airy voice was complimented by a pair of sparkling blue eyes.

"You had a date, ha?" She looked to her father's twinkling dark eyes. Her father's voice had a tone of constant friendliness.

"Mother..." Amber warned.

"You are almost forty, Amber. You can have a date. I'm just curious how it went. He's from Chicago." Amber's mother looked at her father.

"Oh. He a Bears fan?" her father asked, putting a forkful of eggs in his mouth.

"I don't know, Dad."

"Oh. You need to find out," her father replied, not looking up from his eggs.

"He speaks German," her mother chimed in again.

Her father nodded and said, "Well...from what I know, Grandma and Grandpa spoke a funny dialect. Mom said her dad would discourage them from speaking it around any Germans who weren't from Hungary. Something about the Prussians looking down on them and the Ruski-Germans speaking different. I don't think Grandpa was a nice guy. Grandma was real sweet. She made *awesome* soups..."

"Dad? Martin is from Chicago, but his parents were Germans from

Eastern Europe. They came to the US after WWII."

"WWII? Yeah, I don't think German-Hungarians fared too well after the war."

"I know. Martin told me. I think the place your grandma was from is considered part of Romania now," Amber said.

"Martin, huh?" her dad asked.

"Yes."

"Is he handsome?" her mother asked.

Amber blushed.

Her mother noticed. "Heehee. I guess so."

"What does he do?"

"He builds and repairs barns, garages, temporary car shelters, roofs, etc. He owns a property or two in Chicago."

"Is he that Handl fella or the Lindstrom guy? There are only two reputable ones I know of. I thought you paid too much for the guys who worked on your place..."

Amber cringed and answered, "Handl. Martin Handl. And he speaks German and has offered to read the letters addressed to Great Grandma. And it is highly likely I am going to go out with him again."

"Does he seem like the family type?" her mother chimed in, but Amber didn't respond straight away.

Amber gazed out at the yard again, at her father's covered, prized BBQ and the two barren trees at each corner of the wooden fence. As a girl, it had been her sanctuary. She loved it still, even if it wasn't for her anymore.

Strange that now, she preferred her open land and her haunted house.

"He is an only child. He's always been work-focused. It was our first date, so neither of us wanted to talk about starting a family in our forties. Which has never been something that occupies my mind," Amber said, mainly directed at her mother.

Her mother nodded and continued eating. "Not like you have that much time..."

Her Dad finished chewing his bacon and sipped his coffee.

"He's work-focused, huh? Like you. I've heard about Handl. He does good work. Didn't realize he was a German-Hungarian, though. Cool."

Amber looked at her mother. "I have to get going soon, Mom. I'll come over for Thanksgiving."

At her mother's probing look, Amber said, "Martin is probably going to visit friends in Chicago for the holiday. We are only just starting to see one another. He might even put in a permanent garage. He put in the temporary car shelter..." At this point, her father stopped paying so much attention to his coffee. His bushy brown eyebrows lifted up.

Her mother interrupted whatever he was about to say. "Yeah that's how they met."

Then he spoke, his voice slightly louder. "Well, that's good you have a temporary shelter up. I'd told you to do that when you first got the place. And I've heard good things about Handl. But maybe I should talk to him before he puts in a *permanent* garage. I mean, *jeez.*"

"Okay. If we carry on meeting up, I will introduce you to him. Deal?"

Her parents nodded.

They left the topic of Martin alone. Amber helped her mother do the dishes, hugged her parents, then made her way back home, now in possession of the letters.

Being in her childhood home, talking to her parents, and deflecting invasive questions about her involvement with Martin almost made her forget about the ghosts she lived with.

○ॳ ৪০

Martin woke up at eight, after having gotten to sleep at around two in the morning. He had drunk two cups of coffee after dinner and they'd talked late into the evening. It was liberating to be honest about his great grandfather Anton having known Hans and Klara. He had been worried about not getting off on the right foot with Amber.

Now this, with these letters...he had to hold back from driving to Amber's house earlier than they'd agreed.

Calm down, Martin. She had to go to her folks' house.

In some ways, his involvement with Amber was moving too quickly. Her parents already knew about him. That she nearly choked when he said the word 'grandkids' was adorable and reassuring. He didn't want to rush into anything because he hadn't gotten hitched and had kids in his twenties or early thirties like most of his friends had.

Yet in so many ways, it wasn't moving quickly enough. Not *just* because he wanted to kiss Amber for much longer than he had on the front porch.

He felt so damn comfortable with her.

Her lips are really strong. And soft. And sweet. God, that touch of cherry pie taste still clinging to the corners of her mouth from dessert last night...

He could still hear her slight moan when he'd placed his tongue there. It was too much. Far too tempting to open the door and stumble toward that bed of hers.

Not that he was an angel, or even a particularly good Catholic. This was just...too good to rush.

Martin rolled out of bed, and went for a shave and shower. His arms and shoulders ached from lugging the materials for a barn restoration out of his truck last week.

He thought of Hans, childhood friend of his great grandfather, building a barn on his own in a new country. Probably missing his friend Anton. From what his dad had told him, his great grandfather and great-great-grand uncle had made a name for themselves repairing roofs in Temeswar, or Timisoara as it was called now. Once WWI arrived, everything changed.

WWII made everything worse.

Martin walked barefoot, a towel wrapped around his waist, down the carpeted hallway back to his bedroom. Even after a good couple of years, the size of this place was different from the size of his parents' 'decent-for-a-city-sized' house in Chicago. It was massive compared to the apartment they rented when he was a small child.

He dressed and sat at his kitchen table with coffee and some toast. He picked up his phone and dialed his friend in Chicago.

Aaron, his childhood friend answered. "Hey, Martin! How's it goin'?"

"I'm doing alright. How's the house?"

"Everything works just great. I can't thank you enough. 'Course, your folks sure did keep the place in perfect condition too. And, uh, hey...I've been meaning to ask you. I wanna pay more. I know what rent is around here and...this isn't right. Your rate is too low..."

"Never mind that. How are the kids? Is school okay? Still the same as when we went there?"

"Yeah, it's okay. I mean, kids nowadays say 'lol' instead of *actually* laughing, but you know, it's a good school. You coming out for Thanksgiving?"

"Am I still invited?"

"We'd love to have you. Erika was asking. She wants to know if she should bring in an extra cartload of potatoes."

"Very funny. Yeah. I will have a couple of days off. I should be able to get a flight out, but I can't stay long. Is it okay if I stay on Thursday night, though?"

I wanna spend a couple of days with Amber.

"Of course. How come you gotta go so soon? Have you found a bevy of beautiful women over there?" His friend chuckled.

Nope, just one.

Martin realized he'd taken too long to respond.

And now Aaron was silent for a few moments until, "Oooh. You have found a lady friend. Well, well, well. All I can say is, if it's serious, get a pre-nup..."

"Dude, we are not there yet."

Yet. And I can't believe I just said dude.

He had had a couple of 'gold diggers' after him back in Chicago. His dad had invested in property in Chicago, and Martin's move to North Dakota had proven lucrative. He wasn't, nor would he want to be, a billionaire, but he wasn't a poor man either.

"Okay. I get it. I am going to want details when you come over."

Martin laughed. "Okay, well, I'll let you go for now. I'll look into flights and let you know what time I'm coming to impose."

"It's your house, man. Impose any time."

"Well, you are looking after it for me. I'll talk to you later. Have a good one."

"You too, buddy. Bye."

Martin ended the call and scrubbed a hand over his face. If he was honest with Aaron, he could have sold the house to him at a fraction of what it was worth. But his friend needed a spot for his family at the moment, and Aaron wouldn't let Martin get away with giving him charity. Even if he could afford it. So for now, rental it was.

Martin spent a couple of hours going through drawings of structures for work. They were for projects that would be beginning as soon as the ground thawed.

He then spent some time checking on NFL game times, as well as Europa League fixtures. His dad loved 'football,' and Martin had played until he got to college, even though he'd been accused of having the perfect build for American football if he'd been willing to bulk up.

It was only just after forty that he was, admittedly, losing his shape and filling out a bit.

Martin glanced down at his abdomen, suddenly wondering what Amber would think of him once...*if*...hopefully *when* they got close.

Martin noted the time, then stood so quickly he knocked the chair back with such force that it fell over.

Martin swore and set about making his way to Amber's.

Ꮯ8   ᏠᏅ

It was just after one o'clock when he arrived at her house. He couldn't wipe the smile off his face when he knocked on her door. She answered.

Her face and lips were completely white.

"Hi...Are you okay?"

"I'm fine." She smiled. "Maybe too much wine last night."

Martin frowned. She did have a second glass after his one, but afterward, she'd switched to coffee.

She's seen something again.

"Come on in." She smiled, but he could tell it was slightly forced from the way her shoulders twitched and she seemed just slightly out of breath. The color was returning to her lips just a little as he entered.

It felt cold inside. He suddenly shared the anxiety Amber was obviously feeling.

"Did you get plowed after I dropped you off?" He looked at her with lifted brows.

Amber laughed, though there was still a breathless, agitated air to her tone when she said, "No, no. I wouldn't get drunk alone."

"What happened?" he asked as she shut the door and walked to the kitchen to re-set the coffee maker. She seemed to be on autopilot. He cursed himself for taking a moment to notice how well her jeans fit her, as well as the white t-shirt and black wool cardigan. Not too baggy...not too tight.

She turned around and caught him checking her out. She smiled and laughed, her body bending and relaxing against the counter space between the sink and coffee maker.

"Okay, what did happen?" he said.

"I saw her. I got back from my folks' house about an hour ago. I was in the bathroom, washing my hands. In my reflection, it was like she was standing next to me. I turned from the mirror, and she wasn't there."

Martin nodded. The pink tone was fully back in her lips now, and her voice had stopped shaking. Yet with her eyes cast down on the floor, the frequent hints of mirth and pleasure he often caught in her blackish brown eyes were missing. There were purple shadows beneath them.

He walked towards her. At first, she didn't look up, but remained leaning against the counter. When he was inches away from her, he slipped his hands around her back and she instantly leaned into him.

It felt *unbelievably* good to have her so close. Pleasure rushed through his system, swiftly followed by an intense heat that spread through his veins. As though her reaction to his hug caused an embrace within his body.

She sighed with a pleasing humming sound that reverberated against his chest.

Then he lifted his hand to touch the waves of her hair. When he inhaled and his breath caught in his throat at the bliss his fingertips received from the thick texture of her hair, he put his hands on her shoulders.

Now she looked up at him. The desire reflected in her midnight eyes instantly made him her captive.

I don't want to go home tonight. He opened his mouth. Her gaze dropped to his lips.

Then she said, "Martin?"

"Yeah?" Her eyes were still on his mouth. *I love the way she watches me.*

"We…we should start on the letters. I'm…a little worried about moving too…you know…It's…"

He stepped away from her, swallowing. He shook his head from the fog of their mutual physical longing.

"Do you want a glass of water?" she asked, already turning away from him, now facing the sink, retrieving two glasses.

"Yes. Thanks," he said. He looked around the pale blue kitchen towards the rectangular dark wood table. There lay a small bundle of letters.

Whether the room smelled of rosemary or whether he was going crazy wasn't clear to him.

He sat at the table.

"It didn't smell like that before," Amber said, sitting down beside him with two glasses of water.

"No…it didn't. And if you would have been burning rosemary oil within the last five minutes, I would have noticed. I get that we are both… well, past the age of consent, but if we are trying not to rush things, Frau Schreiber is giving us a helping hand."

"Knowing that there is an old German Catholic lady ghost is a bit of an ice bucket, I suppose," Amber said dryly and took a gulp of her water, staring at the letters.

Martin chuckled.

"Well...let's see what she said, shall we?" Martin said with a sigh as he took the first letter.

Dated April 14th, 1912.

'Dear Margaritha...'

Chapter 24

1910. Anton. Temeswar.

"So? Who was she?" Anton's Walter Onkel leaned against the window, puffing on his pipe.

"Who?" Anton asked, then furrowed his brows and took a bite of his bread. The flat he shared with his aunt and uncle was smaller than even his parent's humble home in Bensek.

Right now, it seemed stifling.

The coffee he swallowed didn't help with his rising temperature. Anton had a small bed on the opposite side of the room to his relatives.

"Have some bacon." His Aunt Susannah spooned a few cubes of salty fried meat onto his tiny plate. He stared at the grease soaking into the split piece of bread.

Anton swallowed. "Thank you, Susie Tant." She smiled at him. Ever since he arrived in Temeswar over a month ago, it had been her mission to fatten him up.

His Uncle Walter's hazel gaze stayed on him and the fragrance of pipe smoke mixed with that of the bacon and coffee. This was despite his aunt's insistence that his uncle must smoke near the open window.

Anton looked up at him and Walter said, "The girl whose portrait was so deserving of the last of my oil paints. Such a beauty. And you gave it away to your friends, bound for America."

"I am sorry, Walter Onkel." Anton looked down and sighed.

His uncle shrugged and said, "I don't often get the energy to paint these days. I am happy they went to an inspired source. I'm just curious. I haven't seen this girl in town."

Anton touched his chest. He looked down, not wishing to make eye contact with his uncle. He feared his heart might rip into pieces within his chest.

No, she is far away.

"She emigrated to America too," Anton admitted.

Now he looked up at his uncle. Walter clutched his pipe in one hand and folded his arms.

"Ah. Yes, we considered that once as well, but we have good employment here, and it's risky, changing countries. Even if we went to a city over there, I've established a reputation here. The Kovacs are a good family. They recommend me for roof repair work on other properties. In time, you will learn, and you might progress beyond this."

"I am very grateful for all you and Susie Tant have done for me," Anton said.

"You are a good boy. I liked your mother and father, may they rest in Heaven." His Susie Tant patted him. Even if her fussing was excessive, it had been some time since he'd benefitted from any maternal care.

"So? What was the problem?" his uncle pressed.

"She is wed to another. He took her to America to homestead in North Dakota. He was wealthier, a farmer and an older man. We'd been dear to one another since childhood, but her parents knew I was destined to be a pauper."

His uncle sighed and cast his gaze around the bedsit flat. His aunt kept it clean and with potted herbs and flowers here and there. Paintings of the city and of Bensek from years ago hung on the wall. The first time Anton entered the flat, he could see his uncle had talent.

"Shame, we Handls have yet to find any wealthy nobles who take an interest in the artwork of Bensek's peasants. Nor did we ever master the production of fois gras that the aristocrats so love."

A small corner of Anton's mouth went up. "I'd rather live in a hovel than make a living from force feeding poultry."

Anton thought of Klara's sister Anna, whose cruel nature made her apt at that particular task. Apparently, the small production of the prized pâté was what kept the horrible girl and her mother fed.

Margaritha would jabber away to her father's chickens and ducks. She cooed at them and they followed her. Not once did they peck her. Animals, even most dimwitted, can sense kindness.

His eyes began to sting with unshed tears, but hot embarrassment overshadowed his urge to weep. Anton looked down at his plate and sniffed. He focused on dragging his bread along the bacon grease.

Uncle Walter spoke again, "You aren't over her. I suspect you never will be. Yet life goes on, dear boy. You never know, perhaps your children will have the benefit of going to university, of advancing in this society of ours. But in our culture, marriages tend to happen only between those of the same level."

Anton nodded. "Perhaps." He finished his bread, took a swig of water, and the small family unit began to prepare for bed.

His uncle placed a hand on his shoulder.

"Tomorrow, I will take you to the Kovacses again. They require some work on a wall in the kitchen, and they will only accept decent craftsmanship. He was impressed by how good your Hungarian is. Too many of the village folks were resistant to anything non-German. I love our Swabian culture, but we must also learn the ways of the other cultures we live amongst. We must learn from each other. We'll perish if we insist upon remaining stubborn little islands. Yes?"

"Yes, Walter Onkel."

Anton stood and cleared his plate away.

"Anton?" his aunt said.

"Yes, Susi Tant?"

"The maid in the kitchen likes you."

"Oh." He had met the dark-haired Schwob maid who also worked for the Kovacses. She was being taught to cook and manage the kitchen by his Aunt Susannah. He hadn't exchanged anything other than greetings with her. She was from a different village, but spoke their dialect as opposed to Temeswar German.

It had been pleasant to meet another Schwob, though he hadn't given it much thought.

"Susannah..." Walter warned his wife, albeit in a gentle tone between puffs of his pipe.

"Well...you should know that she has a child," his aunt replied.

"Susi Tant, I am not looking for a wife in Temeswar..."

"Well, the poor girl. She was seduced by a Hungarian count, and thought he would marry her. Poor thing. Lots of people talked, called her names... not me, though. I know her child lives with her parents in Mercydorf for now. She is desperate to have her boy with her."

Anton understood what his aunt was doing, and the tale of the Kovacs' younger maid was quite sad, but part of him wondered how proper it was for Susie Tant to reveal this to him.

"I am sorry for her, Susi Tant. Do her parents speak to her?"

"Yes, but the village maintains a cold stance. Until she finds a man kind enough to marry her, she will always be an outcast. As will her boy."

Anton shook his head and hissed through his teeth. He disliked gossip and small-mindedness on the part of the villagers.

His aunt opened her mouth and moved towards Anton as though to say more, but his uncle's voice cut through his thoughts.

"That's enough, Susi! Of course our hearts go out to the girl, but don't fill the boy's head with such things! Why, if I didn't know any better, I'd say you are pushing the girl onto him!" Uncle Walter wagged a finger at his wife.

His aunt puffed her chest and wagged her finger back at his uncle, as though both were brandishing weapons. This was the first time he'd ever seen them do anything more than playfully bicker.

"You said yourself, there is no point in the boy pining for a girl he cannot have. She is married and halfway across the world. She will have a farm and a brood of her own soon. At least she has a husband to protect her. What does Sophie have? A life of work and witnessing the judgement of her boy for a crime he didn't commit. And as for that Hungarian noble... bah! He will be eating cake and drinking good wine, preparing to marry some pampered lady!"

"No, there won't be any chance of him riding on a white steed and rescuing her from the situation he got her in. You are correct," Walter said. He extinguished his pipe and sighed again.

The sun was going down on Temeswar and some dogs barked in the distance. Despite the humble accommodation, Anton liked living in a city.

His uncle's deep voice leaked into his thoughts. "Oh, perhaps we should have emigrated when we could have, Susi. In America, they don't have such problems with aristocrats hogging all the money."

Anton scoffed. "They don't have titles, Onkel, no. But they do have a class system, and only certain people can do certain things. Others are cast aside. I heard folks in Bensek talk about it. In that North Dakota, horrible things happened to the native people in order to make way for European settlers. When I was in the army, people used to talk about settling in America, just for the benefits that come from being a white man." Anton gestured to the pallor of his face before continuing, wagging his finger.

"No, I will take my chances with the prejudices I am familiar with, Onkel."

Anton's skin flushed. Part of him resented the very land Margaritha now trod on, as though the far away continent itself kept her from his life.

He couldn't intelligently believe every American to be a cruel bigot, but from what he'd read about how closely tied into their history the enslavement of Africans and mistreatment of native people was, disdain grew in his heart and he enjoyed a perverse pleasure in disapproval.

Margaritha won't become like that. Klara and Hans won't. As for Peter...

His aunt and uncle stared at him with raised brows.

Uncle Walter spoke. "It is a shame we can't send you to university, boy...all the reading you do. But for now, I think we retire. We go to the Kovacses in the morning."

"Yes, Walter Onkel. Forgive my outburst," Anton said, nodding.

His aunt reached out and placed her hand over his. "Nonsense, dear Anton. Our world is riddled with injustices, but for now, we must get on with the way of things. Yes?"

"Ja, Susi Tant."

And the extended Handl family prepared for sleep with as much privacy as the small flat would allow.

As Anton rolled over on his small cot to face the wall, his eyes could make out the portrait of Bensek his uncle had created as a very young man.

The heathland and fields.

The old Catholic church.

The wirtshaus, where he'd beaten Michael Koenig for insulting Klara.

Outside, there was a distant sound of wheels and horses on Temeswar's cobbled streets. The smell of budding spring flowers wafted in through the slightly open window, clearing the lingering pipe smoke and bacon smell.

Anton finally drifted off to the miniscule sound of clinking rosary beads, and his aunt's whispered prayers to Mother Mary.

Chapter 25

1912. Hans and Klara. North Dakota.

Many Banat Germans had settled in Hettinger County and the surrounding areas, but Klara heard nothing from Margaritha. Hans had taken her to a Kirchweih at St. Elisabeth's in Lefor this past summer.

There was a huge crowd, many children running about speaking Schwowisch despite many of them having been born in the United States. No Lulay family to be seen. Klara queried several women there, who either did not know of Margaritha or said, "Oh, she is busy with her children. They are only small. And last winter was so hard. I wouldn't be surprised if she lost one of them. You know how that can be."

The woman tilted her head and pushed her bottom lip out in a gesture of pity.

"Yes…" she responded politely, then Klara grew silent. It occurred to Klara that the lady assumed Klara had perhaps conceived yet had not had a successful pregnancy. In the four years of her marriage, she had not been with child once.

Winter had been a hard time in the Banat. This past one in Hettinger County and throughout most of the northern United States had been one of the worst on record. Klara noticed the particularly harsh bite in North Dakota's air when they'd first arrived in the region in springtime a couple of years ago.

Hans proved himself a prudent homesteader.

Hans had taken her to town twice for supplies in the past twelve months. She'd scolded him for spending too much on wood, flour, and feed.

His response had been one of the few times he raised his voice. He knew when to spend and when to keep hold of their purse.

"It's not just us, Klara. All over the northern part of the country, it's been dreadful. Thank goodness we have one another. If we don't get through the winter, we won't have a chance to plant in the spring. An extra piece of wood could mean life or death."

Over the frozen, isolated winter of 1911-1912, she and Hans had kept one another alive. They'd found solace in each other's arms throughout dark nights when the wind battered their new home.

After Christmas, she clung to the hope that she might be expecting a child. The thaw didn't come till almost May. By then, she knew there was no hope for her and Hans to become a family.

Summer, apart from the brief reprieve at the Kirchweih, had been hard work, repairing damage to buildings from the extra harsh temperatures over the previous winter. Now that their house was more or less done, she could begin to make it more pleasant to live in.

Her gaze rested on the lonely prairie, her hands fidgeting with the beads of her rosary. She prayed to Holy Mary that it wouldn't be as harsh this year. They hadn't managed to get to church throughout most of the cold months, and apart from the Kirchweih service, they'd only been twice over the summer.

Klara finished her rosary and went to the bedroom. There she pulled a rolled-up canvas out of a drawer. It was rare to allow herself this luxury of looking at Anton's portrait of Margaritha. To see her dear friend through the eyes of the artist in love with her brought tears to her eyes.

Klara sat on the bed, weeping. The wind whipped around the house and the floor suddenly creaked with Hans's footsteps. Klara quickly wiped her eyes, sniffing and trying to put away the portrait. Whenever he entered the house, the smell of hay, horses, and their dairy cows preceded him. It was a clean smell, as Hans was ever diligent in keeping their barn in good order.

"Anton has such talent. I can't imagine being able to create something like that."

Hans's voice alerted her to how close he actually was.

Klara was so proud of Hans. She'd imagined others expected farmers to have one way of viewing the world. Animals lived or died. They were valuable or not. The fields yielded or they didn't.

Not her Hans, though. He recognized his own practicality, yet comprehended the complexities of life and the need for different personalities and cultures in the world.

"Klara…" he said gently and came to sit beside her.

"You have not mentioned the painting, have you?" he asked her as she looked at it again. Intending to sigh, upon her inhale, her breath shook and a sob escaped her throat. She shook her head and finally placed the canvas back in its protective case.

Hans placed his hand on her arm and pulled her tenderly, as though willing her to look at him.

"I don't know what you mean, Hans. Mention the painting?"

"In your letter to the Lulays. Did you mention that Anton had done a painting of Margaritha?"

"No, of course not. I know it wouldn't do any good. I would like to show her one day though...maybe we should just *go* there." Klara sniffed.

"Klara, Peter has done his best to keep their whereabouts secret from us. I had to ask around for some time before I could get an address. I just thought that if you mentioned the painting, then it would give him reason to forbid her from seeing you. If he thought you were reminding her of Anton..."

"What if he isn't even letting her see my letters?" Klara lifted her hands in despair.

"Keep writing to her, dear. As people have said, she is busy with their children." Hans soothed her, stroking her hair.

Klara went quiet. She didn't wish to ask if, now that time had proved they couldn't conceive, he was disappointed.

Hans's mustache brushed her arm, sending pleasurable shivers down her spine.

"I know what you're thinking..." He paused to move some tendrils of hair away from her neck. The chilly air on her skin was immediately followed by Hans's warm lips.

"And I know what *you're* thinking, Hans. I am having a crisis and you are concerned with frivolities." Yet she leaned into him, smiling.

"It's not a bad way to spend an afternoon..." he murmured between kisses. The feel of his skin against hers ignited such a fire, she couldn't imagine anyone else able to cause this stirring within her.

"I...Don't you have work to do? I have fruit left to preserve. Those apples won't keep all winter." Yet Klara grew warm and languid, her heart fluttering as she squirmed in response to his kisses.

"We are long past harvest time, my love. It's time to practice for the months of winter ahead when all the fields are covered in snow and ice. Perhaps you recall last winter?"

"Yes, I recall. Thank goodness we had adequate firewood." Klara did her best to sound prim and proper, pursing her lips. Against her efforts, her mouth curved up and she giggled, promptly covering her face.

His hand crept up and down her arm, traveling to her waist. Hans squeezed her there and pulled her closer, taking her hands in his.

"When other husbands see their needs fall second, third, and fourth behind the children, I have you all to myself. Why do you assume there is something wrong with you? The issue could, after all, be with me. I always wanted to have you to myself. I am happy, Klara. Come now, you have a moment? Hmm?"

When his vocals vibrated against her neck, Klara sighed and lay back in Hans's arms. Forgetting about the portrait for time being.

CB BO

Hans did have everything he wanted. He wished to protect Klara from heartbreak. He couldn't bear to watch her go through the same tragic existence of his own mother. And he was grateful that he'd been blessed with an affectionate wife. Klara was a loyal, passionate woman. She'd created a beautiful garden, and worked alongside him on the land.

She wasn't precious or soft, yet he treated her like a queen. She'd seemed happy enough in their new homeland, yet his wife rarely stopped thinking about their friend Margaritha or wondering about Anton.

Anton had asked Hans to keep an eye on Margaritha. He had asked around and even noticed the Lulay family once in Dickinson. Margaritha appeared healthy, beautiful still. She cooed at her children and moved with the same stealth as when he'd last seen her.

Peter was beginning to show his age. His hair was receding and the skin around his face sagged. The lines gave him a grumpy, discontented appearance.

Then there was the way he looked at Margaritha. With disappointment.

Hans recognized Peter's hulking frame, saw the older man furrow his brows, sulk and snap at his lovely, younger wife like a large, spoiled child.

But from what Hans could see, there was no evidence of violence and the children also appeared well. Although from what information he gathered from other farmers, the Lulay farm was not particularly successful.

The land they'd chosen was decent enough, though Hans could guess Peter expected immediate results. From what he'd heard, some farmers didn't care for Peter's character. When he was pleasant, it came across as false.

Only fools could believe Peter Lulay was a jovial person. He was always selfish and greedy. Too vain for his own good. It will have come as a shock to him that Margaritha didn't forget Anton and fall madly in love with him after all.

As for Peter's disillusionment with his wife, Hans had no sympathy.

What do you expect, you old fool, when you marry a girl who does not share your affections?

From what Hans understood, Margaritha had one child and was expecting another. They'd made it through the winter.

He didn't want to give Klara the details of when he'd witnessed the Lulay family interacting. He hoped when he took her into town, she might see them herself. Still, it would never do to get her hopes up.

If he shared his own opinion of Peter too much, he feared Klara might curse the man even more.

Hans was happy, with his Klara and his work on the farm.

Now, as he watched his wife buttoning up her dress and retying her apron, he sighed.

"Your hair is slightly out of place," he commented with a smirk.

"That's your fault." She re-tied her hair into a bun, though its thickness and curls made any stern-looking style impossible. That and her cat-like green eyes, which she used to flash at him, gave her a warm yet wild appearance. She stuck her tongue out at him childishly. He chuckled.

"I guess it is." He sat up and pulled on his boots.

"I'll see about you visiting Margaritha, okay? But we have to be careful. Peter Lulay isn't above being difficult. He holds onto old world grudges, and he is still jealous of Margaritha's affection for Anton, I'm sure."

"Yes, well, if I could make some spell to bring Anton over here and whisk Margaritha away, I would!" Her voice was fast and harsh.

"She is a mother now, Klara. She isn't as free as you."

Klara had been turned away from him, still adjusting herself in the looking glass of their bedroom. She straightened herself and he saw her lovely shoulders rise and fall with a resigned sigh.

"I wouldn't want to be free of you, Hans. I've no doubt how she would love to be free of *him*. He's tethered her to him with children. It's unfair to the poor dears too!"

Hans said nothing. He got up and walked behind her, placing his hands on her hips.

"You are certain you don't wish to be free of me?" he said.

"Of course not." The wildness in her gaze settled on him before she continued. "If I wanted to leave you, I would have. I won't leave you, Hans. Ever. And you...won't leave me. Will you?"

Hans's stomach sank at the look on his wife's face, as though something just occurred to her. Like she'd just been informed he was to abandon her.

He kissed her cheek. "My God, Klara. I will never leave you, no." Klara smiled a little in response to him, but something in her eyes told her she didn't believe him.

Oh my darling, Klara. She will always think of Margaritha. That is perhaps why she still is sad.

Hans went to feed the pigs he'd bought when summer arrived, much to Klara's delight.

He racked his brains for a way for Klara to be able to speak to Margaritha, without igniting the ire of Peter Lulay.

Chapter 26

2017. Falling. North Dakota.

'Dearest Margaritha,

I hope this letter finds you well. I wanted to write as I understand how busy you must be with children and the homestead. I wouldn't turn up on your doorstep without an invitation.

Forgive me for not being in touch as it was some time before I had occasion to locate your address.

We are well. Though, things are as I imagined in that Hans and I cannot have a family.

This is not for lack of effort, you understand. As there is little to do during the dreadfully long winters here in North Dakota!

This past one must have been awful for you too. We worked hard to keep our dairy cows and the chickens alive. It wasn't easy but with no field work we were able to focus on the animals. If it wasn't for our animals and for Hans I would have died of loneliness.

During our summers here, Hans has managed to build a wonderful house with the help of some local men. Apparently, Hans is unusual in being willing to work with different groups.

It saddens me to say that when he enlisted the help of some experienced homesteaders of Jewish origin, some people refused to work with him. How sad!

I was nervous about speaking to anyone who wasn't from the Banat. But Hans' English, though it isn't perfect he says, is far better than mine. And many folks around here understand German.

For the most part, the Banaters around Hettinger seem kindly and *welcoming. There is quite a community here! Perhaps we get the same newspapers? Der Volksfreund?*

Hans hated living in the soddy more than I did. I assume you and Peter had the pleasure? Too many bugs. He pushed and pushed until the house was finished. We have a creek not too far away with some trees lining it.

I've worked mostly in the fields and created an adequate garden. As long as there is a garden, there is food. Ensuring that our root cellar was filled has been important.

Hans says he will buy us some pigs this summer.

Despite the winter, I love living here, with so much space to ourselves.

You used to talk about having so much land to yourself when we were girls back in Bensek. Though, if I recall correctly, you wanted run and play, free of chores. I often think of you when I look at the prairie. I hope your children can share your love of so much space to enjoy.

I miss you dearly. I hope you will write and we will be able to visit once again. I await any word from you at all.

Your dear and loyal friend,

Klara (May 1912)

Amber watched Martin place the letter down. His eyes rested on the pile of papers left to be read. They were silent for a few moments.

Amber had watched him scan the letter first, mouthing the words in the dialect. He squinted at the faded letters for a few minutes, then read it aloud to her.

"I'm impressed with your translation skills," Amber commented.

Martin shrugged.

"Mom and Dad spoke it at home, to the point where I was able to take advanced German language classes in college. Dad used to make me watch German films with him. When Mom got upset, it was the only language she would speak. She'd get insecure about her English. It reminded her of a couple of times when folks weren't very nice about her accent. That didn't happen often, but it bothered her more than it did Dad. Dad had to help his Mom out for a few years. He was more resilient about dealing with difficult situations. For the most part..." His voice trailed off and he closed his mouth.

Amber nodded and looked into Martin's dark eyes. "Thank you for doing this."

"It's really okay. It can't be written by anyone but our Klara and Hans here. Bensek is also called Deutschbentschek. It's known as Bencecu De Sus, today. It's part of Romania. In their day, it was still classed as Hungary. That's where my great grandpa was from originally, but the family went to Temeswar for a while." Martin paused, staring at the paper. "There was no mention of my great grandpa, though..."

Amber exhaled through her nose, reaching out to touch the letters. "No. There isn't. But it seems like Klara was hoping for an invite. My dad said something about...his grandma not being allowed many friends. My great grandpa was the jealous type, I guess."

Both of them turned to the wedding portrait of her great grandparents.

Amber said, "This might sound strange, but when I look at her picture, she seems *unhappy*. Lots of old portraits are like that, with unsmiling people, yet I got the feeling she really wasn't content."

"If it was an arranged marriage, then it's likely one of them was happier about it than the other," Martin said, raising his eyebrows as he thought on it more. "Personally, I can't imagine embarking on a lifelong relationship with someone who wasn't interested in me."

Amber's gaze was again fixed on the letters. She was still pondering whether her great grandmother had actually ever read them.

She processed what Martin had just said and shrugged, saying, "Yeah, well...it's nice to think of your ancestors as these great, brave people who lived in hard times. No one likes to think of their ancestors as being bad people. He's my great grandfather, but he wasn't all that nice it seems," Amber said.

Martin cleared his throat. "Yeah...well...I don't like to think about my ancestors being called Nazis or even *loosely* associated with them. But..." His voice trailed off and the wind whistled.

Amber reached out and placed a hand on his wrist. She squeezed and said, "I'm sorry about all that. I've only ever had vague notions of the Old World; my folks weren't in Europe after the war. If any of your folks did fall for that propaganda or pressure...that isn't you. It's up to us to live as better people."

Martin cleared his throat and shifted in his seat. "Yeah...that's a complicated subject. I think some of the family got swept up in it. They had to. State propaganda, and to be honest, most of the Schwobs stuck together. Mom got so angry with me for bringing it up when I was younger. She would refuse to answer...I..." He paused and looked at her hand on his wrist.

Martin smiled and covered Amber's hand with his own. Warmth spread from the back of her hand and rushed up the veins in her arm. She looked up and found herself caught in his eyes. "Martin, I'm sure I have ancestors who committed immoral acts. I'm half-Norwegian. The Vikings weren't known for being humanitarians, but my mom's a nice lady. Still...I understand the Nazi crimes are recent and well documented and... disgusting. I can't imagine you falling for such an ideology...even in the days of state propaganda."

Martin smiled weakly and nodded. "What would we do, Amber? If such forces came knocking on our door?"

Amber said slowly, "Who's to say? We're supposed to be making sure these sort of things never happen again. I wish we could speak to Hans and Klara directly. Hans seems like a good guy, and for a ghost, he isn't that scary."

He sighed, still looking into her eyes. "I can see why my great grandpa would have liked him so much."

Crash! Something collapsed down the hall.

Amber and Martin stood up, nearly knocking their seats over.

Amber was the first to move out of the kitchen, into the living room and down the hall. Martin stayed close behind.

"You're fast," he commented.

"I ran track in college." She spoke monotonously, searching for the source of the crash.

Her eyes widened when she found the cause. It was her easel and canvas that appeared to have been knocked over. Her brushes and coal pencils were still rolling on the ground.

Martin bent down and picked them up. "Ever had that happen before?" he asked breathlessly, his face pale.

"Nope. That was new," she said. And it was. That and having seen Klara's face full on in the mirror were definitely new.

Nothing was damaged or ruined; she only had to re-assemble the easel and place the canvas back on. She stared at the blank, white space then her gaze looked out to the expanse of snow-covered prairie outside her window.

Amber squeezed the back of her neck in frustration, then looked back at Martin. He shook his head, also looking to the white prairie, as though lost. His lips were parted, his eyebrows knitted together.

"I...wish I could explain all this, Amber. I'll stay here if you're worried," he said.

He walked towards her, depositing the brushes and pencils back onto their holders in the easel.

Amber watched as Martin's gaze went to the blank canvas. He ran his hands over the side of it and looked back at her.

"I'm not scared," she commented, her voice unwavering, not removing her gaze from his.

Her knees wobbled a little when he looked her up and down.

"You look amazing in blue jeans, anyone ever told you that?" The words were slow and easy out of his mouth.

"Not for a while." Her voice was less steady now. She blew out a breath and looked at the ground. This was awkward. "Martin, I'm not as freaked out as you'd expect."

Martin nodded and swallowed before opening his mouth to speak. "Amber, I am going to have to get going. I have a lot to do before Thanksgiving. I'm going to Chicago for a couple of days, but…I'll be back next Saturday. How about we continue with the letters after that? I would actually like to hang out next weekend."

Amber smiled. "You don't have to, Martin…"

"Amber, I *want* to. I hope you don't take me leaving now as a sign that I'm not interested, but the atmosphere in this house moves between eerie and sexy pretty quick." He paused and a nervous laugh escaped his lips before continuing, "How about we go for a walk together over the holiday weekend? After I'm back? I have some paperwork to get through and if I stay here with you indoors much longer, it's too tempting to kiss you."

Amber never wanted to tempt someone so much in her life.

"Not…wanting to rush things, eh?" She cleared her throat.

"Right," he replied.

"So…next Saturday then?"

"Yeah. I can be here by noon?"

"Sounds great. I still need your translating skills afterward. Perhaps after we've been for a walk. There's plenty of trails around here."

Amber's lips were just barely closing, after grinning at the anticipation in his voice, when his mouth was on hers. She pushed her fingers into his hair and pulled slightly. A moan escaped her mouth and a rush of blood scorched her cheeks.

Every micro-second of physical contact with Martin was pleasurable.

Having adored the peach tones of his lips for so long, she nipped him gently. Martin groaned and pulled away from her.

His face was flushed and Amber worked to control her breathlessness. She caught a glimpse of Martin's trembling hand as he steadied it on his forehead for a moment.

Martin smiled and chuckled. He said something in Schwowisch, not looking directly at her. Amber could understand that he addressed Frau Schreiber, mentioning his great grandfather...

Her head was still foggy with lust. "What...what did you say?"

"I said I wished she would look after you until we figure out what she is trying to say. That I would be back soon and would look into more news of how Anton was."

"Anton?" Amber asked.

"Yes. That was my great grandfather. I don't know much about him apart from what my dad told me."

Amber nodded. "Wow. Anton. So that's who my great grandma Lulay loved."

Martin smiled and said, "Yeah. Listen, Amber, I'm going to go. I will see you next Saturday." He leaned down and kissed her cheek.

She grinned, leaning into his kiss. "Later, Martin."

"Auf Wiedersehen, Frau Schreiber!" he said to the air, then winked at Amber before leaving.

Amber leaned against the doorframe and watched Martin depart, until his truck disappeared on the rural route and the distant sound of his wheels over the snow-covered gravel faded.

Amber crossed her arms, rubbing them for warmth. She'd been so overheated before, having the door open had been refreshing. Now she shivered.

She closed the door and went into her office. Her easel, with her brushes and pencils, stood upright.

It was as though nothing had happened. Amber organized her tasks for the week.

Martin came across as an average, working guy. Yet from what he had revealed about his business, she guessed that he was relatively successful.

If he was hesitant to get serious, she could see why. Amber couldn't understand going for a guy for his money, but there were people like that. Amber had been careful with her income in her twenties. Throughout her earlier thirties, she'd promised herself that if being independently employed wasn't working, she would have to accept joining a company in a larger city.

That hadn't happened. And that was when she decided to have a very independent career as well as existence in her home state. The comments about 'needing a man,' and her friend Theresa generally questioning her sanity, had never deterred her from doing what she wanted.

Ironic, that if I'd moved to Chicago, I probably wouldn't have ever met Martin.

It also didn't escape that her feelings for Martin complicated her desire to live such an independent life.

She loved Theresa and respected her choice to be a wife and mother, but Amber couldn't see herself doing that.

The complication was...Amber found herself falling for Martin.

"Oh God..." she said out loud, placing her arm on her desk and burying her head in the crook of her elbow.

There were no more 'incidents' that Sunday from the Schreibers. Falling in bed that night, she still wasn't frightened.

Only fascinated by thoughts of Martin, wondering what to do with the warmth in her belly and the intensity her heart felt for this man who'd only recently entered her life.

Amber wondered if she *was* going crazy.

Chapter 27

Martin boarded a plane in Bismarck in the wee hours of the morning. He awoke to a gentle pressure on his shoulder. His sleepy grin was replaced by a blush when he realized it wasn't Amber.

"Did you forget where you were?" The blonde flight attendant smiled.

"'Fraid so. Sorry about that. Which gate for Chicago?"

The flight attendant pointed him in the right direction and asked about his holiday plans. He was polite, but anxious to get on the next plane to catch another half an hour before he was in O'Hare.

He'd spent Monday and Tuesday repairing the roofs of large barns on farms for cattle producers closer to Bismarck.

All of Wednesday was about arranging the springtime construction of outdoor shelters and a small barn at a community orchard.

It was a project intended to reunite impoverished Native American communities with the traditional native agriculture. It was a way to reconnect people who had become out of touch with their land, as well as promoting healthy eating.

He'd talked to some of the locals who helped run the orchard.

"I'm good with structures, but never had a green thumb. I'm from Illinois. I've heard it's tough to grow stuff here," Martin said.

One of the local tribal elders who had negotiated a price, and knew where the best place was to build was, had said, "The earth is good when you are good to her. You have to know what she needs."

Martin nodded, thinking of Amber.

"You got family here?" the local asked him, interrupting his wandering thoughts.

"Um...no. It's just me," Martin replied.

"Not good for a man to be alone out here. God has a way of sending company when you need it. Keep you warm in winter. Shelter for the soul." The older man's face crinkled in a smile.

Martin grinned back. "Thanks. I'll...look out for that." He shook hands with the man and promised to be back in the spring.

The time between having left the Schreiber homestead and talking to cattle farm owners, tribes people, and orchard managers in Bismarck passed like a dream.

You have to know her needs...God has a way of sending company when you need it.

Martin drifted off on the way to O'Hare, wondering what it was that Amber would need from him. He wondered if Amber understood what *he* needed.

More than anything, *he* wondered what he needed. That he wanted Amber in his life was obvious. Did he want to do the whole late marriage and kids thing?

His parents had married and had him later in life. As a child, he'd envied people who had what seemed to him like youthful, carefree parents. His mother suffered from stress and bad childhood memories from her time in the internment camps in Yugoslavia, and refugee camps in Austria. She'd miscarried twice before successfully carrying Martin.

The whir of the plane's engines and the dark cabin encouraged him to drift. Yet his father's voice was in his head as it bobbed about and he distantly sensed the flight's turbulence.

Katy, please. We can talk to the doctor. We can even talk to other people who have visited recently. Won't you at least consider that it might do you good? To see that that time is in the past? I want to see Romania again, and it is safe to visit the Vojvodina region in Serbia now.'

'No! No, Bastian. They will be looking out for us coming back! They think we are all the same!'

'Katy...I beg you. For me. At least talk to someone about it...'

Martin cringed at the outburst he knew was imminent from his mother...

A jerking and plummeting sensation sent his stomach whirling and Martin's eyes snapped open. The weather was making the journey to O'Hare bumpy.

He rubbed his eyes and looked to the side. The plane was packed and the gray-haired gentlemen beside him was staring at him.

Martin raised his eyebrows and said, "Did I snore?"

"No, fella, but you were asking for your mom."

Martin pursed his lips and said, "Sorry. Bad dream."

"It's okay, buddy, just wondered if I should have woken you up or not."

Martin landed and made his way to the CTA where he was able to get a train to the Lincoln Park area of Chicago. His father had invested in properties a few decades ago on Cleveland Avenue.

Martin arrived at the one that had been his boyhood home on Thanksgiving morning.

His friend Aaron opened the door and looked at Martin from head to toe. He turned around and shouted, "Honey? Our landlord is here. He looks like crap too."

When Aaron turned back to face Martin, he extended his hand and with a mischievous grin, said, "Happy Thanksgiving."

Martin pulled the hand closer for a hug and entered the two-bedroom townhouse.

The smell of onions and celery frying in butter mixed with fresh pastry and coffee.

Bottles of unopened red wine lined the counter top separating the kitchen from the living room.

Martin had helped re-vamp the 1800s house for his parents while he was in college. He'd argued with his father about materials and how much to pay for them. It was his father who had insisted on spending more on quality.

It had been his first experience of working with others to make something, that was falling apart, beautiful again.

Footsteps pounded down the stairs, coming to a halt when Aaron's two girls stood beaming in front of Martin, now sitting at the counter sipping coffee.

"Amy, Eva," he greeted with a nod, lifting his cup. "Happy Thanksgiving." He stood and exchanged hugs with the nine and eleven-year-old girls.

"Happy Thanksgiving, Uncle Martin," they replied. "How's North Dakota?"

"Cold. Busy." he responded.

The younger one giggled and nudged her older sister. "Eva wants to know if you have a girlfriend."

Amy shot her younger sister a glare. "Shut up, Eva!" She reached out to yank her sister's braid.

"Ow!"

Aaron's wife Erika turned around from the stove. "Will you girls stop it! Hey, Martin! I'd offer you something stronger to cope with these two, but it's too early."

Aaron leaned against the counter and turned to the girls and back to Martin. "So, do you have a girlfriend?"

Martin smiled.

I'd like to think I do.

He sipped his coffee and cast his gaze around the wooden floors and white walls. The nearest window had a close view of the next brick house's staircase. It was classed as a trendy, expensive part of the city these days.

Martin was accustomed to urban life. Yet after spending time on the Schreiber homestead, entirely surrounded by prairie, a gravel road, a distant creek and trees, being here wasn't as comfortable and 'homey" as he remembered it.

He felt a twinge of jealousy towards whoever had assisted Amber to re-vamp the interior of the old house.

"Hello? Earth to Martin?"

Martin looked up and shook his head. "Uh, sorry. I am seeing someone. She's called Amber. She fixed up a hundred-year-old homestead almost on her own, then realized her car was totally exposed just when the weather was turning. Thankfully, she hired me."

Aaron's eyes narrowed and he nodded. He'd known a lot about Martin's troubled relationship with his father, but Martin hadn't ever told anyone about the reason why he chose North Dakota over, say, Kansas or Iowa as a more agriculturally-based state to expand his business.

"So...you're dating a client? What does she do for a living?" Aaron asked.

"She's a freelance editor and graphic designer. She does cover art and stuff for books."

"And she lives in the middle of nowhere?" his friend responded.

Martin was about to respond to Aaron's question when Erika came over, leaning on the wooden counter. "Martin? I found something I think might interest you. The girls were poking around in the attic, which they shouldn't have been doing, so I'm sorry about that, but they found something." She raised her eyebrows and tapped her fingers on the counter.

"Okay?" Martin cringed. He hoped it wasn't old photos of him as a baby or worse, college photos of him and Aaron. There were only one or two old chests left in the attic of this house. To his knowledge, they were only filled with old photos and the odd unfortunate shirt from the sixties when his parents began dating.

The persistent scramble of pre-teen footsteps reminded him of the mystery thumping in the North Dakota house.

"Omg! Look!" Amy screeched. "It came from North Dakota, addressed to...Anton Handl in Temes...Temes..." She scrutinized the writing. Eva interrupted her sister's attempts at the faded script. "Give it to Martin. We want to know what it says."

Martin took the faded envelope between his thumb and middle finger. Amy still held the worn manila envelope that had encompassed it all these years. He could read the faded yet unmistakable handwriting of his father on that envelope in Amy's hands.

"*Letter to Ota from North Dakota. 1911.*"

His pulse pounded in his ears and his gaze found the peeping girls. He raised his brows at them. "So...you two were snooping around in my folks' stuff?"

Eva's face turned red and she began to stutter. "Uh...um..."

"She dared me to open it! We didn't realize it was private..." Amy blurted out.

Eva sighed and closed her eyes. "Well, we thought it might have been from the people who originally built the house in the 1800s. When we opened it, it was too late when we noticed it was *mainly* stuff from the sixties and seventies. Then we found this."

"And a picture of you and Dad at Halloween in the eighties," Amy added with a grin. Eva giggled and placed a hand over her mouth.

"Oh yeah. It's a good one too," Erika said dryly.

Martin placed the aged envelope down and slapped a hand over his forehead. He sighed and said, "It's fine. But in the future, when you realize that something isn't yours, you shouldn't snoop."

Erika burst in, "That's what I said. But in this case, I thought the discovery might soften the intrusion of our girls on your family privacy."

Martin chuckled and began to read.

Dear Anton,

I hope this letter finds you well in Temeswar and that you are learning your Uncle's trade. Klara longs for news from you.

We arrived safely in Dickinson, ND and stayed with the Petter family for a couple of months until we were able to construct a soddy and begin work on the land which we will eventually 'prove up' on.

The soddy is fine. But I can't expect Klara to keep such a place for too long. Some folks make more of a fuss over the soddy than the house.

I miss the simpler days when we would repair your parent's old roof in Bensek.

There is help available from others in the area. I made arrangements with a German Jewish fellow in Dickinson who knows a thing or two about materials. Unfortunately some around here were awkward that I am accepting the gentleman's expertise.

Do you remember the sentiments of a few of our soldiers about Jews? That sort of thing exists in America too. Shame, as Herr Mayer is most knowledgeable and speaks better German than I do. Ha!

Our Schwowische dialect, though common in Hettinger and surrounding areas, is still seen as 'common' folk speak by some other German speakers.

With help, I've already begun constructing a proper home for Klara and I. This is a challenge as the wind out here is really something.

Klara and I work together to ensure tilling and planting is done each day.

The Lulay family is well. Frau Lulay appears in good health. Herr Lulay is not sociable but is decent enough towards his growing family. How prudent he is with his choice of land and how he manages it, remains to be seen.

Herr and Frau Braun, original Banater settlers in North Dakota who sheltered the Lulays after their arrival, commented on how agreeable Margaritha was. How Herr Lulay is honorable enough, yet they wouldn't care to deal with him in bad temper.

They were aware that Klara and I were not regarded highly by Herr Lulay. Yet upon conversing with Klara and I near the general store in Dickinson, they came to see that Klara was not wielding a witch's broom and I was not a drunken troublemaker.

I miss Bensek's pub being walking distance from our homes. I miss our adventures together as boys. I don't miss the one time we got in a real fight with a certain fellow.

I have the location of the Lulay family, so that Klara can write to her school mate. They haven't settled in Hettinger so their home is not an easy distance from ours. Then again, nothing is within easy distance from us.

The winters are harsher than in the Banat. There are no mountains or forest to act as a barrier from the biting wind and icy temperatures. I am bracing myself for the equal intensity summer offers. You wouldn't think that in a place so cold in winter can get so hot in the summer. But it does.

There is a creek not far from us. Klara and I work together to plow.

Ample supplies and shelter are of great importance. It's like what we would read of the frontier.

It is, as you predicted, a lonely place. But there is community available. There is a church and there will be a Kirchweih.

The prairie can be lonely, but it has a beauty all its own.

I will make what I can of it and Klara already makes good use of her gardening skills.

I regret to say how dearly you are missed. I wish you health and happiness.

I will keep an eye on things here as best as I can.

You notice I include the location of the land of mine and Klara's on the envelope.

Your Loyal Friend,

Hans Schreiber

Hettinger County, ND. June, 1912.

Martin placed the letter down after scanning and translating it. No one spoke.

Martin muttered, "So, that's how Dad knew where the homestead was..." He had never questioned it before. He just remembered his dad's words and he'd written down the address. Martin assumed it had been told to his father by his great grandfather.

"Have you been to the place in North Dakota?" Erika asked, with eyes wider than her daughters.

"Yep," Martin replied.

"And?" Aaron crossed his arms and tilted his head.

"That's where Amber lives," Martin responded.

"Now I can start to really piss you off. Is she related to Hans? That's so weird. Cool, but weird," Aaron said.

"She's *Margaritha's* great granddaughter." Martin cleared his throat.

The family exchanged wide-eyed glances.

"Wow. Well, that's enough family history for us. I would like to meet *Amber*, though." Aaron grinned.

Martin furrowed his brows and stood, stretching and shaking the weariness from his brain.

"Okay. Put me to work, Erika. I am a champion potato peeler." He did a mock 'muscle man' pose and added, "Can I help with the turkey?"

Aaron squeezed his friend's shoulder and said, "I'm doing the turkey. You can do the potatoes and vegetables. We don't have long before the game starts. And if you notice, on the television there, I got that channel with Europa League matches."

Martin grinned and rubbed his hands together. "Excellent," he said. Fueled by coffee, Martin helped the family prepare the holiday meal. He kept an eye on European and American football games.

They ate early, and Martin and Aaron were both asleep on the couch by nine.

Martin had remained dead to the world until the next morning when he found a photo texted to him of he and Aaron snoozing in front of the TV, with a very happy Amy making bunny ears behind them.

Martin chuckled and set his phone down on the wooden coffee table. He was covered in a Chicago Bears blanket and the noises of the city filtered into the room along with the morning sunlight.

He could recall his father shuffling around their old sofa that used to rest in place of the one he was on now. Martin had inherited his father's work ethic.

Sebastian Handl, or 'Bastian,' was never done moving. Or working. Or thinking. He had no patience for 'chilling out' unless there was an important match to watch. Even then, he was all business.

As though he was constantly trying to prove himself worthy of living in this country.

Martin sighed and sat up. He shook his head against the rise of family memories.

He looked at his phone again. Martin frowned.

She hasn't been in touch.

He sent her a message that said, "Happy Thanksgiving. Are we on for tomorrow?"

Martin cringed upon realizing it was an hour earlier in North Dakota than in Illinois.

Then his phone beeped.

His heart rate soared and a smile nearly split his face in two when he saw it was a message from Amber.

'Hope you had a good Turkey Day. I wasn't sure if you still wanted to get together on Saturday. You must be tired.' - A

'I absolutely want to get together as planned. Slept great last night after all the food.' - M

'Bet you did. See you on Saturday. BTW my friend Theresa is demanding to know when I will be back in case you are a psychopath. Funny huh.' - A

'That is funny. Seeing as you live on a haunted homestead in the middle of nowhere and we've been snowed in there together. Not that I minded.' - M

On Friday, Aaron took him to an Irish pub that showed Europa and Premier League matches in the afternoon. Martin spent the afternoon overseeing his friend's more considerable drinking habits and made sure Aaron got home safe before helping Erika out with the leftovers and heading towards the airport.

Chapter 28

1912. Anton. Temeswar.

"Not like that, Anton! One sloppy bit of brick-work could cost me my reputation. You must appreciate how long it has taken me to gain one. Kovacs is a good man, but if you slip, he will notice!"

Anton sighed, set his tool down, and watched his uncle's large hand deftly correct his mistake. Despite the size of the older man's fingers, they were delicate in approach. Anton could imagine how his uncle would do with oil and canvas.

The paintings on the wall of the flat he shared with his aunt and uncle were testament to his talent.

"You see..." his uncle said in between maneuvers of fixing the pointing. "Time and weather will cause the bricks to move. They don't need your assistance to become uneven."

"I'm sorry, Walter Onkel. I will try harder."

"You do well, my boy. But this is an old building. Kovacs recommended us. I don't want him to get any hassle. I've already heard folks whispering about how the Jewish man cuts corners. Bah! They make me sick, these jealous fools..."

Anton swallowed. He loved that Temeswar was home to so many different groups. Bensek had long been populated by mainly Germans.

"Walter Onkel?"

"Hmm?"

"Do you think that the people of Bensek should have embraced speaking Hungarian?"

His Walter Onkel huffed out of his nose. "I don't like these kinds of talks. People have a right to be themselves, but taking a dislike to another based on his background is undignified. No matter how high or low born you are. Take people as they come. I used to think only villagers were like that. If it benefits you to think your blood makes you superior...that's what some will think."

Walter stood, his large-boned frame tense, and he made another 'hmmf' sound then said, "Go to the Kovacs house. Get yourself something from the kitchen. Susi and Sophie are there. Maybe they will have time for your talk."

Anton nodded. His uncle was growing more irritable as talk of possible war with the Serbs was common these days. Anton worked to save his earnings, as well as give his aunt and uncle a small amount for their kindness.

His worn boots clacked over the uneven cobbles and he thought of Hans's letter. Margaritha was okay...but Peter was still a jealous, selfish bastard.

She would like Temeswar. She would be able to see people here. She is in the middle of nowhere. In those cold winters. With small ones to care for.

Anton arrived at the beautiful Baroque house of the Kovacses. He entered the arched doorway and descended into the dimly lit kitchen. Fragrant lamb roasting with rosemary wafted through the kitchen and his mouth watered. There was a huge pile of potatoes and herbs on the counter. This was his aunt's domain.

Yet she wasn't present at the moment.

The fragrance of rosemary always made him think of Margaritha. That and baking bread. She was all things earthy and nourishing. Dark jealousy twisted his guts when he thought of how soon she had conceived with Peter.

The sound of a young woman clearing her throat echoed against the walls. Anton glanced at the dark candelabras hanging about the room and looked to where the servant's table was in the corner. There, he could see Sophie, the Schwob maid, turned away from him, hunched on a table with a quill and parchment.

She sniffed and her shoulders moved. She placed a white hand against the side of her upswept black hair.

"Sophie?"

She turned in panic, stuffing the parchment under the table and spilling ink in the process. "Oh!" she shouted and began to fumble with the ink. "Oh...oh, look what I've done!"

Anton quickly retrieved a cloth and began to blot the spillage and gather the items off the floor. He picked up the parchment, which had only been partially spilled, and his eyes cast themselves over the letter.

"Oh, it will stain...."

To the esteemed descendent of Baron Von Ronai,

I wish to tell you your son does well in our village of Mercydorf. Despite being classed as a bastard, a human reminder of his mother's poor morality.

He is a likable little fellow, who eats well thanks to Hungary's bounty. He will grow strong despite the adversity presented to him at birth.

I realize the impropriety of my statement. I am a lowborn, disgraced woman. Yet I am honest. I know that your love for me was true. And that you only abandoned myself and your son, due to the immense pressure of your noble family.

I forgive you and remember you forever as my love...

Anton's eyes looked to a red-faced Sophie. She grabbed the letter with ink-stained hands and pressed it into her apron.

"Your aunt suggested I write something, even if I couldn't send it. She thought it might help. She told Frau Kovacs she would help me with learning to write, that's why I was allowed the quill. It was foolish. I have much to do..."

"Sophie..." Anton spoke softly. His heart ached for her. He knew too well how it was to love another who, by family obligations and status, was not allowed to proclaim their love for you in return.

"I have work to do," Sophie repeated.

"Sophie, he wasn't right to leave you and your child. It was as much his action as yours that brought about your son's life. He shouldn't..."

"He was a baron's son. The eldest..." She sniffed and squeezed her eyes shut. She had the look of someone whose head was about to explode. He could almost hear the dreadful ringing noise in his ears due to the pressure of suppressing such emotions.

"He was no good, Sophie!"

"No...no, you mustn't say that!" she shouted. "He loved me. I know he did..."

At this point, his aunt walked into the kitchen. "Anton? You've come early for something to eat?"

"I was sent here."

"Ah. Walter is being grumpy again, is he? He goes more and more cantankerous these days." She sighed and said, "Very well. I have some bread and cheese for you, but you must help me carry another sack inside while you are here."

"I will do it, Susi," Sophie began.

"Let Anton do it. It's something he can be useful for. You need to get to work on these vegetables." She cast her eyes over the ink-stained table and tsked.

"I thought you knew how to get the ink on the paper, girl."

"I..." Sophie's hands clenched at her sides.

"It was my fault, Susi Tant. I startled her. I suspect she thought I was Herr Kovacs."

"Bah! He won't mind too much. Long as dinner is on time..."

Anton set about helping with the sacks of flour and potatoes. He ate quickly and his uncle came in, stormy.

"Anton? Come now...I need some help out here. The roof in here is leaking, if you can believe it..."

"Have you eaten?" his aunt called to her husband.

"I have my sustenance with me, dear. This is a mess. Sophie? Frau Kovacs is asking for your help. There is some cleaning to do up here. Anton and I will fix the leak." Walter's quiet curses rebounded against the walls as he ascended the steps to the next floor of the house.

Sophie turned to his aunt and said, "I am sorry, Susi. Will you be okay?"

"I've often worked alone down here. Never fret," she replied.

Anton and Sophie came up the steps to find a panicking Frau Kovacs bustling around the drawing room, pointing at a wet patch on a rug.

Sophie held her hands up, speaking to Frau Kovacs in a soothing manner, and set about rolling the expensive carpet up and gathering cloths to dry the floor.

"Don't worry, don't worry," Sophie cooed. "It's only water. We will be able to put a different carpet there."

"The officer's ladies will come here...I won't have them thinking I'm poorly furnished. They already look down on us! That was our best rug and now it is wet!" Frau Kovacs muttered in Temeswar German.

"It only just started to rain," his uncle said. "Come, Anton, we will have this fixed in no time. Don't worry. Lucky I had finished the other building."

Anton climbed the ladder behind his uncle. He mimicked his uncle's slow yet purposeful movements. His heart raced each time he placed his hand upon a new wet, cold tile, wondering if it would slip.

The rain plopped on their hats as Anton watched his uncle pull an umbrella out of his sack and begin to dab the surrounding area with another cloth.

"The sheath beneath is a bit damaged. This is an old house. It isn't ideal to do it like this, but we will make it last a week or so for sure. Then we'll have to talk to Herr Kovacs about working on the entire roof..."

Anton merely nodded and held the umbrella aloft as his uncle worked.

Walter spoke again as he placed a new, dry tile over the patched sheath beneath.

"So? Sophie is a beautiful young woman. She is a hard worker. A good Schwob girl. Shame that Baron whatever-his-name-was ruined her."

"I don't consider her ruined, Onkel," Anton said.

But she is not Margaritha...

Anton did not realize he spoke aloud.

"She won't ever be Margaritha. No one will. You have to accept that she isn't available for you. You don't make her any less special...by being with someone else. I loved a girl, before your dear Susi Tant. She died very young. At least Margaritha lives on, and she is okay. Remember that."

"Yes, Walter Onkel," Anton said.

Chapter 29

Martin and Amber's boots crunched alongside each other at the grounds around St. Elisabeth's church in Lefor.

"The bell in the tower is from Hungary, or so my dad says." Amber gestured towards the church and slipped her arm through Martin's.

Martin's eyes were hidden behind his sunglasses, but wind-reddened skin stretched in a smile and he nodded. "They probably made it in Timisoara, or Temeswar as my folks called it. It's Romania now, not Hungary."

"Of course." Amber fixed her fleece hat with her gloved hand and nodded. "That enchanted highway is cool, though. Glad we had a detour. I never took the time to really look at it."

Martin chuckled and pulled her closer. "You need to get out more." He nudged her and kissed her cheek.

Amber giggled.

"True. So...do you think my great grandfather had a reason to be jealous of your great grandfather? My dad doesn't remember much about his grandma apart from the food she made."

"Well...there's no way to know how much she returned Anton's affections, but from what I remember my dad saying, his grandfather was a gentleman. I don't think he would have been contacting her after her marriage. She wouldn't have had much say if her parents vetoed Anton courting her. My family was classed as poor. It was hard to get ahead in Europe unless you were high born or got in the favor with one of the aristocrats."

"Same here too, sometimes. Okay, not aristocrats, but there are some old money types around," Amber said distractedly, looking around the fields.

"Well, yeah, there are elite circles here, but it's not the same as nineteenth and early twentieth century Austria-Hungary."

"Martin?" Amber said.

"Yeah?"

"I'm pretty sure that they will have had a Kirchweih here." Amber couldn't take her eyes off the grounds.

The bright sun, which had been illuminating the snow-covered ground, had gone behind a cloud and Amber shivered. She took her sunglasses off to scan the fields.

Martin swallowed. "It's a shame the door is locked. If they had mass today, we've missed it. They might have a service tomorrow."

"I'm not sure. Lefor is turning into a ghost town, not a lot of people come this way."

"You want to walk around the town more?" Martin asked.

"I..." Amber looked around, her mouth slightly open as she walked straight ahead, to peer at the side of the church.

"Amber? You okay?"

"I thought I heard something," she muttered and stopped in her tracks.

"Hmm. Well, they could have had a big Kirchweih here back in the day. Lots of room for a festival," Martin said.

"Yeah..." Amber said, shivering again.

"Let's go have a peek around Lefor. I've always wanted to go to a ghost town," Martin said.

"It's still populated, only a few abandoned houses around," she commented.

"I see. Sun's gone in. You look mighty pale in this gray light," Martin said and put his arm around Amber. Her eyes were cast down and small curls escaped her hat. Martin reached up and brushed at her forehead and temples, trying to push the stray tendrils out of her eyes.

Amber's gaze went to his and she smiled with her mouth closed.

They stood still in the field. Amber squeezed the wrist of the hand that reached to her, and she held his hand against her face.

She said, "Come on, let's go."

"Are you sure you are okay, Amber? Your face went white."

"Oh sure. Don't you find it sad? Knowing that place was once bustling with folks. It felt lonely all locked up and empty," she said.

Martin nodded. "There's communities like that everywhere. Over here, it's a case of the railroad being built on a different route. I heard there's an old bank vault still standing. After we check this place out, I guess it's back to the translating table."

"You got it," she said. "Unless you think it's too cold?"

Martin scoffed. "I work outside in all kinds of conditions."

Amber sat, looking around the town. She knew that it was originally built by Adam Lefor, intended to be a model 'German Hungarian' farming town, dependent on agriculture. Martin was correct—when the railroad didn't have a route nearby, the small town struggled to maintain its population.

"There's a Knights of Columbus club here that still does fish fries and event nights," Martin said.

Amber giggled, happy to be rid of the heavy feelings which overwhelmed her around the church. "You know where all the decent food is in the state, I bet."

"Yep." His boots crunched over the snow.

Though a coating of snow still covered the earth, it was obvious from the overhanging trees and naked, jagged bushes that many of the yards were long unkempt.

Chain-link fences sagged and paint chipped from painted wood houses. Broken windows were a tell-tale sign of homes no longer being inhabited. They walked farther along and though there were a few inhabited homes, the sun's leave of absence weighed on the gray atmosphere.

A smattering of homes had Christmas decorations, and a television inside showed NFL football.

Life goes on. Even after the young people leave. But with no need for a school for youngsters, that's not a good sign for the future.

Amber turned to Martin. "Well, you must be missing watching the game," she said.

Martin smirked and bounced on his feet a little, turning from side to side. "I'd rather hang out with you." He winked.

Amber showed Martin the still-standing bank vault. With the icy air and abandoned homes, there was a frozen in time element to Lefor. She could see a bustling, upcoming town in the early nineteen hundreds. By the nineteen-sixties, the population had dwindled.

She still felt guilty for keeping him from a relaxing afternoon in front of the television after all his travels.

"Okay. We can turn the TV on back at my place. I will let you off the hook of translating. How's that?" Amber said.

Martin nodded and sighed as they turned back towards his truck.

They pulled back onto the highway to head in the direction of Mott.

"Actually, I'm curious to read a couple more letters," Martin said as they merged onto the straight road.

Amber leaned her head back on the passenger side and turned her head towards him. Martin's face was screwed up, as though he was deep in thought.

"What is it?" she asked.

"Well, I'm just thinking...that place. It was different, but in some ways, the feel of it reminds me of the pictures I've seen of my grandparents' villages."

"Yeah, that's how it was intended. Like a German-Hungarian farm village in the Old Country. But the railroad—"

"—never came up here," he finished her sentence.

"I've...heard the old world villages are pretty different now. Not all abandoned. But different."

Martin shook his head. "Yeah. Dad really wanted to go see them. He wanted to take my mom. I just..." Martin stopped and pressed his lips together.

"You feel guilty that you put a stop to it," Amber said.

"You don't understand. Mom *never* would have gone. She had real issues with what happened in Yugoslavia when she was a girl. Some of the old folks went back and it was hard, but..."

"But they went. And it probably did them a lot of good, to see how life goes on, even after such horrible things."

"I guess. I mean...Amber, you don't know the sort of stuff my mom saw. Things got nasty in Yugoslavia before and after the war. If she mentioned it in school over here in the US, her teachers got mad at her. They told her it never happened. Other people would think she was a Nazi and a Holocaust denier. That stung, because she knew they suffered as a result of Hitler's crimes. Mom *hated* Nazis. Romania wasn't easy, but it wasn't quite the same as Yugoslavia. Dad just...never left behind that little boy who missed his grandpa. I was a kid when I first realized my parents had some serious issues with their past. I always figured they were better leaving it all alone."

Amber fell silent. If Martin's maternal grandfather fought in the army on Hitler's side, whether or not he personally held fascist beliefs wouldn't have mattered to the local partisans who had vivid recollections of what some Nazi soldiers did to the Yugoslavian resistance.

"Maybe you should go one day. You seem to feel bad about going along with your mom's refusal to visit. You said other old folks went back and they got something out of it."

Amber watched Martin's hands tighten on the wheel. The highway swished by and Martin said nothing, his eyes on the gray road ahead.

Once the cabin of the truck warmed, Amber took off her gloves and folded her hands in her lap, twiddling her thumbs.

After a few awkward minutes, Martin said, "Maybe. Maybe I should go. In hindsight, I think Mom might have benefited from going. But I was a jerk back then and wouldn't see my dad's point of view. And…I hated how he begged. I thought it was weak. Dad pushed me to work so hard…Mom would bake me stuff. But…I wasn't there at the time they went through what they did in Europe. It wasn't my place to be biased."

He pressed his lips together.

Amber reached out and squeezed Martin's arm. She said nothing for a few moments before she said, "You Chicago folks are emotional."

Martin laughed and cast a glance her way. She winked at him and grinned ear to ear before saying, "I kind of like this about you."

"Thanks, Amber." He chuckled.

"Ah, it's okay. I've got a fridge full of leftovers at my place. My mother made such an enormous meal. We'll have some sustenance warmed up in no time."

Amber didn't feel it was necessary to say much else about Martin's family. Her folks weren't much for digging into raw emotions surrounding family relationships. Her mother always joked about Amber's dad being a man of few words, though both were intelligent and very caring.

Martin and his folks seemed to have more intensity. But then, they hadn't had the quiet, rural American upbringing she and her family had.

They finally arrived at Amber's house. As they walked inside, Amber noticed several messages ping on her phone once they were back on her Wi-Fi signal. Her mother had been trying to call her.

There's either a real emergency or she's being nosy.

"Do you want to warm up the food? I've just got to call my Mom. It's all in the fridge in Tupperware," Amber said.

Martin nodded and went into the kitchen.

"Hello?" her mother said.

"Hi, Mom, everything okay? Is Dad okay? I've been in Lefor and the signal wasn't good."

The microwave hummed in the background as Martin moved the Tupperware around.

"Oh, Dad's fine. I couldn't find my..."

Bang!

The dreadful noise from the kitchen was followed by Martin's swearing.

"Hold on, Mom." Amber rushed into the kitchen.

"Amber? Everything okay?" her mother's eager voice called.

Martin was gingerly taking containers out of the microwave. His dark brows went up and he pulled a small metal object out of some mashed potatoes.

"Did you lose one of your Turkey earrings?" Amber said into her phone.

"Yes. Oh, thank goodness. I paid ten dollars for those..."

"It was in the potatoes, Mom. We just put it in the microwave."

"We? Oh, of course, you have your *friend* with you. What's he called again? Marvin?"

"Martin, Mother. He's called Martin." Amber looked directly at a wide-eyed Martin whilst speaking to her mother.

Meanwhile, Martin stood with his head tilted to one side and an amused look on his face as he went to clean the earring under the tap.

"Martin...of course. Well, I'm so glad you found it. Does he like the potatoes? Your dad told me how to do them Hungarian style."

"Well...we haven't eaten them yet as your earring kind of exploded in them," Amber said, her voice deadpan.

"I think it's okay, though," Martin shouted so her mother could hear him.

"Oh...that's good. Thank goodness. Have you had a nice afternoon? Is he staying..."

Amber cut her mother off. "Okay, Mom. Well, I'm gonna go clean my microwave now."

"Okay, honey. Call me later. Love you!"

"Love you too," Amber said as Martin turned around to look at her again as she said the last words.

He placed the rinsed silver turkey on the counter. He'd already cleaned most of the mess.

"I guess we caught it just in time," he said softly. Amber leaned against the counter next to him.

Martin turned and bent to press his lips to hers. She gripped his shoulder with her left hand, only loosening her grip to slide her hand behind his neck so she could press herself closer.

Then Martin snaked his other arm around her waist. She curved herself and fit snugly into the shape of his larger, warm body.

Then, just to the left, a feeling of tingly cold struck her. They ceased kissing and looked in the direction of the cold air.

It felt like it was coming from the front door, which had been open and promptly shut minutes ago.

A breeze picked up, making the house creak, and they stepped in the direction of the cold, causing more creaking in the floor boards.

'Hans! Hans!' a familiar voice called on the wind.

Klara's voice, Amber thought. She looked at the floor, recalling her dream of imagining that the floorboards would break open. And she feared Martin was not hearing the same thing she was.

"Was that Klara?" Martin said, his previously weather-red face gone white, before he continued, "I heard her say Hans."

"Yeah. That was her..." Amber said.

"Wow. I'll...I'll stay tonight. At least for one night. I don't want to think about you freaked out on your own," Martin said.

Amber laughed, though it was a nervous one, and said, "Sure, we can be freaked out together."

Chapter 30

1914. Kirchweih at St. Elisabeth's in Lefor. North Dakota.

The journey to St. Elisabeth's in Lefor reminded Margaritha of when she and Peter first traveled to the from the rail station in Dickinson. The sky held the same rolling pewter shades. Of course, the land was more familiar now.

She was wearier this time. Plus, they didn't have the children then. One-and-a-half-year-old Josef was sleeping in her arms and four-year-old Caroline sat between her and Peter, leaning on her mother's side.

Margaritha looked at Peter's hands gripping the reins. Caroline scooted even closer to Margaritha, nudging her body, as though wanting to make more of a space between herself and her father.

The repetitive sound of the horse's hooves caused Margaritha's lids to lower.

"God forbid something should happen to the horses on such a frivolous journey," Peter finally said, startling her out of the doze.

"We haven't been to a Kirchweih, Peter. This will be nice for the children."

"They will hardly remember it," he snapped.

"We don't get to socialize often. Caroline has been poorly and Josef only small. I think after all we've been through, it will be nice to see our neighbors."

"Neighbors, bah! It's not as though the couples can collect one another WALKING from house to house. And what have you been suffering with? You and the children have been huddled up nicely in the house, while I've been busy breaking my back without hardly any help."

Margaritha said nothing. She stared ahead, determined to enjoy the festivities when they finally arrived. It would be such a novelty to be surrounded by people. She hadn't even been to visit the town of New England for months.

Peter preferred to travel alone. She understood that bringing the children along was cumbersome and required patience Peter didn't have, so she usually stayed at home.

Then, like a mirage in the prairie, there stood Lefor and St. Elisabeth's church at its center. It *was* similar to a Banat village. She had yet to attend a mass here and had been told that the building was beautiful. It was wonderful to finally see it for herself.

Other wagons were there and a makeshift 'marketplace' had been set up in the surrounding fields.

Josef whined when he woke up. Peter took the boy roughly from Margaritha's arms and held him up. Josef stared at his father with wide brown eyes. "Now you listen, young Josef, we are attending mass. You are not going to spoil it by crying and making us look silly, are you?"

Josef pouted and shook his head. Peter passed him back to Margaritha.

The church was packed. Margaritha wondered if she might faint from lightheadedness, but she daren't complain or ask to go outside. She'd never hear the end of it from Peter.

Margaritha was disappointed in herself for not being in better spirits. She rearranged Josef on her knee, tried to remove the scowl from her face. When she looked back up at the pulpit, the priest smiled at her.

Mass came to a close and the procession outside began. Seeing the young couples linking arms, noting the layer upon layer of the girls' petticoats, unleashed memories from her youth.

Things she hadn't allowed herself to think on for years.

She longed to write to her mother and tell her how a North Dakota Kirchweih differed from a Banat Kirchweih. How the amount of people suddenly gathering around the church reminded her of her home village. That so far away, in Lefor, North Dakota was a community modeled on Banat villages.

Margaritha's mother had recently passed away, and such observations would be lost on her father.

Margaritha's eyes filled with tears.

Oh, what is wrong with me?

Caroline had taken Josef's hand and was keeping a distance from the procession.

"Margaritha? Are you weeping?" Peter whispered. His large fingers gripped her elbow, none too gently.

"It's just...I can't help but think about Mami. It would have been nice to tell her about this."

"Yes, dear, I appreciate that. But if you weep, people will think that you are crying because of me. Please don't draw attention to yourself and make me look bad."

Margaritha sniffled and steeled herself against the rising emotions. She had to reassure herself that at least Peter was keeping his voice kind. She didn't dare admit that she could recall so clearly now, walking beside Anton and how gently he had held her.

How she'd relished every moment of being in his arms. She looked at the uniformed Schuetzenverein members in attendance. Though far more of a social club than a militia, the shooting club made her think of her conversation with Anton at their last Kirchweih.

How she'd dreaded him being conscripted.

And that was during peacetime. Reports from Europe these days were not good, particularly since the Archduke Franz Ferdinand and his wife Sophie had been assassinated by Serbian extremists.

"Peter? How do you think this war will go?" Margaritha asked, still keeping her eyes on their small children, who followed the procession of teenage couples.

Peter huffed. "Oh, I don't know. The Serbs are fools. Austria-Hungary will crush them. Long as it doesn't affect us, I don't care."

"The Serbs only want control over their land. I think it's fair enough. It's sad about the archduke and his wife, they loved one another, but I don't think that they should declare war. So many young men will die... and for what? For pride?"

"Oh, for goodness sake, Margaritha! I knew I should have never let you read that article."

Margaritha snapped her head at him. "What do you mean you shouldn't have *let* me read it? What business do you have telling me what to *read*? I don't know why I talk to you." She huffed and began to move away from him.

He grabbed her elbow again and pulled her towards him. His mustache tickled her ear. "Please, dear. I care about you. Why else would I have allowed you to come here?"

You allowed me to come here because the children and I have barely seen another soul for over twelve months. You were worried I would become half-mad and embarrass you when you were finally ready to wheel us out.

She said nothing and pulled her elbow away as subtly as possible without anyone noticing her aversion to physical touch from her husband.

The young couples erected a 'maypole' of sorts with a bottle of wine attached to it. It was pleasing to just watch the couples dance, for a while.

One young lady was particularly beautiful. She had twinkling light blue eyes that stood out in a face that had gone almost brown from the sun. The wind caused tendrils of sun-bleached hair to dance around her smiling face. Her sturdy partner grinned as he clapped and twirled her around with pride.

Margaritha's heart lightened at such a lovely display. She looked at Peter. He too was watching the girl. She would expect anyone to admire such beauty, but the look in Peter's eyes disgusted her and she turned away.

The ceremonial part was over and it was time to enjoy the food and small market stalls.

She kept a close eye on her children, making sure Josef did not wet himself and that Caroline kept a close hold on her little brother.

Peter, without a word, had stalked off to talk to the members of the Schuetzenverein.

Margaritha crossed her arms and tapped her foot to the music, although she was nervous and shy. It had been a while since she'd been in a crowd.

A familiar voice made her turn.

"Oh, Margaritha, how beautiful you are, my dear. And such lovely children! Finally, we see you at a Kirchweih."

It was Frau Braun. Margaritha had seen her but once since they'd stayed on their homestead after just arriving in North Dakota.

"Frau Braun. So lovely to see you." Margaritha smiled for what felt like the first time all year.

They clasped hands and smiled. Margaritha opened her mouth to speak, but Frau Braun held one hand up to silence her. She then gestured with her other hand to someone on the other side of the field.

Margaritha turned and there she saw Hans and Klara Schreiber, walking towards her.

Klara had hardly changed, apart from her skin looking a shade darker

222 so   Viola Dawn

and her hair a shade lighter.

Hans wore a wider brimmed hat and still had his blonde mustache.

The grass twitched and bent in waves as the wind picked up. Klara's skirts blew against her legs. Her friend had a sturdy, almost athletic appearance now. As the brass band continued to pump out a tune amidst the crowd's chatter, Margaritha ran to her friends.

Her arms closed around Klara first. She laughed and wept with joy at the same time.

"Too long...it's been too long," Klara said, squeezing her back.

The two women let go of one another and Margaritha turned to Hans. He took off his hat and she grinned at him. His pale blue eyes crinkled at the sides. He stepped towards her and took her hands. She noticed that he walked with a slight limp.

"What happened to your leg, Hans? You don't appear as steady on it as you once were." She frowned at his leg.

"Oh well...it would have been worse if I hadn't gotten to Bonesetter Braun. I fell. Klara did what she could before learning of Herr Braun." Hans nodded to Frau Braun, who stood just behind them, smiling at the group of reunited friends.

"It's what he does. He set plenty of bones during his time in the service in the Old Country, let me tell you. And he's sorted many a soldier and a farmer out. I'm just sorry we weren't closer to you when the event happened. Anyway, I will let you folks get reacquainted. You have nice friends, dear Margaritha. Klara is a brave woman. Hans is a good farmer and so kind."

Frau Braun walked back towards the church where Herr Braun was.

Margaritha winked and noticed Hans blushing as he smiled at Klara then back at her.

It was obvious to Margaritha that they still loved each other very much.

"Yes, Hans had an accident earlier in the year, and it's likely he won't ever run too far again, but he hasn't let it stop him. We've done well and have hired help. Hans is clever," Klara gushed.

"He always was," Margaritha added, still beaming at her friends.

Hans shook his head and looked at the ground. "Well, she tolerates me anyway."

Margaritha cast her gaze around for Caroline and Josef. She saw them with a group of other similarly aged children. An older girl had started a mini-procession of younger ones, mimicking the teenage couples.

"They are yours?" Klara saw who Margaritha was looking at.

"Yes. Caroline and Josef," she replied.

"They are beautiful." Klara's smile grew and faded. The lack of mirth in her green eyes was noticeable. Klara cast her gaze down, as though self-conscious. Margaritha could hazard a guess as to why. Her friend loved children and it was apparent she and Hans had not been blessed with them.

"Did you get my letter?" Klara's face brightened and tilted in her direction.

"Letter? No." Margaritha had heard only from her parents back in the Banat.

Hans stood, stroking his pale chin. "Klara must tell you where our place is in Hettinger. It's possible the letter even blew out of the postman's bag. The wind in this country is something else!" Hans smiled before clearing his throat and saying, "Well, I will leave you ladies to talk. I'm interested to know Peter's opinions on the soil here. I miss the grapes from the Banat most of all." He winked at Margaritha. They squeezed hands again and he left, leaving her and Klara able to talk with some degree of privacy.

"So? How is Peter?"

Margaritha turned and saw Peter frozen as Hans approached him. Peter screwed his eyebrows together. It was difficult to tell whether this was due to being upset by Hans's presence or due to confusion at the limp Hans now sported.

"He is well, thank you. He...finds life here difficult. It's been hard to manage. He regrets bringing us. I suppose it would have been easier for him to have a try at homesteading without a wife and children in tow."

Klara nodded. "Perhaps. You make it sound as though it's your fault."

Margaritha shook her head. *That's how he makes me feel. As if everything is my fault.*

"Well, I can understand...I am not as helpful as I could be. And once the children arrived, things grew more difficult. From birth, both of them took turns being poorly. We've been lucky that they've pulled through. I know of so many women losing their children. I can't imagine."

Klara nodded. She stepped a bit closer to Margaritha, lowering her voice.

"Anton wrote to us. He is well. He works with his uncle for a wealthy family in Temeswar. He will want to know how you are," Klara whispered the last line.

Margaritha's belly swam with a pleasure she hadn't experienced since the night she disguised herself as an old woman and sneaked to Anton's house. It felt like more than five years ago. The time and space between this moment and that one seemed more like a century.

I will love you forever...

Margaritha felt Klara's hand squeezing her arm, as though her old friend could sense the thoughts overwhelming her mind.

"We are well. Peter is fine. He cares for us and wants the children to be healthy and successful. He does what he can. At worst, he is moody and unpleasant..." Margaritha now looked down to the bottom of her skirts trailing in the flattened, pale prairie grass. She looked up at the sky's rolling gray shades. She tightened her grip on her shawl.

I don't wish to burden Klara with my disdain for Peter and his for me. I only want Anton to know I am well.

The nearby group of children, including her own, squealed as they played. Someone was being a monster now and chasing the smaller ones. "Tell me, how are you doing? I imagine your garden is the pride of Hettinger County?"

Klara's features split into a grin. "There is plenty of space. Shame the weather is too harsh for grapes. I've planted cherry trees and the fruit is good for pies and jams. My garden gives us an ample supply of cabbages, onions, and carrots..."

Klara shifted on her feet and looked around at the crowd. Margaritha followed the path of her friend's gaze and saw Peter and Hans. Some other farmers had joined them. Peter was talking and gesturing with his hands, becoming somewhat animated about something.

Hans's features were hidden under his hat. He leaned against a wagon, nodding and stroking his chin.

Margaritha sighed and turned back to Klara. "Peter will be jealous of your success. He says the land here is too dry and cold. He..." She paused and laughed to herself. "He is strange. He is embarrassed when Caroline speaks German in town. It's all we speak at home! He says we speak only English in public. But then he sympathizes with Austria-Hungary. Sometimes I feel like, with everything, he waits to see who the winning side is, then he is in support of whoever would make him look correct in everything."

Klara nodded. "Well, one positive of Hans being disabled is that at least he won't be expected to enlist. Even if he did...they wouldn't take him. I hope we remain neutral myself. I worry for those back in Europe. The

Prussian Army is very aggressive, determined even." She shook her head. Then, her eyebrows lifted and she said, "Margaritha? There is something I must tell you..."

"Yes?"

"I do so wish you could convince Peter to come and see us. I would love to show you our home." Klara's eyes looked again to where the men were stood. She continued, though her voice was lower. "I should tell you that Anton is married. His wife expects a child. I can still tell, from his note, how he misses you. Almost every other line was like a hidden question. I should imagine Hans was too vague in the first letter he wrote to him."

Margaritha's head swam. Despite the chilly, early autumn air, a small bit of sweat broke out on her brow. "He is married..." she whispered.

How strange. It isn't as though I didn't expect such a thing. I want him to be happy.

Yet jealousy churned her stomach. Pain stretched across her heart. The smell in the air coming from the church's kitchen ceased being pleasant.

"Margaritha, I know he still thinks of you. But both of you had to move on for the sake of your own sanity." Klara's eyes softened towards her friend.

Margaritha's legs lost strength. The earth below moved and Klara scooped a hardened arm around her waist.

When Margaritha came to again, the faces of Peter, Frau and Herr Braun, Hans and Klara all swam before her.

She could hear Josef crying in the distance.

Peter's eyes had gone black, staring down at her. He turned and hissed. "Hush, Josef, Mama is fine. Caroline, calm your brother please." His tone was strained as he lifted Margaritha to her feet.

"What on earth did you do to my wife, Klara? I thought you would be happy to see one another..."

"I..." Klara's face was screwed up in concern and confusion. She patted Margaritha.

Frau Braun whispered to Margaritha, "My dear? Is it at all possible you are with child?"

Margaritha's head dropped back onto the grass. There was still no sun in the afternoon sky. It was an upwards sea of gray wind with waves of cloud.

"Yes. Possible," she responded after counting the days in her mind.

Peter overheard the exchange between Margaritha and Frau Braun. "It was foolish of us to come. You should have thought, Margaritha. I must take my wife home to rest."

Before she knew it, Margaritha was bundled up along with the children into the Lulay family wagon. She'd hardly had a bite to eat and they had little left with them.

"I will come see you soon, Margaritha," Klara said anxiously.

"Wait until she is better. I will send word when she can have visitors," Peter said abruptly. Any who didn't know him would assume it was concern for his wife that caused his harshness.

Hans hooked an arm through Klara's, pulling her back as she glared at Peter. Hans's blue eyes were like pools of serenity. He tended to remain calm whenever Klara became angered.

"Peter, perhaps it is hasty to leave now. It will be dark in a few hours," Herr Braun suggested.

"We'd already made arrangements to stop somewhere along the way. It seems we shouldn't have come at all. I thought the trip out would do her good." He stopped and placed a hand over his chest, taking a few breaths. He took the reins and continued speaking, this time with a different tone. "They aren't used to this much excitement."

Herr Braun nodded and said, "Please send word when you arrive safely back."

"I will." Peter nodded. Frau Braun gave them a small basket of baked goods, which Peter tried to give back, until Klara insisted that his wife and the children had eaten little as it was only early in the festivities and they would require sustenance along the way.

Margaritha was in a daze as she reached for Klara's hand. Klara reached back. Their hands remained clasped until the jolt of the wagon loosened their hold on one another.

As soon as St. Elisabeth's was out of their vision, Peter began to rant.

"He thinks he is better than everyone. He always has. That Hans Schreiber. He had the nerve to tell ME I planted too late. It wasn't my planting that was the problem. I could have planted earlier...easy for him to say, he doesn't have any children. Ha! The insufferable man can't even sire a child."

Then Peter went quiet. Josef and Caroline snuggled against their mother. Josef sniffled because he had been having such a good time with the other children when his mother took a funny turn.

"Mama? Will we have a new baby?" Caroline asked.

"Maybe, my dear." Margaritha maintained a gentle tone answering her daughter.

Caroline took in a sharp breath and said, "Do you hear that, Joe? We will have somebody new to play with soon. You might get a little brother."

Josef sniffled and said, 'Bruder' in a babyish way, screwing up his chubby face as he mulled over the idea. In the end, he nodded and stopped sniffling.

Margaritha doubted whether she would ever convince Peter to go to a Kirchweih again.

"Don't you agree that Hans is conceited? And that Klara, she hasn't changed at all. Look at how muscled she is. Her chest is more like a man. It's no wonder she can't have children. It's probably *her* who does the work on the farm anyway. Now that Hans is disabled..."

"They can afford help," Margaritha answered, though her voice was small.

"And I suppose it's my fault we don't have help? If you were more organized with the children, perhaps you could help instead of me breaking my back."

He snapped the reins harshly and the horses whinnied in complaint.

All Margaritha wished to do was sleep, arguing that she *did* help wasn't going to help the situation.

Depression settled upon her as the afternoon light waned. They stopped at the house of a German Russian who sheltered them for the night.

Margaritha and the children stayed in their sleeping quarters while Peter drank with the homeowner. From distance, as she and the children drifted off, she could hear Peter's voice. She heard when the German Russian offered Peter some cinnamon schnapps.

Her husband's laughing, drunken voice was foreign to her. When he stumbled into the bed next to her, he pulled her body against his roughly, nuzzling the back of her neck and mumbling how wonderful he thought she was. How beautiful he found her.

She remained tense until Peter began to snore.

They woke late to travel home the next day.

Chapter 31

2017. Amber and Martin. North Dakota.

Martin was laying on his side on the futon in Amber's office. The plug-in nightlight cast a warm glow over the dark wood and the rugs in the hallway.

Creak...

Martin's pulse sped up again and the Thanksgiving leftovers they'd consumed for lunch and supper were not sitting well in his stomach. Every now and again, there would be that noise. He'd already gotten up once to use the bathroom and the only other sounds he heard were his creaking footsteps and the sound of Amber's slow breathing.

How can she sleep in a haunted house? How can she sleep at all...?

Martin, despite being fatigued from travel and an afternoon of walking around Lefor, was unable to drift off.

After their initial kiss in the kitchen before hearing Frau Schreiber calling Hans, they hadn't gotten physical. Apart from her head on his shoulder as she began to drift off. He could still smell her apple-scented shampoo.

They'd sat going through the letters only to find that Klara appeared to have written to Margaritha in vain. Every letter revealed Klara's subtle frustration that her friend was not responding to her, yet the letters were being delivered.

And they'd seen one another at Kirchweih at St. Elisabeth's and Margaritha had taken ill. Margaritha still didn't reply.

Martin rolled over and sighed heavily through his nose. The curtains billowed over the heating vent. He could just make out the shadow of

Amber's easel and canvas.

She'd shown him her most recent work after they made up the bed.

Amber had filled the blank space with colors, creating a piece full of mood and atmosphere, the prairie, her backyard at sunset. With Hans's barn still standing. In the far distance, there was a lone figure, heading towards the creek.

Creak...

Martin's head snapped in the direction of the hall. There were more steps.

"Amber?" Martin whispered, then he said her name again. "Amber?"

No answer. He got up again, his heart pounding and spine tingling.

He reached the doorway and slowly stepped into the hall. The air was much colder than he expected. His breath hitched and his eyes remained open. He walked in the direction of Amber's bedroom again.

It had to have been her.

"Amber?"

He reached her bedroom and found her sleeping soundly, breathing steadily. Earlier she'd been so drowsy, her head lolling onto his shoulder, that he insisted they retire. Seeing her so drowsy tugged at his heartstrings in a way he'd never experienced before. Finding a woman his age *adorable* wasn't something he expected.

He stood in the doorway of her bedroom, his pulse starting to slow. Someone had definitely walked past his bedroom door. Amber's soft breathing, and the way her slender arm stretched out of her quilt, suggested that she hadn't moved for some time.

He watched her for a few moments. She was beautiful in her sleep, graceful with loose, wild blonde hair and long limbs. She had the bone structure of a supermodel.

Yet her character likely wouldn't allow for such a profession. She valued her solitude and privacy too much.

Here, she was tucked away like a fairy princess hidden amidst a sea of snow-dusted prairie. Living with the restless, albeit kindly, spirits of an old couple.

Watching her on her bed, he could have painted her. Though, more tempting was the thought of kissing her.

Martin decided it was best he turn back to the office/guest room and try to get some sleep. He wouldn't be able to stay here tomorrow, since he had to get to the office early on Monday.

He sighed quietly and looked around the room, keeping a safe distance from his sleeping beauty.

Martin gasped when he saw the back of an old woman, with curly gray hair pinned up at the back, staring out of the window.

"Oh..." He drew back. Then there was a loud bang and Amber's eyes opened. She sat up, her eyes wide and startled, and placed a hand over her mouth.

Bang!

It happened again, appearing to be coming from beneath the bed. Martin rushed to Amber, placing his hands on her arms. He looked to the window.

No one was there.

Despite his blood turning to ice, he flipped the light on and looked beneath the bed. There was nothing. He put his ear to the floorboards, wondering if he would hear any scurrying or anything, and there wasn't a sound. The wind blew against the side of the house, making the walls creak, yet there was no sign of any disturbance beneath the wood or coming from the ground.

There was a crackling energy in the room, and it was still colder than usual. Amber turned to him and said, "There's nothing...nothing, Martin. That has happened...a few times..." She was out of breath and had a hand placed over her chest as though to calm her racing heart.

Their eyes locked as Martin was still kneeling in front of her bed after listening to the floor. He looked at her trembling hands and thought of them lovingly painting an image of the prairie as Klara would have seen it years ago. As she would have watched Hans walking past his barn, out towards the creek to fetch water for the animals.

Martin placed his hands over hers. Her skin as freezing and he squeezed her. Her shoulders relaxed.

"Martin?"

"Yeah?"

"Would you stay in here with me?"

He bit the inside of his lip. "Yeah." His voice was croaky and he felt lightheaded.

"Geez, it's cold..." He coughed as he got in beside her. He didn't exactly feel like hot stuff in his boxers, socks, t-shirt and sweater that he'd worn all day.

Even after all that had just transpired, he was grateful for having spread some toothpaste around in his mouth and rinsed before getting into bed. He settled himself behind her and pulled her close.

To his relief, Amber relaxed in his arms, nestling closer to him for warmth. If he didn't believe in the possibility of an old lady ghost watching them, he would have found this situation far more exciting.

Now, both were still slightly spooked and somewhat conscious of not being alone.

Spirit lady or no, he pulled her up against him and nestled his nose in her hair. Amber sighed.

"You know, Amber...you could come and work from my place if you wanted? You could come home with me? Have a break from this?" He bit the inside of his lip again.

"I know you don't believe me, but I'm not that scared here. I know who they are. I just need to find out what happened..." Her voice grew groggy.

"Do you sleep so soundly when you're alone?"

She didn't immediately answer. Then she said with a sleepy sigh, "It can vary. But I'm okay."

"Hmm. Well...I'm looking forward to getting a few hours of sleep now," he said, feeling more secure next to her, although he didn't want to say that. The younger, hormone-driven version of himself would have been horrified.

"Goodnight, Martin," Amber said, the previously tense muscles in her back pliant, curved to fit the shape of him.

"Goodnight, Amber."

And as he drifted off, he thought of Amber's painting being the view that Klara would have seen from Amber's bedroom window. Martin loved art; he would spend time at art museums in the city to clear his mind between classes when he was in school.

Now, the notion of Klara Schreiber keeping a watchful eye wasn't quite as disconcerting. He began to drift off, with Amber snug against him, her soft snoozing breaths as close to him as ever.

Chapter 32

1914. Anton and Sophie. Temeswar.

"So? Will you paint me?" Sophie called Anton from his pallet and he looked up at his wife, who stood with one hand on her waist. She smiled and moved towards him gingerly, her large belly making maneuvering in their tiny flat awkward.

She laid a hand on his shoulder to steady herself and they both surveyed the painting of his home village. The one he hadn't finished before as he'd used the last of his supplies on the portrait of Margaritha. Now, he was able to finish it.

A small hand laid itself on his leg and said, "Tati? You paint me next?" It was Marcus, Sophie's son whom he'd adopted as his own. His 'noble' father had soon married another aristocrat and sired 'legitimate children.' Sophie and Marcus were expendable, despite Sophie's hopes that one day her handsome nobleman would return to her.

"Perhaps, Marcus," Anton said, trying to imagine the fields surrounding Bensek. He could still see the Koenig family's large back garden and the porch surrounding their house. But when he'd been walking away from his village towards the train, he'd been too distraught over leaving Margaritha behind to take a final look at anything.

Sophie's voice cut into his thoughts again as she addressed their boy. "I don't think Daddy draws portraits anymore, darling."

Anton grit his teeth. It was a sore subject. Sophie caught him, trying to sketch Margaritha after they'd married. It had been so long since he'd looked at her, yet she was clear in his mind. There were times it was a torment not to sit and draw her.

Sophie was beautiful, and he cared for her deeply. Yet as his wife admitted, it was fate which brought them together. Not true love.

"Come, it's time for some supper for grownups," Sophie said, lighting some more candles after putting Marcus to bed. Anton moved to sit at the small table beside their bed.

He stared at the stack of papers beside the door and shook his head. The news these days was grim.

Sophie noticed his gesture and began to speak. Anton held a hand up as he retrieved a pillow from their bed and set it behind his wife.

"You won't go, will you? You don't have to. We need you here," she said.

"I don't agree with the war, but it would be dishonorable not to be of service. I will stay until you have the baby. My aunt and uncle will make sure you are looked after. And perhaps your parents will come to stay?" He glanced down at Sophie.

Sophie's large brown eyes filled up, glistening in the candlelight. She sniffed and turned away, crossing her arms before beginning to slice some bread.

She spoke, "Perhaps we should *all* just go to Mercydorf. It will be safer there. Only Germans there. There will be no crazy Serbs with guns. Bah! The Serbs are animals! Starting this war."

"Sophie, don't distress yourself. I don't like that they assassinated the archduke, but I can understand their disgruntlement with the Hapsburgs, annexing their territory without any consideration of the wishes of the Serbian people. Let's be honest...Austria-Hungary wants war with the Serbs, they always have wanted to crush them."

"Well, they have no choice. They've killed the archduke and his innocent wife! I can't believe you would have any sympathy with those Serbs. Someone glared at Marcus and me at the market yesterday. He looked like a Serb." She waved her finger, gesturing to her face.

"Sophie..." Anton admonished gently. "Please, think of the baby. You are getting flushed."

"Very well..." She sighed and winced, placing a hand on the side of her belly before muttering, "I just think we will be a bit better off if we got out of the city. A few other Schwobs look down upon us for working for a Jewish family." As soon as Sophie uttered the words, she pressed her lips together and looked down. As though ashamed of her own words, yet unable to apologize for them.

Anton, shaking his head, "I know what nonsense you would say, and I don't care for such talk. We must rise above such petty hatefulness."

Marcus rolled over on the tiny cot, inches away from their bed. Anton wasn't quite sure how they would manage once the baby arrived, but at least they had privacy. He'd saved for them to have their own place, rather than put his aunt and uncle to any more trouble.

He knew they would have a bit more space if they moved back into a Schwob village like Bensek or Mercydorf. Perhaps even Rekasch, where to his knowledge, there was a successful wine industry. Kovacs was a wine merchant, after all. Perhaps there was work at the vineyards for his family.

Mulling the prospect over, he said, "We have to be loyal to the Kovacses. They've always given my aunt and uncle work, and Herr Kovacs will come across hard times now. With things heating up politically between differing groups, their Jewish faith might work against them business-wise. There's always been prejudice...but I've no wish for us to be part of it. They need our help around the home, and Frau Kovacs has been kind to you."

"She has. I will never forget her kindness when she found out about my situation, and they were generous with us when we wed," Sophie admitted and sighed. "Still, I would rather be in my home village..."

"I...I understand, dear." Anton poured more water into their cups and spooned an extra helping of the bean stew into their bowls. Sophie began to clear up once they'd finished when Anton insisted she lay down.

"You need rest, Sophie," Anton said.

"Nonsense, Anton. My mother carried on with her work right up until she delivered. I did with Marcus as well." Her words were tight, clipped as they came from her mouth. Anton noted the sheen of sweat on her forehead and insisted she lay down.

It was Anton who quieted Marcus and tidied their small flat while Sophie tossed and turned in their bed. Sleep had become quite difficult over the past months. Anton couldn't help but think of Margaritha, whom he knew had more than one child now. He imagined she would carry on as well. Margaritha entered his thoughts more than he could admit to anyone.

He cursed himself for his disloyalty to Sophie, but he would never get over the worry for his lost love.

Sophie cried out, "It's time! For sure, it's time!"

Marcus whimpered a little and Anton said to his adopted son, "Don't worry. Mama just has some work to do before she brings us your baby brother."

"Oh...imagine having a baby during a war..." Sophie grunted and blew a breath out of her mouth.

Anton summoned the neighbor, who would bring the midwife along with his Aunt Susannah.

His aunt and the stout midwife bustled in. He'd never seen his aunt look so 'business like' outside of the kitchen. Uncle Walter waited outside the door to take Marcus while Sophie delivered.

When his son finally arrived, Anton said, "We shall call you Sebastian. Sebastian Martin Handl."

Chapter 33

2017. Approaching the Holiday Season. North Dakota.

Amber and Martin pulled up at the entrance of Sunnyslope Cemetery. As soon as they emerged from the truck, snowflakes floated down to land on them. The air was cold, yet lacked the accompanying bitterness.

Amber slipped her arm through Martin's as they found themselves at the Catholic end of the cemetery where Hans and Klara were buried.

"Geez, it's quiet," Martin said.

Amber laughed. "It's always quiet."

"No, I mean, there's no wind. Nothing. Last time I was here, it was windy as hell." Martin's booted feet made light crunching noises over the path.

Snowflakes landed with gentle precision on Amber's nose and cheeks as their feet moved in unison. Amber startled when Martin's bare hand reached out to stroke flurries off her face.

"Sorry. Didn't wanna touch your face with my cold glove," Martin said.

When she looked at him, the corner of his mouth was turned up. Amber sighed.

When they'd woken up together a couple of weeks ago, their combined body temperatures created such heat beneath the heavy quilts, it was like being cocooned in an electric blanket.

Martin's warm skin still had that musky, soapy smell, even after an afternoon of walking and a restless night.

The way he'd buried his face in my hair and murmured something I couldn't even understand...oh dear...

Yet they'd gotten up, changed and washed separately. Martin had coffee and eggs, then had to get to his office for a few hours. She thought she'd entirely lost his interest once he read his e-mails. Then he'd stolen one last kiss, nearly bruising her lips before dashing to his truck. Her sheets smelled of him the next night, as though they'd been intimate.

It was odd, to think of such things in a snowy graveyard.

"You're blushing," he said.

"Oh." Amber reached up and touched her cheeks.

"What were you thinking about?" Martin asked.

"Oh...nothing much," she said, warm beneath her wintry layers.

"Hmm. I missed you. I'm gonna have a quiet week pretty soon, over Christmas."

"You going to Chicago again? To see your friends?"

"They are going to stay with his wife's parents up in Wisconsin. He said I could go and stay at the house, but I'm not sure if I want to go on my own. And Christmas is a funny time to be in the house you grew up in, minus your parents." Martin cleared his throat and looked away.

"Oh. I...am kind of expected to go to my folks' place on Christmas Eve and Christmas Day."

Amber winced.

They'd only been seeing one another for a couple of months. Was it appropriate to bring him to her parents? And what would they think of her going with him to Chicago? Was he hinting he would want her to go with him?

"So...would you want to go to Chicago? If you had company?"

"Chicago is crazy at Christmas. Fun, though. Might be nice for a weekend," Martin said.

Amber took a deep breath. "Would you like to come to my folks' place for Christmas? It's okay if you don't."

"I... Sure. I wanna see what earrings she sports for Christmas," Martin said, a hint of delight in his voice.

"They are pretty special. She wears a glittery neck tie too." A wave of relief passed over her that he wasn't freaked out by her suggestion of meeting her parents.

"Would you like to come to Chicago for a night or two? It's fun."

Amber's heartbeat pounded in her ears and she swallowed. She mumbled, "Sure..." Then stuttered on the words, "Haven't been to Chicago for years. It would be cool to visit with a native."

Martin nodded as though he wasn't sure he believed her response.

After that last kiss...I was sure we would head back to the bedroom. This time...oh, geez. Amber, you are nearly forty, for goodness sake. And your lousy Catholic status never bothered you before. You can have a weekend away with a guy.

They approached Hans and Klara's graves. Martin laid down the small Christmas wreath between the old stones and said, 'Frohe Weihnachten,' murmuring something else in the language she'd never had a chance to learn and couldn't understand.

"Is it...really that different from the German they teach in high schools?" Amber said.

"A little. Some of the words are very different, and the dialect even varied from village to village. Most Schwobs can speak decent German, even if standard native German speakers wince when they hear it." Martin sniffed.

When Amber looked over at him, she saw he was wiping his eyes and bobbing up and down as though nervous.

He's crying.

Amber put her arm around him. "Hey...it's okay. You don't have to meet my mother." She attempted half-serious humor.

Luckily, it worked and he chuckled a little, sniffing. "Nah...it's just, um...my folks passed away around Christmas time. Speaking the language and graveyards and stuff...ya know. Memories."

He sighed and Amber dug in her bag for a tissue. She passed it to him and put her arm back around him. She kissed his cheek.

"You don't have to read any old letters if you don't want. We can go into Mott and grab a bite?"

"A bite might be nice. But I'll still take a look at the letters. And, um... Amber?"

"Yeah?"

"There's no pressure, you know. For you to go or not go to Chicago with me. And if you do go...I don't expect anything. Even if we won't have our usual chaperone." He gestured back to Klara's grave.

Amber looked at Martin and saw the melted snow flakes mixed with hastily wiped tears on his cheeks. The flakes landing on her lashes made her blink quickly.

Again, Martin's bare hand reached out to wipe them away.

Amber swallowed and said, "I appreciate that. I'm not a city person, but I would like to see Chicago again." She continued to wipe her face with her gloves.

"Good thing you're not wearing mascara," he said.

"You too, I guess," Amber commented.

"No need. I have gorgeous lashes naturally."

"Well, aren't we just full of ourselves?" She giggled as they turned around.

You do, though, she thought.

Martin chuckled and they walked arm in arm back to the truck.

C3 &

Later, Amber and Martin sat on her couch with the letters on the coffee table. Martin had already scanned the text and worked out the faded sections.

Dearest Margaritha,

I hope this letter finds you and Peter well. I understand the farm with three young children will keep you very busy. I should imagine your eldest, Caroline might even be helping you with the two little boys. She was a sweet, beautiful thing when I saw her at the Kirchweih at St. Elisabeth's.

I had hoped we would see you at one of the Kirchweihs since the last time we met. Yet, since the war began, it seems anything involving our language is not encouraged. My English is better these days but thankfully many neighbors still speak German.

Hans was quite happy to find he does not qualify for the military in this country since the incident with his leg. I told him not to attempt joining. The thought of him in the military again frightened me. He insisted it was dishonorable to reject the call to service.

I told him, he could even wind up fighting with someone we know. The enemy is not only the Prussian Kaiser but our own Hungary.

I wish America would have remained neutral. Things won't be the same now. I've heard of scorn being given to those who speak our language in places where they are more mixed with English speakers.

Our farm is doing well. Hans has built two barns and a smokehouse with the help of some laborers. At threshing time, migrating laborers are a blessing. I never cook so much in my life! But we are grateful. Hans does well to say his speed is limited.

A fellow came, from the south. He spoke English. He asked Hans why he was still called Hans. Hans replied that is what his mother named him. The man seemed to think he should change his name to John. True, a lot of people here have done so, so they sound more like English names. The Petter brothers from Glogon, who sheltered us when we first came to this country, are now called 'Peters.'

This fellow, he worked hard enough but his manner worried me. Hans says it isn't unusual for people to feel this way during times of war. He is happy we are not in a place where there is tension between Serbian and Austrian. That would be worse, he says.

Hans is ever steady during difficult times. I thank the heavens he is not a soldier in this horrible war. I pray for all who are. Yet selfishly, I worry about my Hans leaving me all the time. I couldn't bear to be without him.

I long for news from you, and hope to see you soon.

Ever your dear friend,

Klara.

Hettinger County. December 1917.

Chapter 34

1918. Threshing Season. Margaritha and Peter. North Dakota.

Margaritha stood over a large pot of potato soup and checked on her strudels in the oven. Caroline often had to distract Josef and Jacob while their mother cooked for the threshers.

She would prepare a cucumber salad later, as something cooler to have in the afternoon. As Caroline chatted to Jacob in the background, she gave him a piece of cucumber to quiet him. Margaritha's thoughts strayed to her friend Klara. The Schreibers' farm was well known in Hettinger and Stark County. Hans was clever, but Klara was a hard worker and apt at growing things.

She would discuss using the moon and stars, as well as paying attention to the immediate weather reports, even back in Bensek. Now, staring at the vegetables on her counter, Margaritha smiled to herself and imagined that Klara's place would be even more abundant with fresh food.

There was no way to know for sure. Margaritha had received no letters from Hettinger, even though she was sure Klara mentioning having sent a letter when she'd seen her at the Kirchweih.

Jacob had proved a most demanding baby, although all the children had taken turns taking poorly. Caroline tried so hard and had been wise beyond her years since learning to walk, yet Margaritha was determined to allow her daughter to enjoy childhood and not spend it all caring for her brothers.

"Caroline, why don't you take Jacob out? Find where Josef is. Go run around. Just stay away from the threshers, yes? Then you can help me sprinkle sugar on the cakes later."

The front door opened and large, booted feet sounded on her floor.

Peter's bushy brows furrowed in a scowl. Margaritha was accustomed to him taking little notice of the children unless they irritated him.

"You wrap her in cotton, Margaritha. She will be ten soon enough. She should be doing more of the cooking now, not out playing."

"She is a little girl who needs time to play just as much as her brothers," Margaritha said.

Peter snorted. "And another thing, for goodness sake, will you start speaking more English around the children! That is the language of this country. That is the language they should speak!"

Margaritha slammed her hands on the counter and glared at Peter. "Of course. They will grow up speaking two languages. What a dreadful thing! I recall you were one of the more outspoken ones when Hungarian was taught in our village school instead of German."

She took a step back at the reddened look in Peter's face.

Knock, knock, knock.

Peter swigged some coffee and went to the door.

"Hello?" Peter boomed. Margaritha sniggered at his accent, even though he would correct her pronunciation of English words all the time.

A wiry, small young man stood on their front porch. "You Mister *Luli*?"

"Lulay. Yes. It's a French name. Are you here to work?"

"Well, yes, sir." He spoke with a certain irreverence and squinted at Peter.

For a moment, neither man spoke. Then Peter cleared his throat and crossed his arms.

The young man took his hat off slowly, tilting his head. "Where are you from, exactly, Mister Lulay?"

"My family and I came from Hungary, almost ten years ago now. My family was French before that. We are Americans now. Would you like to work here or no?"

"I would, sir. I just...Well...There sure are a lot of Germans up here. I wasn't old enough to enlist, but, boy, those Prussians are something else."

"Hmmm. Come inside. My wife and daughter will prepare some breakfast," Peter said.

Margaritha blushed and fixed her hair. Though she was accustomed to men being around at threshing time, having visitors always caught her unprepared. Many of the men spoke only English, and she wasn't completely bilingual yet.

"Yes, come. Ve have lots food, ja. You like strudel? Coffee?"

The boy couldn't be more than seventeen. He looked at Margaritha as though she was an alien, then turned to Peter. "She don't talk English much?" the young man asked.

Peter grumbled and waved dismissively. "Forgive my wife. Her mind is slow and she hasn't grasped the language as easy as the children have. What was your name again?"

"My name is Paul. Paul Johnson. I don't think I'll take any of that... strudel if it's all the same with you. Never liked foreign food. I'll try your coffee."

Margaritha bristled at Peter's speaking of her as though she was some dimwitted fool who couldn't communicate. She addressed Paul while pouring him some coffee.

"Vehr your parents, dey come from?"

Paul took the coffee from her without making eye contact. "My folks is dead."

Peter grunted and Paul followed him out to the fields.

C3 ⁂

Later, Margaritha took Caroline out to deliver some dressed lettuce leaves and a separate cucumber salad, with some pitchers of water.

Most of the threshers thanked her and smiled, patting Caroline on the head. "You a good cook like your mama? I'd come back here every year just for the food," one of them said.

Caroline giggled and said, "Papa says Mama is a lazy cook. She makes lazy noodles." The men laughed at the child, and the mother and daughter smiled and walked away.

Most of the men were either boys still or much older. Before the war, there were more fit and able-bodied men. Yet these 'misfits,' as Peter called them, still rescued them every year. They did hard work for not a great deal of pay. Margaritha had heard that Hans Schreiber paid his workers well. Peter was a spendthrift.

Later, Margaritha was clearing up near a small group of the men, including Paul.

Paul's tones stuck out to her, his quick, sharp way of speaking. She couldn't speak English brilliantly, yet she understood most well enough.

"Well, I don't care. Least Mister Lulay wants to be a real American. There is a fellow here called Hans. What kind of a damn name is Hans? Who keeps a name like Hans nowadays? Damned murdering Kraut bastard. I wish I'd been old enough. I'd have shot some of the bastards, you bet."

"I heard Schreiber is a good fellow, even tried to enlist. That wife of his wasn't happy, though. His leg's bad anyway. There's a lot of Germans around here, has been for a while. They're good enough farmers," another thresher said.

Paul replied, "Huh. I bet he only wanted to get in to sabotage the army. There's a threat of that, you know, with all these Germans..."

Margaritha kept her eyes on the grass as she walked back to the house. The men hadn't noticed her.

Murdering bastards...Hans couldn't be any further from being a murdering bastard.

Margaritha did not like Paul one bit, and she intended to tell Peter. Yet, whenever she wanted something doing, Peter would be sure to go against her.

Just like when she'd requested to visit the Schreibers. He'd insisted, "You have far more important things to be doing than going to gossip with some old friend."

It was true her daily duties did not allow for many day trips. There was always something to do.

Margaritha sighed, entering the ever-working kitchen. Dinner was next, then doing her best to clean up and prepare the children for sleep and another busy day.

Her mind went to the uniformed soldiers she'd seen caricatured in English papers. Peter always snatched the Volksfreund local German language paper from her. He wanted her to read the English papers, saying they couldn't draw attention to themselves.

This struck her as ridiculous given that many of their neighbors spoke German. Not only Banat Germans, but southwestern North Dakota hosted an abundance of Germans from Russia.

Margaritha wondered if he didn't want her reading anything about Hans or Klara, and their successful farm. He tended to avoid any topics that would lead to a discussion about Hungary. He'd only allow short references to her own family, telling her not to dwell on missing them as there was no point.

No point thinking about the past.

He certainly won't want me to think of Anton.

Anton...

Her chest clenched merely thinking his name, even after a decade.

She wondered if he had joined the Austro-Hungarian forces. Tears stung her eyes and she placed a hand over her heart.

Is he even alive? Would he have been drafted? Perhaps some ailment like Hans's stopped him. If only I could speak to Klara...Why hasn't she written to me?

Margaritha winced and turned to look outside. The view before her was one of empty fields, not so different from the picture she'd painted in the Handl home as a child.

She could hear the men shouting to one another nearby. It was nice, having so many people around. Peter's voice was dominant, booming as he instructed the men.

She turned away and sighed.

How would it be, to live in a city, where people were constantly around?

Margaritha wasn't sure she would like to live in the city all the time, yet for a moment, she imagined herself strolling down a busy cobbled street on Anton's arm.

Shaking her head and arranging some clean plates on the counter, she blew out an angry sigh.

What a wicked thing to think, Margaritha! Perhaps this is why Peter won't even talk about Bensek.

Bensek, had she been able to stay there, seemed like a dream now. After ten years of regularly going months without seeing another soul outside Peter and the children, living in a village again, being walking distance from a local store, a neighbor, the church...It seemed perfect.

She wondered if Anton ever finished his painting of Bensek.

Anton...

Her heart ached again and she willed the yearning to ease as she continued her work in the kitchen, but the feelings wouldn't cease. Tears welled in her eyes and anguish overwhelmed her.

Margaritha fell to her knees before the table, swallowed by emotions.

"Mama?" Caroline's small voice sounded behind her.

"Oh...I just dropped something." Margaritha wiped her eyes and battled with her breathing.

"Are you okay, Mama? You made a strange noise. Shall I get Tati?"

"No!" Margaritha's voice came out more forcefully than intended. She placed a hand on her daughter's shoulder and said, more gently, "There is no need to alarm your father."

"Okay, Mama," Caroline said. Throughout the evening until it was time for everyone to go to bed, she noticed her daughter casting a wary eye towards her.

Like there was some part of her mother she'd only just found out existed, and the girl had no idea how to address it.

Chapter 35

2017. Martin and Amber. Chicago.

They'd arrived in Chicago late Friday evening.

Amber placed her bag down on the hardwood floor of Martin's Chicago townhouse. A tree stood near the window in the living room, and twinkly fairy lights hung down the spiral staircase near the kitchen.

"So this is where you had Thanksgiving?" She looked at Martin as he fidgeted with the heating.

"Yep. This is where I had my teen years. But it sure didn't look like this when I was a kid. Mom had flowers and herbs like...everywhere."

"Looks like it's had a heck of a makeover, it's so modern. Still has a woman's touch, though. Your friend's wife and the two little girls who found Hans's letter have had something to do with that?"

"Yep," Martin responded.

Flashing lights lit up the side window and a siren wailed down the street. Amber stood there, waiting.

A warm hand squeezed her shoulder and Amber jumped. "Oh!" She laughed a little and said, "I thought this was a good neighborhood." Amber smiled, though nerves made her heart beat faster.

"That's fairly normal. It was an ambulance, though. I thought you've been here before?" Martin said.

"Not for a while. It took me time to adjust then too. I spent more time in Minneapolis," Amber said, a blush heating her cheeks.

"Don't worry, I'll protect you." He winked.

"You are too kind." She grinned.

"You wanna go out for dinner? Or order in?"

"Wow. It's nine p.m. So many options..."

The tree lights twinkled beside the television, and with the street lights outside, alongside the glowing Christmas décor flashing against the hardwood floors, the atmosphere was very inviting.

Martin took a big whiff of the air and screwed his face up. "Really smells like cinnamon in here. I hope those girls didn't leave a candle going..." He went to investigate, but came back shaking his head. "Nope...but they've even got Christmas cookie soap in the bathrooms." He laughed.

Amber smirked. "It's sweet how tolerant you are of children."

Martin grinned. "So? Shall I show you around or should we order in? There's a great pizza place nearby."

Amber shrugged. "Well, sure is cozy in here. I think I'd like to stay in and order a pizza. Can't do that at my place."

Martin smiled. "Perfect. I will order and then we can freshen up and settle in. There is a bathroom just to the side by the door and there's one upstairs."

Amber entered the bathroom, taking note of the twin dark glass effect sinks and the purple wallpaper. She splashed some cold water on her face and looked in the mirror. She wondered if Frau Schreiber might have followed her there and if she would appear in the mirror like she had back home.

But there was no sign of Klara. Or Hans, whose letter to Anton had resided here in the attic for so many decades.

Amber entered the girl's room, with its white walls and mahogany looking borders and frames. There were two twin beds covered by girly duvets. Amber giggled at the posters of pop stars with handwritten slogans on them. She changed into sweatpants and a black hoodie, taking her hair out to brush it and then clip it back from her face.

Martin emerged from the upstairs bathroom in similar attire, with his University of Illinois hoodie. His heavy five o'clock shadow and laugh lines were the only giveaways he wasn't a college student anymore.

They smiled nervously and sat down on the cream and beige-striped sofa. Amber noticed that Martin smelled like soap and toothpaste.

He brushed his teeth before we eat.

Amber fidgeted on the couch for a moment, then excused herself to brush her own teeth. She re-emerged and sat down with a big sigh.

"You brushed your teeth too, huh?" Martin chuckled. "You smell minty."

Amber blushed, pressed her lips together, and replied, "Well...I caught on that you did. I didn't want to offend you with my smell."

If Amber were to admit, before he picked her up, she'd shaved her legs, exfoliated, moisturized, put on perfume, flossed, and rinsed twice. And she was wearing matching underwear.

For the first time in a while.

Now, nerves made her chest tight. She'd expected her mother to make more of a fuss when she mentioned Martin was taking her out of town. Instead, she'd received a, *"Well, you go have fun, honey. That's great. I can't wait to meet him!"*

When Amber pushed her mother with, "Is that all you have to say?" She'd just said, "Honey...you are old enough to make your decision to sin or not. Personally, I say go ahead and sin."

Amber shook her head. Her mother hinting that she approved of her getting intimate with Martin was a bucket of ice water.

"What's up?" Martin interrupted her thoughts.

"Oh, I was just thinking about my mother. She is really excited to meet you."

Martin grinned. His lips spread and paled into that peach color she found so appealing. Amber swallowed.

"You want a beer?" he said.

"Beer sounds good." She shivered beneath her hoodie when he removed his body heat to retrieve two bottles from the fridge.

Martin removed the tops and passed her the drink. She took a long sip of the cold, hoppy liquid.

"Was your Mom hoping I'd get you pregnant this weekend?"

She choked on the beer. Martin patted her back and she laughed in between coughs.

"Oh...gosh..." When she finally stopped coughing, she said, "I never thought of that. Oh, geez..." She leaned back onto the cushions, took another sip of beer, swallowed, and sighed, feeling more relaxed.

Martin scooched close, a smile on his face. "It's cool. I was pretty nervous too. How about we just eat our pizza, have a couple of beers, and enjoy one another's company."

"Pregnancy is optional, huh?" Amber teased.

Martin chuckled, though it was with a nervous edge.

"Now I guess I'll tell *you* to relax. I'm not entirely sure I want to be a mom, nice as kids are and all that. I might consider a cat or a dog, though. And that's a maybe."

Martin drew out an exaggerated sigh of relief. "My feelings are similar. I like kids and animals, but even getting a damn fish is a commitment I'm not sure I want."

At this point, they both had their feet on the coffee table, sitting side by side on the couch. Amber's muscles were starting to unwind, like the way she felt after a hot bath, languid and drowsy.

The sounds of the city faded into the background, and sitting beside Martin made being in such a foreign, urban atmosphere less jarring.

She was still smiling when she turned her head back to him and found his face inches from hers. His eyes were brown, yet a shade lighter than hers. Amber had always been told her eyes were coal black.

Martin's voice was husky and low when he said, "You've got intense eyes, like black coffee. For such a calm person, you have dramatically good looks."

Amber giggled softly. "Thanks, I think? Your eyes are a softer color than mine. I was told I have demon eyes. Yours are more like milk chocolate."

Martin smiled at her and bit his lip, pulling at the peach tones of his mouth. Amber stared and her mouth watered, her pulse quickened and blood rushed to her face.

She scooted closer. Within seconds, their lips were against one another's. They both sighed with relief. To finally be kissing one another. They'd been busy with work, anxious about traveling, negotiating extra busy airports, and being in a very different environment together.

Martin's mouth moved from hers and traveled down her face towards her neck. He'd angled his body towards hers and Amber acquiesced by turning and tilting her head back. His whiskers scratched the skin on her throat as he kissed her. When his tongue snaked out to lick the flesh on her neck, already raw from his five o'clock shadow, Amber shuddered with pleasure and reached for Martin's shoulders.

She was sure he would leave a love bite at this rate. Martin's hands went to her hair. He grabbed two handfuls, not roughly, but as though he was savoring the texture. Then her head was back into the cushions with Martin's hands cradling it.

"Amber..." He sounded hoarse, as though unbearably excited. She pulled at him to bring his body closer to hers, anxious for more contact.

All rational thought was leaving her. In one swift move, she straddled

Martin's lap. His mouth was slightly open in surprise, and what she hoped was joy, when she brought her lips down on him again.

His groan was music to her ears. Martin's hands started to move to her backside, pressing her to him. Amber sighed when his lips found her neck again.

Then the doorbell rang. They pulled apart. Martin's face was red with embarrassment and she realized his predicament of being less than acceptable to answer the door.

"Hold on. I'll get it," she said. As Martin had insisted on paying for the flights, she wanted to get the food this weekend.

"Amber..." Martin said. She figured he was trying to stop her. She shushed him, grabbed her purse, and went to the door. The delivery boy had a strange, wide-eyed look and cleared his throat as he gave her the pizza.

The delivery boy seemed to be trying to not look at her as he took the money.

"Okay. Thank you," she said with a smile.

The boy pursed his lips and nodded. "Have a good night." Then he went back down the icy steps to his car.

Amber shook her head. "He was strange." She returned to Martin, who was still on the couch with one hand under his chin as he looked up at her.

"Amber, you'd better look in the mirror. I'll get some plates," Martin said. He stood with a slight wince and went to get plates.

Amber went into the bathroom and instantly slapped a hand over her mouth. Her mouth and cheeks were reddened, her lips swollen. And her hair...that was something else. The clips she'd put in before were more than out of place and to her eyes, it appeared she'd been struck by lightning.

Amber quickly readjusted herself before stepping back into the living room.

She sat next to Martin and got a piece of pizza. He was quiet, then got himself a piece and presented them both with a napkin before they started eating.

After a mouthful of pizza washed down with a swallow of beer, Amber said, "Well, guess he figured out what I'd been doing, huh? Think he'll gossip with all his pizza boy buddies?" She took another bite, looking at Martin.

Martin laughed and said, "I'm sorry. I'll, um...I'll shave. I guess my whiskers left a mark."

"Don't bother. I like it. Long as you don't go for the Santa look, I can deal with that stubble any day."

Martin chuckled, saying, "Good to know." They clinked their bottles together in a toast.

The food was delicious, with sausage and mushrooms and a rich tasty sauce. "This is by far the best pizza I've ever had. I love the Italian sausage on it," she said.

"Thanks," he responded. Martin put on the television and flipped through the channels. The history channel advertised a marathon of WWI and WWII documentaries. Images flashed of soldiers in trenches. The earlier twentieth century images were replaced by 1940s photos of prisoners in concentration camps.

It was a heavy contrast to the warm, festive townhouse they now sat in. Amber sighed.

"Hey, Martin? Why did your mother not want to go to Europe if other folks from your parents' group were going?"

Martin was silent for a while. He put his pizza down and said, "Before the Russians officially arrived, some local partisans came and murdered her father and grandfather. Like I said, Yugoslavia post-WWII was not an awesome place to be considered....well anything remotely German. Her mother and her eventually escaped and got to Austria. I guess she didn't want to return to the scene of the crime. She seemed to have really been scared by the hatred directed at her as a kid."

Footage of the atomic bomb dropping on Hiroshima was playing as Martin continued to talk. "Mom always said her family hated the Nazis, couldn't wait for them to leave the village. They assumed that when the partisans and Russians came, they would be considered loyal Yugoslav citizens. Her dad was forced into the German army when Hitler was short on reinforcements from the Reich. My grandpa had done what he could to avoid conscription. Eventually, they caught up with him, pulled a gun out, and told him he was in the army now. He assumed when he explained this to the Yugoslav partisan comrades, they would have some sort of sympathy. They didn't. Mom just never got over it. She was a little girl when it all happened. Thankfully, they had some cousins in Chicago so they were able to apply for refugee status. But it took a while. Lots of waiting and unpleasant conditions."

Amber reached out and placed a hand on Martin's knee. "I'm sorry."

"It's okay. I like to think she's at peace now. War and extremist nationalism suck. When the Nazis came to the villages, they really screwed things up for the Schwobs, getting a bunch of farmers and craftsmen to swallow fascism. I don't have a lot of love for communism either. Tragic as it all is, after what the Nazis did, you can kind of see where all the hatred and desire for retribution came from. There's no country full of angels verses a country full of demons."

"There's also no perfect form of government," Amber said. "People are so different. Even in the same groups, people will disagree with how things should be run. And that's when times are civilized."

"I agree with you...but let's change the subject. I really want to show you around. Listen, I wanna take you to an art museum tomorrow. Then we can hit Michigan Avenue. We can visit the Hancock Building. I'll take you for a cocktail in the Signature Lounge. That sound okay?"

"Sounds amazing. Are we gonna drive?"

"Hell no. Public transportation all the way, baby," he said with a playful smile.

Amber laughed.

After another slice of pizza and another beer, Amber was stuffed. She washed the plates and sat back down, content but also sad for Martin's family history. Even if he didn't experience such horrors firsthand, he'd grown up with someone who had.

Amber moved close to Martin, but didn't move to kiss him. She wasn't sure if he wanted to continue from where they'd left off. She wasn't sure if they should. Relief washed over her when he wrapped an arm around her shoulders and pulled her close.

"Is the house warm enough for you?" he murmured in her ear.

She leaned her head on his shoulder and replied, "Yeah."

"Good. Because if I get in bed next to you tonight, I won't keep my hands to myself."

Amber nodded. "Good to know. I like sleeping in the same house as you, though."

"I really...really enjoyed before, Amber."

"Me too, Martin."

"But I meant what I said. There is no pressure on you regarding...you know..."

"I appreciate that. Does that mean we can't make out?" she said, then instantly wished she'd kept her mouth shut.

Martin laughed. "Well...would you be partial to a beer and pizza-flavored goodnight kiss?"

"That's one of my favorite types," she whispered, their faces now inches from one another.

Martin leaned in and delivered just that.

Chapter 36

"Klara! Klara! Where are you?" Hans called for his wife. She poked her head up from the cellar, carrying a jar of pickles. The house smelled of fragrant chicken soup and baking bread. Fresh noodles hung from a makeshift beam near the cellar.

Hans grinned when he saw his wife's face. It had been a long journey, and the cold always made his bad leg ache.

"You're back! I was getting so worried. It got dark an hour ago and I thought you would have frozen. I've prayed and cooked and prayed and cooked." There was laughter in her words as she set the jar of pickles down and came towards him with open arms. Klara's fears for his safety and well-being, though at times excessive, always reminded him of how important he was to his wife. How much she loved him.

He wrapped her in a hug, grateful she wasn't angry with him for causing her worry.

"I'm starving. The house smells wonderful. Let me go and make sure my horses have enough to eat in the barn and I will come enjoy dinner with my bride. I have a wonderful surprise for you! You will be so happy."

"Oh! Is it a letter from Margaritha?" Klara asked as she placed a fresh loaf of bread on the counter.

Hans sighed. "No, my dear, not from Margaritha. Let me check on my horses. They worked hard bringing me back to you."

"Yes, very well, but hurry. I'll set out your soup and it'll go cold." She bustled about the kitchen, tidying any crumbs and dirty dishes. He shook his head. She was rarely off her feet.

Hans walked out to the barn, cursing his stiff, damaged leg. He spoke to his tired horses, ensuring they were covered and that they had plenty to eat. He rubbed one down before straightening its blanket. "Well done, you beauties."

Hans cooed in Schwowische to his companions. It occurred to him that both he and Klara had slowly started mixing English in with their daily speech, alongside their native language. He stroked one horse's nose and said, "Well, I suppose you will be a bilingual horse. Or do you prefer English? Well, let me tell you I am so happy that my friend from Hungary has written to me. He survived the war! Isn't dat great?"

A knock on the barn door caused Hans heart to leap into his throat. It was a heavy knock, not like Klara's gentle tap. "Hello?" Hans eyed where he kept his gun beside the door.

"Hello? Mister Schreiber? I...I hope you don't mind. I heard you in here and I didn't want to worry your wife. It's me. Paul? Paul Johnson? I helped you with your threshing?"

Hans walked to the door and saw the man—thin, red, and chapped from the cold. His bony, jutting chin and squinty eyes gave him the appearance of an older man. Paul Johnson couldn't be much past twenty by now.

"Hello, Paul. You look dreadful. Have you walked here?"

"Well...I had a horse at one point, but lost it in a poker game. I managed to hitch a ride halfway to the area. Then I remembered you and Missus Schreiber's place. I hope you don't mind me putting you out, but I got no place to go."

Hans was wary. He'd told him last season that he wouldn't require his help with threshing. Paul didn't care for any non-whites, Jews, Catholics, Native Americans, foreigners, and due to the war with the Kaiser, he seemed to have a current dislike to anything German. Hans never cared for Paul's opinion on how he should change his name.

"You can stay with us for the night. I can't let you back out in this, you'll die. Town is miles away and the next farm isn't close either. My wife cooked soup."

"I appreciate it," Paul said. "In fact, I had some of your foreign cooking. I worked for a Mister Lulay near New England last threshing time. Said he's French...sounds like you when he talks."

"Hmm. Yes, we came from the same village," Hans said as they walked to the house.

He cringed, knowing Klara wouldn't be happy he was bringing Paul in.

He re-entered the house with a completely different feeling than before. "Klara?"

Klara was still smiling, setting out their supper, the kitchen still fragrant yet tidier now. She looked up and when her wide green eyes found Paul's pitiful figure, her expression froze.

"I didn't know we have guest? Hans?" Klara's brows were high.

"My name's Paul. You might not remember me. I worked for you once, but this is a popular place of employment come threshing time. I guess Mister Hans had enough help last time."

"Ah. You look so cold. Have soup, it will warm you. Sit." Klara said the words without a smile. She looked down, as though to keep her expression hidden, but Hans could clearly tell his wife was afraid.

"Thank you, ma'am. I wouldn't mind having some of your food. I was telling Mister Hans how I ate some of Missus Lulay's food. I don't like foreign food, but I guess the Lord intends to teach me to be grateful."

Klara squinted at him, like she didn't quite believe him, then gave a closed mouth smile and nodded. Hans sighed and helped himself to some food. He knew that Klara, though she had grasped basic English over the years, was not fluent and when folks spoke too fast, she struggled.

"You speak to Margaritha? Missus Lulay?" Klara surprised Hans with querying Paul so openly. He didn't trust the man. Hans learned early in his life and during his military service that once a person expressed a dislike for others based on their race or creed, it was a long, near impossible road to convince them to change.

"Yeah. That Missus Lulay isn't a bad cook. Mister Schreiber? I see you still have a limp?"

"I will always walk strange, but at least I can walk. Not like some of these poor boys coming back home," Hans said.

"Ja, so sad. My heart hurt for dem," Klara said. Hans feared his wife's extra strong accent might grate on Paul. Then, he thought perhaps the man had seen the light after all and wouldn't be a bigot forever.

Then Paul spoke. "Well, it's a shame what those Kraut bastards did to our boys, but that's the price to defeat the Beast. Some countries invite evil. Us Americans, we never will."

Klara pursed her lips and took a quiet spoonful of soup. Hans had so looked forward to telling her about the letter from Anton over a quiet supper together, but it seemed he would have to wait until Paul was asleep. It was a frigid January night, so he would have to bed the man down in their parlor. The thought didn't sit easy with him. Klara's voice interrupted his thoughts.

"War is sad. No matter who die. Big men in charge make war, everybody remember dem in da books. Small men not in charge die, nobody remember dem. Big mess then for poor women and children left to clean up all alone. Ja, dat's true," Klara said and continued to eat her soup.

Paul put down his spoon. "Well, I sure thank you for your hospitality. I'm afraid this might have too much spice in it. I'm sure you people like that. My stomach can't handle it. Mister Schreiber? If I could bed down near your horses?"

"Oh. You can sleep in the parlor. It's too cold out tonight."

"I have the constitution of a horse, Mister Schreiber. I'll be right in the barn," Paul replied.

"He is like horse but can't eat pepper?" Klara murmured just loud enough for Paul to hear.

"Klara, hush," Hans admonished, then said, "Please, I don't want to find a frozen man in the barn tomorrow. I'd be in the Lord's debt."

"If you have a spare blanket, I can assure you I've slept in worse conditions. I've been up north for a while, workin' in factories. You won't find me frozen in the morning."

"Okay, then." Hans set about making sure Paul had enough dry blankets and that he was on the floor above the horses and other livestock, so enough body heat would rise up to the straw pallet in the loft of the barn.

Hans even questioned whether or not to leave Paul a firearm, just in case any coyotes came near. His stomach twisted with unease and he rubbed at the stiffness in his leg.

"Well, I can't say how comfortable you will be here, but you should make it through the night. The offer of staying in our parlor still stands." Hans looked the man in the eye.

"No, sir. I can sure tell Miz Klara doesn't like me. You should be careful, though. She sounded like one of them Bolsheviks. I don't blame *you*, though, Mister Schreiber. Women talk too much these days."

"Hmm. Well, give us a holler if you need something. Goodnight," Hans replied solemnly and set off back to the house, trying to hide his limp.

He was relieved, in a way, that Paul wouldn't be in the same place as he and Klara. It would allow them to discuss the matter of Anton's letter.

Klara had finished clearing by the time he came in. With anxiety heavy on his chest, he didn't thank her for the glare she shot him whilst walking past and into their bedroom. She undressed quickly, furiously brushing out her hair and braiding it tightly. Hans normally enjoyed watching her womanly bedtime preparations.

She still said nothing, fastening the top button of her flannel night gown. After her initial glare, Klara had not looked at him at all.

Hans cleared his throat. "Klara?" he asked.

"Oh, am I allowed to speak now?" she said sharply in their language.

"Klara, listen. I don't trust Paul. We have to be careful. I did not expect him tonight."

"No, neither did I. How could you hush me in front of him? Bah! The Americans are just as guilty of this blind nationalism as the Germans are. All these stupid people. They don't like Jews. They don't like Serbs…Serbs don't like them. Bah! Round and round they go, like fools." Klara made a furious circular motion with her fingers in the air. "This isn't over." Her voice rose and Hans made a shushing gesture again.

"Klara…there are a few like him. I believe he is dangerous. I don't like him being here at all, but we cannot turn him out. We would still be classed as foreigners here, he is a native…" Hans tried to explain to his wife, but when she became impassioned like this, there was little reasoning with her. In many ways, he was happy they'd left Europe. That she could find peace here in her garden.

"Native? He is not native. No…his grandparents killed all of them. Ha! I don't like him! Turn him out and let him die!" Klara shouted.

"Klara!" Hans scolded in a tone he rarely used with his wife.

Klara bunched her hands into fists at her sides, her green eyes illuminated by her fury. "Don't you shush me! The world would not miss a man like that!"

"Klara…please." Hans held his hands up. "The war is still fresh in people's minds here. I don't want our surprise guest to hear us ranting at each other in German."

"Okay, I speak English then. I speak English. That Paul can go to Hell! Stupid boy who only listen to stupid people! What does he know about Margaritha? Why don't you take me to my friend? Stupid war! We might have a friend who died for Hungary. You remember? Anton was not bad, and he fought for the Hapsburgs! Not because he loved them, but because he was a citizen and would do his duty! Why is this man in our barn! I don't care if he *dies* in the snow! You? I care!"

At this, Hans promptly crossed the bedroom floor and grabbed his wife's wrists. She kept her body stiff as a board as he jerked her to him. He spoke in a low whisper. "I have a letter from our dear friend, Anton. If you will stop ranting like a fool, I will read it to you." He released her wrists.

Klara stepped back and looked down. She was silent and sat on the bed, her hands folded. Hans wondered if she would weep. Instead, she looked up at him and said, "Forgive me, Hans. I do feel that way about the war, but I realize now my haste in carrying on so."

Hans sat beside his wife and put his hand over hers. "Klara I understand why you are angry. It is bad luck that fellow came here."

Hans laid his lips on Klara's cheek, tenderly kissing down to her throat. Klara's breath hitched when his fingers found the top button on her thick night dress.

He whispered in her ear, "Come, my love, we will forget this quarrel. Let's read the news that comes from our friend and then perhaps I can forgive you properly before we sleep?"

Klara giggled and laid her hand over Hans's. He brought it up to his lips.

She said, "Do you need ointment for your leg? I have plenty."

"Later, dear..."

They settled down together and began to read.

Dearest Hans and Klara,

I trust this letter finds you well. I'd wished to send you a letter to tell you of my well-being in time to wish you Merry Christmas. It took some time before I could settle down to write.

I recall learning of Hans' injury. I assume this is why I did not meet my friend on the battlefield.

I am very grateful for this.

I have been away from my dear Marcus, my dear son Sebastian and my wife Sophie for some time. I came home to find my Walter Onkel gravely ill, and my Susie Tant in a frail state. Age has caught up with them and the war has been difficult for those at home too.

I have seen things I would rather not have seen. I have watched men behave in a manner which brought sickness into my mouth. I have lived through conditions I'd rather not detail. I killed men.

Throughout it all, I didn't have time to think on why I was there. I just knew that I couldn't ask others to do such things in my stead. Yet there were many moments, when cowardice beckoned me and I cursed myself for being there. If running away had been an option, I would have gladly done so.

Alas I live, and now back in Temeswar, I haven't time to think on what I did and saw. I must carry on for my family. It seems I will be the head soon now that Onkel is so unwell.

I miss you and Klara greatly. I miss more innocent days. Yet if such horrors can take place in our time, perhaps there has been a darkness brewing in man we hadn't noticed in our youth and the innocence of life was only an illusion.

With the defeat of Austria-Hungary, things have changed. There was a brief declaration of a Banat Republic. This would have been great for the Schwobs, yet it lasted but a day. Temeswar is now part of Romania. So is Bensek as it happens. Other Schwob villages belong to Yugoslavia. Only a few are still in Hungary.

People still walk around and speak their languages as normal. Sophie wishes to go back to her home village of Mercydorf, I think she is nostalgic for village life.

I'm not sure I can face it knowing you two won't be there. But life goes on. And I am well by the Grace of God.

All my best to you both and please send my warmest regards to our fellow Bensekers,

Your Loyal Friend,

Anton Handl.

December 1918.

Hans put the letter on the bedside table and looked to his wife.

"Romania? So, are we Romanians now?" Her eyes were wide.

"No, my love, we are Americans now. I am joyful our dear friend is alive. Yet, from the sounds of it, our Banat is changing beyond recognition," Hans said.

"I miss his kind smile. How I wish he would have whisked Margaritha away. Curse that Peter Lulay!"

Klara helped Hans out of his trousers and applied medicinal ointment to his leg.

"Klara..." Hans said as they both got into bed and beneath the quilts to warm themselves after she'd tended to him.

"Hmm." *Americans now.* "Tell that to your friend Paul out there," Klara said, blowing out the candle and turning her back to Hans.

Hans scooted behind Klara and put his arm around her. She relaxed against him, obviously deciding not to shun him. Hans had decided to leave the matter to rest, when his wife's quiet voice came out into the dark air. "Do you think he will survive?"

Hans was confused. "He has survived, Klara. He wrote to us."

"That's not what I mean, Hans. What he will have seen and done, from his letter, it will haunt him. Do you think he will be well? In his mind?"

Hans was silent for a minute, thinking on the matter. "Anton has always been able to find the beauty in the grimmest moments. If he wasn't well in himself, he wouldn't have even mentioned his troubled thoughts. We will pray for our friend."

Hans kissed his wife on the cheek and settled down behind her to sleep. The wind whipped over the prairie and he suddenly popped his head up. He was certain he heard retreating footsteps in the snow.

The horses whinnied. Hans got up with a groan and looked out the window and could see no signs of movement in the darkness. Only the sound of the wind. He'd learned over the past decade that the wind over the fields had a way of playing tricks. He never told Klara at first how much it frightened him.

To his great shame, it had been the wind which startled him to the point of falling and permanently injuring himself. As passionate and caring as Klara was with him, he wondered if at times she found him to be less of a man.

"Hans?" Klara said from the bed, startling him from his thoughts, likely wondering what he was looking at.

"Yes, my dear?"

"Aren't you going to forgive me?"

"Forgive...Oh!" Hans chuckled, relieved to be distracted from the worries of the world. Those of the strange man in his barn, and his dear friend, thousands of miles away in the Old Country.

Hans prided himself on being a sensible, solid fellow. He knew if one was ever presented with joy and happiness, it was to be accepted with gratitude.

"I do love you, Klara. And of course I will forgive you."

Hans got into his warm bed next to his wife.

Chapter 37

2018. A Persistent Message. North Dakota.

Martin lay in bed, staring up at his ceiling. He'd met Amber's parents twice now. Her mother was a funny woman, with themed sweatshirts and earrings for every holiday. Having been a teacher before retirement, she now made jewelry and seasonal shirts as a hobby. According to Amber, even on normal days, she rarely wore anything unless it had a comical phrase or image on it.

Before they even entered Amber's parents' house in Mott, his girlfriend turned around and held her hands up, gesturing that she had to tell him something. Martin sighed with his hand on his heart, now that he could call Amber his *girlfriend*.

'Martin? My mother will be wearing love heart earrings. With glitter. And a pink shirt with a giant sparkly red love heart. She goes all out in February. She says it's a grim time of year so she likes the color.' Martin shook his head and chuckled, recalling that the woman even wore pink leggings.

Her father had a landscaping business and had been a part-time assistant football coach. The first thing Martin noticed about him was his size.

And the fact that he didn't say much.

'Dad just likes to be outside, working. Even in the cold. Like you. He stays in and reads the paper a lot more now though. He loves standing outside and talking about the weather,' Amber told him.

Amber's dad had passed on a more subdued nature to his daughter, yet she still possessed enough of her mother's quirkiness. She was a beautiful combination of both parents, who seemed decent and loveable people.

He wondered what Amber would have thought of his folks. If she would have found his dad's fidgety, loving, and sometimes needy nature to be disconcerting. What she would have thought of his mother's steady yet intense nature. They were funny at times, though often it was without realizing they were being so.

His mother was horrified by any food waste and didn't understand people who didn't consider how much they would actually eat when cooking. Once, after he'd started making money, he took his parents out to a fancy restaurant in one of Chicago's best hotels. His mother asked what would become of the food customers didn't take home in a 'doggy bag.' The waiter informed her that for health and safety reasons, they would have to throw it away.

His mother became so upset they nearly had to leave. Amber's mother, with her stacks of labeled Tupperware and dangling earrings, would have amused Katy Handl very much.

Valentine's Day was tomorrow and he hoped to head over to Amber's for the evening. Even if just to cook together. He would happily sleep on her futon just to see her smile behind a wine glass and kiss her lips just once. That was all he wanted...for now.

Martin's phone started to buzz on the desk beside him. He leaned up to see who was calling him. "Amber..." He picked up the phone. "Hey, what's up?"

"Hi, Martin?"

"Everything okay?" Martin asked. Her voice was shaky and quiet.

"I...I keep hearing it. The banging. It's beneath the bed and I can't sleep...It's like she's agitated..."

"Okay. I'm coming over. Don't worry. Everything is going to be fine." Martin hung up, got his coat, and jumped in his truck.

 C3   80

Once he got off the main highway and into Hettinger County, the snow made a near impossible barrier to see the road. If it hadn't been for his phone and GPS, he might not have made it.

He laughed with nerves and relief when he finally got to the single lane gravel road that led to Amber's place. Martin got out of the truck and realized the headlights were still on. Reaching inside to press the button, he was looking towards the front of the house.

A pale face with light blue eyes stared back at him. Martin swore and started to shake.

"Hans?" Martin was frightened to move from his truck, but the cold and his worry for Amber forced him to do so.

He flipped the lights off, locked the car, and darted to the house, terrified of being stuck outside with an uneasy ghost.

"Amber?" Martin knocked on the door. Amber answered it, looking pale and shaken.

"Oh my gosh, I was so worried. I can't believe you drove in this. I shouldn't have called," she babbled. He came into the house, not even wiping his feet, and wrapped his snow-matted, coated arms around her. She buried her warm face against his neck.

Then she jumped again. "Oh! It's Hans!" she gasped. "Did you see him?"

Martin turned around and nodded. They could both see Hans's shape. He was wearing only a shirt and trousers with suspenders, as though it was summer. The brim of his hat didn't move despite the frigid, ruthless wind. He nodded at them and turned away.

"Wait! Please!" Amber said, starting in the ghost's direction. Yet it took only seconds for him to disappear into the darkness.

"Come on, Amber, let's shut the door," Martin said.

"I just don't understand it..." Amber started to say.

Martin was taking off his coat and boots, his gaze flickering between the door and the window. He shook his head and looked back to Amber. "I gotta admit...it was kind of stupid of me to drive out here, but I was so worried. You never sound scared like that. And it was like he was checking I got here okay..."

"I'm sorry I called you. I was drifting off in bed. I've been sleeping so great lately. Then the banging kept happening. I got scared. I swear it is from beneath the bed, but then...it's like something is really wrong in that cellar too."

"Well, we know they aren't buried here, don't we? We've been to their graves."

"Yes, that's right, but...Martin?"

"Yeah?"

"I think we need to look into how they actually died. From what I can see, they weren't really elderly. Klara was around fifty-five...but I am not actually sure how they died. I did find some records of them in US censuses but no death certificates."

"They might still only be kept at the church. Shall we go see the priest tomorrow? To see if there are any records of how they'd passed away?"

"Yes. I think we should. I've looked online and I can't find any record of Klara or Hans' death."

"That's a heck of a romantic Valentine's Day. I was thinking more candlelit dinner." Martin grinned, though the anxiety hadn't quite dissipated.

"Well, we can do that too."

"Well, then...Miss Amber Kilzer? Would you be my Valentine?"

"I'd love to," she said with a smile, though there were purple, bruise-like shadows beneath her eyes. Martin slipped his hand through hers pulled her to the couch.

It was Amber who took the fleece blanket and wrapped it around them both. She snuggled close to him, as though hiding from the rest of the room. She shivered and Martin rubbed her slender back beneath the fleece until her shaking eased.

"Relax, I'm here. We're going to figure this out. You don't have to do this alone." Her teeth chattered from time to time, not due to the cold, due to the tension of being afraid and anxious.

"Martin?"

"Yeah?"

"Do you really think I'm stupid for living out here alone? The other day, I thought maybe I should move."

The question surprised him. In the months that he'd known her, Amber had been confident and happy that there was a purpose in living here. There were times he tried to convince her to leave, but she'd insisted on staying. Now, it was he who understood that something had to be sorted out before Amber could leave.

Before Hans and Klara Schreiber could be at peace, Amber had to discover something. But what?

Martin placed his palm on her head, savoring the feel of her short curls. He opened his mouth to reply, then the word froze on his tongue. There, in the opening between the kitchen and the living room, stood Frau Schreiber.

He wanted to bid her good evening or say something in the dialect he'd spoken at home. Klara was so real. Her green eyes were vivid, wide as though she was trying to see *them* more clearly. Her head was tilted to the side, and he could see gray wisps of her curls floating in a phantom breeze.

The old woman put her hands up in a gesture, moving them slightly as though to say 'stay.' Martin nodded and held Amber close. Amber seemed to sense and see nothing.

Klara Schreiber's appearance seemed to be only for him on this occasion.

"Martin, I don't think I can do this. I thought I could, but I can't figure out the noise. What does it mean? I've looked and looked. It's not like there is a body buried here or some secret passageway."

Martin held Amber close. He kissed the top of her head. When he looked back up, no spirit of Klara Schreiber stood there.

"Don't worry. We'll figure this out. Let's find out about how they passed away, then we'll go through a couple more letters."

Chapter 38

1925. Anton's Nightmare. Temeswar.

Tiny, jagged rocks stabbed at Hans's and Anton's faces. The scurrying of retreating small feet sounded then faded by the time he and his friend could look to the source of the mysterious flying stones.

A fellow soldier marching behind the two friends said, "We should string the little bastards up. We are here to assert Hapsburg authority, not to take abuse from Serb brats."

"You can't blame the children for hating us. In their minds, they are heroes and we are villains," Hans replied, and wiped the blood dripping from his temple. Anton knew Hans hated the views of many of their fellow soldiers.

The stinging injury and irritation grated on Anton when they spotted a dark-haired boy who stuck his tongue out at them and ran away. Anton shook his head and bid his fellow soldiers to leave the boy alone. There was no way to prove the child was the one responsible for their cuts.

That had been peacetime, but tensions were building.

Years later, Anton found himself in the same village. The same homes that likely hid their assailants now lay in ruins. The stench of rot and unwashed bodies caused bile to rise in his throat.

The corpse of an enemy soldier hung from makeshift gallows. Anton vomited. He realized the body couldn't belong to anyone older than seventeen or eighteen. It could have been the same boy who stuck his tongue out when he and Hans had been on patrol.

Anton was on his hands and knees on debris-filled mud. Scraps of metal dug into his palms.

"Hans!" he'd shouted for his friend, fearful of why he wasn't there.

Had Hans even come into the village with me? Is he even alive?

Anton realized that he'd forgotten that Hans wasn't with him during this war. Hans had emigrated to America years ago. Anton wished to speak to his old friend.

Needed to speak to his old friend.

The body attached to the noose swung ever so slightly and Anton's nose and throat stung from his previous retching. It was so difficult to move. The air was as thick as the mud he'd knelt in. Going into a conquered village should have been a respite from the trenches.

How could he get out? Nothing made sense at all. His old friend Hans tended to keep his head, even in difficult circumstances. "Is Hans here?" he asked.

"Hans!" Anton shouted. When he turned to his fellow soldiers, they were different men. Their faces were blank, stunned by the horror of war. Hunger, thirst, and exhaustion had long since become companions.

Anton sat up, lightheaded and coated in sweat. He was in the flat with Sophie and the boys.

Sebastian slept next to Marcus. Marcus knit his brows together, and Sebastian wiped his eyes.

"Anton...you were talking in your sleep. This keeps happening! The children are terrified." Sophie mopped his forehead.

"Sophie...I want to emigrate." Panic rose in his chest.

"Anton, please. It's as you said, we owe our loyalty to the Kovacses. We don't have money to go. The war has been over for years. Perhaps we should get you to a doctor."

"What can a doctor do? Every night, I go back to the war. It's a memory replayed as though it was yesterday." Anton was just catching his breath. Sophie reached for him again and he pushed her hand away.

"What's wrong with Tati?" Sebastian asked.

"He has nightmares from being a soldier," Marcus whispered to his little brother.

"I don't ever want to be a soldier," Sebastian mumbled.

Anton sighed and pushed himself out of bed. He felt hollow inside, walking towards the window of their flat. Looking outside at the cobbled streets of Temeswar he'd once found so beautiful. Now he didn't see the same thing.

A sense of foreboding and sadness threatened him.

"No. Don't be a soldier, boys..." Anton swallowed, trying to compose himself in front of his sons.

"If I was a soldier, I would be brave. I wouldn't be frightened of anything," Marcus said.

"Marcus, hush! Your father is upset," Sophie said.

"He is not my father! Not really. I am of noble blood. I would be strong. I wouldn't cower like this." Marcus had recently uncovered the truth about his birth.

Sophie glared at her firstborn, but Anton held his hand up and shook his head. He never rose to Marcus's adolescent taunts.

"Sophie, I think it would be best if in the future we would emigrate."

Sophie nodded. "Perhaps in a few years, we could go back to Mercydorf? Things will be more peaceful there. Perhaps it is being in the city which strains your nerves. Anton, I simply cannot leave the country of my birth," Sophie said.

Anton turned from the window and said, "What country?! Romania? Hungary? Austria-Hungary? The Banat? Our 'country' lost the war, alongside thousands of lives. The Hapsburgs are done. We were never important to them anyway! You should know that more than anyone! Why not start afresh?" Anton said.

Sophie crossed her arms. "I suppose you are anxious to go and see *old friends* in America? What was she called? *Margaritha?*"

Anton's blood boiled. He bit back a retort that she would hate to leave the Banat as she hoped to see the great love of her youth, the Hungarian nobleman who had abandoned her. Hoping to be relieved of their common, impoverished life.

Every time Anton mentioned emigration, Sophie was resistant. Part of their wages went to her elderly parents, and her plans were to take residence at her childhood home in Mercydorf. Anton did care for Sophie's parents, but he felt they were stuck in the same position and it would never change as long as they lived in Europe.

Uncle Walter and Aunt Susannah had passed away within two years of one another, and he'd felt particularly lost since his Susi Tant passed away. Alone.

He turned to Sophie. "Yes, I did know a girl called Margaritha once. I also had friends called Hans and Klara from Bensek. I would love to see them again. They run a successful farm in America! But most importantly,

I feel America might hold better prospects for the boys. At least for our grandchildren, Sophie."

Her eyes filled up. "Anton, please. Let's go to Mercydorf. The village doctor will see to you and life will be quieter. It will be better. You will see."

Marcus spoke, unable to be left out of his parents' conversation in their small living space. "Yes, perhaps we should go to America, Mother. Seeing as you married a commoner, it might be better. I'm tired of working for the old Jew. We'll never get out of this small flat," Marcus said bitterly.

Anton walked towards Marcus.

"Why would you say it in such a way? The *old Jew,* as you say, has looked after us, kept us employed. When your mother was distraught with heartbreak over the man who sired you, the lady of the house cared for her. She even made arrangements for you to come live with us. Oh, how you've changed. Once an innocent child...now that you are nearly a man, you disappoint me by talking nonsense! Where is your *noble* father? He won't come to rescue you! You are a fool to hold onto this dream," Anton said, hurt by his adopted son's words.

"You can't tell me this!" Marcus charged towards the door. Sophie screeched and went to hold onto Marcus. Sebastian bit his hand to fight back tears. He released his hand, shouting, "Don't go, Marcus! Don't run away, please."

Marcus turned to his half-brother and looked down. His jaw tensed and all could see how he fought with himself.

"Very well...Father. Forgive me. But some of the boys tease me for being a Jew's servant, like it is the worst thing ever. And they call me a bastard."

Anton placed his hand on Marcus's shoulder. "I understand it isn't easy for you. I do love you as my own. We mustn't let anyone interfere with our family." Anton sighed again and turned to Sophie,

"Perhaps it will be best if we do move back into the country. If the climate here is shifting, perhaps...we will be better being around our own people."

In that moment, Anton realized he could no longer hold onto the past, onto a dream of seeing Hans and Klara again. He wasn't sure he could live in a Schwob village without his old friends. He knew that it would cost him dearly to repress the memory of his first love.

Yet he also knew there would be no sanctuary from nightmares or from the endless sadness in America.

None of them could afford to remain in love with the past. Sophie couldn't either. A distant view of what was a selfish nobleman's seduction. A romantic notion of the man returning to claim responsibility and be part of his son's life.

The texture of Margaritha's curls and the picture she drew of lands she had yet to see with her amber-toned eyes would have to fade into fantasy.

The dream of seeing his dear friends who lived near her, yet who couldn't even visit his love due to a jealous, selfish man, must remain a dream.

A marriage, sons, and a brutal war separated him from his friends. From love.

So, Anton decided to do what was necessary to keep his family happy and together. If that meant moving to Mercydorf, that is what they would do. Otherwise, they would break apart in this ever-changeable world. He owed it to his family to stick together.

He embraced Marcus and then Sebastian. He said to them both, "One day, you will have children, and your children will have children. We owe it to one another to remain a family. As God intended us to be."

Chapter 39

2018. Valentine's Day. North Dakota.

Sunlight shone through Amber's bedroom curtains, and she watched the dust particles float in the beams of light. She rolled over onto her back and reached one arm out to the side of the bed where Martin had slept next to her.

Martin's smell was soapy with an essence of male deodorant and warm skin. Smiling, she realized how accustomed to his scent she was becoming. Amber turned onto her side and studied the head imprint still on the pillow.

Groggy due to sleeping so heavily after being nervous and panicking about agitated noises in the house, Amber listened. There wasn't a sound now. She sat up, looking around.

Where is he now?

Amber wondered if he had to leave for an emergency meeting. Checking her phone, there were no messages...apart from a confusing text from her mother who had yet to turn off her autocorrect function. Amber began replying, encouraging her mother to turn off autocorrect and text slower.

Then the floor creaked. The house groaned from the force of a sudden gale. The sunbeams and the warmth they'd brought into the room were replaced by a gray.

Amber swallowed. "Hello?"

The noise picked up and Amber's heart began to pound, then Martin appeared in the doorway holding two steaming cups of coffee.

"Morning." He smiled. "Sorry...took me a while to figure your coffee maker out and I had some e-mails to answer on my phone." He walked towards her. The stubble on his cheeks alongside tousled hair made her forget to scold him for making her think he was Klara or Hans haunting again.

"I couldn't even smell any coffee. My senses are all messed up. I thought you'd gone for a meeting or something."

"No, not today. It's Valentine's, remember?"

"How could I forget?" Amber replied. "Did you sleep okay?"

Martin nodded. "Yep. I like having sleepovers with you."

Blood rushed to her cheeks. Last night was not the first time she had slept in Martin's arms. They hadn't gotten intimate, hadn't crossed the line into passion.

It was the first night she panicked about where she lived. It was the first night she thought of leaving the homestead.

The bed sank with Martin's weight and she heard him set the coffee down on the bedside tables.

He cleared his throat and stretched out beside her, leaning against the headboard.

"I got you something," Amber said. She smiled and got up, retrieving a wrapped canvas from where she'd laid it, alongside the gift basket she picked up. She smiled, walking back into the bedroom where Martin still sprawled on her bed, his eyebrows up.

Amber plopped herself down next to Martin and showed him the wrapped canvas.

Martin unwrapped the flat parcel and then his mouth dropped open. Amber bit her lip, suddenly conscious that he wouldn't like it.

"Wow...it's the art institute in Chicago." Amber had used oil on canvas to beautiful effect. There were two figures at the bottom, walking beside one of the lion statues. The faces weren't detailed, yet it should have been discernable from the smaller blonde and larger dark-haired figure that it was her and Martin, linking arms exiting the Institute. They'd spent a long time on Michigan Avenue on the Saturday they were in Chicago together.

That weekend, Martin caught on that Amber preferred the museums and the aquarium to shopping.

Martin stared at the painting for a while. "That's amazing, Amber. I don't know what to say. You've got the detail of every step. Even all the different shades on the bronze lion. Wow. And that's us...just walking outside."

"Well...I had a wonderful time that day. You were so nice, showing a country girl around. I wasn't sure if you would like it, so I got you a brewery gift basket too. If you don't like the beer, I'll drink it." Amber giggled.

Martin laughed lightly, but couldn't seem to stop staring at her work. His cheeks were turning red. He cleared his throat.

"I'd got you something too. But I forgot to bring it. Obviously..."

Amber interrupted him. "Yeah, I understand. I rushed you over here. Sorry about that."

"Well, I was going to come over here this morning anyway. But thanks for the painting. And the beer. I'll share it with you," he said. "Amber, why don't you come over and stay at my place tonight? I think it's important for you to stick this out, but how about, just for tonight, you stay at my place?"

He reached for her hand and stroked her wrist with his thumb. Amber stared at Martin as he pressed into her skin. She sighed and smiled.

"Are you sure you can afford the time off today?"

One corner of Martin's mouth went up. "I can spend Valentine's Day with my girlfriend. Can't I? I can give you my gift too."

"Sure. I'll help you with your nice beer basket."

"That sounds like a deal." Martin chuckled.

"We need to have a word with the priest too. Remember? What the death records say about Hans and Klara at the church," Amber reminded him.

"Sure. We can stop there on the way to my place."

C8 8O

Snow was high on the ground on the side of the road, but the plows had already been through. Martin knew Amber paid them a bit extra to take care of the gravel road that led up to her driveway.

He imagined the place being buried in snow, if she did decide to stop living there. Who else would buy it? It would finally deteriorate into the prairie.

Martin and Amber stopped along the way to St. Vincent's church to pick up some flowers to place on Klara and Hans's graves.

"A Valentine's Day present for them," Martin said, kneeling to brush some of the snow off their gravestones. He laid the blood red roses on the ground before them.

"I hope she doesn't mind me spending it at your place, having another chaperone-free sleepover," Amber said.

"I will be a gentleman as always. I promise. Even once I get you in my lair." Martin did his best villainous laugh.

Amber laughed. "So...I suppose we are going to have to discuss business eventually. You are getting booked up for work. Will you have time to build a garage for me?"

"Sure. But you don't have to use me...you know," Martin said.

"Yes, I do."

"Okay, yes, you do. I'll kill anyone else who tries to do building work for you," Martin said. He was joking. He wouldn't kill anyone. He would be jealous, though.

I've never been so unreasonable about a woman before. Martin shook his head. Amber had giggled when he said that.

"Don't worry. I've already thought about it and I will use you. I considered selling the place last night. But even if I do, it needs a garage."

"So Klara can haunt someone else?" Martin raised an eyebrow in her direction.

"Not that I think so much of myself, but I don't think she would haunt somebody else," Amber replied, her eyes resting on names inscribed upon the stones.

Martin nodded, remembering how the old woman had appeared to him and not Amber. Pleading with him to encourage her to stay.

"Well...let's see if the priest can dig anything up. Not literally of course." Martin winced.

"Oh please, no."

Martin cleared off a few of the fresh flurries that had fallen onto the graves.

They drove back to the church. There were a couple of cars there, though mass wouldn't begin for a couple of hours.

Amber and Martin walked into the quiet church, engulfed by the familiar musty smell of an old place of worship. All churches over a certain age all had a similar smell. Martin was brought right back to his childhood to one of the few times he'd recalled getting upset with his mother.

He'd been a teenager. They were learning about WWI. His dad was working overtime and his mother wanted to attend Saturday mass. He went along as he wanted to ask her some historical questions while it was just the two of them.

'Mom?'

'*Ja?*' She'd always spoken Schwowische by default, even when he began the conversation with English.

'Do you remember any old people who talked about WWI? They served in the military, right? For Austria-Hungary?'

'No. All I remember is my father being taken. I don't remember much about Ota. He tried to stop them from taking my father. They shot him. After the war, there wasn't much left of us.'

'I know that, Mom. I know all about the starvation camps and how horrible it was. I'm asking about WWI. If you don't know anything or remember anyone talking about it, just say no.'

'The soldiers, they came and they took everything. They called us Fascist Schwobos and told us they would ruin us. They did. But we came here.'

'I understand all that, Mom. You and Dad told me about the camps and the partisans. It's just that we are working on WWI right now. Our family must have been there. I wanted to talk about what service was like for the other side.'

'I wasn't there. I don't know,' she'd said.

'Yeah...but any of the older people?'

'What older people? The ones who were shot or the ones who starved to death? No. They never talked about that.'

'Geez, Mom...I know about the...'

'No, you don't. You don't know. You weren't there. I was.'

Martin bit his lip. He tried asking his father, wondering if his Ota ever talked about his time in the service.

Martin's father, Bastian Handl, had been named after his father, Anton Handl's son, Sebastian Martin Handl.

'Dad...Mom won't answer me about WWI. I just want to know.'

'She won't answer because she won't know. And the partisans took the people who would have known about that time when she was a little girl. Ota never talked about it. I just remember his drawings. He liked to paint and draw. He didn't talk much about being a soldier in WWI.'

Someone tugged at Martin's arm. He shook his head from the cloud of memory and looked at Amber.

She tilted her head and said, "You okay? You look like you got lost."

"Yeah, I'm fine." He smiled.

Footsteps approached and a portly, smiling priest greeted them. "Well, hello. I'm Father Zenf. What can I help you with?"

Amber answered, "My name is Amber Kilzer. This is my friend, Martin Handl. We actually want to see the death records of a couple who are resting out in the Catholic half of Sunnyslope."

"Ah...I see. Well, I can help you with that. Who exactly are you looking for?"

"Hans and Klara Schreiber."

"Ah...Schreiber. Their house is still standing, I believe. The Schreiber homestead," Father Zenf replied.

"I know. I live there," Amber said.

Father Zenf smiled. "Beautiful land around there. They chose well when they came to this country. So, you're the loony who fixed the place up? And who is this gentleman?" The portly priest looked between them.

"He's my b...my b...." Amber's pale face went pink.

Martin raised his brows and looked her way.

"Your boyfriend?" The priest's eyebrows went up above a mischievous grin.

"Not rolling off the tongue, is it? What happened? Did you forget Valentine's Day?" Father Zenf said to Martin and chuckled.

Martin smiled and rubbed Amber's back. "Well...it's a long story."

When he looked at Amber, he saw she had her lips pressed together. "I've never said the name out loud. But yes, he is my boyfriend. It's okay to say that, right?" She looked at Martin.

"Yeah. It's really okay." Martin's cheeks heated when he remembered waking up with her nestled against him. Years of Catholic education and upbringing suddenly rained down on him as he blushed in front of the priest.

"Well...I now pronounce you boyfriend and girlfriend." He laughed, then continued, "Well, step into my office. We do have files from the forties."

They cast one look at the ornate alter where Father Zenf would be delivering mass in a few hours.

Their coats rustled yet their footsteps remained silent as they walked into the room where older records were kept.

"Have a seat. It might take me a few moments to dig up the record," he said. The room was filled with the scent of old paper.

The priest went into another room for a few minutes before returning with a large, old book.

Father Zenf now donned spectacles and delicately turned pages. "Ah!

Here we are..." He scanned the words until finally saying, "Come on and have a look." He gestured for them to come closer.

Martin's heart beat with anticipation. He could hear Amber's unsteady breaths.

Father Zenf spoke again. "This is when their funeral masses were held. There wasn't much time in between their deaths. From what it says here, they had a joint mass arranged by a friend. By a...Missus Lulay."

Martin swallowed. "Lulay?"

"Yes...services arranged by Missus Margaritha Lulay of New England."

Amber asked, "Does it say anything about how they passed?"

Martin glanced at Amber's hands in her lap. She wrung her slim fingers together as though the seconds before Father Zenf answered were a torment.

"I'm afraid not, dear. You'd best head to the library and check out old newspaper articles. There's no mention of survivors or descendants. My grandpa used to talk about Hans Schreiber. He was a good farmer, apparently. My grandparents liked to talk about all the older folks who lived in the area."

Father Zenf shrugged as he put away the old book and said, "Well, sorry I can't be of any help."

"No, that's great, Father. Thank you for your time." Martin shook the priest's hand. Amber did as well and they headed in the direction of the car.

Amber's eyes looked ahead as she nimbly slid into his truck. She was obviously mulling something over.

"So. The library, eh?" Martin said. She looked at him as though waking from a daze.

"Guess so. That might have to wait a couple of days. It will take some time to scroll through weeks of old articles and the different papers. They are closed tomorrow. Plus, I might have to ask my dad about some stuff. I am sure if I jog his memory a little, he will remember more than his grandmother's soups," she said.

"How about a dinner in Dickinson at my place?" Martin said.

"That sounds great," Amber said with a smile as she leaned back in the passenger seat.

Martin glanced at the curve of her neck and sighed.

This being a gentleman thing is a challenge.

"What's wrong?" Amber asked. He realized it was likely a result of his sigh.

"Oh, nothing. I, uh..." He paused and laughed. "Okay, Amber. I'm gonna be honest with you. I was checking you out. You're gorgeous." He cleared his throat and started the engine.

Amber still had her head against the seat, unaware that it was the curve of her throat driving him crazy.

Then she crossed her long legs and Martin swallowed.

Amber said, "It's okay. I'm always checking you out. But we are in front of church right now, so behave and take me to Dickinson." She turned in his direction and winked, a slow smile spreading across her pale face.

"Yes, ma'am." Martin took the truck out of park and they rolled out of the parking lot, heading toward Dickinson. The afternoon light shifted occasionally and sometimes created a blindingly bright, sparkly prairie, like some ethereal realm their eyes could hardly cope with. Other times, it was a stark expanse of blank land topped by an unforgiving gray sky.

"Wouldn't it be useful to make use of a time machine, yet be invisible to anyone there? I wish I could just observe some day to day stuff from over fifty years ago," Amber said, watching the shifting light.

Martin nodded. "Well, I think it would be interesting to see some things. But there is a lot of stuff my family witnessed that I don't think I could deal with seeing..."

Amber's cool, slender hands slipped over his on the steering wheel. "I didn't intend to be insensitive."

"Everyday life, family interaction. Not war time or tragedies or huge events. Just the day in, day out life of our people before social media. But a lot of that is lost. Mom's memories were dominated by the bad stuff. I think my dad was kind of in love with the past. He still remembered it via the eyes of an innocent child."

"Hmm...*In love with the past*. You know, sometimes I think I'm in love with the past, and it's becoming more obvious to me that I don't understand it. It is literally trying to communicate with us and I'm struggling to understand," Amber said.

The engine still hummed and they had hardly seen another vehicle since leaving St. Vincent's. It had been a day of graveyards and nearly empty churches and now a nearly empty highway. It was as though they were the last two people in the world.

Martin reached one hand out and squeezed Amber's knee. "It'll be okay. We found each other, didn't we?"

He caught Amber's smile, her head turned towards him as she replied, "Yeah...yeah, we did."

Chapter 40

1938. Peter's Deception. North Dakota.

Winter's chill still clung to the fields around the Lulay household. Patches of ice-hardened snow clung to the earth like scars. Margaritha's foot dipped into one of their damaged floorboards and she cursed, shaking her head. Her home was clean enough, but the chipping paint and rotting wood distressed her with every glance.

Margaritha stood over the pot of boiling chicken and swallowed. Her mouth kept watering. She'd been doing her best to convince Peter to sell the farm while they still could get a decent price for it. They were in a better position than many, but if Peter insisted they stay much longer, they wouldn't be.

She'd carefully counted every cherry, every cabbage leaf and onion. Over the past ten years, many farmers had to abandon their homesteads after decades of work.

Margaritha sighed, remembering the past year. A calf died. One of the horses broke a leg when stepping into an iced-over creek. Money had been increasingly tight. Josef and Jacob had both abandoned any thoughts of further education in order to work.

Caroline had become engaged to a local boy of Schwob descent this year. The door creaked open and Margaritha turned to her daughter, whose light blonde hair was piled high on her head. The future in-laws were coming over for dinner.

Her only daughter had grown into such a beauty, and Margaritha was happy for Caroline to have found love. The boy's parents were from a different part of the Banat, but she'd recognized their dialect straight away.

Margaritha's memories of any references to the villages outside Bensek were foggy.

"You look beautiful, my dear." Margaritha reached for her daughter.

Caroline hugged her and said, "It smells wonderful, Mother. Can I help?"

Margaritha smiled. "No, dear, it's all ready. Not much for a Sunday dinner, but this is about as good as I can do." The soup was thin, but potatoes and onions had to be used sparingly these days.

"It's fine, Mom." Margaritha noticed her daughter staring longingly into the pot, like she used to do as a child and she'd been playing out all afternoon in the fresh air. "I'm so hungry," Caroline said with a rushed smile as she turned away from the soup.

"I hope they don't think we are being stingy." Margaritha stirred the pot and smiled again.

"No, not at all. Elmer's parents have had a terrible time. He...he is thinking of joining the army." Caroline stumbled on the last words.

"Hmm. Josef mentioned this. Says they will pay for food and that maybe they will be able to send money home," Margaritha commented.

"What do you think about that?" Caroline asked.

Margaritha sighed. "I don't want them to give us money. I think it is honorable to serve your country. But I..." Her mind drifted to memories of Anton in uniform. How he'd left for his duty and she'd feared he would never come back.

She worried for him now. There had been no word from the Banat for nearly twenty years. Her parents were both gone. Her brother had sold the farm and immigrated to Argentina after WWI. The last she'd heard of him was that after surviving the war, Michael had been determined to live a life of excitement.

"Mama?" Caroline touched her gently and Margaritha roused from her daydream. "Are you alright?"

"Oh. Yes. I'm okay. I was thinking of something from a long time ago. Will you go and see what your father and brothers are doing?"

"Sure, Mama. Oh. I forgot. I wanted to get you something." Caroline placed a book on the table.

"Oh, how can you afford this?"

"It is from the library, Mother. It costs nothing. It's poetry in English. I know Papa said he wishes you would speak English more and with less of an accent. I thought you might like this poetry. It's by Elisabeth Akers

Allen."

"Ah..." Margaritha nodded. She hated Peter's constant criticism of her accent. How she hadn't worked hard enough to speak English properly and this perhaps had held them back. She stroked the binding of the book, opened it and noted the smell of the pages.

Margaritha turned to Caroline and said, "Thank you, dear. Maybe when the memories fade of that war with the Germans, I will teach you to speak German properly. You and your brothers picked up too much slang. My mother could speak standard German as well as Schwowische."

Caroline giggled. "Okay, Mama. I will go find the boys and Papa. They are probably tinkering in the barn. If the priest is coming as well as Elmer and his parents, they probably all need to change if they've been doing that."

Caroline kissed her mother and went outside.

Margaritha sighed, looking at her humble kitchen. She wanted to be alone whenever the strange homesickness happened. Her memories of Anton had never faded. She'd forgotten details of the land outside Bensek, of what their Hungarian-speaking school master had tried to impart upon them, but Anton's face and the feel of his arms around her...the memory of that never left.

She wondered if his wife loved him as much as she would have. Margaritha slammed her hand down on the counter so hard that the wooden spoon jumped in response. How could Hans and Klara never write to her?

She'd tried to write to them, but Peter grew so angry with her, he knew just what to say to put her off. She'd heard that despite the Depression, they still had their farm and were reasonably well off. Peter despised Hans, likely out of jealousy.

Margaritha's heart sank as she imagined that her friend might have left her behind after all. Perhaps Peter was trying to protect her from rejection. She'd had no choice but to cling to him in such hard times. It wasn't as though she could go and get her own house. Not when they could barely afford the one they had.

She bit her lip and began to set the table in readiness for company coming. Even the priest would come and give his blessing. It was supposed to be a happy time for the family.

Yet Margaritha couldn't rid her chest of the pangs of loneliness. She cursed herself for being a disloyal woman. How she longed for the company of her parents, of Hans, Klara, and God forgive her, Anton.

She opened the book and scanned the words, the smell of its pages bringing back memories from her school days.

She began reading the English words out loud. "Backward turn backward oh time in your flight. Make me a child again. Just once more tonight..."

"Ja, dat's true," she said aloud in English, sniffling while setting the table.

ℭ ℨ

Caroline clutched her wrap tightly around her shoulders. It was April already, but the cold was so bitter, it froze the inside of her nose.

Her boots barely sank into the swaths of frozen snow clinging to the ground.

She could hear her brother, Josef, saying something to her father.

"Dad, we want to join. There is trouble over there with this Hitler fellow. He's crazy. He's poisoning minds."

"Joe, I need you *and* your brother here. I'm not getting any younger. What will your mother do?"

"If you hadn't burned so many bridges being stubborn with folks, you would be able to get a bit more help, but you've been hardheaded and stingy."

"What do you know? Hah!" Caroline heard her father shout back.

"Dad? I think Mom has a right to read these. I can mostly understand 'em, you know," Jacob commented.

She shivered and stood still before the barn. *Read what?*

Her father's angry voice made Caroline jump.

"People shouldn't be writing German letters to her! That Hans and Klara Schreiber, they probably agree with that Hitler guy. I read them. I know..." He started to cough and splutter, then continued, "I know...it's for her own good she doesn't read these. That Hans Schreiber will ruin us."

"Dad, stuff like that was pretty bad down in Nebraska, but up here, there's still so many German folks. None of them were on the Kaiser's side back in the war. Look at Elmer, the army sees *his* language ability to be an asset," Josef said.

Caroline couldn't take it any longer. She knocked on the door and stepped in. Her father and two brothers looked to her with wide eyes, as though they'd been caught breaking something.

Caroline took a deep breath and said, "Read what? Are you hiding something from Mama?"

"The Schreibers have been writing to her. You know, the couple in Hettinger who Mom and Dad know from the Old Country. Dad has been keeping the letters."

Meanwhile, her father was continuing to cough, holding one hand over his mouth. His face was red with the effort of suppressing one of his fits.

Her father looked at her and said, "I have good reason. The Schreibers are not to be trusted. They were a bad influence on your mother, and you shouldn't let her read them. Ever!"

Caroline nodded, but said calmly, "Mom misses the Old Country. It's been a long time since whatever happened. Why won't you let her visit with old friends?"

"That woman, Klara? She practices witchcraft. You don't know! She would bring God's wrath to us."

"Oh, Dad, come on..."

"You will never show her those letters. Never! Even after I die! They will only hurt her. You want your mother to suffer? Then show her the letters. The one time we saw them, at the Kirchweih, Klara made your mother faint, she was so upset."

Caroline could remember her mother turning poorly at a community event once, but little else.

"Why didn't you just destroy them, Dad? If you thought they would upset Mama? Did you think you might see some secret in there as to why the Schreibers were so successful?"

Her father went purple, holding his breath for a few moments. Caroline thought he might strike her, he looked so angry.

Her father exhaled and continued his rant, "I was going to! I kept them as proof of...as I feared Hans Schreiber had unpatriotic sympathies! He was always strange, I never trusted him. You promise me. Promise your father you won't show her those letters. I can't handle her being upset now. She will be heartbroken. Right before we prepare for your marriage? And your brothers enlist in the army? You...You two..." He gestured to her brothers. "You will go away in the service and leave me and your mother all upset? Over some old letters? If they want to come here, I won't stop them. But they never have. Shows how much they care! Now, they think they are better than us. It's been hard enough these past years. Bah, I should have just destroyed them. I forgot all about them. Then Josef found them." He waved his hand in fatigued disgust.

Caroline pitied her father. She understood he somehow felt aggrieved by her mother, yet she never understood why. Mama was a good cook and had looked after them. She certainly hadn't had time to be disloyal to their family in any way.

What did happen? she wondered.

Then they heard voices outside the barn. Her mother was calling. Elmer and his parents and the priest had arrived for supper.

Caroline couldn't wait to marry Elmer. Even if she dreaded him going a way to be in the military, she loved his sense of loyalty to the country their parents had brought them to. He was classed as a hero already, with his ability to translate German being a valuable asset.

"Right. I came in to tell you all to come in anyway," Caroline said.

Her father nodded and walked out ahead of them. He muttered the words, yet pronounced them clearly enough, offering a Schwowische warning. "I don't want to hear talk of these letters. Ever."

Caroline and her brothers followed their father out of the barn and back towards the house.

Chapter 41

2018. The Wurst Shop in Dickinson. North Dakota.

Amber and Martin stopped at a shop and restaurant in Dickinson called The Wurst Shop and German Kitchen.

It was packed with early Valentine's Day diners, and decorated with hearts and Happy Valentine's Day banners.

"Wow...this place is busy," Amber commented as they negotiated the line for ordering.

"Yep. I come here for breakfast or lunch sometimes. Tonight, I thought we'd grab some steaks to cook at my place."

"Mister Handl! How are you, sir?" A man wearing a chef's hat and a huge grin stood behind the counter.

"How's it going? I thought I'd come in here 'cause you guys needed business. I guess not." Martin gestured at all the customers.

The man chuckled and said, "Always happy to see you, but we are pretty full of lovebirds today. Who is this you have here?"

Amber smiled and jumped a bit as she felt Martin's arm reach around her shoulders and pull her close. Martin said, "This is Amber."

"Didn't know you had a girlfriend."

"Yep. We're after some steaks to cook at home."

The man's eyebrow raised and he nodded. "Sure."

They got their meat alongside some takeout side dishes.

They stepped out of the brick building, and Amber shivered from the rush of cold after being in a heated restaurant packed with bodies and hot food.

The skies ahead were gray as they pulled up into Martin's house. Amber looked at the dark blue paint on the wooden, Victorian house.

"This is an old neighborhood, huh? Lots of Victorian stuff."

"Yeah. This place has had a couple of makeovers. I did most of the work here around two years ago. It's not a bad neighborhood."

"You've done a great job. Just from the outside, it looks good. Do you have servants?"

Martin chuckled. "I can assure you that in 'Victorian' or even 'Hapsburg' times where our families were, my ancestors did not have servants. The Hapsburgs sure did, but not the Handls."

They approached his front door and Martin unlocked it, holding it open for her.

She could smell varnished wood and new carpet.

There were cream-colored couches and dark wooden tables.

"You have good taste. May I use your bathroom?"

"Sure, I'll start getting our food ready."

"Sounds good. I'll help, only be a second," Amber replied.

Amber took off her boots and padded along the carpet towards the bathroom. She looked to the side and noticed the paintings along the wall. At first, she wondered if the land and cityscape oil on canvas were paint by numbers pieces of décor. But she noted the detail. Martin had done all of them.

He'd painted scenery of Illinois forest preserves, gardens, Wisconsin lakes and sunsets. Amber thought they were the kind of look that would have stood out to an art patron in Europe in the late nineteenth century. Martin had a flair for color and detail.

Even as she pulled and turned the crystal effect bathroom tap to wash her hands, she could see the work in her mind and could hardly wait to look again.

He'd signed each piece with a tiny signature, "Handl." She went to find Martin, excited at having seen his work.

She walked past the wooden staircase and handrail. She could hear plates, knives and forks being shuffled.

Amber was still smiling when she walked into the kitchen. Martin was rubbing salt and pepper on the fillet steaks and he looked up at her.

"I love your work," she said, unable to keep the smile from her face as she approached him.

A reddish hue spread across his face and he looked down. "Yeah, I, um...used to paint a lot. I haven't been doing a lot over the last couple of years...At one point, I wanted to be an artist. Dad was actually okay with it, but Mom insisted I go to school and learn a trade too. She always liked my work, though. Want a beer?"

"Yeah, please," Amber said and looked to the small breakfast table by the window. There, hung on a dark blue wall, was a framed photo of three people.

"Who is this?" Amber asked as she stepped closer, skirting around the breakfast nook.

A younger, still handsome, more mischievous Martin in a cap and gown smiled at the camera. A tall, slim man with salt and pepper hair stood on one side of Martin while a smaller woman with pulled up, coifed hair and a shy smile clung to his other arm.

"Your dad looks like he is tearing up. Must have been an emotional day."

"It was."

Amber jumped, not realizing that Martin had come up beside her. She turned and Martin held two open beers. She grasped the bottle from his hands and their fingers lingered as they brushed up against one another. They both took a sip, maintaining eye contact.

Martin was the first to look away and back to the picture.

"I was the first person in our family to go to college. Dad wanted to go, he did really well in school and everything, but he never got around to going to college. Mom put all her energy into raising me. She worked helping Dad manage the properties, she was pretty into church, and keeping the house spotless. She worked as a cleaner until she was in her late fifties. Then Dad had done so well, we were doing alright. She always missed living in the country. That's one thing she liked to remember about Europe, the fields and stuff before she knew anything bad was happening. I did some of the paintings in the hall for her. She always loved landscapes. Dad could paint too."

Amber nodded. "They look like really nice people."

"Yeah...they were." Martin sighed as he looked at the photo, then he turned back to her.

"I'll help with the side dishes. I'm good at warming things up." She grinned.

"Well, these should be seasonal earring free." Martin winked.

Amber giggled and said, "Cheers."

"Cheers," Martin replied and they clinked bottles.

Amber watched Martin's Adam's apple bob up and down as he swallowed.

Her eyes went up to his face. "You have a beautiful home, by the way. I'm impressed."

"Thanks. It's a little too big for me. Actually, when I saw that the Schreiber place had been taken, I chose another route and bought this place as an investment. I am going to sell it when the time is right."

"What if nobody buys it?" Amber asked.

"That's a chance I will have to take, but I've got faith. More folks will come to live out here, and when you think of what a place like this would cost in, say, Chicago...it's crazy. This would be a good option for a family. And if nobody buys it...I guess it will turn into a beautiful ruin." He shrugged.

One corner of Amber's mouth turned up, but her heart sank a little. "That's sad...when places become ruins or ghost towns. I know people are fascinated by that kind of thing, but it's tragic."

Martin set his beer bottle down on the counter in front of her and placed a hand on her shoulder blade. "Hey, I didn't mean to bring on the darkness or anything."

"Oh..." Amber forced a laugh. "It's just that it's hard not to feel that way as you get older. Like when we were young, things seemed better. And looking at the world, lots of people think that way back in the day, things were better. Not that they necessarily were. It's just rose-tinted glasses. With our relationship...it's all new yet we find a connection via abandoned houses, death records, and graveyards."

"I know how you feel...but the present and the future isn't all bad. Is it?"

Amber turned to face Martin directly and his hand moved to her upper arm. Amber glanced down at his hand and then back towards him.

She reached both her hands out to cup his face and leaned in to kiss him. She'd barely given Martin a moment to protest. His lips were cold and wet from a recent sip on the chilled beer bottle. When he wrapped his hands around her waist and pulled her tightly against him, she understood he didn't find her advance invasive.

Amber had never been this way with boyfriends in the past. Then again, she'd never felt this intensely.

"Oh, God, Amber…" he said against her in between kisses. His stubble scratched her face and she wrapped her arms around his neck.

They sank to the floor of the kitchen, the room filling with the sounds of their kisses. Martin's breath was becoming heavier. Amber leaned back into the hard floor, euphoric with pleasure as Martin's weight pressed her body down, his scent and the sensation of his mouth and hands engulfing her.

"Martin…Martin…"

Then he suddenly pulled up, looking down at her with brown eyes glazed and darkened by lust. He said, "We…we should move…This isn't…"

Amber knew he was going to insist they move to the bedroom.

"Amber…we should…we should move. I've wanted to…" Then he fell upon her again with a passionate kiss on the side of her neck.

Amber pressed and arched against him, giving him more access. "I don't care…Here, Martin…let's be together here."

Martin only groaned in response.

Then, Amber's phone rang. Fearing that she might answer it accidently due to the maneuvering happening against her pocket, she moved her phone and set it as far away as she could.

Martin's eyes followed her movements, hungrily. Then, his darkly excited expression shifted and he grit his teeth and winced. "What?" Amber asked, wide-eyed.

"It's your dad," Martin replied.

"Oh, geez…He never calls." Amber winced and Martin moved off her as the phone continued to buzz.

She answered after clearing her throat. "Hi, Dad."

"Hi, honey…I, um…I got your message about my grandma arranging the Schreibers' funeral. Well, you know how my mom's state of mind wasn't all that good at the end. She obviously gave those letters to your mother not long before she died, when she got confused…" Her father stopped talking and cleared his throat. "I, uh…I always liked my grandma. But I didn't know that she had much of a past or anything. She made… *awesome* soups."

"I know, Dad," Amber said as Martin propped himself up beside her on the kitchen island.

"Your Grandma Caroline was a lovely woman. She didn't have much, and you know…she'd lost my dad, Elmer, in the war."

"Oh...of course. I...had forgotten about that." Amber blushed. She hadn't thought *that* much about her immediate family history. She'd been thinking so much about Hans and Klara.

"Yeah. I don't make a fuss. My stepdad was okay, but Mom never quite got over Elmer. He was a good guy, I guess. War hero and all that. I think he did secret stuff because he could speak German. He flew several missions over Germany. She got his body back. It was right at the end of the war. The family liked to think that he was responsible for bringing down Hitler."

"Wow. Well, thanks for that, Dad. I knew that, but...I've been distracted. Martin and I were actually going to check something out at the library to see if we could figure out how Hans and Klara passed away."

"Yeah, I just couldn't remember my mom mentioning them. She talked about my Grandma Margaritha a lot, she loved her dearly. I never heard much about Grandpa Peter. He died before I was born. He was a lot older. Anyway...when you get a chance, I can show you stuff about Elmer Kilzer."

"Thanks, Dad. I'll probably be in Mott the day after tomorrow."

"Oh. Where are you now?"

"With Martin." Blood rushed to Amber's cheeks.

You are nearly forty, for goodness sake.

Her dad cleared his throat. "Oh. That's nice, I guess. I'm cooking your mother dinner."

Amber widened her eyes, then pressed her lips together. "Wow. I'm impressed, Dad."

"I wanted to try. She is usually the cook. Gotta do something."

Amber heard her mother in the background. "He's making pork chops! Can you believe it?" And she heard her mother's giggle, which Amber recognized as the one she'd hear as a child after she'd gone to bed and her parents were celebrating an anniversary or birthday.

"Dad? Have you given Mom spumante?" Amber said.

"She likes spumante. It's Valentine's," he said, almost deadpan as if she couldn't hear the smirk in her father's voice.

Amber looked at the clock in Martin's kitchen. It was almost six. She sighed.

"Okay. Well, you two have a nice Valentine's Day." She wanted to end the conversation.

"You too, honey. I just...I knew there was something I wanted to tell you. In case you forgot about Elmer."

"Yeah. I remember Elmer, Dad. You wanted to tell me before you and Mom got too tipsy? Well, don't start any fires in the kitchen." Amber cringed, thinking of her parents acting like college students and the passionate moment she had just shared with Martin. The mental images made her a little squeamish.

"We won't. Bye, honey."

"Bye, Dad."

Amber hung up, put her phone down, and placed a hand over her face. "Oh, geez."

"What is it?" Martin asked.

Amber enlightened him on the conversation with her dad. Martin leaned back while listening.

When he had gotten the gist of everything, Martin said, "I guess that's our bucket of ice water for the evening. Wow. I would have thought the Valentine's Day spirit would have left us to it."

"Martin...it's a holiday for chocolate companies and florists," Amber replied snarkily.

"And good butchers...and liquor stores," Martin threw in and Amber laughed.

He helped her off the floor. Amber was still going through everything in her mind. "I knew my real grandpa died in the war. Grandma remarried a few years later and he was a decent enough guy, he passed away ages ago."

"So, he flew a plane over Germany? Elmer?" Martin asked.

"Yeah. His parents were Schwobs, I think. He could decipher some of the Germans' codes."

"Hmm. It's odd to think our recent ancestors would have been enemies."

"I'm sure your grandfather wasn't happy about being forced to fight for Germany once they invaded Yugoslavia due to his 'ethnic status'," Amber replied.

Martin nodded. "I'm really not sure how my mom's dad felt about fighting against the Russians as an ethnic German yet still Yugoslav citizen. I'm not totally sure what happened to my dad's dad, Sebastian. It was kind of strange, because Romania switched sides right at the end. But he never made it to America. He was born right at the beginning of WWI. My dad really was more bothered about his grandpa, my Great Grandpa Anton. I think Anton spent more time with him in Romania."

"Anton..." Amber said, lost in thought. "I mean, it's nice that my dad remembered his real dad, but...it doesn't shed much light on how Great Grandmother Margaritha came to arrange Hans and Klara's funeral."

"Yeah..." Martin said.

"So, where were we?"

"I was about to make love to you on my kitchen floor," Martin said with a sigh.

Amber blushed and said, "I was heartily in favor of that. Then my Dad called. Who is currently in the process of wooing my mother with spumante and likely overdone pork chops."

Martin laughed. "In a way, I'm glad we got interrupted."

"Really?" Amber turned to him with one eyebrow lifted.

"Yeah...Amber?"

"Yes?"

"When we do make love for the first time, I would like to take you to bed. I want it to be...premeditated, not a moment of madness. You are here as my guest and my date. I want to be ready. I like...literally want to spend the whole evening together, both of us knowing and understanding that we will end it in each other's arms. Not hiding from a ghost or talking about our family's history. Just you and me. I feel like that will be part of the beauty of finding each other at this point in our lives. Yes, we are free and we are adults, but...we know each other and ourselves and can work together to get the most out of being together. Neither of us are virgins but...I've thought about you a lot and I want it to be special."

Martin's cheeks turned red.

Amber's stomach fluttered with an anticipation that wasn't edgy and restless. It was pleasurable in itself. "You do seem to have thought about this a lot."

"I have. And right now, I can tell you that college me would be horrified."

"I think he might be impressed, actually. Give the younger you a little credit. I'll look forward to our moment, Martin. Right now, I'm so..."

"Hungry?" he finished her sentence.

"Very," she replied.

"Let's get dinner ready. I've got to give you my present afterward."

Amber grinned. "I'm excited about this. I didn't expect you to get me anything."

They enjoyed the steak with the warm potato salad and cold cucumber salad they'd picked up from the German Kitchen in Dickinson.

After eating, they settled onto Martin's couch with a final glass of wine. Amber never thought of herself as the type to be part of a couple. She had laid her head down in Martin's lap. Martin stroked her hair absently and her eyes grew heavy as he traced the texture of her curls with his fingers.

It was sensual and soothing at the same time. She could imagine what intimacy with him would be like.

True fulfilment won't happen in such a rush...

"Amber?"

Martin's low voice lulled her out of her dose and she turned from her side to face him, her head still in his lap as he looked down at her for a few moments before speaking again.

"Do you want your present now?"

"Is it a pillow and blanket?" she responded sleepily and he grinned at her.

"Come here..."

Amber sat up and Martin took her hand. He led her up the stairs to his study/home office.

She looked around the dark wooden floors at the desk. Against the wall was a dark green couch.

"That folds into a bed, by the way. I will make it up for you."

"That's my present?" She had turned from him, looking disappointedly at what would be her bed for the night.

"No, this is..." Martin said behind her. She turned and her jaw dropped. "You've...You've drawn...me?"

And it was a portrait of her in her own home office, at her desk. She was wearing her glasses, looking at the viewer as though interrupted yet not displeased. It was the way she would look at Martin. He had every detail of the room down—her bookshelf, the texture of her curtains, the blanket on the futon, and the mess that was her work space.

"It's like you've got every nook and cranny memorized. Even the rug on the floor....my canvas and easel. Even the details just outside the window... in the distance. It's like the painting is alive. And that's me. You could do cover design work, you know."

"Geez, thanks," Martin said quietly.

"You did a portrait of me...That is...so cool. And it's flattering. Makes me look industrious and attractive." She let out an unladylike laugh, covering her mouth. She was flattered, yet slightly embarrassed and overwhelmed. The *detail* on her face and of her work space. The things she saw every day. It was *almost* unnerving. She'd feared that her painting had been too intimate...but she'd mainly focused on the art institute and had drawn a couple that could be viewed as them but not close up.

"You *are* industrious and attractive. I just...wanted to show you that I...think about you a lot. And you are completely burned into my head," Martin replied.

Amber opened her mouth, yet couldn't think of what to say. She was about to say 'thank you' when Martin's mouth was on hers. His hand slipped beneath her sweater, caressing the skin of her bare back.

She clutched at his shoulders, slightly shocked yet not entirely displeased by the sensation of his hands on her flesh. "Martin..." Her voice was unsteady, and she felt suddenly nervous.

He stepped back, flushed. "Okay. Let's get you ready for bed."

"Right...pre-meditated." Amber was breathless.

"Yep. Planned and executed."

"Well now, you aren't gonna kill me, are you?" Amber said, unable to keep the nerves from her voice.

"No, Amber..." Martin laughed and blushed. "I guess that was a stupid thing to say."

"No. I think a bit of anticipation and planning could be fun. I'm with you on this."

"Good, I hope so. I'm tired of being alone on this one."

Amber giggled and said, "You are definitely not alone."

Amber tried to help Martin make the bed, but he insisted on preparing it for her.

When it was ready, Martin leaned in and kissed her on the cheek before backing away quickly. "Goodnight, Amber. Happy Valentine's Day, and thank you for my present."

"Happy Valentine's Day to you, Martin. Thanks for having me over, for the steak, and for the painting. You've made me very happy."

"You're welcome." Martin smiled shyly and nodded before hesitating, then slipping behind the door to go to his own room.

Amber sunk onto the mattress, remembering how she'd debated with herself whether to include her and Martin as a couple on her gift painting to him. She knew that on her piece, they were hardly recognizable. But she'd been so relieved when Martin saw the pair outside as them.

His words echoed in her mind...

I like...literally want to spend the whole evening with you, both of us knowing that we will end it in each other's arms.

She recalled his fingers in her hair and soon drifted off.

Chapter 42

1938. Fascism and a Baby. Mercydorf.

Anton sat in the Wirtshaus with Marcus and Sebastian. Sebastian's wife, Magdalena, was busy bringing Anton's first grandson into the world. Marcus's wife Eva and her newborn child passed away three years ago and Marcus still was not over the loss. Hence, the coming birth of another child was seen with trepidation.

Marcus was now part of the Romanian military and was home on leave. He placed his hand on his worried younger brother's shoulder. "Don't worry, Sebastian. She is a strong girl, she will pull through. Eva, God rest her soul, had always had a weak constitution."

Anton smiled, took a sip of his wine, and said, "Yes, don't worry, son. Your mother did just fine bringing you two into the world, so never fear."

Sebastian nodded, though his face was white.

Marcus looked to his father and said, "So? How are you finding Mercydorf, Father? Do you miss Temeswar? I have been away so often, I… haven't asked you."

Anton knew his adopted son was only trying to combat the tension in the room. He did his best to respond.

"Mercydorf is a pretty village. Since the death of your grandparents here, we have worked hard and made something of your mother's family properties. She never told me of course that her parents were one of the better off. I…never wanted to be a farmer. I wanted to be an artist or a builder. Being in the Banat amongst lots of other Schwobs has been a good thing, but I do miss all the different cultures in Temeswar. I…miss the Kovacses. I haven't heard from Mister Kovacs for some time."

"Ah yes," Marcus responded. "They were kind to my mother, when her parents cast her out to teach her a lesson. Still, it's better you are not working for Jews anymore. That kind of thing is frowned upon. It will be better for our status as a family."

Anton frowned. He was used to this kind of talk, but lately, it had become more extreme. Anton had his suspicions that the Kovacs family had emigrated. Many Jews he knew spoke of going to France or America, where the climate was less hostile.

Sebastian stared at his wine. "I think...yes...it's better. Soon things will be much better for the Schwobs. Things are really looking up in Germany. The economy is improving everywhere. For my child...things will be better living as a German in Romania."

Anton's eyebrows lifted. "Well, that's not really what I mean, of course. I am sad that I don't hear from Kovacses. And I am sad if he has had to flee. He even put in a good word with other merchants for some of our products..."

"Oh, Father, please!" Sebastian sat back and said with a tone that bordered on disgust. Anton's brows knitted together when he realized that Sebastian had now drained his third cup of wine.

"Sebastian, come now. Are you drunk already?" Anton asked with disappointment.

"He always was a lightweight." Marcus chuckled and slapped him on the back.

"No, no. I mean...Father, you are too humble. Think about it. We, as Germans, came here and made these successful villages. We transformed what was a Turk and Slav ridden wasteland into the breadbasket of Europe. Look at the Transylvania Saxons and how successful they have been. For years, the other groups have been jealous of us and our productivity. Hitler...he appreciates this. He sees us. He will see that *my* child will get the way forward it deserves. Not working for some Jew like you had to, when you and Walter Onkel were obviously more skilled and intelligent and deserved better."

Anton's stomach churned. This was what he had been hearing too much of lately, yet it shocked and horrified him to hear the words coming out of his own son's mouth. After years of a difficult adolescence with Marcus who mourned the father who abandoned him, Sebastian had been a quiet and obedient child. Yet watchful. Anton always assumed this was a due to a quiet intelligence. Now he saw how his son yearned for recognition and status.

"Don't look so surprised, Father. You've always been of such a liberal mind and far too tolerant for your own good."

Anton's heart pounded. From the last the women had told him, Magdalena was doing well with the birth, but it would be a few more hours. This *should* have been a happy occasion. But for Anton, he could hardly find the will to speak. He didn't want *those* words to be coming from his own son's mouth.

"You...you believe that madman? That Hitler?" He could barely keep control of his own voice.

Sebastian nodded, his eyebrows high. "Yes, I do. He has made great changes in Germany. He has made things better for the German people. After *you* lost the war, lost the empire and became a slave to the Jews, Hitler wants Germans to rise. He saw what was wrong. We, Schwobs in the Banat, in Poland and in the Balkans, have long been underappreciated. Things will be better for my son."

Anton shook his head. "These are not the words of my flesh and blood. Your wife is in agony right now, and you are thinking of how superior you are because of your ethnicity. We have always been proud of success, but not like this...not with thoughts like that..."

Sebastian said, "Well, I am not a boy, Father. I have been a man for a while now. You've been too busy slaving away like a fool to the Jew or blubbering in your sleep to notice."

Marcus said, "Sebastian, that is enough! I know I've had words with Father in the past, but this is too much. This isn't like you. We might be of German ancestry, but we are Romanians."

"Bah!" Sebastian said. "Romania. Hungary. Yugoslavia. Whatever. In my heart, I am a German. We speak it at home. It is the language my son will speak..."

"I am horrified." Anton finally said his feelings out loud. Sebastian looked at his father as though he thought he had been jesting before when he expressed his discontent. Sebastian's face altered itself into an expression that Anton hardly recognized.

Marcus said, "Be careful, Sebastian..."

"I will be. I will see that my family has a secure future. Magdalena's relatives are poor as anything in America. There, the liberals, socialists, and Jewish capitalists rule everything. Hardworking, decent Germans don't stand a chance. If the Fuhrer calls me to fight for his vision, I will."

A knock on the window made all three men turn. It was Sophie. Her beaming face was a stark contrast to the mood on the other side of the glass. She didn't appear to notice.

She gestured for them to come back to the house.

Anton watched his wife look back at the men in her life. She said, "You should be proud of your Magdalena. She has done so well. I didn't expect your son to arrive so quickly."

"A son? Congratulations! I am an uncle! You are a grandfather! Come... let's forget any unpleasantness here..." Marcus put his arm around his younger brother.

Anton caught Sophie looking at him. The two brothers walked ahead of their parents, and Sophie fell back beside Anton. "What is it?"

Anton, pleased as he was about the arrival of a child in their family, was still very disturbed by his son's feelings. "Sebastian embraces Fascism. He likes that Hitler character's views..."

"Oh, lots of people feel like that. Don't worry, Anton. If war will come, it will come and go. Just like the other one. Marcus does well in the Romanian military, we have a successful farm, and your nightmares are much better, aren't they? From all the fresh air?"

Much as Anton had grown to care for and appreciate his wife, she did have a way of dismissing the most serious of issues. When he found her crying on her own, lost over the memory of being whisked away by a handsome nobleman only to be forgotten about the next day, she said, "Well...Anton...it's good we have one another. And we have our boys. We will be fine..."

Anton said, "Yes. This is a beautiful village. We are lucky." Yet disgust over Sebastian's words remained in his stomach.

They eventually came to the now Handl family home to find a healthy baby boy in the arms of Magdalena, who appeared well as the midwife fussed around her.

"So, Sebastian? What will you call your son?" Anton asked.

"I think he will be called Sebastian, like me. But we will call him Bastian so we don't get confused. Bastian Anton Handl."

Anton looked down at the latest addition to the Handl family, snoozing in his mother's arms.

It was true that right now, this child was born into more prosperous situation than his father. However, Anton did not care for the ideology that seemed to circle their village like a poisonous mist. Lurking like the toxic gases he'd managed to avoid during his time as a soldier in the Great War. But he'd witnessed the effects of such gases. Poor men who had been burned from the inside. Vile, painful deaths.

Live by the sword. Die by the sword.

Anton vowed to protect this child from the mist that, even now, sought to destroy his family.

Chapter 43

1944. Elmer. North Dakota.

Margaritha was happier these days, living in the town of New England rather than being alone on the prairie. A couple of years ago, they had to give up the pretense of being able to keep the farm going. Peter's health, however, went from bad to worse once they got settled in their small house in town.

She'd heard from the boys, Josef and Jacob, and thanked Heaven that they seemed well and that they had survived the war thus far.

Knock, knock, knock.

It was Caroline and the children, along with the town doctor, an elderly Irishman who came to make sure Peter was comfortable.

Caroline and Margaritha chatted with one another while the small children napped.

"Mama?"

"Yes, dear."

"Elmer and I might move to Mott, when he comes home. There is a house there he has his eye on. There is a shop that I could get work in too. You could come and stay with us."

"That sounds good, my dear," Margaritha replied.

The doctor emerged and said, "Dear lady, I know you are Catholics. I think soon it will be time for the priest. There is little else I can do for him apart from keep him comfortable until the Lord calls him. I'm sorry."

Margaritha looked up into the kindly old gentleman's twinkling green eyes and nodded. She touched his hand. "Thank you, Doctor. You have been good to come to us and ease my husband's passing. Please let me know if there is anything I can do for you. Can I get you some coffee?"

"No, ma'am. I'll step outside. I think he wants to speak to you alone, Caroline. You being the eldest child. Give him a minute or so to come 'round."

"Yes, Doctor," Margaritha replied as the man went to smoke his pipe on the porch. It was ironic that Peter fell victim to cancer of the lungs. He had rarely smoked. The Irish doctor's pipe smoke wafted in through the screen door.

The fragrance of the smoke reminded her of the Old World. She was sure Anton's father smoked a pipe, as did her father and grandfather when she was a girl.

One corner of her mouth turned up when she looked up to find her daughter looking at her.

"Mother? Do you think you will join us in Mott? It's not so far. You won't have much reason to stay here. Mother? You seem distracted," Caroline said.

"Oh...that smell reminded me of the Old World. Of people I haven't seen for decades." Margaritha sighed. She wanted to change the subject and said, "I will be happy when this war is over and your brothers and husband are back. I will be happy when your father's suffering is done. This has been a very drawn out illness. I don't think he deserved *this*."

Caroline's head was tilted as she continued to look at her mother, as though some suspicion plagued her mind. "The doctor seems a very nice man," Caroline finally whispered to her mother, who widened her eyes at what her daughter could be suggesting.

"He is. He has been very good to us as since we came to this house and your father became sick. It is lucky we moved to town when we did. Yet if you are both going to Mott, then perhaps it is best I go. Even if it is all the way in Hettinger."

Then Margaritha's mind stopped. *Hettinger is where Klara and Hans are!*

"Caroline..." They both turned to the sound of Peter's weak voice. Margaritha felt a pang of guilt, thinking of her old friends whom her husband had long since forbidden her to see. She'd never grown to love Peter in the way she knew a wife should love a husband, but she'd remained loyal and had catered to him as best as she could.

"Caroline..."

ℭℨ   ℬℴ

Caroline walked into the bedroom to find her father. "Daughter..." he said feebly.

Caroline sat in the chair beside the bed and leaned close to her father.

"I am sorry...I don't leave your brothers a rich farm. You must tell them this, if they come back alive. And I must ask something else of you. The letters. Do you have still have them?"

"I..."

"Destroy them. Never show them to your mother. She will hate me. I cannot bear it upon my soul if she would hate me so. She would only suffer from seeing them. I wanted to protect her. Please promise me. And do your best to be a good and obedient wife. Don't associate with anyone your husband does not approve of. Try and improve your cooking, but don't eat too much. You are a pretty woman still."

"Yes, Father. And don't worry, I will look after Mama." She pressed her lips tightly together after speaking.

"Yes, yes. She will be fine, but don't show her the letters. She will only be sad. Even after so many years, that Schreiber woman tried to hold onto your mother's affections. She would have stolen her from me."

"Rest now, Father."

"Tell your mother to get the priest soon. The doctor is right. I won't be here much longer."

"Yes, Father. I will give Elmer your best when he comes back."

At this, her father barely responded. She'd hoped he would acknowledge her worry for her husband and brother's safety. She'd hoped he would be more troubled over her mother's well-being once he was gone. Though it hurt to see her father so ill and vulnerable, it grated on her to have him far more concerned with how his reputation would fare when he passed.

Caroline kissed her father's cold, clammy forehead. She arranged the vase of flowers beside him, took one last look, and exited the room.

She could hear two men talking. The mailman and the doctor. The baby was just starting to stir.

Margaritha stood at the door. She turned to her daughter and came towards her with open arms.

"I am sorry. I am so, so sorry, my dear."

Caroline felt her knees give way. Elmer had been confirmed as dead. Her mother soothed her and kissed her forehead, then the children began to fuss. Margaritha and the doctor helped to get Caroline to the other bed.

Tears stung her eyes yet didn't fall. Her body was useless as she stared out at the open prairie, just out the window.

This can't be happening.

She knew mothers and wives who lost men in the war, yet Elmer had survived for so long. She had been so proud of him. He'd been so handsome in his uniform. The thought of him ruined, broken beyond repair, was not something she could accept. She stared out at the window.

The glass seemed to crack from the force of the wind. Even in town, the wind was brutal in its assault on any manmade structures.

Caroline stared at the white blanket. Now, she was trapped in an icy cocoon, stunned and distant.

Until her mother's hands were on the side of her face. "You have to stay strong for your children. Elmer would want you to. He was a good man. Don't go away...out *there*." Her mother gestured to the expanse outside, which seemed more desolate now than it ever did on their farm in the country. "You can mourn, but you must stay *here. There* will come for you soon enough."

"Yes...yes, Mama," was all Caroline could say before sobbing in her mother's arms.

Chapter 44

2018. The Library. North Dakota.

It was getting to that time of year, mid-March, when everyone started making jokes about forgetting what summer looked like. When the thought of stepping outside in shorts and flip flops in the same location was so absurd, the only thing one could do was jest.

It was another icy week and Martin drove to Amber's place. In the end, they imagined that the library in Mott might have more of the local area newspaper articles they wanted to find. Plus, they were going to have a visit with Amber's parents.

He was about ten minutes away from Amber's place as the song *Nice and Easy Does It* played on the radio. He had kept to his own promise of not rushing their physical relationship, and savoring what they were becoming. He admitted to himself that their bond was becoming entwined, and wasn't just a passing infatuation.

He'd pursued relationships based on immediate personal attractions before and they ultimately led to disappointment. Not in the women themselves, though in recent years, he did have those who were after his money. Yet most of the time, it was in the lack of any depth to their relationship.

After initial lusts were satisfied, there was always the inevitable dulling. The realization that they did 'couple things' after refusing to stick with one-night stands. The 'couple things' moved from exciting and novel to obligatory frustrating compromises.

The fitting into society types of actions. The 'this is the path society expects a young couple to take' types of actions. Don't be too old-fashioned, but don't shun tradition either. Honor your parents...but be cool too.

These days with social media, everyone had a public profile. Not that Martin wanted to go back to 'the good ole days,' but...he wasn't sure about the direction the world was taking either.

Those consistent experiences, alongside his father's last wishes, alongside a business decision to get out of a highly expensive area and make his own way in a less populated, less expensive area, all pushed him to North Dakota.

Those things ultimately pushed him towards Amber, who he saw for the first time in a church. Neither of them subscribed to every ideological aspect associated with the institutionalized religion they'd been raised with. In the past few months, he'd realized that both he and Amber were independent thinkers. Neither of them cared for subscribing to whatever was the popular or trendy viewpoint, simply because it was 'the thing to do.' Neither did they disagree with any points of view simply for the sake of being rebellious or argumentative.

He thought of his great grandfather, whom he knew resided in a vastly changing environment, where anti-Semitism and irrational nationalism grew from something in the background to government policy. And anyone who didn't fall into the correct ethnic, religious, political, gender roles had to run and hide or die trying.

How many loves throughout history must have died at the hands of society in the grip of madness?

He adored Amber's bravery, yet any notion of her being threatened stirred him in a way he could barely process. He was happy her family left Europe before the wars.

Martin wouldn't dare utter the words to even a priest in confession, yet after seeing Amber in the church, he had all the usual reactions of wanting to pursue a woman and then some.

Yet something said to him, *Wait...just wait. You'll see.*

Whether that *something* was his dad, his mom, his great grandfather, Hans or Klara, or something much bigger, he wasn't entirely sure.

But as he pulled up outside Amber's, next to the temporary car shelter he'd installed, he was sure about something.

Martin Anton Handl was hopelessly in love with Amber Margaret Kilzer.

☙ ❧

Amber looked at Martin, who kept his eyes on the road as they headed into Mott. "Are you okay?" she asked.

He swallowed and looked at her briefly before looking back at the road. "Oh yeah. I'm okay."

"I know it's a weekday and I can go do this alone. You can just come over for dinner at the weekend..."

"Amber, I'm in love with you."

"I worried when you kept your hands to yourself...Thought you were getting sick of me..." She folded her hands in her lap and looked down.

Amber did her best to keep her expression under control. She *loved* being with Martin. She was far more attracted to him than towards anyone else she'd encountered in her lifetime. Though she hadn't had many relationships in the past, she'd never experienced being in tune with someone the way she was with Martin.

But was this some sort of obligatory thing? Should she feel pressured to be with Martin forever simply because they had a shared heritage, including two ancestors who may have once been sweethearts?

Would her happy, independent life be compromised once she admitted how deep her own feelings ran?

That was just it. Her feelings *did* run deep. Very much so. She wasn't the sort of woman who would love lightly or for the sake of tradition. She stared at the gray, salted residue on other vehicles in Mott. At the piles of dirty snow.

Long gone were the twinkly holiday lights, yet spring hadn't shown itself with any evidence of warmth or greenery. This was where she was always strongest. When other folks despaired about the weather, about the depressing atmosphere of late winter, Amber got her head down and worked.

She found pleasure in the smallest of things, and didn't long for luxury items or tropical getaways. She'd never been needy for attention or approval. All she'd ever wanted was the freedom to work, keep her home, and enjoy the fresh air. Amber never expected to find such pleasure and contentment with another person.

Martin interrupted her thoughts. "Amber? It's okay if you don't feel the same. I mean, I'm hurt, but I won't—"

"I love you too," she replied.

Martin switched off the engine and turned to her. He looked around the library parking lot, then he leaned in and pressed his lips against hers. He applied steady pressure and angled his head. Placing soft kisses along her cheek, he stopped when he got to her ear and whispered, "I'm so happy. You make me so happy..." Then he kissed her cheek again and leaned back. "Shall we go do some research?"

"Sure, let's go have a hot date in the library," she replied.

"Actually...there's a lot to be said for libraries and hot dates." Martin winked as he got out.

Amber took Martin's arm and just before they got into the building, she said, "This isn't some huge city library where there are places to get lost in, so you better behave." She lowered her voice on the last words and reached around with her other arm to give his abdomen a squeeze.

Martin tenderly wrapped his gloved fingers around the arm that held him and said in a low voice, "Speak for yourself. I'm a good boy. I only meant that I think libraries are cool places."

Amber giggled and they found the librarian who guided them to a spot where they could look through old Hettinger County Newspaper archives from 1945, around the month when Hans and Klara died.

C3 &O

Martin scrolled through German language papers and columns from the 1910s and 1920s. They were both curious if there would be any mention of Hans or Klara.

"Hans was respected in the area. Oh...there's a comment here from your great grandfather, Peter Lulay. Look...see there?" Martin pointed.

"What?" Amber's eyes were sore from staring at the small print on the screens.

"Your great grandfather, Peter Lulay. Someone interviewed him about how things were for Banaters in North Dakota. He said...'Some folks get lucky. Others have to break their backs to get any success.' And this is the same article that mentions the success of Hans Schreiber in 1921. This reporter was going all over southwest North Dakota, trying to gauge how German Russians and German Hungarians had fared since arriving a couple of decades earlier."

"Wow...he didn't really like Hans, did he?" Amber said.

"Yep, because he had been buddies with Anton back in the Old Country. And I think we know why he didn't like Anton," Martin replied.

"Hmm." Then Amber found a headline and said, "Martin?"

"What is it?"

"Look..."

The headline read: 'Local farmer killed by migrant worker. Wife died shortly after.'

"A local farmer, Hans Schreiber, was shot by a passing migrant worker by the name of Paul Johnson, now imprisoned. Grown children of Mrs. Lulay found the couple after encountering Johnson, who was at a local tavern boasting about killing a Nazi. The two recently returned soldiers, Josef and Jacob Lulay, said they became suspicious when he spoke of where the Nazi was.

"The Schreibers lived in southwestern North Dakota since 1909. A supporter of American veterans from the first World War, Hans gave employment and work experience to many battle weary soldiers in the years leading up to the Second World War. Having suffered from a wounded leg himself, the result of a farming accident, he said he needed the help from his fellow Americans, immigrants and natives alike, and that he wanted to help his adopted country.

"The mass will be arranged by friend, Mrs. Margaritha (Peter) Lulay, at St. Vincent's church. It was Mrs. Lulay who found Mrs. Schreiber in the cellar of her homestead. Mrs. Lulay had this to say about Hans, 'Believe me...I knew Hans and Klara from the Old Country. They would have hated the Nazis. For him to die as a result of one man's madness is a tragedy.'"

Amber looked at Martin, the tears falling down her cheeks. She placed a hand over her mouth, and Martin wrapped his arms around her. "Oh, Amber...I'm sorry. All this time, I wondered if it was an accident that killed them both. They died at the hands of some disturbed bigot."

ᙣ   ᛒᚩ

After an early dinner with her parents, Martin headed back home to prepare for the rest of the week. Amber's father couldn't recall his grandmother mentioning anything about the Schreiber tragedy. Then again, he said they had been through so much with the loss of Elmer and they didn't discuss him often either.

"Grandma was just always happy and sweet. Mom never talked about sad stuff much. She always used to say, 'If you don't laugh, you'll cry.' But I don't recall her mentioning anything that had anything to do with stuff that upset her." Amber's father shrugged. "They were always busy working and putting food on the table. No time to dwell on tragedies, I guess."

Amber was happy that her dad seemed to like Martin. Her mother absolutely loved him.

When Amber got back home, she sat down in her office to spend the evening working, making up for her day off. She'd placed the painting of herself up on the wall.

Part of her was still unnerved by the detail in it. The textures and atmosphere Martin had been able to capture. It was an odd thing, to be grieving for Klara and Hans.

Yet that's how it felt, after discovering the circumstances of their death. She had asked for a printed copy of the article and had it set on her desk while formatting a client's manuscript.

The house groaned from the wind outside and Amber said out loud, "I am actually pretty anxious for spring to arrive. It's been cold for too long." She shook her head, admonishing herself for going 'soft.'

A creak sounded in the background and Amber absently looked towards her easel by the window, outside of which the dark, dormant prairie lay.

Klara stood with her hand on the easel, and Amber could just make out the outline of Hans outside.

Tears slipped down her cheeks and plopped onto the floor.

She didn't take her gaze away from the two ghosts. Their expressions were not angry. It was as though they comforted her...

"Oh, I'm sorry...I'm so, so sorry..." Amber wept until the Banater spirits disappeared.

Chapter 45

1944. A Walk to School. Mercydorf.

Anton sat at the desk in his and Sophie's bedroom in Mercydorf. The family had done reasonably well once leaving Temeswar and focusing all their efforts on Sophie's family farm. Magdalena, who had always been a quiet, nervous woman, had taken well to motherhood, yet was often too busy with work to spend much time with her son.

This left Bastian with Anton. All of the news coming to their village was that the Fuhrer was close to victory and they must maintain hope. Yet Anton, though there were no conflicting reports available, understood that things couldn't possibly be as the news portrayed them. Else the word of mouth reports of fighting between communist partisans and German soldiers wouldn't have been filled with such fierceness.

Marcus had fallen at Stalingrad as a soldier in the Romanian army. Anton was filled with regret for never having spent enough time with his adopted son. Sebastian, little Bastian's father, hadn't been heard from for over a year. To Anton's horror, his youngest son pledged his loyalty to the German army and happily accepted the obligatory draft for ethnic Germans, or Volksdeutsche, as the German army referred to them. He saw it as his honor.

Sebastian's decision had led to rift. Anton was disgusted. "You are ashamed of your heritage!" Sebastian had accused him.

"I am not! But my heritage does not revolve around hating anyone who isn't like me. That isn't heritage. It's small-minded bigotry with manipulative words and obsession with military might! I raised you to be more intelligent than this! For God's sake, you have never even been to Germany!"

Sebastian, who had always been a clever boy praised by his teachers, narrowed his eyes at his father and said, "Be careful, old man. You are going to be taking care of your only grandson. Do it for my wife and son, and for Mother's sake. You can be an idiot all you like. You lost the last war with your weakness! It is old Jew-loving fools like you who lost the Austro-Hungarian Empire!"

Anton recalled the blood draining from his face as he backed away from his son. "Austria-Hungary was a multi-cultural empire. It was the stupidity of its elitist, deluded rulers, and unreasonable extremists like *you*, who caused the downfall." Anton backed, away, feeling faint. "You… you cannot belong to me. You cannot."

"I belong to the Fatherland. We all do. It's our only hope, and I'm going to fight for it."

And that was the last thing he had heard from his remaining son. Where Sebastian was now, none of them knew. He'd never written, having been swept up in the leaflets and shouting voices on the radio. Anton heard that there was a way to get alternative news, yet no one in his family would even speak of it.

His heart was heavy as he went through smaller sketches he'd done whilst away at war, which his son had accused him of losing.

"Ota?" a small voice sounded and Anton turned to his seven-year-old nephew standing in his doorway.

"Good evening, Bastian. Aren't you supposed to be in bed?" Despite the reprimand, one corner of his mouth turned up.

"Well…yes, but there is something I want to ask you."

"What is that?"

"Will you walk me to school tomorrow? I am nervous. Oma or Mama could, but…I would like you to."

"Of course, dear boy," Anton replied, still distracted by the articles scattered on his desk.

"Ota?" Bastian said again.

Anton turned to his grandson with raised brows. "Yes, Bastian?"

Bastian walked towards the desk and pointed at the papers on it. "Who are you drawing?"

Anton's heart melted and he went right back in time to when Marcus queried about Anton's painting and drawing.

"I…Well, actually, I like to sketch and paint. These are sketches of the people Ota used to work for in Temeswar. This is…my parents, your great grandparents. I like to remember people's faces. And these two...their names are Hans and Klara Schreiber. Hans was my best friend when I was a boy. He moved to America with his bride, Klara. I have missed them so. But once I sketch someone...I don't forget their face."

Bastian nodded, looking at all the pictures. He surprised Anton by hugging him and saying, "They all look like nice people. Goodnight, Ota."

Anton hugged the boy back and said, "Goodnight, child."

ᴄᴈ   ᴥ

Anton walked proudly beside his grandson on the way to the schoolhouse.

"I wonder if I will be as tall as you one day, Ota."

"Perhaps. And maybe you will be a strapping, strong man like my Walter Onkel. He had huge hands and was so broad in the chest. Yet he was nimble and deft as anyone, he must have been on every rooftop in Temeswar. He taught me everything I know."

"Is that why our roof has never leaked?" Bastian asked.

Anton chuckled.

One of the Volksgruppe representatives passed them, a young man with a staunch step and his chin jutting out.

"Heil Hitler!" the youth saluted and looked to the boy.

Bastian frowned then pressed his lips together and was about to raise his arm in the traditional salute.

Anton reached down to his grandson and gently pressed Bastian's arm back down.

He looked to the Volksgruppe member and said, "Forgive me. In this village, we always addressed our elders with the greeting Gruss Gott. I promise my grandson won't make the same mistake again. Now, Bastian, greet this young gentleman properly. He is testing your manners."

Bastian performed a shy and confused, "Gruss Gott."

The man stood in front of them, tilted his head, and said, "No, no, he would have been correct the first time. You old fool, do you think you are being clever? He must do the proper salute."

Anton smiled and said, "Ah, well. Once this war is over, I hope that we will still have our manners. That is a part of my heritage I am most proud of, and I always greeted my elders properly as a boy. Once the Fuhrer is victorious, I am sure he would agree."

The man's eyes widened and his nostrils flared. He stood back and puffed his chest out. "You are a disgrace and you will pay for this insult."

"Bah! Go away. If you are so passionate, you should be at the front, serving the Fuhrer. My son certainly is."

"Ah, of course, you are Sebastian's father. Your son talked a lot of sense. Good day to you." Anton and Bastian nodded and watched the man walk away. Anton thought since he had lost one son to this war, and another to this Fuhrer, he had a right to at least express his disdain for the cowardly sorts who hung back in the villages, not fighting or defending. He had little but disdain for those who hid in the villages and only enforced the propaganda.

"You are very brave, Ota," Bastian said.

"Well, I don't know about that. You see, Bastian, there are people who should never be let out into society. People who bully children, women, and the elderly. They are cowards. It's worth remembering that cowards can be cruel in order to appear brave."

They arrived at the schoolhouse. Anton told Bastian he would collect him later.

He was halfway home when he felt a hard shove from behind. Anton didn't have time to register what it was when a blow came to his back. He groaned in pain.

He opened his eyes to see the pair of boots in front of him. He winced and prepared for the blows. It wasn't long before they came. As consciousness slipped away, he heard a shrill cry in the distance.

Chapter 46

1945. Klara. North Dakota.

Klara sat up in bed, clutching her chest. Breathless, she looked to the side of her bed and saw Hans snoring next to her. She patted him on the arm. Terror struck her heart, despite seeing him beside her.

"Hans?"

Hans rolled over and slowly opened his eyes. "Klara? What is wrong? Are you not feeling well?"

Hans's brows knit together and Klara was aware that she took too long to answer. She licked her dry lips and said, "I am fine. I had a bad dream."

"Perhaps you should rest. It's only a couple of days until threshing. You will need your strength." Hans sat up and rubbed her back. She could feel him scrutinizing her. "Do you need a doctor, Klara?"

Admonishing herself for worrying her husband, Klara took several deep breaths and closed her eyes. "Really, I am fine. It is only cooking and baking for me today. I just had a dreadful dream. I called for you and you did not answer."

"Oh...Klara." Hans sighed. "You and these dreams. You've always been a sensitive soul. There are many dreadful things happening in the world right now. This war has been bad. I remember a lot of people not liking Jews when we lived in Bensek, but that Hitler, he wanted to get rid of them all, murder them! Maybe you are sensing all the trouble. Don't worry. It won't reach you here, and this war is done now anyhow."

He kissed her forehead and got out of bed. Klara watched him limp towards the chest of drawers. His bad leg was always worse in the mornings, particularly in recent years. Yet once he moved around, his limp was less noticeable.

Her heart had calmed and Klara caught her breath. She removed the covers and sat on the edge of the bed. A cool morning breeze blew in through the partially open window. Later, the temperature would rise as the men worked in the fields. It was hard labor, but Hans mainly only oversaw things and paid men to help with the threshing.

"Hans? When was the last time we heard from Anton?" Klara asked.

Hans stood in front of their bedroom window. He rubbed the top of his head while turned away from her. "Oh…" he said. "It's been quite a few years now. I got the feeling that he struggled after the first war."

Klara stood and stretched. She shook her arms and legs, feeling lightheaded. She sat down on the bed suddenly and blew out a breath.

Klara willed herself to speak so as not to trouble Hans that she wasn't well.

"I can't shake this feeling of dread, Hans. Even though the war is over. I hope Anton and his family are alright."

An hour later, there was a knock at the door and there on the porch stood Paul Johnson. He was still small and wiry, yet he was clean-shaven. He took his hat off and Klara noticed his hair looked recently washed. Last time she had seen him, he appeared greasy and matted.

"Missus Schreiber? I hope I'm not bothering you and Mister Schreiber. I…I wanted to offer my services free of charge. You see, I found Jesus. Jesus taught me about forgiveness and…my pastor suggested that I help my fellow man, instead of helping myself."

Klara clenched one of her fists on and off at her side. She was normally a clearheaded person, but this twitchiness as a result of the nightmare was interfering with her ability to think clearly.

"How…how…nice…."

Hans appeared behind her and said, "Mister Johnson? We aren't quite ready for threshing just yet. I've got some men coming in a couple of days. We would be grateful for some help then, but I'll pay you for your time, of course. I don't accept slave labor."

At this, Paul Johnson put his hand up. "Now, Mister Schreiber, I owe you. I know I've been rude in the past. You see, I…I have to confess. I've been so full of hate. I hated all the different types coming into my country. I hated 'em because I always felt they were stealing my country from me and trying to turn it into somethin' foreign. But now I see. I have seen the light. We are all God's children. I know you…Catholics would understand that. You believe in Jesus, don't you?"

Klara's eye twitched and she looked at Hans, whose expression did not betray that he had heard such a heartfelt speech.

Hans said, "If I said I didn't believe in Jesus as you do, would you still feel so charitable? Or would you wish to make a problem with me?"

Klara's heart raced again.

"Hans..." she said, so softly she wasn't sure if Hans could hear it. Paul swallowed and smiled.

Paul said, "Well, Jesus teaches to forgive unconditionally. So...I suppose that's what I do."

Hans looked to Klara, then back to Paul. He said, "Come, Mister Johnson. Let's step outside and I'm sure I can find something for you to do. It's kind of you to offer."

Klara nodded and went to the kitchen to sit down. As a girl, she'd been able to skip breakfast easily. Now if she did, she felt sick to her stomach and lightheaded. Soon, the men would come for threshing and it would be necessary to have enough food prepared to feed them while the work was happening. She had plenty of pickles and preserves in the cellar.

She descended the stair case with a flashlight to collect the necessary items for food, thinking that once she had a slice of bread with some jam, she'd feel better.

The air in the cellar wasn't as cool as normal. It was as though it offended her lungs and her breath was not cooperating. Then, her flashlight went out.

Yet there was something else. Unspeakable panic. Terror seized her heart and vision, and her thoughts were no longer under her control. Blackness consumed her.

ঙ‍ও   ঙ‍ও

"Klara!" a voice called. The first sense to return was her hearing, then scent. Sadly, she could smell filth and an urge to wretch rose within her. The voice talking to her was too high.

"Hans..." she said, but one side of her mouth would not work.

A light flooded the room and she saw what appeared to be an older version of her friend, Margaritha. Margaritha who had not ever replied to her letters. Margaritha...The portrait. But she would get Hans. Hans would help her find it. At least finally, she would be able to tell Margaritha about the portrait. She had to.

Her mouth would not work.

"Oh, Klara...my dear friend. My dear friend, I am here now. I am sorry.

I am so, so sorry," Margaritha said in their old village dialect.

"M....th...Hans!" Klara called.

"Klara, please, don't try to talk. My sons found Paul. They haven't been back long from the war. They found this madman saying he had done the Lord's work...that he killed a Nazi. He was crazy. I always knew he was crazy...I wish so that we would have reported him."

Suddenly, Klara realized, in a rush of clarity, that something bad had happened to Hans. That she had to get upstairs. She had to show Margaritha something. She had to find her husband.

Yet the clarity didn't remain and the heaviest of sleeps overtook her. Her last thought was that when she woke, she would do what she had to do.

Chapter 47

2018. 'Pfiat Eich.' Chicago.

Martin landed in Chicago over a month after the trip to the library with Amber. He had a meeting with a property developer from Wisconsin who wanted to build traditional barn-themed taverns and restaurants throughout the upper Midwest.

Martin accepted the meeting with the man, as he insisted that quality was important to him. He wanted the structures to stand the test of time, and not wind up as some ex-bar and grill type place on empty, unkempt parking lots strewn across the Midwest.

"I heard that Handl's Structures is worth using..."

He was going to stay at a hotel in the city, in order to work in the evening.

Even though it was a few states over and with fairly similar weather, if marginally less extreme, northern Illinois seemed like a million miles away from North Dakota. He'd been unable to control himself in front of Amber. It had only been a few months and now, he felt as though he'd thrown himself at her.

Not in a physical way, of course, though the heat between them was undeniable. She'd confessed to loving him in return, but he still couldn't help but wonder if she said it due to feeling obligated after he spilled out how much he adored her.

Amber had been heartbroken to find out what happened to Hans and Klara, and so had he. They'd finally figured out what happened to the Banater couple who'd been haunting the homestead Amber had lovingly fixed up.

Unlike a lot of Schwobs, Martin, until recently, hadn't felt compelled to look into the fate of his family. Everything was buried in the sorrow of what happened between the end of WWII and in the years after. The camps, the refugee period, the years of Communist rule in Romania and Yugoslavia. That was all too heavy and wasn't an easily digested topic unless you had family involved.

It upset him that his mother never felt comfortable discussing what happened to her and her family as a child in Europe. She'd been terrified of being mistaken as a Nazi sympathizer. Martin admitted to himself that he held back talking about it in history class. The shame of being remotely associated with the Nazis wasn't something he ever risked as a younger man. The very idea of being associated with them was sickening.

The Nazi perpetrators of ethnic cleansing committed crimes so vile, the anger over such knowledge would live on forever. There were known, documented cases of unspeakable cruelty. Mere examples of the sort of thing that went on for years as the war raged on.

His mother's shocking childhood memories, the cruelties she had witnessed in former Yugoslavia, were viewed as penance for the Nazis' crimes. His mother hated Nazis, and she swore her family wanted them and their influence out of her village. Yet when the German occupiers and Nazi propagandists were gone, having fled along with locals who embraced the ideology and theories of genetic superiority, it was mostly the innocent and naïve who remained.

And it was often them who paid the price at the hands of vengeful partisans, unsavory Red Army soldiers, yet ultimately an international post-war agreement allowed for such events to take place.

There were always exceptions, helpful Romanians and Hungarians; Yugoslav partisans who didn't want the murders, only political change; Russian soldiers and officers who stepped in when cruelties went too far; families in Germany and the United States, who reached out and helped loved ones escape the madness of post-war Europe.

If such people hadn't existed, people who did the right thing in the very worst circumstances, he and his family wouldn't be around at all to even hesitantly tell their tale.

There were older folks in the Danube Swabian community who were still seeking brothers, sisters, and cousins who they'd lost contact with in the chaos of fleeing Europe.

Still lost in thought, a breeze picked up that reminded Martin of North Dakota. Spring was in the air. There were definitely buds on the trees, and the last remnants of snow and ice were melting.

Martin walked along Michigan Avenue and through Grant Park, places his mother would take him for a picnic lunch on the weekends when his father was still working.

He walked into the area where the Art Institute was, headed in the direction of the Field Museum and Shedd Aquarium.

Martin met with the investor at a nearby burger restaurant. On their way out, they saw a rather short, slightly overweight woman with two redheaded children and a fairly tall British-sounding man. They were laughing and taking turns speaking in some exaggerated English accent.

They thanked him for holding the door for them and he guessed from the woman's flushed cheeks that she'd probably had a couple of drinks. The family were obviously on a break from out of town. The dad asked him where the Field Museum was and Martin pointed the family in the direction of where he'd just been walking.

After meeting the gentleman from Wisconsin, Martin decided that it was a great opportunity as the man wasn't building on any controversial land, and he wanted his structures to mean something to people. He kept his politics to himself, but always made a point of never working with anyone who was willing to roll over underprivileged groups for the sake of 'progress.' For a lapsed Catholic, Martin gave a lot of credence to the concept of karma.

After the meeting, Martin stopped at a florist and went to a nearby Catholic cemetery.

He approached the graves of his parents, Sebastian 'Bastian' Marcus Handl and Katherine 'Katy' Maria Handl. His eyes welled up and Martin sniffled, bristling at the emotions that rose against his will. He wished Amber was there to place an arm around him.

In days gone by, he would have been horrified by a woman witnessing his display of emotions.

He laid the wreath at his parents' graves and spoke to them in Schwowische. He wanted them to know about Amber, how he wished they could have met her and told her all sorts of things about Banater culture that he'd never bothered to ask his parents when they were alive. He told them about North Dakota, about Hans and Klara, and how he hoped they were happy where they were.

How he was sorry for any hurt he caused them in his life. They only ever encouraged him to do well. He stood before the stones and pulled a handkerchief embroidered with his initials out of his pocket. Emotion threatened to choke him, but he managed to wave the handkerchief and place it beneath a rock in between the stones.

His final words in dialect were, "Pfiat Eich." Meaning, *'Bye, you two. See you.'* He was sure he would see them again one day.

Martin left the cemetery, happy that he had been to speak to his parents.

Yet it's not like they are there...They aren't there...

Martin began the long walk back to his hotel. Much as he had grown to love his quieter life in North Dakota, he did enjoy the long anonymous strolls one could take through the streets of a city.

He looked up at the trees lining the sidewalks, watched the branches and delicate buds sway in the breeze.

Staring ahead into the people walking in the opposite direction, suddenly his heart jumped within his chest. His father and mother were arm in arm, smiling at him. It happened so fast that he didn't have time to properly study the faces, but it was them.

Then again, maybe they were just a friendly old couple who bore a resemblance to his parents.

He turned around and there was no sign of the two. The hair on his arms, even beneath his layers, stood on end, the goosebumps spread along his limbs and his scalp tingled.

He readjusted his position on the sidewalk. His phone buzzed and he looked at the message. It was from Aaron.

'Hey buddy, we still meeting for breakfast tomorrow before you go? I had a look at the other house down the street. They seem to be doing a good job on restoring the floorboards. The tenants found a post card from some place called Maria Radna. It's got that German writing on it, but it mentions 'Ota, Anton Handl. Thought you might want it. Think it slipped out a while ago. See you tomorrow.'

Dad was always going between the houses when he was working on them.

Then he had a message from Amber. 'Hi, hope the meeting in Chicago went okay. I was thinking, if you don't mind...I would like to know what happened to Anton. And the weather here is forecast to warm up. Maybe you could get started on something a bit more permanent?'

The tingly feeling was still present, and Martin slowly started to calm. One corner of his mouth went up. He made his way back to his hotel. Once there, he sat down at the desk in his room and began to compose a letter.

Chapter 48

1944. Maria Radna. The Banat.

Anton's head still caused him a lot of pain whenever he became too stressed. Sophie asserted that they were Romanian citizens, and that Germany's actions didn't matter. King Michael I of Romania would gain favor with America and the United Kingdom, and things might be as before, with a benevolent royal ruler and administration that would allow them to carry on with their lives as the Hapsburgs had once done.

"Besides, we haven't done anything wrong," she added.

"Mami, you are being idealistic and you underestimate what the Russians will want, and their influence here," Magdalena countered.

It was Magdalena who had begun to grow twitchy as reports of revenge killings in Yugoslavia began to circulate. The fighting there between German forces and partisans had been brutal and cruel.

Now, the tides were truly changing and surely anyone who still thought Hitler would be victorious was a fool. She had found an ally in Anton. She had relatives in Chicago, and if she could get to a place where it was safe to contact them, they could eventually emigrate.

It was Sophie who insisted they stay. The farm had done well, and she imagined they could expand even more after the war, once the situation was politically stable. She imagined King Michael would save and spare them all. Anton bristled and imagined her old infatuation with Marcus's father drew her to a worship of nobles and royals. Sophie had been a loyal wife, but he knew she'd never recovered from her first love. As for Anton, he still thought of Margaritha. He had her portrait in his head.

Sophie's continued stubbornness grated on him.

"I am not a Nazi. We never were! My Sebastian, God rest his soul, was manipulated by the Germans. They used him. My Marcus is also dead. We owe it to them to do well in our homeland. To stay near them." Sophie's dark eyes glistened with tears.

Magdalena said, "Mami...we have to leave. I miss Sebastian, the man he was before this madness. You don't want to know what I've heard from Yugoslavia. In a way, I am glad he perished on the battlefield and not at the hands of vengeful partisans. This is only the beginning. Believe me, our penance for allowing the Nazis in our village is coming."

Sophie gestured dismissively. "I never wanted them! And anyway, even if the Russians come, they will keep a tight lid on the partisans. That communist nonsense won't last. We will have a new government, a time of peace, and we can get on with our work."

Just then, they heard shots outside. Anton grabbed Bastian from his bed, his head throbbing, and told the women it was time to go. Bastian was sleepy and confused, as he clung to his grandfather.

Sophie still protested, but Anton insisted they at least, for the night, move to the next village while the fighting was so close. Summer's warmth had departed and there was a chill, so Anton wrapped his grandson up in his warmest coat.

With a speed and stealth that surprised all of them, the family gathered some small provisions and moved out of the house. More shots were fired. Anton was certain one whizzed past his ear. His stomach clenched and bile rose in his throat. He winced against the onslaught of memories of bullets and battlefields from nearly thirty years ago.

It was Sophie's voice that pulled him back into the moment. "Anton, I can hear them. I can hear Russian. I...They are so close."

Anton put his arm around his wife. "It's okay, my dear. It's okay. I've heard German soldiers much closer..." Anton realized the madness of the situation. It was the German army, the one he'd resented being present in his village and in his family life, who would be their savior.

The instigators of the situation they now found themselves in. The darkness surrounding them was both friend and foe. It protected them, yet he couldn't see Magdalena and Bastian, who must have run ahead.

Anton's ears began to ring and panic rose in his chest. It was difficult to tell if bullets were really buzzing past his ears or it was an internal attack he was experiencing.

Sophie jumped beside him and he looked to her. His heart sank at the look on her face. She sank onto the cold field.

"Sophie!" he cried, forgetting it was necessary to keep his voice low in case any hostile soldiers were nearby.

Magdalena and Bastian were beside him. Magdalena tried to keep Bastian behind her as they helped lay Sophie down. She reached out to Anton, who grasped her hands.

"You were right..." Sophie's voice was a strained, unnatural whisper.

"Don't talk, Mami...please don't talk," Magdalena pleaded.

Sophie shook her head and said, "You must go...You must...take Bastian. I have always cared for you, Anton. You have been...good husband." She lay back and closed her eyes. Anton knew he would never again speak to his wife in this life.

He looked all around, and listened close. He heard German soldiers shouting. "Go back to your homes! It isn't safe outside anywhere!"

Then retreating footsteps in the fields, but whether those footsteps were friend or foe, Anton couldn't tell. For now, the shots seemed to stop.

The next day, they made arrangements for Sophie's burial. There had been one other civilian killed in the crossfire, and both families were anxious to lay their loved ones to rest.

Afterward, Magdalena approached Anton and said, "I have made arrangements, Tati. With the assistance of a Romanian friend, we will be able to get across the border. We will first shelter at Maria Radna."

Anton had always wanted to visit the large monastery near the Hungarian border. From there, he knew they would manage to get into less dangerous territory, where Magdalena could contact her relatives. They could get sponsorship and thus be able to emigrate.

"It might take time, and it won't be easy, but we can't stay here."

"No...No, we cannot," Anton replied.

"I will understand, Tati, if you don't want to leave now...after..."

"No, Lena. We need to go. Sophie realized this too. I'm just sorry it was too late."

ભ ಶ

It took them three days to reach the Basilica of Maria Radna. The word was that the monastery near Lipova, close to the Hungarian border, was a safe place.

Anton's head throbbed often and Magdalena insisted they stop frequently to rest. What Anton refused to admit to his daughter-in-law and grandson was that his chest pained far worse than his head. He imagined it was something to do with having lost his wife in such a sudden and traumatic way.

Yet a small part of him suspected another cause. They saw the monastery turrets reaching above the distant, nearly bare trees, like beacons of strength in any weather. Tears stung Anton's eyes. How he would have liked to paint such a beautiful sight.

"Bastian, you must take this image with you somehow. Perhaps there will be a postcard or something. You must ask the friar. You could...you could..." Suddenly, Anton's breath didn't allow him to speak anymore.

He faltered on the path, and Magdalena and Bastian helped prop him up.

"Oh...you are a strong boy, Bastian..." Anton was impressed that his grandson, rather than weep at their plight, was persistent in ensuring that what remained of their family remained intact.

Anton said a quick prayer before they knocked on the entrance. There, a Franciscan monk greeted them in Romanian. "Good afternoon." Then he spoke in a low voice, "Is this all that remains of your family?"

It was Bastian who replied. "Please...my Ota isn't well." The friar's bushy eyebrows went up when he saw the small boy. He quickly relieved Bastian and hoisted Anton up as he promptly moved the family to some sparse, but comfortable and clean enough, sleeping quarters.

"I will get him some water. A lot of the time, it is just dehydration..."

The friar hurried off. Anton could see that they weren't the only people there. Out of the corner of his eye, he saw Magdalena with her arm around a distressed woman who had fled alone. She had nothing left in the Banat. Her husband had gone to fight for Germany too and had also perished at Stalingrad. She greatly feared the Red Army's retribution against her, the wife of a fallen ethnic German soldier.

Anton listened as the woman recounted what he had feared. "People think that just because they are Romanian or Yugoslav citizens, the Russians and the partisans won't bother with them. But it's not true...."

Anton clutched his heart and looked to Bastian. Bastian held his hand. The friar came with some water, and Bastian helped him drink. The water eased his parched throat, but the liquid in his body seemed pointless. His heart beat grew agitated and his arm ached. It felt as though the blood had drained from his body, leaving him utterly weak, sick, and breathless.

He squeezed Bastian's hand to get his attention. He whispered so low that only the boy could hear. "I will need the good friar to give me last rites soon, dear boy. But let me tell you...no matter what, you and your mami need to get to America. To your relatives there. If you manage to get a postcard of this place, perhaps you could go to bring it to Hans and Klara, my friends...look in my suitcase. They will be so happy to know I reached this fine place. For I doubt anyone in America knows anything of us. Remember, Bastian, always, that love is stronger than hate. Your oma and I, we looked after each other. I loved your father...but I was ashamed of him, of what he became. My only way now to make amends for that is through you. Always..."

Then speech became impossible and he grew wearier than ever.

"I will miss you, Ota. I won't forget you. I won't forget."

Bastian's sorrowful voice reached Anton's ears and he squeezed his grandson's hand one last time.

He could hear Magdalena weeping in the distance, then the Latin words of last rites were the final thing he heard in the way he was accustomed to hearing things, even as a sickly child. Even as an injured old man.

Light and warmth suffused Anton, and he no longer worried about the past.

Chapter 49

2018. Amber and Martin. North Dakota.

On the homestead, things had been quiet. There was the odd waft of rosemary as Martin and Amber sat together, watching television or cleaning up after dinner.

Now, Amber was at her desk, editing a manuscript for a client in New York. The sun hadn't been up long and was casting its rays into her office.

Knock, knock, knock.

Amber opened the door to a grinning Martin, and the rest of the crew who were there to begin the work.

"Mornin'," he said.

"Morning. You guys want coffee or anything?" she asked, though she knew the answer.

"No, we've got thermoses and stuff. We're good."

John smiled and nodded. Martin introduced the other crew members, who would assist with the digging and pouring the concrete.

They all smiled, shook Amber's hand, and went out to the chosen spot. The skid steer started up to begin the work on the area that had been marked out for digging.

Martin hung back on her porch while the crew started work.

"They all seem to like you," Amber said.

"You sound surprised," Martin said.

She laughed and held up her hands. "No."

Then Martin's face turned serious. His brows knit together and he said, "So...nothing happening at the moment?"

Amber pursed her lips and sighed. "No. It's...strange. We've smelled rosemary, but that's it. Maybe they're at peace now that we know what happened."

Martin nodded. He'd already shown her the old postcard of Maria Radna on which Martin's father wrote, 'Where Ota died. 1944.' Martin had been sad as he'd understood far too late that this was why his father pushed his mother to go and at least visit Romania.

"Hmm. Well, I'll go make sure these clowns don't make too much of a mess in your yard," Martin said as he leaned in, touched Amber's arm, and kissed her cheek. His lips lingered on her skin for a few seconds. When he broke away, she yearned for more physical contact.

The skid steer became a steady sound in the background, along with the spring winds. Summer heat hadn't arrived yet, but spring warmth sure had. Amber itched to get outside, but work had held her captive to the screen for weeks.

The crew hardly came in apart from the odd bathroom break, and Amber even ate her lunch alone. Martin had suggested that she hire or enlist the help of a student or someone who could do simpler editing and digital formatting for her so she didn't get too bogged down.

In truth, she still felt weighted down by a long first winter in her house. Surely a few outdoor activities would brighten things up. Amber stood and stretched her long arms above her head. She went into the kitchen and made a sandwich, then she stepped outside to grab the mail.

Breathing in the crisp spring air, Amber glanced at the workers and saw Martin staring at her. One of the other men waved a hand in front of his face to get his attention and Martin laughed.

She blushed and hurried inside to eat her light lunch, opening her mail. Most of it was the usual junk, but then an envelope caught her attention.

To: Ms. Amber Kilzer

    Schreiber Homestead

    Rt. 2

    Hettinger, Co.

    North Dakota

From: Martin Sebastian Handl

Amber gently opened the envelope. Martin had handwritten a letter, using a gothic style of writing, yet thankfully it was in English. The floor creaked and Amber's head whipped around. All was quiet indoors. Only the skid steer carried on. She got up and quickly checked the hall, then peeked outside. A couple of the people were eating sandwiches while Martin stood gesturing to John in the skid steer.

Deciding she was alone, Amber sat back down and began to read the letter.

Dearest Amber,

You could be from Mars and I would still love you.

In some ways, I feel like I was born to love you. The feelings I have for you, are not common. They aren't from the reckless lust of youth. They aren't from fear of loneliness or any other strange pressures.

I am in love with you in a way that no longer scares me. You've haunted my dreams and dwelled in my heart. The greatest thing about it, is that you're real and with me.

A complicated past and restless spirits have led us here.

For years, I looked at my heritage as something full of pain, loss and regret. After meeting you, I've revisited it with a more open mind and have been able to lay my own unhappy memories to rest.

Separation, wars and cruelty are common occurrences throughout history.

Now, history has brought us together.

I do believe the past has taught us a lot and will continue to do so with its uncovered stories and forgotten events. Not only our own history and culture, but others have stories to tell.

For now, let's leave it to the historians and focus on the future. We are lucky to find ourselves entwined with one another in America. We are privileged to be allowed to love one another as we both desire.

Soon summer will be here and it won't be time for heavy hearts.

I am very much looking forward to making Spaetzle for you, if you would be so kind to make Paprikasch.

Perhaps Hans and Klara will join us, or we can at least toast to your first summer living properly in the home they so lovingly built.

I cannot think of a place I would rather be than anywhere with you.

I love you Amber Kilzer and if you will have me, I am yours.

Love,

Martin

Amber's hands were shaking as she placed the paper down beside her half-eaten sandwich. How many times had they sat here and read the letters from so long ago?

They hadn't wanted to rush things. It hadn't been a year since they'd met. Yet how long was the appropriate time to wait before discussions of marriage, intimacy, and commitment came up? Two months? Three months? One year?

Who cares! I love him. I'm not scared of that anymore.

She stood up, slowly. Excitement and giddiness pulsed through her, and it was the oddest, most liberating sensation. The wind seemed to pick up and Amber looked outside. The men were still working, but she couldn't see Martin.

A hand rested on her shoulder and Amber turned. "Martin..."

But it was Klara, who hadn't made an appearance for many weeks. The older lady smiled with kind, twinkling green eyes.

"No...thank you..." Klara said in accented English.

Amber blinked. The accent on the woman's voice was detectable, as was her polite tone. When she opened her eyes, Klara wasn't there anymore. Amber pushed a hand into her tied-back curls and went into her office. She sat back down, then looked behind her, wondering if Klara would appear again.

"'No, thank you,' eh, Klara? Okay. Not sure what you mean by that."

Amber threw herself back into her work. Hours ticked by. Eventually, her stomach growled and reminded her that it was after six now.

Knock, knock, knock.

Amber went to the door and saw only Martin there with a wide grin. "Hey. Got your letter. Where's the crew?" she asked, though her voice was breathless.

Martin raised an eyebrow and looked around. "Oh, they are finished for the day. You, uh...You hungry? I thought maybe we could start cooking now."

Amber, beaming, placed her hands on either side of his cold, stubbled cheeks and kissed him. She pulled him in and Martin offered little resistance.

The door was still open.

The evening's spring air blew into the house. Amber found herself on the floor beneath Martin's weight. It seemed they had forgotten about dinner. Her stomach growled again though, reminding them, and they giggled in between kisses. Amber had practically forgotten about Klara's appearance and message.

The words 'I love you too, Martin' were on the tip of her tongue.

Then, a loud BANG sounded. It shook the floorboards. Martin and Amber scrambled to get up off the floor.

Amber remained on her hands and knees, feeling the vibrations of the floor. Martin tried to pull her up, but she insisted.

"I will tell where it's coming from this way..." She scrambled along from the front entrance and crawled her way to her bedroom, keeping her palms in contact with the floor. This was where she often heard the thumping.

She leaned down and looked beneath her bed, no longer frightened but like a madwoman on a quest. Her eyes widened.

"Martin!" she cried. He was beside her. "Help me move the bed."

Together, they moved the bed and the banging lessened. It was more like a steady knocking now. "Let's take the floorboard up," she said.

As they worked together, thumps and knocks continued, as though encouraging them that they were in the right place. It took some time to do it without doing too much damage.

There, carefully wrapped in many disintegrating layers, was a satchel wrapped in waterproof oilcloth.

Amber and Martin looked at one another. "She wanted us to see this. Whatever it is."

Gingerly, they removed the oilcloth and unfastened the satchel. The canvas had been packed and protected so carefully, it miraculously unrolled without much damage. It was a marvel.

Martin and Amber gasped. It was a portrait of her great grandmother, Margaritha. At the bottom was a signature: *A. Handl.*

"He did love her..." Martin said.

A chill went up Amber's spine and a wind swept through the room. Not icy cold or eerie, but cleansing. Amber and Martin both turned to the bedroom doorway and there was Klara with the same smile on her face.

She said something in the German dialect of the Banaters to Martin. He did his best to smile and nod, yet he kept his mouth slightly open and didn't appear able to speak.

Klara turned away, in the direction of the door. They had left it open. They both followed the spirit.

Klara Schreiber finally left her house. Amber expected her to disappear, but her form remained. Then, from behind the car shelter, stood Hans. He nodded and tipped his cap to Amber and Martin.

He gestured to the digging and did a thumbs up.

Klara ran to Hans and they linked arms, moving past the digging, the car shelter, and out past the gravel road.

"Who is that?" Martin said.

"Who?" Amber squinted. Then she saw it. Another couple, standing together. One was a very tall, slender man, and beside him was the lady in the portrait, Margaritha. Finally, with her long-lost love, Anton.

They were there to greet Hans and Klara at last and guide them home.

Amber felt Martin put something in her hands. It was a handkerchief. "You should wave it. It's traditional when bidding farewell." Amber's mouth was dry, but she licked her lips and waved the handkerchief while standing on the porch of the Schreiber homestead next to Martin. She turned and saw Martin doing the same.

Amber and Martin stood on threshold of her open door and watched as the spirits eventually disappeared.

Martin closed it and turned to Amber, who moved close to him. They wrapped their arms around one another. Amber could feel Martin's heartbeat.

"What did Klara say to you, Martin?"

Martin swallowed and said, "She said...Thank you for the invitation to dinner, but she will leave us sweethearts now in peace..."

"Oh...she was reading your letter," Amber said.

They were alone.

She looked up into his warm brown eyes and Martin smiled in the way he did when his lips spread into that appealing peach color.

Martin leaned down and pressed his lips against hers. He kept his mouth closed at first. She felt his stubble and the texture of his skin. Then, he prized her lips open with his, increasing the pressure. His fingers slipped into her curls.

The thump-thump-thumping of his heartbeat against her body excited Amber. She pulled at his shirt, untucking it from his jeans.

Her knees weakened when his tongue brushed hers. He tightened his hold, pressing her body against his. Amber became out of breath against him and Martin's breath had quickened. He pulled away and her eyes rested on his. The glazed, impassioned stare in his eyes mirrored hers. His lips glistened from their intimate kiss, and she felt the twin effect on her own now sensitive mouth.

Amber slipped a hand beneath Martin's shirt and gently brushed her nails up the bare, heated skin of his back.

"I love you too, Martin. I'm all yours."

He smiled again, stroking her hair, and said, "I love you so much, Amber. Let's get dinner going. We're all alone, finally, and we've got all night together."

The vibration and intent in his voice got into her blood and Amber knew this would be the brilliant opening night of their happy future together.

The End

Author's Note: The History

Hans, Klara, Anton, Margaritha, and Peter all lived in what is today Romania. At the time when they were there together, it was part of Hungary.

Almost all characters in this story are fictitious, apart from 'Herr Braun' or 'Bonesetter Braun,' whom the Schreibers and Lulays encounter in North Dakota.

He was a pioneering Banat German settler in North Dakota, who was known for his ability to set bones and help with other injuries. The author read about him in the book *From the Banat to North Dakota* by David Dreyer and Josette Steiner Hatter. The author also read about Adam Lefor, whom the town of Lefor, North Dakota, is named after.

If Anton and his family would have stayed, as 'ethnic Germans' in Romania, they would have been viewed as enemies of the state, whether or not they collaborated with the previous pro-Nazi occupying forces.

Reference is made to Martin's mother being a Banat German from former Yugoslavia, which is today Serbia. In the Vojvodina region of Serbia, there were many villages similar to Bensek or Mercydorf, where ethnic Germans had lived for generations, having been invited by the Hapsburgs in the eighteenth century to settle and work the land.

The status of the ethnic Germans who remained in Yugoslavia was particularly low due to atrocities committed against Yugoslav citizens by Nazi soldiers; sadly; including a regiment of soldiers recruited from the Banat's ethnic Germans.

The ones who remained in the Russian-controlled zone of Europe, imagining that because they had not been part of such atrocities and war crimes they would be able to return to normal life, were sorely mistaken.

There are similar histories involving villages in other Eastern European countries, who found themselves at one point overtaken by Nazi German forces, called upon to embrace Hitler's regime as they were 'Volksdeutsche.' Some did. They waved Nazi flags. They participated in the murder and disenfranchisement of Jews and Slavs.

Many did not, and took dangerous steps to protect those they had lived in harmony with for generations. Yet vengeance came knocking on all ethnic German doors in the guise of Russian soldiers and communist partisans.

In a circle of bravery and kindness, Slavic people, Russians, Romanians, and Hungarians took steps to help their ethnic German neighbors who were having their turn being disenfranchised and persecuted. The numbers of ethnic Germans persecuted, though tragic, does not compare to the Holocaust such comparisons are unhelpful in the author's opinion. However the fact that both happened should remain in historical knowledge.

It is that circle of human bravery, kindness, and the transcendent power of love that deserves celebrating and writing about and exploring. Yet the human capacity to forget such things in the wake of zealotry or extremism and to embrace vengeance and cruelty must never be forgotten.

The author's maternal great grandparents and their families left the Banat region of Europe to homestead in North Dakota between 1893 and 1904. What they would have thought of what became of their villages in the decades after their departure cannot be known.

Because of this, she had to enlist the help of many people.

Author's Acknowledgements

I would like to thank my North Dakota-born, Danube Swabian descendant relatives for helping me out with their memories of my grandparents and others who had more knowledge of 'The Old Country' and immigrant life in North Dakota.

Aunt Cheri, you have been so helpful with the North Dakota details, and have always answered my questions about where stuff is and what's the norm in the state these days. Thank you for reading my manuscript.

Aunt Cathryn, thank you for sharing memories of your childhood in North Dakota. I particularly enjoyed the stories of you running between 'Aunt Lena and Uncle Tony' and then to your mother who would translate their requests.

To the cover artist, Aunt Edie, who read the manuscript along with Aunt Cheri, offered advice, and lovingly painted an oil on canvas portrait based on a photo of her own mother, my grandmother Katharina Margaritha Peters (nee Burghart). Thank you.

Thank you to Troy Larson, a North Dakota native, publisher, author, and photographer who took the time to answer my questions about Lefor via Twitter.

Visiting the website, www.ghostsofnorthdakota.com is worthwhile.

I must give thanks to certain members of the Danube Swabian community who were very kind with offering resources and answers when there were aspects of the culture and history I didn't understand.

Nick Tullius, author of *My Journey from the Banat to Canada*, and Stephanie Angerer, author of *Valerius: The Little Star* were particularly helpful with language and culture questions. Many of the scenes in the book couldn't have been written without their assistance.

Jane Moore, whom I contacted via the Danube Swabian Helping Hands website, was also instrumental in guiding me to the correct resources, particularly with historical questions about Deutschbentschek (Bensek).

Joseph Stein, archivist for the American Aid Society, was very kind and helpful me when I requested sources and information about post-war and refugee life for Danube Swabians.

Rita Schiwanowitsch has shared details of how things were in the villages populated with ethnic Germans in former Yugoslavia and how it is there today. Thank you, Rita, and I wish you all the best in getting a marker placed to remember your grandfather in his home village.

Thank you to Heidi Groesche, not a Danube Swabian but a very kind lady from Germany who translated an article on weddings in Deutschbentschek for me.

Thank you to authors Abigail Owen, BR Kingsolver, and Carmen Stefanescue for beta reading for me.

Thank you, Mia Darien for your support in encouraging me to finish a story in the first place, valuing my writing enough to ask me to contribute to your short story anthologies, and your editing and helping me out with my continuity issues.

And thank you to my family, who have patiently tolerated my rambling about Danube Swabians, the Banat, ghost towns, and North Dakota.

Thank you, Mike, for telling me what a skid steer is.

Resources

List of historical, biographical, and some fictional resources relevant to Danube Swabian history and culture.

My Journey from the Banat to Canada by Nick Tullius

Bread on My Mother's Table: A Danube Swabian Remembers by Ingrid Andor

A Pebble in My Shoe: A Memoir by Katherine Hoeger Flotz

Last Waltz on the Danube by Dr. Ali Botein

Back to the Banat by Victor Wendl

Nadirs by Herta Muller

The Passport by Herta Muller

The Hunger Angel by Herta Muller

A Terrible Revenge: The Ethnic Cleansing of East European Germans 1944-1950 by Alfred-Maurice de Zayas

From the Banat to North Dakota by David Dreyer and Josette Steiner Hatter

The Great Chicago Refugee Rescue by Raymond Lohne

Danube Swabian Helping Hands website: dvhh.org

Podunavske Svabe/Danube Swabians a film on Youtube.com by Mandragora film.

About the Author

Viola Dawn is obsessed with ghosts, vampires & history. She loves love and prefers to write deep, meaningful encounters or explore the torments of unrequited desire. She's also a poet who loves to read historical romance, erotic romance, paranormal romance, ghost stories, and some light horror. She writes the sort of thing she would enjoy reading. Originally from Illinois, USA, she's been an expat for many years and now lives in the UK with her husband, children and dog.

You can find her at:

https://violadawn.wordpress.com/

@ViolaDawnAuthor

Made in the USA
San Bernardino, CA
11 May 2019